# CRY OF THE SHIFTERS

# CRY OF THE SHIFTERS

## BOOK I
## THE SILVER KINGDOM

## tayla jean grossberg

AIONIOSBOOKS

*This book is dedicated to Michael Grossberg.*

# PROLOGUE

"KILL THE GIRL."

The boy barely heard the hoarse whisper as he stumbled and fell, dropping his father's sword to the cold earth. A hand had grabbed his ankle and held him like a bear trap. Dylan pulled backward and kicked hard. He felt the hand, slick with blood, release its grip and slide to the ground. It came to rest beside his father's sword.

Dylan's eyes found the owner of the hand, lying still beside the sword. It was his uncle. And he was dying.

"Listen, boy. You must... k-kill... g-girl..." repeated his uncle, his voice growing softer, weaker, broken.

With those words, the boy's world began to shrink so that all he could see were his uncle's sky-blue eyes staring up at him and reflecting the big blue sky above.

The boy didn't understand the dying man.

All he wanted to do was to take his uncle's hand and comfort him in those last moments, but he could not. He was supposed to be a hunter, like his father, and he had to do what his uncle asked of him.

He didn't need to understand anything.

So he continued to stare at his uncle who raised a trembling hand and extended it: he was pointing. But to where? And at what?

Dylan stood up and looked across the battlefield. His legs were shaking because he expected one of the corpses to get up and attack at any moment. He recognized some of his uncle's men. He did not know any of them well but he had watched them training and knew they were seasoned warriors. They had not paid him much attention when they'd trained and now they never will.

Dylan looked past the dead bodies of men and shifters. Partly hidden behind some brush, he saw one body lying apart from the others.

"Uncle, is that—?" Dylan stopped as his uncle's breathing stopped and sky-blue eyes forever closed to the cold blue sky.

A tear rolled down the child's cheek. Then he blinked away all the other tears that wanted to follow and looked toward the body behind the brush again.

He had an order to obey.

So he picked up his father's sword and held it out in front of him, expecting a fight. Dylan walked among the bodies and tried not to focus on the dead shifters' animal-like features. He tried to walk past all of them as fast as possible. His breath quickened but he refused to let out the terror he felt inside. He refused to let his father Liam and his aunt Lillian, who were searching for survivors nearby, see that he was scared. Shifter guts squelched beneath his feet and he left a trail of bloody footsteps behind him.

When he reached the body, he saw that the girl was his age or even younger. He had expected her to be bigger, older. Her golden hair was spread out over the ground around her. Her eyes were sealed shut. If not for the slow rising and falling of her chest, he would have thought her dead.

"*Kill the girl.*" His uncle's final command replayed in his mind.

*Very well.* He took a deep breath as he gripped the sword with both hands and lifted it high above his head. *I can do it. I can.*

His eyes drifted down to her face. Her cheeks looked soft. Her eyelids fluttered. Is she dreaming? Dylan shook his head. He wasn't supposed to be thinking that! He was supposed to kill her!

Kill her.... But then she would be dead. *Like my mother.* Murdered. *Like my mother.*

Dylan looked down at her again. He wondered if she had a mother. Would her mother miss her if she died today—died by his hand?

Slowly he lowered his father's heavy sword to his side, its tip stabbing the earth.

She was harmless. Dylan sighed heavily and then trudged up the hill, dragging the sword behind him. When he reached the top, he stopped to look back.

The girl was gone.

# CHAPTER 1

TEN YEARS LATER.

Her leaf-colored eyes flew open. She sat up and studied her surroundings cautiously.

The bed was small but comfortable. It had a single pillow that was filled with feathers. Animal coats had warmed her during the night. She shoved them off and they dropped to the ground.

The room was small too. It had a chest of drawers made of dark wood. Its bottom drawer was open. A shirt spilled out of it and pooled to the floor. Next to it was a dresser. Its door was closed so she could not see what was inside.

The girl swung her legs out of the bed. Her bare feet touched the stone floor. She looked up at the window. Sun rays smiled into the room.

*Where am I?*

4

Hesitantly she looked down at herself. The clothes she wore were dull, worn soft with age. She touched them as if they were foreign. The shirt she wore was a cream color. Maybe some time ago, it had been white but now it was stained by dirt. The pants she wore were short and torn. They were a dark brown and more figure-hugging than the shirt. The girl stopped looking at her clothes and stood up. Her legs buckled and for a moment she thought she would fall over. She didn't.

She took a step on the stone floor, followed by another shaky one. She walked toward the mirror that hung above the chest of drawers. She looked at the mirror, wide-eyed—she did not know the girl who stared back at her.

The girl was tall and lean. Her leaf-green eyes looked wild and a bit tired. The golden hair just touching her shoulders was tangled but clean. Her lips were full but unsmiling. She did not have freckles but had one beauty spot at the right corner of her mouth. She had prominent cheekbones.

The girl tilted her head to the side. *Pretty. But who am I?*

Then the room's wooden door opened. She jumped at the creaking sound and spun toward it. She did not know what or who to expect.

"Caitlin! You're awake!" a high-pitched child's voice yelled.

*Caitlin. Is that me?*

A little girl ran inside and threw her arms around the bigger girl's waist. She clung like a tick. The older girl didn't know where to put her hands, so she dangled them awkwardly in the air. She didn't know the kid and felt no need to hug her or be hugged by her. She stepped back but the kid would not let go. So she lowered her hands to push the clingy thing away. Her fingers touched its hair, but she could not muster the courage to shoo it away.

The kid's hair was thick and long and dark brown. Caitlin awkwardly patted her head.

"You can let go now," she said tightly.

The girl squeezed hard and then let go. She looked up at Caitlin with adoration and a toothy smile and then stuck her hand into her pocket to pull out a small package. It was wrapped very roughly in brown paper secured with twine. She handed it to Caitlin.

Reluctantly the older girl took it. Caitlin looked from the brown package to the big smile and gleaming eyes. "What is it?" she asked. She held the packet at a distance as if it was an unwanted or dangerous thing.

The kid rolled her eyes and giggled. "You have to open it to see, silly!"

Caitlin shifted it to her other hand. Holding it made her feel even more uncomfortable. "Why are you giving this to me?"

The girl frowned. "Because it's your birthday," she said in a very adult, matter-of-fact tone. The kid looked to Caitlin to be only about six years old.

"Oh," Caitlin said awkwardly.

"Don't tell me you forgot! NO ONE forgets their own birthday!"

Caitlin's eyes went back to the package. She slowly pulled at the bindings and opened it. Then she lifted the gift out. It was a handmade beaded necklace. In the middle of the strand were two wood-carved girls. The taller one was holding the shorter one's hand.

"I made it myself," the little girl gleamed. "Or well, Dad helped with the carving."

Caitlin looked at it. It was clearly made by a six-year-old: it was sloppy. She did not want the gift and she did not appreciate the effort. It was stupid, ugly, and would look ridiculous on her.

She touched the two figures. "Are they us?"

"Of course they are!" The child danced around the room, clearly very pleased with herself. When she came to a stop she was out of breath. Then as if she only now realized that she had given the present hoping that Caitlin would be pleased by it, she asked: "Do you like it? Do you, do you?"

"Huh?" Caitlin asked. She had been so focused on the kid dancing that it took her a moment to realize she was referring to the necklace. She forced herself to nod, although she actually thought it was atrocious.

The child smiled again and ran to the door. Once at the door she turned back and said enthusiastically, "Come on! Mom made you breakfast!"

Caitlin did not reply.

When the little girl left, the room was uncomfortably quiet. It felt as if the walls were closing in. She looked around. *Is this my room?*

*Caitlin.* She repeated the name that still sounded unfamiliar to her ears.

Then she heard the clanging of pots and slowly started making her way toward the door. She walked out of the bedroom into a short, narrow hallway. The house was small and humble. It was not very impressive, beautiful, or big.

Caitlin followed her nose. *Something smells good— really good.* Her stomach rumbled. She felt like she had not eaten in days. She walked a little farther down the hallway which opened up to a cozy dining hall and there next to it, was the source of the amazing smell —the kitchen.

"Good morning, dear!" a woman said as Caitlin entered the kitchen. The kitchen walls were greasy and made from the same stone as the rest of the house. The interior was rough and built to last a long time. Whoever constructed the house did not take beauty into consideration.

Caitlin looked around and realized she lived in a single-story house, one that had plenty of windows to make the most use of the natural light—and therefore save on candles—and wooden shutters to protect the family from the rain and the cold. Ample but simple wooden chairs and tables furnished the interior.

Caitlin clearly did not live alone. *There is this*

*annoying six-year-old and this woman.* She looked at the woman crouching before the fireplace. A thirty-year-old version of the six-year-old, her wide fore-head, strong jawline, and dark hair matched the little girl's. She wore leather boots, a long skirt, and a smile. She had warm, soft eyes, and in her right hand she held a frying pan. The frying pan was charred, like the open fireplace she used as a stove.

"Happy birthday!" She put the pan down on the blackened stone hearth before standing up to hug and kiss Caitlin.

Caitlin nearly pulled away but quickly stopped herself. She forced a smile and wondered if it looked as awkward and out of place as it felt.

"I was going to bring you breakfast in bed," the lady said, "but then Maggie just couldn't wait to give you your present."

Maggie giggled.

Caitlin looked down at her hand. She had forgotten that she was holding the beaded necklace.

"Can I put it on for you?" the lady asked, gesturing at the necklace.

"Sure," Caitlin said after a pause. She handed the woman the necklace and turned around. Turning her back on a stranger, who was tying something around her neck, made her feel even more uncomfortable, vulnerable. The lady fastened it and told her to turn around.

"It looks beautiful," she said more to Maggie before

looking straight into Caitlin's eyes. "Your sister put a lot of effort into making it for you."

"My sister?!" Caitlin exclaimed. Her eyes darted to the unfamiliar child. *This kid is my sister?*

The lady didn't realize that Caitlin was asking if they were related. She thought Caitlin was asking if Maggie had made it all by herself.

"She did most of the work on her own–" the lady said.

"All of it! I barely helped with the woodwork," a large man interrupted as he walked into the kitchen.

"Daddy!" Maggie yelled, running toward the man with outstretched arms. He scooped her up and cuddled her to his chest before pretending to drop her. She laughed and he put her down carefully.

*He is gentle.*

"Birthday girl."

*Oh damn.* He was looking at Caitlin now. Her feet felt heavy as she met his eyes. He then walked toward her and hugged her. It was a big, long hug from which she could not wait to be free.

When the bear hug ended, he did not let go completely but draped one arm over her shoulders loosely.

"Daisy darling," he called to his wife.

"Yes, Gerald?" she smiled sweetly.

"That smells good."

"I was about to ask Caitlin to set the table for us," she said, looking at her elder daughter.

Caitlin did not move. Her eyes were wide and her face was pale.

"Caitlin?" Daisy asked.

"Oh yes, sure," she stuttered as she moved away from her father. *These are my parents?* She looked from the one to the other. The man was hairy. He had a beard and bear-like arms. But he wasn't fat or very muscular. He wore dull clothes and fur shoes. The woman was thin and much shorter than he was. If they were her parents, she looked nothing like them.

"Darling, are you okay?" Gerald asked.

"Hmm? Yes." Caitlin felt her cheeks redden. Then she remembered that her "mother" had asked her to set the table. But she did not know where anything was. The house was strange. The cupboards were unfamiliar. Luckily Maggie came skipping back into the kitchen and opened a wooden cupboard that revealed wooden plates and took four of them out.

"Thanks for the help," Caitlin managed.

Maggie grinned, "Don't get used to it! I'm only helping because it's your birthday."

Caitlin walked toward the shelves that lined the wall next to the fireplace. She breathed slowly, guessed that the cutlery would be in the drawer, and opened it slowly. She had guessed right.

"Are you feeling alright?" Daisy asked.

"What?" she blurted out sharply when she realized the woman was talking to her.

"That's no way to talk to your mother, birthday or not." Gerald said, trying not to sound too firm.

There was a moment of silence and she wondered

11

if they expected her to apologize. She did not feel like apologizing. So she just looked at them awkwardly.

"Are you feeling alright?" Daisy asked again.

"I... I'm just a little sleepy," she lied and hurried out after Maggie, passing through the small dining hall and then out through the front door.

The fresh air welcomed her. A small square wooden table stood outside, with four simple chairs crowded around it. There was only just enough room for a family of four.

A few steps from the house were modest wooden pens filled with chickens, and Caitlin heard a goat bleat. She looked back at the house and saw that its roof was made of grass, like most of the houses Caitlin saw nearby. *Are they all farmers?* she wondered.

Caitlin looked closely at the neighboring houses. All of them were made out of the same stone and most of them had small pens containing animals. There were big trees everywhere and the grass was a bright green. *I can hear rushing water.*

She turned in a half-circle as she took in the little village they lived in. All of the houses were small but had spacious yards. The gardens were filled with ferns, trees, vegetables and herbs, and some hidden flowers. She guessed people here rose with the sun.

WHY CAN'T I REMEMBER ANYTHING? she exhaled in frustration.

"What are you looking for?"

"What?" Caitlin jumped at the sound of Maggie's voice.

"You look like you are searching for something," the six-year-old said.

"I'm not," Caitlin responded. She felt lightheaded so she sat down at the table.

"I'll go get the cups," Maggie said and skipped back into the house.

She returned and placed ceramic cups on the table. She was followed by Daisy and Gerald and the smell of food.

They all sat down around the little table, and Gerald waited until everyone's plates were full before he scooped some eggs onto his plate. Caitlin's stomach rumbled. The bacon looked crispy and made her mouth water, but she took a bite of bread first and then washed it down with water.

Maggie giggled.

"What?" Caitlin asked as she realized the six-year-old was laughing at her.

"You eat like a pig!" she said, but not in a mean way —her voice was joking.

"Maggie!" Daisy exclaimed, but Caitlin could tell that she agreed with the six-year-old from the way Daisy looked at her.

"It's true!" Maggie said to her mother before turning her attention back to her older sister. "You'll never be a lady or a duchess if you eat like that!"

Caitlin felt her cheeks flush as she wiped some egg off her face.

Maggie took her cutlery and sat upright. She cut a

small piece of bread and daintily popped it into her mouth. She chewed slowly and neatly and dabbed her mouth with a cloth afterward. "I am going to be a lady one day," she stated.

"You already are," her dad said sweetly, knowing that there was no place in the castle for a peasant like his daughter.

"Like a *real* lady," Maggie continued. "I'll wear nice dresses and have jewelry and servants."

The parents exchanged a weary look. Caitlin had a feeling that this wasn't the first time they'd had this conversation with the little girl.

"And I'll wear a crown," she touched the top of her head to indicate where she would place her crown.

"The ladies of the castle don't wear crowns," her mother told her gently.

"Then who does?" she asked.

"Only princesses wear crowns or, in our case, the prince."

Maggie took another small bite of food while thinking about this. "Daddy, how do I become a princess?"

"It's something you are born into," her father said wearily.

She looked disappointed. "So there is no way to become royalty then?"

"You could marry a prince..." Caitlin said.

"Then I want to marry the prince one day," she decided. She touched her long, brown dress. It did not have a corset or any embellishments. It was dull and boring and not fit for a princess.

"I'm sure Crown Prince Reagan has more than enough ladies lining up to marry him," Gerald said.

"You are much too young to be thinking about marriage anyway," Daisy stated. Then her eyes went to Caitlin. "You on the other hand..."

"What?" Caitlin sputtered, nearly choking on her bread.

"Don't talk to you mother like that!" Gerald growled. He hated having to remind his children to mind their manners. They were poor but that was not an excuse to be rude.

"I don't want to get married!" Caitlin screeched almost rising from the table.

"Caitlin!" Gerald found himself reprimanding her again.

"I was sixteen when I got married," Daisy said smoothly. "It's a great age."

"But you need a strong man," Gerald added. The anger had gone from his voice. It was replaced by a hopeful and energetic tone.

Caitlin felt suffocated. Her stomach turned. Suddenly she regretted eating. She shot up from the table, bumping her leg in the process. "I need some air," she blurted out and darted away from the house.

She ran away from the village—away from people. She ignored their voices calling after her and ran deeper into the trees.

If she had known what she would find, she never would have left the breakfast table.

# CHAPTER 2

CAITLIN RAN UNTIL she could no longer see her family's little farmhouse. That was her family back there—a family she didn't remember. *It was all too much.*

She had no idea where she was going, but she was going there fast. She was fit. Her long legs did not ache and she felt like she could run forever.

When she finally slowed to a walk, she became aware of her surroundings and realized that she had lost all sense of direction. She had not stuck to any path that could lead her back. *I don't want to go back.*

She wondered if a lot of people got lost out here. If they did, what had happened to them? Surprisingly, she was not scared. She felt safer out in the open than she did inside the small house. Out here she could breathe in the clean, fresh air. It cleared her mind and gave her a sense of freedom.

Her surroundings were beautiful. The trees were green and lush, as was the thick grass that grew here. She spotted a willow tree and walked through the grass toward it. As she grew closer, she heard the sound of white water.

She had reached a river. It wasn't that big, but something told Caitlin that it ran into an even bigger one. *Am I guessing or remembering?*

She walked to the river and washed her face. The water was cool and fresh and clean, like the air. She started walking along with its current, and her memories carried her away even farther than the river could.

The word *marriage* spiraled around in her thoughts. She was sixteen and her parents wanted her to get married. They weren't wealthy, so they probably wanted a man to take care of her. Should she honor the wishes of parents she didn't know or love?

As she looked at the river, her thoughts continued to race with its rushing waters. *If I get married, what does that mean? Am I supposed to start a family?* Her thoughts went to Maggie and the idea of having kids made her stomach turn. She wondered if she was about to be promised to someone, a boy who, just like her parents, she could not remember. Maybe that was why they brought up the whole marriage idea in the first place.

When Caitlin looked up, she snapped out of her daydream. She had reached a bigger river. It was magnificent. Powerful water gushed down from the mountains.

In the distance, Caitlin could see a waterfall. She started toward it, walking cautiously; if she fell in, she would surely drown or be crushed by the rocks.

She was almost there when something to her right caught her eye. It was a splash of red that stood out against the lush green landscape. She walked toward it. Like paint, it was splattered against the river's rocks and trees.

Caitlin grimaced. *Blood.*

Her instincts told her to take a step back, but she did not. She was intrigued, so instead of running away, she continued toward it. There was a lot it. Slowly, she moved the tree branch that blocked her path forward, as if it might be dangerous, and walked deeper into the copse of trees. She did not walk far before finding—it was an arm! A human arm severed from someone's body.

Caitlin stood there. But instead of being terrified like most people would have been, she was curious. *What did this?*

She took a step closer to examine it. *It looks like it's been ripped off, not cut off by a sword.* Caitlin wondered what kind of animals lived in these woods.

*There's more blood.* She wondered if she would find the rest of the body, and if so, what should she do then? She could go and tell Gerald, but she might not even be able to find her way back to the village.

A groan escaped the forest. It sent chills down her

19

spine, and a flock of birds flew from the trees. They soared away into the sky.

Caitlin was aware of her heart hammering in her chest as she walked in the direction of the groan. Then she found him. A man. She guessed he was her father's age. Both of his arms were still connected to his shoulders, so the severed arm belonged to someone else.

His blood-stained hair, with its streaks of gray, clung to his face. His cheek was bleeding. Sweat dripped from his brows and tears leaked from his eyes, mixing with the blood on his face. There were claw gashes all over in his tattered clothes. His hands clutched his right leg, and blood pooled around him. The grass he was lying on was ripped from the ground in clumps. She wondered if he had done that out of frustration and pain.

"Girl!" he screamed when he saw her.

She froze. Her lips did not want to form words and her legs wanted to run away. She was about to turn and go, but the man started talking.

"My son..." he looked at her with hope in his eyes.

She thought about the arm. Then she shook her head and watched sobs shake his crumpled body. His body shook and shook, but she felt no need to comfort him.

"Help me," he mumbled the words and then screamed them when she continued to do nothing. "Help me!"

"Who are you?" she asked.

"Don't you recognize me through the blood, Caitlin?" he asked.

With or without blood, she had no idea who he was. She remembered how small the town looked. That probably meant that everyone knew each other. Maybe she was supposed to know him. Maybe he was someone important to her. Or maybe not.

"Please help me get back home," he begged.

She looked down at him. Although she did not feel the need to help, she slowly walked closer and bent down. "You're bleeding very badly," she said matter-of-factly.

He took off his shirt and she helped him to wrap it around his leg to stop the blood flow. A huge chunk was taken out of his leg.

He put his arm around her shoulder as she helped him up. She was stronger than she thought she would be. In contrast, he was very weak. He stumbled but she kept him upright.

"Don't faint on me!" she said. "You need to help me to get home."

"I know a shortcut," he said.

She started walking in the direction he showed her. She decided to take this opportunity to learn as much as she possibly could. "Are there any more of you out here?" she asked.

"No," he said with tears in his eyes. "It was only my son and I who came fishing this morning. We were here before the sun was up."

She nodded and helped him over some rocks. *My journey will be slow with him,* she sighed. *I wonder if he will die in my arms.* The thought irritated her. She did not feel like carrying him so far if he was only going to die anyway.

"What happened?" she asked.

He closed his eyes a moment and then spoke through clenched teeth. "We started fishing and it came out of nowhere!"

"What did?"

"A bear," the man said and then started sobbing again.

Caitlin turned her eyes toward the trees and did not try to comfort him. "I thought bears usually keep to themselves. They only attack if attacked or when they feel threatened."

"We didn't threaten it!" he protested. "We didn't even have time to. It came from the other side of the river and swam across just to get to us! My son... he tried to fight when it attacked. But it got his arm... and my leg. It tossed me into the trees like I was nothing. Then I heard my boy's screams...."

Caitlin wondered if the man was delusional. He was losing a lot of blood after all.... *Bears don't just attack.* But then she looked at his bloody shirt tied around his wound. *Something did that.*

She hoped they were close to the village. The man was getting heavier and heavier in her arms. He went quiet for a while.

"Are we almost there?" she asked.

"Huh," he groaned. "I feel tired."

"Don't you dare fall asleep!" she said.

"Just follow this little side river," he said. "It's the branch of the Big River that runs through our River Town."

Caitlin looked at the small tributary and wondered how many villages relied on the Big River and all of its branches for water. The trees were beginning to thin and the rocks had grown smaller.

She walked on and then became conscious of the man's silence. His head was hanging even more and his eyelids were drooping. "I'm sorry about your son," she said, desperate for him to talk and stay awake.

"I hate it," he said.

"Hate what?" she asked.

"The very thing that caused all of this!" His voice was soft but filled with rage.

At *least he's talking*, she thought. "The bear?"

"No," he said. "The bear was a victim too!"

She frowned.

"It's the very thing the king told us about! The thing he banned!"

"What?" she asked.

"This attack was the act of one thing and one thing only."

At that moment his legs gave and he fell onto the dirt footpath that led to the village. Caitlin tried to stop his fall. Although she managed to slow it, his

23

knees hit the ground hard anyway. She gently laid him on his back, realizing he could not walk anymore.

She looked up and the village, with its stone houses and grass roofs, came into view. She knew she had to run for help. Time was precious. But she did not move. She wanted to know what he had to say first.

"What caused the attack?" she asked.

"Magic," the man answered. He started coughing and his eyes slowly closed.

*Magic.* Caitlin did not know why, but that word made her flinch.

# CHAPTER 3

THE MAN'S NAME was Joshua Forbes. His son, Henry, had not returned home. Caitlin did not think that he was going to either.

The villagers lifted his body from the ground and took him to the healer's house. Caitlin watched them go. She could see the house from where she was standing. It did not stand out from the other houses. It had stone walls and a grass roof, like Caitlin's house. Nothing about it indicated that it was a place for people to be treated.

"You should go with them," one of the villagers told her. "You found him. Everyone will want to hear the tale and I doubt he will be able to tell it all himself."

Caitlin's eyes stared blankly at the shaking man as he was carried away. She wondered if he would survive another day. Following behind the crowd slowly, watching them all, she thought they swarmed around him like flies around dead meat.

"Joshua!" a woman yelled frantically. She had thin, blond hair and weary eyes. Her small figure pushed through the crowd toward her husband.

"Oh! Joshua!" She wailed as she reached out to grab his hand.

"Candice," a friend put a hand on her arm. "Don't slow them down. He needs a healer right now!"

Candice stepped back and let the villagers carry him into the healer's house. She stared longingly after him. Once he disappeared from sight, she shook her head and tried to pull herself together. "Who found him?" she asked, her eyes searching the faces around her frantically.

Caitlin kept quiet standing beside the healer's house, but the villagers turned in her direction and Candice's eyes met hers. Caitlin did not want to explain herself. She did not owe anyone anything.

"You?" Candice asked and walked closer. "What happened?" she said, grabbing and shaking Caitlin's shoulders.

Caitlin stepped back onto the village footpath to escape her grasp. She did not like people touching her or invading her personal space. Her irritation flared up and she considered smacking the woman on the side of her face.

"What happened?" Candice asked again.

"She will tell us all tonight at sunset," a sharp voice said.

Something about the voice was familiar. It was, in

fact, the most familiar sound Caitlin had heard all day. Caitlin turned so that she could see who it belonged to. The old man had a gray beard and leaned on a walking stick. He was wearing a long coat and brown boots that were fit for hiking or horseback riding. She did not know him.

Some of the people mumbled their greetings. Others bowed their heads in respect. They all moved out of the way so that he could walk through them. He was the village leader, and his name was Campbell.

"Caitlin, you will address the village tonight." His eyes met hers. "You need to tell us everything you know."

Her throat felt tight with nerves as she nodded. She did not even know who she was or where she was! *What can I tell them?*

She did not respond but instead turned around and forced herself to walk away, not run away. She walked faster as she felt Campbell's eyes burn into her back. She walked past many houses but did not see anything new. She heard a few horses neigh. Then she heard a familiar high-pitched voice coming toward her.

"Sister!" Maggie ran to her. "You're back! Why did you leave?"

"Uh..." she said. Caitlin felt shaky and did not want to explain to a six-year-old what she had just been through. She did not want to be there and considered running away again, but then she met Gerald's concerned eyes.

27

Her father walked up to her and pointed out the obvious. "You are dreadfully pale."

"Something happened," she said to him.

Her father arched an eyebrow.

Then she blurted it all out. She told him of her walk, the severed arm, and what Joshua had told her. "He ended up telling me it was Magic."

Maggie gasped, "You said the M-word!"

Gerald's eyes widened and he grabbed Caitlin's arm, dragging her into the house. Caitlin didn't resist and Maggie followed them.

"Daisy!" Gerald's voice echoed through the house. Once inside, he slammed the door and closed the wooden shutters. It felt like he was barricading them against a siege.

"Sit down!" he barked. "And tell your mother what you told me! Maggie, go to your room!"

Daisy sat down next to Caitlin on a wooden bench. She took her daughter's hand in hers. This only added to Caitlin's nerves. She repeated the story while contemplating her escape in the back of her mind. Gerald stood still with his broad arms crossed and Maggie shuffled out of the room.

"You'll be speaking in front of the villagers at Sunset Point," Gerald said.

It was the meeting place for the village. It was where the townsfolk gathered to talk about their crops and animals, and on rare occasions, they talked about someone's death or accident. Women often had to stay home with the children. Sometimes, they assembled to voice a complaint or tell a story.

"I'll take you there while your mother and sister stay home," her father said tightly.

"Gerald," Daisy said and stood up. "We should come with you. If this is M—" she stopped herself. "If this is what Joshua claims it is, then we are in trouble. The king will have our village burned!"

"Or the villagers will stone our daughter," he said bitterly and anxiously scraped his hand against the back of his head.

"What?!" Caitlin croaked. "Why?"

"Because you were part of the events."

"But I wasn't there when it happened! I just found them!" she said defensively.

"I know, honey." Daisy said and squeezed her hand. It was supposed to be comforting but Caitlin found it made her even more uneasy so she pulled her hand free. Daisy spoke in a whisper, although no one could hear them inside their house. "Magic is dangerous. You know how many people have been killed for just witnessing it. Hunters even kill their own kind if they were touched by Magic."

"Did you tell anyone?" Maggie asked unexpectedly. She had been hiding in the hallway, eavesdropping.

Caitlin smirked; she knew Maggie had never gone to her room like Gerald had told her to.

"Maggie! Go to your room!" Gerald boomed. "This isn't a conversation for a child!"

Maggie chose to ignore her father—something she rarely did. "If you didn't tell anyone about Magic, then no one knows."

"Maggie, for the last time, go to your room!" Gerald was on his feet but Maggie was faster. He reached for her and missed. She ran to her older sister.

"I don't want them to take you!" she started crying. "So if they don't know, don't tell them! Just lie at the meeting!"

Her little hands tangled in Caitlin's shirt. "I know you aren't a witch. I know you wouldn't do anything bad!"

Her father dragged her to her room and then came back. His face was pale.

"Caitlin," her mother asked hesitantly. "Have you told anyone anything?"

Caitlin shook her head.

Her parents exchanged weary looks. "You can't seriously expect her to take the advice of a six-year-old!" Gerald said.

"Honey, think about it. It's sound advice." Daisy said. "What good can come from saying the M-word?"

Gerald held his ground as she approached him. Her hands touched his face gently.

"Joshua is probably going to die. And if he doesn't, everyone will think he was delusional from the loss of blood. There was no Magic! So let's just keep the story simple." Daisy turned to face Caitlin. "You will tell them that he told you a bear attacked them and say nothing more."

Caitlin nodded. She wondered if she should tell them that she had no idea who she was. That she did not even know them. That she did not know this life or any of these people.

But her parents' faces were weary, and the atmosphere was tense.

*Maybe I shouldn't tell them yet....*

# CHAPTER 4

SUNSET POINT WAS a tree-shrouded hill at the edge of the village. From the top of the hill Caitlin could see everything. On the right, a few miles away, the Big River flowed behind her house. Across the houses in front of her she could see the footpath where she had carried Joshua into the village, and behind her was another river. She could see a forest that lead to big mountains on her left, the sinking sun behind them. It was a beautiful sight, River Town, but Caitlin felt too nervous to appreciate it.

She walked silently up the narrow footpath to the top of the hill and looked around like she was a mouse trapped in a cage. *There is nowhere to run, nowhere to go but up.*

Chairs hewn from rocks sat at the very top, arranged in concentric circles around the center of the grassy knoll. The wind blew cold up there. The trees cast their shadows on the villagers as they talked and chose their seats. The majority of them were male.

Campbell was standing at the very center, his eyes scanning his people before coming to rest on Caitlin.

*His eyes are dark*, thought Caitlin.

Campbell motioned for her to come and stand beside him. He didn't smile when he beckoned her and Caitlin felt like his coldness might freeze her. She looked up at Gerald, who was standing next to her. He gave her a gentle push. Slowly she walked through the rows of stone chairs. Eyes turned to her and she felt sick. Gerald took a seat in the front row and saved a seat for her next to him.

"Can everyone please take their seats?" Campbell asked with a rusty old voice. He did not need to talk loudly. Like dogs, the villagers obeyed. He didn't look at Caitlin, nor did he say anything to her. But she was smart enough to know when someone didn't like her.

"Quiet now," Campbell said as he clasped his hands together. The villagers obeyed again.

Caitlin's stomach turned. She didn't like being told what to do, but nevertheless she listened, just like everyone else. She stood a few steps behind the old man. Many questioning eyes that looked on him now turned to her. The people waited. They were eager to hear what she had to say. She wondered if anything violent had ever happened in this village. By the looks of the people, this was an isolated incident. None of them looked like they knew how to fight. She tensed and felt the strong muscles in her arms. *Do I know how to fight?*

"Thank you for gathering here tonight," the village leader said solemnly, his hands still clasped together. "As most of you know, we are here to talk about the deaths of Henry and Joshua Forbes."

Some heads nodded.

Caitlin let that sink in and sighed. So had Joshua died. She wasn't able to save him. She went through all that effort for nothing. Trying to save someone had gotten her into this terrible situation. *No good deed goes unpunished.*

The old man took a breath and paced through the grass slowly as he talked. It wasn't a nervous pacing. He was fully in control. He looked at the villagers with calm and certain eyes as he spoke.

*He is dangerous.*

"They went fishing this morning. They left before the sun was up, according to Candice Forbes." Campbell's eyes met the widow's.

The frail, blond woman was sitting in the front row. She had her arms wrapped around herself, appearing even smaller than she had earlier in the day. Her eyes were red and she didn't look at Caitlin.

"Then Miss Caitlin Wilde found them. Or what was left to be found. She brought Joshua back, but he died from his wounds before he could tell us what had happened." He paused again to let the words sink in. Caitlin wondered if he was enjoying making this as

34

dramatic as possible. "We are here tonight to discuss their deaths and then decide what action to take."

He stepped back and put a soothing hand on Caitlin's shoulder. She bit her lip and wanted to shrug it off. "Speak child," he said.

Caitlin's eyes darted around from person to person. Her palms were sweaty, and her bottom lip shook. She couldn't speak.

"It's alright child," Campbell said calmly. But his grip tightened. "Tell us what happened."

"I..." she said and then stopped because of the lump in her throat. She stood up a little taller and cleared her throat. "I went for a walk this morning. I was walking by the Big River when I saw the blood," she swallowed, "and then I found an arm... and then I found Joshua."

A whisper spread among the people. All eyes were fixed on her. She shifted her weight from one foot to the other and then moved away from Campbell's hand. He looked slightly surprised but turned his attention back to the audience.

"Hush now," Campbell said to the villagers and then turned back to her. "Please continue."

Caitlin hated this. She hated speaking in front of a crowd. She felt like this was a circus and she was the starring act. Part of her wished she had just walked away and left the man there. *Why did I try to help him? It's not like he meant anything to me.*

"I helped him home. He didn't say much to me. Just that it was a bear attack," she tried to get the words out as fast as possible so that this dreadful moment would pass. She took a breath and stared at the forest next to her.

"Bear attacks are uncommon," someone said in disbelief. Caitlin looked toward the skinny boy with the mouse-like face.

"But not unheard of," another said. He was sitting next to the mouse-faced boy and Caitlin guessed that they were friends.

"Don't sound so excited, Conrad. Bears are dangerous," mouse-face spoke softly.

"Don't sound so scared, Albert," Conrad said louder.

"Is that all?" Campbell said and faced Caitlin. He did not pay much attention to the boys bickering; neither did the villagers. His eyes were big, cold, and menacing as he looked at her like he could see right into her soul. He stared at her as if he would know when she was lying.

But something inside Caitlin told her that she could lie. That she had lied many times in her life and that she was good at it. So she looked into his eyes unblinkingly and said, "That's all."

He stared into her eyes for a little longer after she spoke. He looked as if he was waiting for her to say more, but she didn't.

Caitlin just stared right back.

His eyes narrowed as he held her stare and then he nodded, allowing her to go and sit down next to her father.

36

Caitlin hid a sigh of relief as she sank back into her stone chair. Gerald touched her arm, giving her an approving smile. She did not smile back and pulled her arm away instead.

Then Campbell asked the town's healer to join him in the circle. The healer, who had also been sitting in one of the front rows, rose to his feet and scurried to their leader's side.

"Healer," Campbell said. "Will you please tell us about your patient?"

The healer's nod was jerky. He was a pale, clean-shaven man with round, saucer-shaped eyes, like those of a frightened animal. He stood center stage, as all eyes turned to him, with his fingers intertwined to stop their twitching. "When J-Joshua came in this morning, I thought he would surely b-bleed to d-death," the healer began. "He had already lost too much b-blood. But it wasn't the loss of blood or his wounds that k-killed him."

He hesitated. It was so deathly quiet. Everyone focused on his every word and sat forward in their seats. The healer swallowed before continuing. "The man was m-mad..."

The crowed murmured again and Caitlin sensed Gerald stiffen beside her. His eyes were fixed on the anxious healer. He gripped his stone seat's sides, his knuckles white, and Caitlin knew he wished the healer would stop speaking.

"He was mumbling at first... b-but it became clearer

and clearer what he was s-saying," the healer paused. "He said what happened was the doing of M-Magic."

Chaos broke out. People yelled and cursed. The healer dodged a stone that was thrown his way. Caitlin couldn't believe how the peace and quiet had quickly erupted into a violent uproar.

"Quiet!" For the first time Campbell raised his voice. He looked at the healer and asked, "Was he infected with Magic?"

"Y-yes. So b-bad that he even tried to k-kill m-me."

Caitlin frowned and sat back in her seat with her arms crossed. Joshua wasn't violent when she found him in the woods. *How could a man so weak, a dying man, try to kill someone?*

"How did he attack?" one villager asked.

"Did he cast a spell?" another asked.

"N-n-no," the healer's voice shook so much that Caitlin could barely understand him. "He w-was like a w-wild animal. L-like a b-beast! He ran t-toward me... He t-tried to b-bite me... He w-wanted to scratch my eyes out."

The talking got louder again, and Campbell was struggling to regain control of the crowd.

"I had n-no choice but t-to..." He hesitated before finishing his sentence, "P-put him out of his m-misery."

"You murdered my husband!" Candice screamed. The widow jumped to her feet in anger and pointed her finger at the shaking healer.

"I had no choice!" the healer yelled, and tears formed

in his eyes. "He w-was infected!"

"Then how do we know you aren't?" Candice asked bluntly.

"Quiet!" Campbell ordered.

Once again everyone became quiet. Their eyes burned into the healer with fear and hatred. He was a good man. He had helped many of them. He had saved many of them. He attended to their kids and to the elderly daily. But he saw, for the first time, the distrust in their eyes.

Magic was not a game. Magic was unforgivable. Magic was dangerous. So dangerous that the king himself burned entire villages that used Magic and posed a threat to themselves and others.

"P-please," the healer begged futilely.

"Burn him!" Candice yelled. "He must burn! He is infected!"

No one objected. Two men restrained the healer. Caitlin wondered why they even bothered. The man was a whimpering mess. It was clear that he was not going to run or fight.

"We burn the healer. We hunt the bear and burn it too," Campbell decided. Caitlin felt her heart skip a beat when he turned his eyes to hers. "We burn everyone associated with this."

"I only t-told you so that you know I had nothing to d-do with it!" the healer yelled at the same time that Caitlin's dad yelled, "Run!"

Gerald jumped to his feet and shoved Caitlin to

start running down the footpath. They were in the middle of the circle and had nowhere else to go.

Caitlin tried to push past the people, but she felt a woman grab her hair and pull her back. She yelped and shoved the woman away, only so that another could grab her again. She slammed her elbow back and hit the woman in the nose. She heard a crunch, followed by a scream. Although the sound was satisfying, she didn't look back to see the bloodied face. Instead, she pushed forward to the next row of chairs and knocked over two people.

"Let go of me!" she yelled as she felt another hand yanking her hair. She spun around and her fist flew through the air, hitting the man in his Adam's apple. He grabbed his throat and was pushed back by the mass of people fighting their way forward to seize Caitlin.

Nearer the center of the circle, Gerald swung punches but he couldn't fight off the mob. Someone hit him. He fell to the ground as kicks and punches rained down upon him. They were like wolves tearing at an injured stallion.

Someone threw Caitlin to the ground. So she kicked the attacker's legs out from under him. He fell and cursed. Caitlin turned to look at their escape route: they were not even halfway through the rows of stone chairs. *We can't win.*

The mob grabbed Caitlin and Gerald and then tied their hands behind their backs. They would be dragged down the hill.

"Find the healer's family and the Wilde family," Campbell instructed. "They will burn at the stake after we've killed the bear."

Caitlin glared at him with hate in her eyes. He smiled back at her. *So this is what he had planned.*

The villagers had their hands on her arms. They pushed and pulled her toward the bottom of the hill, where she tripped. They let her fall and roll through the dirt and the grass.

Rolling didn't hurt. If she had fallen hard in one spot, it would have hurt. Rolling was fine. When she came to a stop, she was amazed to find herself on her feet and not at all dizzy. But she had no time to run. Two men seized her arms and walked her through the succession of trees. *It's dark.* Caitlin kicked and jerked trying to get free but the men just squeezed her arms tighter. She could hear her muscles screaming in agony.

The men refused to even look at Caitlin as they brought her into a clearing. They were treating her like an animal. The villagers lit torches and hurried to get their knives, swords, bows and arrows. The ones who didn't own any weapons returned carrying pitchforks or wooden sticks. They chanted and yelled like barbarians.

Caitlin looked around frantically. Some people her age avoided her eyes. Were they friends? She tilted her head to the side. *If we were friends, we aren't anymore.*

Caitlin gasped as she saw the stakes. They reached into the sky. They were made of thick wood, and

41

although they weren't sharp, they reminded her of knives. There were so many of them.... *Why are there so many?*

She heard an old villager laugh and say, "It's been years since we've had a good roast! I remember a time when we used to burn witches weekly!" This made all the villagers cheer.

Caitlin's heart hammered in her chest as she was lifted up and tied to one of the stakes. She looked to the stake on her right. Gerald refused to meet her eyes.

*We're going to die.*

Then it sunk in: this was her fault. If only she had stayed at home that morning, she would never have found Joshua and this would never have happened. She was the reason her family would get killed. She was the reason Maggie would die at the age of six.

A whimper escaped her lips. Maggie and Daisy were at home. She imagined the men banging on their front door and breaking it down. She imagined them dragging Daisy and Maggie from their home and then burning it to the ground. To the right of the cluster of trees, she saw smoke and in her heart she knew that it was their home.

Minutes later, a wailing mother and daughter were dragged through the trees to the clearing. Daisy's left cheek was bruised, and a man was pulling her by the hair toward the stakes. Maggie was screaming hysterically. It was the worst sound Caitlin had ever heard. *Think, you have to THINK.*

42

She watched as the men forced the rest of her family against the poles and tied ropes around them. A whimper escaped her lips. She wanted to scream. She wanted to beg. She wanted to pray.

But in her mind, she knew that no one was coming to save them.

# CHAPTER 5

THE VILLAGERS HAD the weapons. They had the numbers. They had the will. They would have their way.

The women stayed inside their houses that night. Some locked their doors while others left them wide open, confident that their men would return home safe and sound. Mothers told their children that they had nothing to fear, swearing that their fathers would protect them from the beasts that dwelled in the dark.

Stories were told that night. Some mothers told their children about the Age of Magic. They told about the terrible things that had happened before they were born. About people who shifted into animals and devoured kids. About mermaids who drowned men for fishing in their rivers. About witches who cast spells that made people go insane.

Once upon a time, Magic was used freely and it nearly ended the human race. Those were the days before King Leonard sat on the throne, before he so bravely overpowered the Witch King and restored peace and safety to the kingdom. Everyone with Magical blood was executed. Magical beasts were hunted and killed. Men who supported Magic were exiled. If any Magical beings like faeries or elves survived, they fled.

The kids smiled, comforted by the tales of their brave king and his fearless knights. Most of them fell asleep with happiness in their hearts.

Unlike their fathers.

The men's hearts were filled with rage and hatred. They stomped through the trees and followed the river into the night. Their torches lit their way and the crescent moon hung high in the dark night sky.

Anger, confusion, fear reigned, all because of one word—Magic. The men feared Magic because they did not understand it. But even more, they feared their king and what he would do to them if they failed to destroy whatever Magic had infiltrated their town.

No one knew where in the woods they would find this Magical bear, but they were sure they would find it. Each man pretended to be more fearless than the next while they marched along the river. The group patrolled for some time but still didn't find anything resembling a Magical bear.

"Where are we going?" a short man called from the back of the group. His name was Bernard and he was used to being ignored. He was insignificant. He was not surprised when another villager talked over him:

"How do we know where the beast will be?"

"This is the place," a much quieter voice answered Bernard's question. His name was Craig and he also stayed at the back of the group. These two men were good friends and always supported each other.

The air smelled of dry rust and the men followed Craig's gaze to the blood that stained the ground.

Everyone was alert instantly and they fanned out from the river to the surrounding trees. They searched, but to their disappointment, they found no evidence of bears.

"What if it moved to the next town?" Bernard asked.

"Then we should warn the villagers," Craig responded.

"No," another argued. Of course he only spoke to Craig—no one ever spoke to Bernard. "If the Magical bear has moved on, it is no longer our problem."

The men went deeper into the trees, but soon they grew tired, hungry, and disappointed. There was no bear. The crowd lowered their weapons.

"Let's go home," one man said to his friend. "This is stupid."

"What if it comes for our children?" a voice screeched from somewhere.

"There is no 'it'," the man snapped back and in irritation.

Slowly, man by man, they stared, turned around, and began to shuffle home. But the man leading the group hesitated and looked at his fellow villagers. Was it too soon to give up? Yes, he was scared of a wild, crazy bear. But he had one fear bigger than this —disappointing his father. His father lay at home, sick in bed. He was old and not the fighter that he had been in his younger days. He expected his son to lead the search and to fight if necessary. He expected him to keep them all safe. The tall and lean young leader was only twenty years old, but he wanted to prove himself.

He stood by the river. His feet were getting wet from the spray. Slowly he climbed onto a rock to get a better view of the wild water. As a child he used to jump from rock to rock. He only did this in the branches of the Big River, where the current wasn't as strong as it was here. If he fell in at this point, he would be washed downstream. And if the rocks didn't break his bones, he would drown.

But he wasn't scared. He jumped to the next rock and found himself in a deeper part of the river. He looked down at his feet. He trusted his body. One more rock, then he would have a really nice view.

"Don't do it."

He didn't have to turn to know the voice of his dear friend Albert. When they were growing up, Albert was always the protective and responsible one. He was the one who believed in rules. He was a thin man, with chicken-like legs and a small, mouse-shaped face. Conrad wondered if his friend felt weak and power-less and if that was why he was always afraid of getting hurt.

47

"You could fall," Albert pointed out the obvious. He held a pitchfork in his right hand but no torch. In the dark, his friend couldn't make out his face and his body disappeared in the shadows of the rocks.

"I won't," the man-boy said as he turned and jumped.

"Conrad!" Albert let his friend's name echo through the trees.

Conrad steadied himself and looked back. His feet were safely planted on a rock. He put his hand on his father's sword that hung in its sheath by his side and smiled. "Relax."

Albert clenched his jaw and his nostrils flared as he exhaled. "I'm walking back. Don't fall in."

Conrad watched him turn and leave. Then he looked out at the river before deciding to make another jump. The night seemed peaceful as his torchlight shined on the rocks in front of him. He jumped to the first rock and landed safely.

Then he decided to jump to a different rock farther away. He launched himself. His feet touched down but he bobbled and almost lost his balance.

One more jump to a lower rock and he would be on the ground. He took a deep breath. He leaped. His feet touched down. But this time the rock groaned.

Conrad froze and the hairs on his arms stood up. This rock wasn't hard like the others. It was soft. It was furry. It moved.

His eyes widened, and his knees started wobbling. He was standing on the bear!

A terrified scream escaped his lips and the bear roared. It got to its feet and Conrad lost his balance. He fell to the ground. He didn't have time to get away. The bear lashed out. Its claw slammed into the boy's face, ripping it off.

"Conrad!" Albert yelled. He'd changed his mind about abandoning his friend and returned just in time to hear Conrad scream, but he was too late to save his friend.

Albert stopped in his tracks as he laid eyes on the beast. This was not a normal bear. It had the huge bear body, and the fur. It had sharp, deadly claws and long yellow teeth. But its eyes weren't those of an animal.

Albert stared right into the bear's human eyes before it killed him too.

A man emerged from the forest path and yelled, charging the bear. Someone screamed. More men followed. The bear stood on its hind legs and attacked.

It was a blood bath.

The bear ripped the first two men in half but more men kept coming. Soon the men were cutting and spearing the bear. But it continued fighting. It slashed out; they jabbed. It snarled; they screamed. It bled; they bled.

One man chose to stand back. He was small, much smaller than most men. He didn't stay back because he wanted to put a plan, a strategy, into play. He stayed back because he was scared. His hands shook as he hid behind a tree, watching people he'd known his whole life get ripped to shreds. He had come along on this hunt, but he didn't think they would actually find the bear.

His legs shook so much that they crumpled under him. He clutched his knees to his chest, folded himself into a ball, closed his eyes, and tried to slow his breathing. He was too scared to run. He was too scared to move. All he could do was try to not get noticed.

He didn't need to look behind him to know that the bear was there, so close by. He could hear it ripping the villagers apart.

When he opened his eyes, he noticed a bow and arrows just a few feet away from him. He guessed the owner was dead. His eyes lingered on the weapon. His grandfather had taught him how to shoot when he was six, and he was now very good.

But he wasn't brave. He had never been brave.

He heard another man screaming, dying. Chills ran down his spine. He was so scared that he couldn't stop the tears from rolling down his cheeks.

They had lost so many men.... This bear was not normal. A normal bear would be dead by now. Another thought struck fear into his heart: What if they failed to kill it? Then it would surely go to the village and kill more innocent people, including his family.

His eyes found the bow again. He had to do it. He breathed and counted to three before leaping to his feet. He rushed to grab the bow and then jumped back to hide behind the tree again, his eyes squeezed tightly shut. No one had even noticed. He was too scared to feel ashamed.

The young man knocked the arrow into the bow with trembling hands and willed himself to stand. He stepped out from behind the tree.

The bear was right there. Men were attacking it from all sides. It was swinging, slashing, and biting. Not once did it stand still. It was close enough for an easy shot, but he would surely miss if it kept swinging its head like that.

He took aim, exactly the way his grandfather had taught him. He breathed in deeply through his nose and then let the arrow fly as he exhaled.

This time the bear noticed him—but too late.

His arrow hit the bear in the eye. It burrowed through one eye socket, straight into the bear's head. The man watched the bear fall to the ground. They had won!

But no one clapped and no one cheered. The man looked around him. Bodies were everywhere. He vomited.

"Nice shot," someone said to him, but he didn't hear.

Slowly men started walking home, thankful that the fight was over.

The man who shot the arrow stood still for a while. He still felt too sick to walk.

Then the high-pitched scream of a woman rang in their ears. Everyone spun around simultaneously as something emerged from the trees.

The men stared. Was she a woman or a bear?

She—it—had human eyes and a human mouth, but bear teeth. Her body was large and bulky with a bear's fur. Her fingers were clawed but still in the shape of hands. Her voice was filled with rage. "You killed him," she growled and then attacked.

The surviving men didn't stand a chance. She attacked like she was a trained assassin, flipping and jumping through the air as she sliced through men's bodies. It didn't take long for her to kill all of them.

When all the men went still, she let her eyes linger on the dead bear who had once been her partner. "They killed you," she said, "so I killed them all."

All but two—Bernard and Craig.

"What have we done?" Bernard choked to his injured friend who he cradled in his arms. Craig had a deep gash in his stomach and blood slowly leaked into the mud.

"Run... village... Must... warn..." Craig managed to gasp before losing the strength to speak.

Bernard grasped his injured friend, holding him while trying to stanch the blood leaking from the gash in his side. He didn't want to leave, but he knew Craig was dying. And he had his own wife and kids to protect. So he placed a hunting knife in his friend's hand and ran into the night.

The bear lady saw Bernard run and followed him. As she sprinted past the dying man, she felt a sharp jab to her legs. She screamed and fell.

She looked at her leg, ripped the knife from it, and locked eyes with the man. Her claws slashed through his throat.

Craig died, alone and scared, at the claws of the bear lady.

Then she stood up tall. A leg wound would not stop her from getting her revenge.

# CHAPTER 6

CAITLIN LOOKED DOWN the row of stakes, seeing Maggie, Gerald, and Daisy restrained.

"Miss Wilde," Campbell said as he approached her, speaking in a low voice. The stakes were spaced a good distance apart, so only she could hear what he had to say.

She struggled against her bonds, but they were wrapped tightly around her body. They were so tight she couldn't even take deep breaths. She was panting.

Some of the men from the village stood close by. They were out of earshot. These men had laid logs and kindling at her feet and doused them with oil earlier. They were just waiting for the command to burn her.

She glared at Campbell as he stopped a few feet away from her. He had a patronizing grin on his face that she wanted to smack off. *Ugh.*

"It's interesting that they chose that name for you," he said, looking at her. His eyes darted up and down.

"It does suit. You always were wild."

"What do you mean 'they chose my name'?" Caitlin asked. She focused on the trees ahead of her.

He came closer and stopped, inches from her face, his sour breath moist against her cheek. "It's not the name I would have chosen. I would think a name like this would perhaps bring back memories. It might bind you to your wild side—the side that should be repressed."

Caitlin's eyes bored deep into his soulless ones and refused to look away. She would not let him intimidate her. She was almost glad the ropes held her in place. This way, she couldn't back away from him even if she wanted to. She did not want him to see her fear.

Campbell studied her face. "This is one thing that hasn't changed about you," he continued. "You still don't show fear." He leaned even closer and whispered, "But tell me, Miss Wilde, do you feel it?"

The lie rolled off her tongue before she had time to think about it. "No."

"No?" he said. "That's strange. You are *human* after all.... Fear is normal. Fear is good. Fear keeps us alive."

"I don't think fear will be getting me out of this," she sneered.

"No," he laughed out loud, making Daisy, Gerald, and Maggie turn in their direction, trying to hear what Campbell was saying. "Fear won't. So what will?"

"Are you trying to figure out if I have an escape plan?" she raised an eyebrow.

He shrugged and then walked around her, making

a show of checking the ropes binding her to the stake. "One can't be too careful. I never know what goes on in that mind of yours."

*Neither do I.*

"I knew you would die sooner or later. But I honestly didn't think it would be on your first day."

*First day?* She tilted her chin up abruptly, stopping herself from shaking her head in confusion.

He sounded like a mad man. So she chose to indulge in his madness. "What, you're not even going to miss me?"

"I'll miss all the fun we had," he confessed. "All the things you don't remember…"

She looked to the ground and instantly regretted it. He would see this as submission. But she was not submitting, she was thinking. She so wanted to ask what he was talking about, but she stopped herself. She wouldn't give him the satisfaction of seeing her lost and confused. She had to hold herself together.

He leaned in again. "Do you really not remember?"

"Remember what?"

"Who you are! Or do you really think you're just a common farm girl? Have you looked at yourself? Have you seen how much stronger your body is than everyone else's? Or did you not think that far because you were told not to?" Campbell scoffed.

She squirmed.

"I honestly had my doubts that it would work on you. You were always much stronger than the other children. You were always the survivor. And just look at you now. You were defeated by untrained peasants." Campbell made a tsk-tsking sound and smiled as he gripped her face in his hand, his fingers digging into the flesh of her cheeks. He was in her face now. "You don't remember me, but I will never forget you. I always thought I'd be the one to kill you, and now here we are. I get to watch you burn, the way monsters like you should burn."

*Enough!* She slammed her forehead into his face.

Campbell screamed and backed up. Blood spurted from his nose.

Caitlin smirked. *He deserved it!*

"Light them up!" he bellowed.

At that moment, a man covered in blood came running toward them. Straight from the woods. He was alone and carried no weapons.

"Help! Help!" Bernard yelled as he ran.

His screams attracted attention immediately. He saw their leader and rushed toward him, stopping right in front of Campbell. Panting, he tried to catch his breath.

"What happened?" Campbell asked, tilting his head up to stop the blood from leaking out of his nose.

"The monster! Half bear, half human!" Bernard wailed. He pictured Craig dying and his heart ached.

"Where are the other men?" Campbell asked, dabbing at his bleeding nose.

"Dead. All dead."

People came closer to see what all the fuss was about.

They formed a tiny circle around their leader and Bernard.

"All of our best men were there!" one of the villagers said, panicking. "The beast is coming here!"

Campbell knew they didn't stand a chance. The only people left in the village were women, children, and the sick and elderly. If the men with their weapons could not kill the bear, then the remaining villagers did not stand a chance.

Caitlin could not help but feel triumphant. These people wanted to execute her when she hadn't done anything wrong. *I hope the bear eats them all.*

"What do we do?" The people turned to Campbell.

He looked at all of them, more frustrated than scared. Caitlin expected him as their leader to piece together a master plan. She expected him to stay calm and help them. He did none of these things.

"Run," he told them.

The word hung over them like a cloud. It took a few seconds for all of them to react: they just stood there as if waiting for him to say more. As if expecting him to take action. When they realized he would do nothing, they scurried away like vermin.

The first scream was loud and painful. It sent the villagers running. More screams followed as the bear lady tore down doors and killed everyone in her path.

Campbell walked toward the nearest torches. He would have to burn them now if he wanted time to escape himself.

Caitlin fumbled with the ropes. But they refused to

loosen. Sweat broke out on her brow. She heard Maggie crying hysterically.

Caitlin looked up, and her eyes caught movement in the trees. She squinted and saw a silhouette—but it didn't look human. It had four legs. It was too small to be a bear. *What sort of a wild animal comes to a town filled with noisy humans?*

Campbell was walking back toward them, holding a flaming torch in his hands. The flame danced around menacingly and reflected in his murderous eyes. "And so it ends," he said, approaching Caitlin's stake and pile of kindling first.

Daisy started crying, Gerald started yelling for Campbell to stop, and Maggie started screaming while looking at Caitlin, horrified.

No one noticed the animal moving slowly out from under the trees. It was a gray wolf. It charged at Campbell who then swung his torch violently back and forth to ward off the beast. The wolf dodged to the left and snarled.

Caitlin could see the fear in Campbell's jerky movements. He backed up a few steps and wielded the torch in front of him like a sword. He swallowed hard. "I know what you are," he said to the wolf.

Any other girl, tied to a stake to be burnt as a witch, would have thought that Campbell was mad to speak to a wild animal as if it were human. But Caitlin studied the wolf. She saw its expression change as if it understood human language.

It drew its lips back and revealed strong white canines. It started circling the scared man. He swung his torch at the wolf but it simply skipped to the side. It snapped its jaws at the man but the man moved out of reach just in time.

Then they heard a roar.

Both man and wolf turned in the same direction at the same time.

The bear lady stood in the midst of the dead villagers. She would be upon them soon.

Campbell looked at the wolf and then at Caitlin and the stake and then at the torch. He had to take the chance. *The girl can't live!*

He drew the torch back and the wolf jumped forward as he swung. He let go. The wolf jumped up to catch the torch in his mouth, like a dog catching a stick.

But he missed it by a few inches.

The torch landed on the pyre laid at Caitlin's feet, touching the oil on the wood and kindling, igniting the pile, and spreading flames down the entire row of stakes.

The wolf snarled at Campbell, knowing very well that if he killed him now, he wouldn't have time to save the people who were tied to the stakes.

Campbell turned and ran. He would saddle his horse and flee this godforsaken town.

The wolf ran to the older girl first. He bit into the ropes and pulled. Caitlin wiggled and squirmed until its teeth sawed through the rope. The ropes sagged and she shoved them off.

"Thank you," she breathed.

The wolf looked at her as if to say, "My pleasure."

They broke eye contact when the bear lady roared again, sending shivers down Caitlin's spine. She turned her head in the bear's direction. The beast was unlike anything she had ever seen—powerful, rabid, and bloodthirsty. Saliva dripped from her mouth and blood dripped from her claws. She was coming for them.

Caitlin glanced at the people who called themselves her parents. *There's not enough time to free all of them. I should just leave.* After all, nothing good ever came from her trying to save people. So she turned to run away, but—

"Caitlin!" Maggie screamed, "Help me!"

The little girl's voice struck her like a punch to the gut. Caitlin couldn't leave her.

The bear spotted the wolf as the wolf charged fearlessly at her with his mouth wide open. He jumped and bit at the air. Then she slashed, just missing him with her claws. As he sped faster, his massive paws tore hunks of turf out of the ground. She started chasing him into the trees. He was like an annoying insect to her—like a fly that needed to be swatted.

Catching the stench of burning hair, Caitlin diverted her attention from the battling animals to the quickly spreading flames. She didn't have much time. She looked around for something sharp. There was nothing close by.

She ran toward the villagers' carcasses and found a knife on one of them. She ran back. Her whole family was screaming. She cut Maggie's bonds first and then moved to Gerald.

"No!" he said. "Cut your mom's first!"

She did as instructed and then freed him too. They hurried away from the stakes. The fire was out of control. Caitlin could tell it was going to consume most of the village along with the bear lady.

Daisy picked Maggie up in her arms and started running away from the flames.

"There—a cart and a horse!" Gerald said, pointing to a stable.

The horse was big and spooked. Its eyes rolled white and it trampled the ground beneath its hooves. It reared slightly in its paddock and whinnied.

"Daisy! Get the tack on!" Caitlin said, taking charge. "Gerald get the cart!"

"Where are you going?" her father asked.

"To get supplies!"

Caitlin knew they wouldn't last long without food or water so she ran into the nearest house and grabbed as much food as she could. She filled some waterskins and found bread and apples. She ran back to the cart and loaded these in the back where Maggie was seated.

The horse reared again and Gerald was struggling to hold it. He did not let go.

"Get on! Go!" Caitlin yelled to him as she jumped into the cart.

He jumped smoothly into the driver's seat and then slapped the reins to urge the horse on. The horse took off with such force Caitlin thought the cart might break free.

*We did it. We got away!* Caitlin released some of her tension and looked around as they drove past the houses and continued down the road. The village was on fire. Everything was in ruins. Everyone was dead.

*But what about the wolf? Where is it?* Her eyes darted from house to house, tree to tree, until she saw it. The bear had sunk its claws into its sides. She lifted the wolf up above her head and threw it into a tree.

Caitlin watched the wolf stumble to its feet. Her heart was thumping so hard that she felt like her chest would explode. *I'm no heroine. I'm no warrior. This might be my only chance to get out of this alive.*

With every passing second, she was getting farther and farther away. Away from what she knew she had to do...

Then she heard the wolf cry out in pain. It didn't look to her for help, the way she had looked to it when she was tied to the stake.

Caitlin inhaled deeply and then jumped from the cart.

# CHAPTER 7

CAITLIN HIT THE ground hard. The impact knocked the breath out of her lungs. The Wilde family screamed her name but she was too focused to hear. *Get up.*

She was running in the direction of the wolf howl she'd heard, back to where she and her family were going to be burned. Her whole body felt heavy; her pace was slow at first. But as she breathed in more air, her pace quickened.

Caitlin stopped as she neared her destination. She saw the bear grab the wolf's front leg and underbelly, watched her throw the wolf into the trees behind the stakes. Its body disappeared into the shadows. She hoped that it was still in one piece.

"Hey!" she yelled and swung her arms in the air to get the bear's attention.

*It worked.* The bear lady looked at her, growled, and

took a step forward. Caitlin gasped—she had no weapon, no backup, and no plan.

Caitlin cursed, turned on her heels, and ran with her heart pounding in her throat. She ran away from the shadows of the dark trees, trying to lead the bear in a direction opposite of where her family's cart was going. *I have to distract the bear, buy them time to get away.*

The bear was fast. She could feel the ground thundering and shaking as it ran. Her ears were filled with the bear's ragged breathing and wondered how long it would be before she was knocked to the ground with a fatal blow from those massive claws.

Don't look back. If she dared to look back, she would lose speed and surely be caught. *Keep moving.* Caitlin jumped over several corpses. *This one animal wiped out an entire village.*

The bear was getting too close, so she turned sharply to the right. *I'm not faster, so there is no point in sprinting until I'm exhausted.* She couldn't outrun the bear but maybe she could outmaneuver her.

Stumbling and losing speed, the bear tried to turn too but was too big to turn as fast and as quickly as Caitlin did.

Good. This gave Caitlin time to search for an escape. She was now close to the middle of town, heading north.

*I hope that wolf ran away.* Her mind flashed an image of the wolf being flung into the trees.... *Is it even alive?* Caitlin shook her head trying to focus. Twice in one day she'd tried to save someone and maybe the wolf would end up no better than Joshua.

Her eyes darted to the stables. The fire had reached one end of the building. Flames ate at the wood, spitting up black smoke that made the horses choke and kick at their stable doors.

Caitlin hid behind the nearest house. She held her hand over her mouth to stifle her breathing. She heard the bear's paws crunching over the leaves that covered the ground a few yards from her on the left side of the house. She looked toward the stables again. The bear was limping. She had an injured leg. That was the only reason why she hadn't caught Caitlin yet. *If I can get onto a horse, that's my best chance of outrunning this creature.* But how would she get there without being chased?

She heard the bear approaching and tried to flatten herself against the wall. She tried to quiet her breathing and calm the heart hammering in her chest and listened as best she could. She heard the horses whinny and kick. She heard the fire crackle as it burned closer and closer to her. She heard the wind howl through the trees. But nothing was louder than the steady footsteps coming toward her.

Caitlin took a deep breath. She moved to her right, planning to go around the house full circle, waiting for the bear to pass. She moved as silently as she could, tiptoeing around the leaves on the ground and came to a stop just short of the corner of the house. *Bear lady should be just around this—*

"I know you're there," the bear growled. "I can smell you."

Caitlin quickened her pace. The stables were now in sight. If she ran now, the bear would definitely hear her and follow. So she cast around for ideas. *Why am I so calm?... How do I beat this bear?*

The bear knew where she was. The girl was right around the corner. So the bear lady pulled back her lips in a bloody smile, in anticipation, and jumped. *Kill.*

But there was no girl.

The bear paused and tilted her head. Where had the girl gone? She snarled and started searching in blind fury, slashing everything in sight. She was so angry that she didn't even think of looking up. If she had, she would have seen Caitlin, sitting high up on the roof of the house.

Caitlin watched as the bear lady ran up and down the rows of houses and then disappeared in the wrong direction. *It's now or never.* She dropped to the ground and ran toward the burning stables. She opened the doors to the stalls and horses dashed out in panic.

The bear lady heard the noise of hooves pounding the dirt and started running in the stable's direction. Caitlin spotted her and realized that there was no time to saddle a horse. She opened all the stables except one, the last stall. She opened the door just wide enough to get in. The white stallion tried to push past her, but she wouldn't let him. *Sorry but no, boy. You're my last chance.* She shut the door and moved to his side.

The horse was pacing around the stall, which made

it really difficult to mount. She didn't have a saddle knob, so she grabbed a fistful of mane and jumped, swinging her leg over and pulling herself up.

The horse reared. She had to lean forward, wrapping her arms around his neck and squeezing her knees into his sides, to stay on his back. Caitlin was afraid that he would bump his head on the stable roof and injure himself if he didn't calm down.

As his hooves touched down, she kicked open the stable door. He was out in a flash, running through the stable hall. Caitlin heard creaking all around her as the roof started to collapse. She kept her eyes fixed on the exit. *We're going to make it.*

Burning wood bits showered down around them but the spooked horse didn't stop. He jumped. Caitlin wanted to throw her hands up to the sky as they soared through the air. *Freedom.*

The bear struck.

Caitlin felt the wind from the impact on her face. The bear's claws sunk into the horse as he was about to land. A terrible, agonizing sound was ripped from the horse's mouth as he fell to the ground.

Caitlin was splattered with blood. She lost her balance and fell forward, landing on her stomach and rolling over in time to see the stallion get to his feet. Blood gushed from his side where a piece of flesh was missing. He sprinted away. *He might bleed to death.*

The bear stood on her hind legs. Caitlin shook and wiped blood out of her eyes. The bear lady took a step forward. Caitlin reached for a burning stick she found on the ground. She waved it at the bear as she got to her feet.

The bear charged. She ducked, lost her balance—along with her burning stick—and fell again. She rolled to avoid the slashing claws and gnashing teeth.

Caitlin hurriedly looked around her for another weapon. She needed something better. Then she saw something that might work: a pitchfork that was used to scoop hay. But it was behind the bear, leaning up against a burning house. A *sword would have been better, but that will do.*

The bear charged again and she managed to move around it. She ran straight toward the pitchfork, but she didn't make it in time. The bear's claws slashed out, and she allowed herself to fall. The bear ran over Caitlin, stumbled over her shoulder, and fell, crashing through the burning house.

Caitlin pulled herself to her feet. The adrenaline that coursed through her body numbed the pain in her shoulder. Caitlin found the pitchfork, thrown by the side of the house. *This is it.* It was big, bulky, and not an easy weapon to wield.

The bear walked out of the burning house and, as Caitlin expected, charged again. Caitlin waited until the last moment. She stood up tall and held her ground until the bear was upon her. Then she dropped to her knees at the same moment the bear lifted its claws and tried to rip open her face—but found only air. With her body weight falling forward, the bear couldn't avoid the pitchfork that Caitlin aimed to its abdomen.

The bear roared.

As Caitlin felt her weapon enter the bear's flesh, she fell to her stomach so that the flailing arms and claws wouldn't scratch her. She crawled through the bear's hind legs and got back onto her feet. She retreated several steps and then stopped.

Caitlin smiled as she watched the bear die.

# CHAPTER 8

I ACTUALLY DID IT. She alone killed a creature that an entire town couldn't kill.

She looked around. Embers were swirling in the air. River Town was burning. She felt like she was standing in the middle of a battlefield and not a peaceful farming town. Bodies decorated the ground like flowers should. Black smoke filled the air like clouds should. Caitlin didn't feel any remorse, like she knew she should.

*Let the place burn! These people wanted to kill me when I was innocent. They wanted to kill a six-year-old child too. And for what? They deserved to die.*

"Caitlin..." a voice made her jump.

"Geral–Dad?" Her eyes widened. "You came back?"

"Of course I did!" Gerald said as he ran toward her. He dropped his sword to the ground and embraced her. "You stupid, stupid girl!" he said, squeezing her tightly. "Stupid and brave," he added softly.

She didn't hug back and patiently waited for him to let her go. When he finally did, he looked into her eyes. "I can't believe you did that."

She shrugged as if it was nothing.

Gerald looked at the bear, "I've never seen anything like it."

"What is it? Is it human or bear?"

"It's both," he said and studied the fork in its stomach. "You did this?"

She nodded.

"All by yourself?"

She nodded again, resisting the urge to roll her eyes.

He walked around the bear. "That's amazing."

Caitlin's knees felt weak. She didn't speak any more than she needed to. Luckily for her Gerald wanted to do all the talking.

"Your mother and sister are safe. They are on their way, probably past the northern boundary of the village now. But their horse is slow, so we will catch up with them quickly."

Caitlin didn't really care about that. *I don't care if I never see them again. They mean nothing to me, but... I suppose I mean a lot to them.* She sighed and looked at Gerald. He had come back for her. He could have fled but instead he came back. He valued her life more than his own.

"I didn't see anyone left alive," Gerald said pitifully and shook his head. "It killed them all. The king was right about these beasts."

Caitlin looked at the bodies and then at the fire. Most of the town had burned down because most houses had thatched roofs. Some plants and trees were very green and remained untouched by the fire. They didn't burn easily.

"These beasts?"

"Shifters, Caitlin. They're Magical creatures. They look like humans but have the ability to transform into animals. It's usually triggered by rage. Once they're in animal form, their animal instincts take over and they lose all control."

"Does this mean I killed a human?"

"It means you killed a monster."

Caitlin stared at the bear. Its huge, bulky body was shrinking into something small and bony. Something more human. The matted fur was disappearing and pale white skin appeared. The deadly, dangerous teeth shrank to normal-sized yellowish teeth. *It isn't a bear anymore. It's a woman.* Caitlin's chest felt tight. "I killed a person."

"No," Gerald said and strode over to her. "No," he repeated, squaring her shoulders so that she faced him. "You killed an evil monster. The world is a better place because of you."

"She looks so normal," Caitlin observed.

"That's how they fool you into thinking that they are harmless," Gerald said.

Caitlin felt no guilt—only victory. The bear attacked first. It was kill or be killed. And Caitlin didn't want to die.

"Where will we go?" After the words left her lips, she realized that she was completely lost. She might as well travel with them until she could remember more about herself.

"To the castle in the clouds, Sky Castle. We are refugees now."

Caitlin let those words sink in.

"I'll look for more horses," Gerald said but Caitlin was already walking away. "Where are you going?" he called after her.

She didn't answer.

Caitlin walked fast, aware of the pain that was creeping into her body as the adrenaline wore off. She was heading in the direction where she last saw the wolf—the stakes.

She slowed her pace as she neared the trees behind the burned stables. She realized that the wolf might be dead. *I don't want to see him dead. I tried so hard to save him. Maybe he ran away.* Or maybe that was wishful thinking.

She walked past a few rows of trees. The fire hadn't reached the forest and she didn't see the wolf. She breathed fresh air deep into her lungs and sighed. *If there isn't a corpse, then it isn't dead.*

Her eyes scanned the forest behind the stakes, coming to rest on a body with pale white human skin that looked different from the other bodies she'd found around the village.

She walked closer to the body. A young man—*Oh,*

*he's naked!*—lay in the grass with his eyes closed. He had a beautiful, strong jawline with a dark stubble and black hair hung over his eyes. He had scratch marks in his sides.

Caitlin bent down next to him. *Could it be...?* She smirked. *I do owe him.*

She searched for clothes. The closest ones were on dead people. *The dead don't need clothes.* She eyed a nearby corpse that was about his size, pulled the pants off, and then looked to the naked young man. Her cheeks reddened. She felt awkward and was thankful that he was asleep as she put the clothes on. To her relief, he groaned but didn't wake up.

"Caitlin!" Gerald called. He was too focused on her to notice the unconscious and half-naked young man.

"Over here!" she responded and waited for him to find her. This was a small town and everyone knew everyone. Gerald would know who the man is.

When he found her, she asked, "Who is he?"

"I don't know," Gerald confessed, "but he's not one of us."

Gerald was turning away. It was clear that he cared only about his family. He was not going to make a stranger his responsibility.

"We can't leave him," Caitlin protested.

"Sure we can and we will."

Caitlin knew she couldn't tell Gerald what she thought the man was. Nor could she tell Gerald that he had saved their lives. Because despite that, she knew Gerald would kill him if he knew the young man was a shifter.

"If we leave him, he'll die from his wounds," Caitlin said.

Gerald was in no mood to argue with his daughter. She had always been a bit of a rebel. She had never liked listening to him or taking orders. And she was the most stubborn person in the world.

Gerald considered dragging her away from the shirtless man. But then he looked at Caitlin closely. *She is exhausted. She is hurt. And she fought a battle that no woman should ever have to fight.*

"Fine," Gerald said. "But you'll be taking care of him."

Caitlin gently ran her finger over the man's dirty face. *I don't mind.*

# CHAPTER 9

WITH EVERYONE DEAD in the village, the Wilde family scavenged the supplies they needed from the houses that didn't burn down. They also found a bigger cart to carry everything. Unfortunately because all of the other horses had run off and their load was too heavy for one horse, they would have to walk most of the way.

They also had to rummage around for extra clothes because their house and all their belongings had burned to the ground. Caitlin didn't know how many clothes she had owned, and now it didn't matter. She touched the rough weave on her sleeve and looked at what the rest of her family was wearing: their garments all had the same simple, homespun look and she wondered if Daisy had woven the fabric and sewed them herself.

Caitlin entered the healer's house, still untouched

by the fires, and went through multiple medicine shelves but she did not recognize any of the mixtures. She wasn't even sure if any of the bottles even contained medicine or something else.

"What are you looking for?" Maggie asked. Her voice startled Caitlin. The little girl loved following Caitlin around as if Caitlin was a queen that deserved attention and admiration.

"Nothing," Caitlin said instinctively.

"Then why are you moving from house to house?" Maggie asked with a raised eyebrow.

She and Daisy had come back for Gerald and Caitlin after everything had gone quiet. Gerald had scolded them for not following his behest to start their northward journey without them. Daisy chided him, putting her foot down and saying that they didn't want to leave the people they love most in the world behind.

"I'm looking for medicine," Caitlin said as she ransacked another shelf.

"Is it for the man that's sleeping on our horse cart?" Maggie asked.

Caitlin nodded.

"He isn't one of us," Maggie said. She didn't sound resentful like Gerald had. She just sounded a little cautious.

"Are you saying I should have left him to die?" Caitlin retorted, thinking that Maggie probably took after her father.

"NO! Of course not."

Caitlin pulled two bottles from the cabinet. She had no idea what they were for.

"You really should pay more attention when Mom teaches us about medicine," Maggie said. "Those are no good."

Maggie was too short to reach the top shelf, so she climbed on top of a chair and searched through the items. She pulled out some bandages. "We will definitely need these," she stated and then she went through the medicine bottles and selectively chose some. "We'll also need a bucket of water to wash his wounds with."

"You sound like a healer."

"I told Dad if I can't grow up to be a lady, I want to grow up to be a healer." But Maggie's eyes were sad as she said this.

"I think that's a good dream to have."

"Daddy says I should be more realistic. He said only men are allowed to be healers."

*Oh, that's the reason for the sadness.* Caitlin nodded in understanding. "Well you can always be a healer's helper. You'll be great at it." *But it's so unfair!*

Maggie smiled sweetly and walked with her older sister back to the cart. It was loaded with food and water and their clothes. The horse was tied to a tree and stood waiting patiently, away from the fire and burning houses.

Caitlin put the medicine and bandages in the cart and then studied the young man. He was still asleep. Gerald had helped her to lift him onto the cart. He

79

was tall and didn't fit properly. He had to bend his knees so that his feet didn't dangle off. *I wish he could be more comfortable.*

She had put some pressure on the man's wounds earlier with cloth she found and was able to stop the bleeding, but his wounds should be cleaned and properly bandaged as soon as possible.

"We should get going," Gerald said, interrupting Caitlin's thoughts. "I know it's nighttime, but we shouldn't stay here. We can rest tomorrow."

"How far is the castle?" Maggie asked.

"Far," Gerald said. "It might take a week or two to get there. It all depends on how fast we travel."

"It's going to be hard cleaning him while the cart is moving," Caitlin said. "Can't we wait just a little longer?"

Gerald shook his head. "You can clean him as we go."

Caitlin jumped on the cart and helped Maggie up. Some of the water in the bucket spilled as the horse started moving. They were on their way. It was a gravel road and the cart shook as the horse pulled it. It was going to be a long and uncomfortable ride.

Caitlin looked at the man who lay there limply. His head shook from side to side as the cart moved. He had lost a lot of blood and a dark purple bruise was forming on his cheek. His body was covered with dust and his fingernails were bloody. She dipped a cloth into the water then squeezed the water out and sponged his chest.

"You should start with the wounds," Maggie rolled

her eyes. "You have to do the most important things first." She took a cloth as well and started washing.

Caitlin noticed how clumsy she was compared to Maggie. Caitlin's stokes were too rough, too hard, and yet she failed to thoroughly clean his wounds. In contrast, Maggie worked quickly, gently, and competently.

Caitlin ran her cloth over his abdominal muscles. *He is beautiful.* She let go of the cloth and gently touched his hard abs with her uncertain fingers. She wondered if she had ever touched a man's body like this before. He felt strong and lean beneath her hands. She traced his muscles and went to his dirty face. She softly wiped his bruised cheek and closed eyes. Then her hand moved to his chin and mouth. *Pretty lips. They aren't thick or full, and they aren't too skinny either. Have I been kissed before?* Caitlin touched her lips.

"He will need stitches on his left side," Maggie said. "And we need to make sure the wound is not infected."

"How do we do that?" Caitlin asked the six-year-old dumbly.

"With this," Maggie said. She picked up a bottle with orange goo in it. "It's the same stuff Mom uses every time I scrape my knees. It burns a lot, but it works."

"Do you think it will wake him up?"

Maggie looked at his face. "No, he is going to be asleep for a long time."

They used the orange goo to disinfect all his wounds. The man didn't flinch or groan. Caitlin wondered if he took a blow to the head that knocked him out cold.

"Now stitches," Maggie said.

At the sound of the word stitches Caitlin's hand trembled. She took a needle from the medicine bag that she'd packed. She held the needle in one hand but did not have any thread.

"We can use some of Penny's hair," Maggie suggested.

"Penny?" Caitlin asked.

"Our horse," Maggie said proudly. "I named her."

"Don't get too attached to her," Daisy said. She was walking beside Gerald in front of the cart. "We might need to sell her for money."

Maggie pulled a face. "But I've always wanted a horse!"

Her parents didn't respond.

Caitlin jumped off the slow-moving cart and jogged to Penny's tail. The horse was very tame and didn't kick her when she pulled out some hair. She just swished her tail, annoyed.

Caitlin climbed back onto the cart.

"Finish up back there," Gerald called. "I want you two off the cart so the horse doesn't have to drag extra weight and tire too soon."

"Almost done," Caitlin replied.

Maggie was really good at this. She pulled the hair through the needle and started stitching. Caitlin had to look away as the needle went through the man's skin. Her stomach felt queasy. His other wounds weren't that bad, but she'd have to keep checking them for infection and apply salve every day.

When Maggie finished, she washed her hands in the bucket and emptied the water over the side of the cart. Then both girls jumped off. They left the man lying in the cart, with his eyes closed and head resting on a pillow. They had covered his body in blankets and put their own jackets on as they walked into the night.

"Who do you think he is?" Maggie asked.

"I don't know," Caitlin said.

In her mind she pictured the gray wolf. Beautiful, strong, fearless—animal. Caitlin knew it was even more than that; it could understand her language.

She thought about the bear lady. Like her, the wolf was a shifter as well, but they were not friends. The bear lady would have killed him if Caitlin hadn't run back to help.

She thought of how violent and crazy and deadly and bloodthirsty the bear had been. Then she pictured the body of the lady—the woman she had killed. *Does this mean I killed a human?* She replayed her words in her mind.

*It means you killed a monster.* She could still hear her father's response. So if shifters were monsters and she saved this man who shifts into a wolf, did that mean she saved a monster?

*I still owe him my life. I'll help him heal and then we'll be even.* Nothing would go wrong, as long as the people she traveled with didn't find out what he really was.

# CHAPTER 10

"IT'S WEIRD THAT he came to River Town. No one ever goes there."

"Why?" Caitlin asked, as if she had not been born and raised there.

"Because it's boring!" Maggie giggled. "And in the middle of nothing." She started picking flowers as she walked. "He doesn't even look like one of the river folk."

Caitlin looked at him again. The moon's light was shining on his face. He was much paler than the people she had seen in the town. He was also more muscular, like a warrior and not a farmer. She agreed that he was not from River Town. If he was a traveller, it would not make sense for him to go there either—there was not much to see and do. Unless he was just passing through the town.

"Where do you think he is from then?" Caitlin asked.

"It's hard to say," Maggie said as she picked a white flower. "But I'm sure there isn't a lot of sun where he's from."

"Maybe he was traveling somewhere," Caitlin thought out loud, "and he was just passing through."

"Well, he chose the wrong night," Maggie said.

They walked in silence for a little while. Their parents led the way, and they kept to the main road. It was safer to stay on the known roads than to wander into the forest. The girls followed behind the cart.

"I am not mad at you, by the way," Maggie said out of the blue.

"For what?" Caitlin asked, confused.

"For running away this morning."

A small wave of guilt hit Caitlin as she thought about little Maggie who had been tied to a stake because of her. Her little sister could have died right there and it would all have been her fault.

"If you hadn't run, we wouldn't be going to the castle right now!" Maggie twirled. "I'm so excited! I've always wanted to see Sky Castle."

Caitlin swallowed. None of these places sounded familiar to her. She looked at the six-year-old who was smiling wider than Caitlin had ever seen her smile.

"Tell me about it?" she indulged.

"Well it is supposed to be spectacular. It's high up in the Whispering Mountains. It is so high up that it is covered in clouds and overlooks most of the kingdom!"

"That sounds like quite a view."

"I wonder if I will be scared up there?" she talked on. "I have always been sacred of heights. You, on the other hand, are like a bird!"

*So I am not scared of heights,* Caitlin thought to herself. *What am I scared of then?*

"I wonder if we will get to meet Prince Reagan! Or King Leonard! Or Queen Isabella! I wonder who Dad will tell our story to so that they take us in...."

"I don't think he will be speaking to the king himself," Caitlin said.

"I wonder if the queen will make me a lady?" Maggie continued. "Did you know she has the power to do that?"

"Well, she is the queen...."

Maggie sighed. Her left hand clutched the flowers she had plucked. "It must be amazing to be the queen. Don't you think?"

"No," Caitlin said. She thought about the big responsibility of being queen. And she would always have to look perfect. And talk perfectly. And walk perfectly. And wear gowns so tight that she could barely breathe. "No, I don't want to be queen. Or a lady of the castle," she said.

"Is that why you cut your hair off?" Maggie asked.

Feeling self-conscious Caitlin touched her short hair and then looked at Maggie's long locks. Long hair was a sign of youth and beauty. All the ladies in the palace had long, beautiful hair. Caitlin couldn't remember cutting her hair. "I cut it?" she asked.

"Yes, Mom was furious!" Maggie reminded her. "She

said that you looked like a warrior instead of a lady."

"Do I?" Caitlin asked, looking down at her lean body.

"No," Maggie said. "You are beautiful."

Caitlin smiled at her little sister. Although she didn't remember the kid, Maggie already had a soft spot in her heart. She was so kind and way too good for this world. Caitlin wondered how the castle folk would treat them. She hoped it would work out for the better. She hoped that Maggie would be happy and get the things she wanted.

"Maggie," Daisy said. "You need to sleep."

"But Mom!" Daisy said.

"No 'buts'," her mom replied sternly. "We have a long journey ahead of us. You never go to bed this late anyway. And you'll need your rest."

She helped Maggie into the carriage and covered her with fur blankets. They were careful not to wake the sleeping man, but Caitlin didn't think he would wake up anyway. He'd slept through the ride and all the talking.

"Will you tell me a bedtime story?" Maggie asked.

"Not tonight," her mother said. "I'm too tired."

Caitlin walked next to her mother while Gerald led the horse. The cool night air felt good against her skin. Her legs were tired but she kept walking. Her green eyes went to the sleeping man as a snore escaped his parted lips.

"I'm surprised you saved him," Daisy said.

"Yeah?" Caitlin said softly.

"It's an unusually kind act for you."

Caitlin looked at her a bit baffled. *Am I that unkind?*

"I didn't mean to be cruel!" her mom said quickly. "It's just... You've never been very... caring." She chose her words carefully. "It's always Maggie who helps people and saves animals. Do you remember when that bunny that got his foot stuck in a trap? Maggie was crying and you told her that we should just leave it to die?"

"I don't remember," Caitlin said.

"Well it was only two years ago!" Daisy said.

"What happened?" Caitlin asked.

Her mother smiled. "You saved the bunny, because your sister asked."

"At least that story had a happy ending," Caitlin said. If her mother heard the bitterness in her voice, she didn't show it.

"Sweetheart," Daisy said, touching her arm, "this is going to be a big move for us. I'll need your help with Maggie."

"What would you like me to do?" Caitlin didn't feel like helping anyone right now. *Unkind people don't help others.*

"She looks up to you for guidance. She follows your example. If you're happy, she's happy. I know moving to a castle won't be easy for any of us. And we will be outsiders. We will have to work hard for little money. We can do it. But I am worried out Maggie...."

"Go on," Caitlin urged. She tried to sound more interested than she actually was.

"She is only six. You know she's always had these crazy big dreams of becoming a lady or marrying a prince. I've never had the heart to tell her that her dreams won't come true... that she, like us, are peasants and nothing in the royal family's eyes."

"You're scared she will get her heart broken in Sky Castle?"

Her mother looked down at her feet as she walked. Then she looked to the little girl who had fallen asleep in the cart moments after closing her eyes. "Yes, I am afraid that this move will destroy all of her dreams."

"It's good to dream, but better to dream realistically," Gerald said as they caught up to him at the front of the carriage.

"So we'll need you to be on your best behavior," Daisy said kindly. "Please try to act like a lady."

Caitlin grimaced. Her mother was asking her to do the impossible.

"It's a pity you cut your hair," her mother continued. "I'm sure we'd still be able to find you a fine husband."

Caitlin's stomach turned. Luckily Daisy didn't keep talking about getting married and the awkward conversation came to a welcome end.

Gerald told them to take turns sleeping so that they could travel faster. So Caitlin got into the cart. There wasn't a lot of space, among the food, water, clothes, and two sleeping bodies, but she managed to squeeze her lean frame between the man and her small sister. She was really tired and wondered how long her mom would let her sleep before waking her up so that they could trade places.

She closed her eyes and sleep came easily. She wanted the sleep desperately—but not the nightmares that came with it.

# CHAPTER 11

IN HER NIGHTMARE, she was a little girl.

Her hair was lighter and longer than it was now; it hung down to the middle of her back. Her face was rounder and younger. Her skin was soft and she had no freckles from the sun. Her tiny hands clasped a glass bottle. The only thing that was the same about her was her green eyes.

She had six bottles arranged in front of her on her desk. They all looked identical, except for the different colored fluids they contained. The teacher told the students that three of the six bottles contained poison. Their task was simple: they had to identify the three bottles that did not contain poison and then they had to drink down all their contents.

They had been studying poisons for the past few weeks now. They had written several papers and even concocted their own poisons. Everyone had debated what ingredients to mix for their poison to be more deadly. It had been all fun and games—until now.

The classroom was big and it did not have any windows. The walls were made of stone and the roof sat high above their heads. Candles and torches provided enough illumination for the students, although those with poor vision had to squint to see sometimes.

The classroom went silent. Kids stopped talking, joking, or playing. Everyone focused either on their own work or on trying to copy someone else's. The teacher walked around the room, carrying a selection of antidotes for the children who chose the wrong bottles to drink.

Caitlin had studied hard. She knew what she was doing. She smelled the first bottle and detected the faintly earthy, musky scent of one type of poison—an easy one to identify. If she drank it, she would not die. It would only make her very sick, and depending on how much she drank, she would begin to hallucinate. She moved that bottle to the left side of her desk and then picked up and smelled the next bottle. It smelled like water. She dipped her finger in it and stirred. She slid it to the right side of her desk, thinking that it was safe. The next one was safe too. And then she found one that had a purple shimmer to it when she stirred. It was another poison. This one would cause painful stomachaches.

She finished first in the class—as always. On the left

side of her desk were the three bottles that contained poison. On the right side were the three that were safe. She smiled, clearly pleased with herself.

The girl sitting opposite her—the one called Stacey —noticed that Caitlin had finished. Her expression changed from ambitious and focused to frustrated. She glared at Caitlin, like she usually did when Caitlin finished first. She hated that she could never beat Caitlin at anything. Even when Stacey had studied for hours and hours, Caitlin always seemed to do better.

"I hope you got it wrong," she snarled under her breath.

Caitlin tried to ignore her but failed miserably. She did not like it when people picked on her, and Stacey was always picking on her.

Distracted, Stacey had stopped sorting through her own bottles. If she didn't pick up the pace, she would lose her chance to finish in second place too. But it didn't matter to her because all positions behind first meant she was a loser. "I hope you drink poison and die," she whispered.

Caitlin kept her eyes in front of her. Her face was calm, but her mind was not. Punching Stacey would only get her in trouble again. Instead of fighting, she raised her hand for the teacher to come and check her work.

"The teachers won't let us die," another student whispered. "They are always saying how they need us!"

The teacher walked up to Caitlin with a pleased

smile. She was always pleased with Caitlin's work because Caitlin was an A-student. "Are you ready to drink?" she asked.

Caitlin looked at her teacher's body language. Her shoulders were relaxed and her hands weren't near the antidotes. Caitlin knew that she had passed the test even before she started drinking.

The kids in the class turned their heads, all eager to see if she would pass or fail. Some were tired of her and hoped that for once she got it wrong. Others were looking in awe, wishing that they could finish a task as quickly as she did.

"I am," Caitlin said confidently and drank the contents of the three bottles that sat on the right side of her desk without hesitating. Now all she had to do was wait. She gave the teacher a beaming smile.

As the rest of the class continued to sort through their bottles, Caitlin leaned back in her seat with a bored expression on her face. The problem with finishing first was that she had to wait for the other kids to catch up. There weren't many students but they were always so slow. What was she supposed to do with all this time? Her eyes went to Stacey.

"You're doing it wrong." Caitlin lied easily. She knew this girl was gullible and jealous. She could manipulate her as easily as she could breathe.

"Shut up," Stacey snapped back.

But Caitlin saw the flicker of doubt in her eyes. Although Stacey desperately tried to hide her jealousy,

Caitlin knew it was burning like a fire inside her. She saw how Stacey glared at her. She saw how Stacey tried to copy everything she did. She also saw how Stacey always tried to bring her down. So Caitlin whispered harshly, "You will be the one to drink the poison. Soon you will be rolling around the classroom floor."

Stacey bit her lip. She had sorted all her bottles. There were three bottles on the left side of her desk and three on the right side.

"Everyone will laugh at you," Caitlin pressed on.

"Stop it," Stacey said in a tight voice.

"Fine," Caitlin leaned back and smiled as she saw the girl's shoulders tense. "Don't listen to me, although I got it right."

Stacey hesitated. Her eyes darted from the left side of her desk to the right before she decided to give in. "Fine! Which one is wrong?" she whispered so that the teacher didn't hear.

Another student, seated at the front of the classroom, finished and drank his. It only took seconds before he started choking, catching the teacher's attention. She rushed to the boy, who was writhing on the floor, and tried to force the antidote down his throat.

Caitlin wasn't focused on the gagging boy. She was looking at the bottles on Stacey's desk. She saw the little bit of purple in one bottle. "That one," she pointed to it. "It's clean. Safe to drink."

Stacey lifted it obediently.

"Swap it with this one," Caitlin said and pointed to one of the clean bottles.

Stacey did that, and Caitlin hid her smile. It was so easy to get people to do what she wanted if she just stayed calm and took the time to plan her actions.

Stacey didn't thank Caitlin and her hands were shaking slightly before she raised one into the air to signal the teacher.

The teacher stood by the poisoned child a little longer —he was now sitting up with his head between his knees recuperating—before making her way over to Stacey. Her face was tense.

"Are you ready?" she asked.

Stacey nodded.

Caitlin tilted her head to the side, wondering why she was so stupid. How could she not see the teachers worried eyes? Or her hand on the antidote bottle?

Stacey hesitated before drinking her two clean bottles and then slowly tipped poisoned one into her mouth and swallowed.

Caitlin smiled as she counted in her head: *one monkey, two monkeys, three monkeys...*

Then Stacey grabbed her stomach, tried to stand but couldn't, and fell to the floor. She screamed in pain and started rolling around. Some kids jumped to their feet while others froze in their seats. Stacey wrapped her arms around her stomach. The teacher bent down and forced the antidote into her mouth by clasping her hand over Stacey's lips while pinching her nose closed.

Stacey swallowed involuntarily and moments later she stopped squirming.

"You drank the most obvious poison," the teacher said while getting to her feet.

Stacey's face went red with humiliation. She struggled to get to her feet and didn't look at Caitlin once.

A tall, gangly girl sitting behind her had watched the entire incident without saying anything. She didn't like Stacey who had always been mean to her. But maybe she should have spoken up when she saw that Caitlin had tricked her? Guilt started eating away at this girl. By the time the class ended, she ran to the teacher and told her what had happened.

When the kids left the classroom, the teacher held Caitlin back to speak to her. Caitlin approached the teacher and glared at the tall girl who was making a quick exit out of the classroom.

"Sit," the teacher commanded.

Caitlin sighed and flopped down into a chair. She looked up at the teacher with a blank face.

"Is it true?" the teacher asked her. "Did you tell Stacey to switch the bottles?"

"No," Caitlin said and looked straight at the teacher with wide, unblinking eyes.

"Are you sure?" the teacher asked.

"Why do you always want to get me in trouble?" Caitlin asked. "I'm at top of the class. I am your best student."

"And my meanest student," the teacher added coldly.

There was silence. Caitlin wasn't going to confess.

"Why did you do it?" her teacher persisted. "She is no competition to you."

"But I didn't do anything," Caitlin said calmly and smoothly.

The teacher took a seat beside her. "I saw you do it. Another student didn't have to tell me for me to know." The teacher studied Caitlin's face in silence before continuing. "I've never seen anyone lie the way you do," she said. "Do you ever feel guilty?"

"I don't feel much," Caitlin said evenly.

"That's another lie," the teacher said. "You feel anger. You feel hate."

Caitlin clenched her fists.

"I understand that it's not your fault. It's in your blood."

"Am I being punished?" Caitlin asked.

The teacher looked at her for a long time. "Don't hurt any more children."

Caitlin got up and left the room without another word.

"Wake up, darling." Daisy gently shook her daughter's shoulders. "Wake up."

Sixteen-year-old Caitlin opened her eyes. She sat up and rubbed the sleep out of her eyes. It was dawn and they were still moving. She was still in the cart. Maggie and the young man were still asleep in the cart next to her.

"Is it your turn to sleep?" she asked Daisy.

Her mother nodded and climbed into the cart.

As she climbed out of the cart, Caitlin's legs felt stiff and her mind felt foggy. But she remembered her dream as clear as day.

# CHAPTER 12

CAITLIN'S SHADOW TRAILED her in the moonlight as she walked to the front of the cart where Gerald was leading Penny. Penny had a calm nature and she was strong working horse. She was perfect for the long journey to Sky Castle but she would still get tired. Caitlin wondered if they would stop to let the horse rest soon. She had been walking for hours and was nervous because of the fires that burned down the stables and most of the village. The horse also needed some sleep.

"Did you sleep well?" Gerald asked her, his voice full of concern.

"Yes," she said.

The dream still troubled her but he didn't need to know that. She didn't feel that they were close enough for her to confide in him. Neither did she want to think about the things that bothered her. So she redirected their conversation. "Are *you* feeling alright? You have been walking for hours."

"I'm fine," he said and then clenched his jaw. "I will rest when your mother wakes up. It is best if we keep moving."

She nodded. Gerald was a determined man, but not stubborn. She had a feeling that if she asked nicely, he would give her whatever she wanted. She did not want to keep walking. "Will we stop soon?"

"It's a two-day walk to Waterfall Haven," he said. "It's a big town where we can rest. Maybe we will even find travel companions to join us on our way to the castle. It is always better to travel in a group. We will be much safer that way."

Caitlin thought of the bear and saw the wisdom of his plan to continue traveling. Her legs could keep walking for a long time if they had to. But she didn't feel like running away from any crazy beasts. "What do we have to fear?"

"Besides common thieves and bandits..." Gerald said, his thoughts straying to the bear. He'd never seen a creature like that before and shuddered at the idea that there might be more. "Magic. That's what I fear most and that's what we need to warn our king about."

She was surprised that he said that word out loud. Maggie had reacted to it as if saying it was worse than swearing. Maybe Gerald said it now because no one else was near enough to hear him.

"But won't the king have us burned? The way the villagers wanted to?" Caitlin asked hesitantly.

"The king is a smart man," he said. "He will be able to tell that we have nothing to do with Magic. He has fought against it all his life."

"Tell me his story," she prodded.

Her father looked at her. "You want me to tell you about how he came to rule the Silver Kingdom?"

She nodded.

"Didn't they teach you this in school?" he asked.

"Refresh my memory," she asked innocently.

"Very well," he breathed in deeply. "King Leonard has been ruling for twenty years now. He was born during the Age of Magic, during the days of the Witch Prince. The Witch Prince was a wicked, cruel thing." Caitlin could hear the disgust in Gerald's voice. "He was born a royal and his family had been ruling for centuries. Magic and man lived together in peace because his father had strict laws. But the Witch Prince hated man. He had no respect for those who did not have Magic blood. He didn't like our horses because they couldn't fly. He didn't like our dogs because they weren't devilish. He didn't like our very existence."

"And he was going to inherit the throne from his father?"

"He was the older child so he was supposed to," Gerald said. "But his father sensed the evil in him so he was forced to ban him from Sky Castle. The throne would go to the younger prince. The Witch Prince didn't like this. In his fury he killed his younger brother and that same night he slit his parents' throats when they were asleep."

"What?!" Caitlin said, with goose bumps on her arms.

"The Witch Prince was powerful and feared. He had anyone killed who spoke against his taking the crown. After he killed his family, he crowned himself the Witch King. He sat on his father's throne and enslaved those without Magic. He killed us, hurt us, and tortured us just because we were different from him."

"That's terrible," Caitlin breathed.

"King Leonard, our current king, was born a normal man. He has no Magical abilities whatsoever. He grew up poor and his father died a slave. He had a terrible childhood full of hardship and suffering. His mother died when he was only sixteen at the hands of a sorcerer. So he was conscripted along with other men without Magic and forced to fight in the king's army. He gained the loyalty and trust of these men, and together they crafted a plan to overthrow the Witch King.

"He formed an army, and more and more men joined him. They rose up and overthrew the Witch King. He was burned alive in front of the army. We now celebrate the day of the Witch King's death as Freedom Day. That was the day that King Leonard took the throne and saved us all."

"Didn't any of our neighboring kingdoms come to help with the battle?" Caitlin asked.

A look of disgust crossed Gerald's face. "The Silver

Kingdom is much bigger than the Forevermore Kingdom. But the Forevermore Kingdom has more natural resources that make them richer than us. During the Age of Magic, King Leonard asked them to fight beside us. They said they would but showed up only after the fight was over. Some believe they were waiting to see which side won so they could side with the winner. There has been a fragile peace between us for years now. The royals of the Forevermore Kingdom visit us once a year on Freedom Day to show that we stand united against Magic. I think that they want to overthrow us and take our lands for themselves, but they don't have the numbers. We have the men and the might to take their kingdom, but since they have done nothing to start a war, it would be unwise for us to attack first. Attacking first and for no reason would make the other kingdoms despise us."

Gerald realized he had trailed off a bit. "Anyway, our king banished Magic and got justice for all of our people who had been killed or enslaved. Since then the dangerous people with strange abilities have been burned and killed and hunted. There are few left."

"But there are some left," Caitlin said. "Like the bear lady."

"Yes," Gerald said. "And just look at what she did! She slaughtered an entire village."

"So what will the king do?"

"He will most likely send hunters to see if there are any more such foul creatures."

"But are all of them bad?" she asked.

Gerald gave her a shocked look. "Caitlin, you saw that thing with your own eyes! It's not human. It doesn't have a conscience. It's a killing machine."

Gerald and Daisy had been tied to their stakes facing the opposite direction from Caitlin so they didn't see the wolf help her. She wondered what Gerald would think of that but was wise enough not to bring it up. Little Maggie had been facing the same direction as Caitlin. She wondered if her sister had seen it or if she had been too panicked. Maybe her eyes were closed during the whole thing? But if she had seen something, she didn't say anything about it...

Caitlin willed herself to look into Gerald's eyes and not look back at the man sleeping in the cart.

"Anyone who mixes with Magic, or helps Magical beings, are hanged! You never ever want to get caught up in something like that. It is an unforgivable crime," Gerald's eyes were serious. "Do you understand?"

She nodded.

"Is there anything you want to tell me?" Gerald asked.

"Why do you ask?" she answered with a question.

"Because ever since yesterday morning you've been distant."

She didn't know how she could tell him that she didn't know who he was. He looked at her with loving eyes. He treated her as if he had been caring for her since she was a child. He talked to her as if she was the most precious daughter in the world. She couldn't tell him. "A lot has happened," she said lamely.

"You have these moments when you look around in confusion," her father said. "It almost looks like you don't know where you are or who you are."

"And who am I?" she asked.

If he was her father and he noticed a change in her behavior, perhaps he could tell her more about herself. Maybe she could even figure out why she couldn't remember anything.

"You are Caitlin Wilde," he said. "You are my beautiful elder daughter who was born and raised in River Town. You are a stunning young lady and I love you."

She didn't say anything back. She knew her face was pale. She looked down at the ground as if it was speaking instead of Gerald.

"If you ever need to talk to me, about anything, don't hesitate," Gerald said.

She could tell he meant it, so she answered with a nod. She didn't feel the need to sound like a crazy person and tell him that she woke up, on her birthday, and couldn't remember her life before that. She couldn't tell him that she didn't know him or Daisy or Maggie. That she hadn't even recognized her own face!

And she couldn't shake the feeling that she didn't belong here.... "Does amnesia run in our family?" she asked.

The question caught Gerald off guard. He looked confused as he answered her. "No, it doesn't."

She bit her lip and didn't look at him as she continued to her next question. "Have I had any accidents lately?"

"What do you mean 'accidents'?"

"Like... have I maybe had a head injury?"

"Does your head hurt?" he responded with a frown wrinkling his forehead.

"No..."

"Then why would you ask such a question?"

She shrugged. "Sometimes it just feels like I can't remember...."

"What is it you want to remember?" he sounded a bit worried.

She swung her arms at her side and her voice was soft. "I don't know."

He looked at her, waiting for more, but she didn't know what else to say. "It feels like there is something I forgot. Something important and I can't remember what it is."

"If it was important, you would not have forgotten," her father said. "Unless of course, you don't want to remember."

It was her turn to be confused. To her relief, Gerald explained his statement. "Our brains sometimes block out memories that are harmful to us for our own safety."

"Do you mean to say that maybe something really traumatic happened and I don't want to remember it?"

"Well, dear, in River Town nothing ever happens," he said with his eyes crinkling.

They walked in silence for a little while, and she felt the long grasses tickle her ankles as she walked. Her mind was still racing.

"If your head hurts, blame it on your mother." Gerald immediately caught her attention. "I think she might have dropped you on your head as a child," he continued and he let out a soft, rumbling chuckle.

She smiled. "That was a lame dad-joke."

He shrugged. "But it made you smile, didn't it?"

Caitlin heard a groan come from the back of the cart. Was the young man awake?

# CHAPTER 13

CAITLIN LEFT GERALD'S SIDE and walked to the back of the cart.

The man was trying to sit upright. His face was pulled into an expression of pain and confusion. His hands pressed down beside him as he tried to push himself up.

"Don't," Caitlin said and put her hand on his arm to stop him from moving. In a flash his other hand locked around her wrist and pulled it from his arm. He laid his wide eyes on her.

"I didn't mean to startle you," she said and looked up from her wrist that he gripped so tightly.

His eyes found hers. They were as gray as a foggy mist. She felt like she might fall into them and get lost. For a moment she just stared into them, forgetting about the iron grip he had on her wrist.

"Who are you?" he growled. "Where am I?"

"I'll answer all of your questions," she said calmly and then she looked at his hand. "But first, please let me go?"

He hesitated but did as she asked. Then he rolled to his side and propped himself up on one elbow trying to get up again.

"Don't try to sit up," she said. "You are injured."

He lifted the blankets and looked at the bandage. "How bad is it?"

"It will be alright, but you need to rest," she told him. "I think the medicine might help to make you sleep."

"I don't want to sleep," he said. "I have to be alert."

He looked over his raised shoulder at Daisy who held Maggie in her arms. They were both sound asleep. His eyes lingered on them and he seemed to relax a bit.

"No one will harm you here," Caitlin said. He turned his attention on her. She saw no hint of trust in his eyes. "My family and I are farmers. My name is Caitlin Wilde—"

"You were tied to the stake," he interrupted.

She nodded.

"How is your town?"

She didn't know if he was being sarcastic or if really wanted to know. "Destroyed," she said. She was aware that her voice was emotionless. There was no hint of her feeling traumatized or frightened.

"You don't sound very sad, witch-girl."

"I am not a witch," she retorted.

"And apparently not a healer either," he growled.

Caitlin felt the anger rising in her stomach. *What an ungrateful man! I saved him, and this is how he thanks me?! By calling me names and complaining!* "We did the best we could to help you, with the few things we had," she said, trying to sound calm. She didn't want to raise her voice and wake Daisy and Maggie.

"It feels like I am on fire," he said.

She hopped into the cart. It was easy to get on because of their slow pace. Unfortunately, with four people aboard there wasn't a lot of space.

She stooped over and fumbled through their things. It was hard to see in the dark but after a few seconds, that felt like forever, she found the salve. "This should help," she said, turning to face him.

"Should?" he asked worriedly.

"Relax, I know what I am doing."

"It doesn't look that way."

"Then what does it look like?" she said as she stood with one hand on a hip, the other brandishing the jar of salve.

"Like you're about to fall."

"What?"

The cart shook, and sure enough, she lost her balance. He reached out and pulled her back just before she fell off. Grunting from the pain that the jerking motion caused, he barked, "Will you please sit down!"

She didn't thank him as she sat and crossed her legs. He pulled away the blankets so she could get at his bandages. Caitlin eyed the soiled bandages and then began to remove them roughly.

"Can you be gentle?" he asked. He didn't say it in a mean way. His voice was pleading.

"Stop being so overly sensitive."

"I'm not overly sensitive."

She tried to keep her hands from shaking as she fumbled with the lid on the jar. *Am I nervous?*

The man looked at her with raised eyebrows and for a moment she thought she saw the edge of his mouth lift up into half a smile.

"What?" she spat at him. "The cart is shaking!"

"I didn't say anything," he said in a charming voice.

She focused her attention on the lid of the jar. She tried to look confident and calm and this time it opened when she twisted. She almost sighed with relief.

But opening the jar was only the beginning.

She looked at the man's pale chest and wounded sides and tried not to stare as she dipped her fingers into the salve. She touched his side and he flinched but didn't make a sound. She put the salve on as best as she could and wrapped him up again. She saw that she did a sloppy job with the bandages as he struggled to sit up. He groaned and didn't thank her.

"Where are we going?" he asked.

"To Waterfall Haven," she said. "We are going to rest there and then make our way to Sky Castle."

"You do know that witches aren't welcome there either, right?" he raised an eyebrow.

"That was a misunderstanding," she said defensively. "I'm not a witch."

"Prove it."

"How?"

"We tie you to a stake and set it on fire. If you burn, you weren't a witch."

"But I'll be dead."

"Then that would be tragic," he said with sarcasm.

"If I die no one will tend to your wounds. Then you will die."

"That would *really* be tragic," he said genuinely.

"There must be another way to prove that I'm just a human girl."

He thought about this for a moment as he watched her sitting beside him on the cart.

"Okay then. How about by not casting any spells."

"What?"

"Witches cast spells. So if you don't do any, you're not a witch."

She looked at him, confused. "So do I just carry on with what I was doing?"

"Yes. What were you doing?"

"Sitting."

"Okay. You just sit there then."

She paused and realized he had a sharp, sarcastic sense of humour. "You don't really think I'm a witch, do you?"

"Of course not," he laughed. "I'm just messing with you."

"But you met me when I was tied to a stake about to be burned," she made the moment serious. "Isn't that where you would expect to meet a witch?"

"No witch is dumb enough to get caught and then burned on a stake," he said.

Something had changed in his voice. It was more serious too. A part of her was hoping he would elaborate on the subject.

The seriousness disappeared and he managed a weak smile. "Do you have any pain medication?"

She rummaged through the medicine that she had stolen from the healer's house, doing her best to look like she knew what she was doing. She had no idea what any of the bottles or salves were.

"I think it might be this one," she said lifting a bottle.

"You think?"

"I know," she corrected.

"You're wrong," he said. "Don't you recognize that color?"

"It's a pretty pink color," she pointed out the obvious.

"It's an emetic. That means it'll make me vomit everything that's in my stomach—and quickly," he said with a deadpan expression.

"Really?" she gasped and nearly dropped the bottle.

"How would I know?" He bit his lip. "'It's YOUR stuff."

She glared at him.

"Well, since neither of us knows what it is, I'd feel better if you took the first sip."

"But I'm not sick or injured," she stated.

"–yet." He looked at the bottle in her hands. Then he spotted another one. "Hand me that one."

She did as he asked. He opened the bottle, smelled it, and took a few sips. "Caitlin," he said in his serious voice.

She braced herself for a *thank-you*. "Yes..."

"Don't become a healer," he said flatly as he lay down on his back again.

She managed a smile.

He closed his eyes. The medicine was already making him sleepy.

"You didn't tell me your name," she said.

"Rafe Grey," he yawned. Minutes later he fell asleep.

# CHAPTER 14

THE JOURNEY WAS slow, but they at last arrived at Waterfall Haven. Rafe slept during most of the journey. He was still too weak to walk. The medicine he was taking blunted his appetite, along with his good will. So he didn't speak much to anyone, aside from a stray snide or sarcastic comment.

He didn't mention wolves or Magic. He spent most of his time staring into the sky or observing the Wilde family. Sometimes when Maggie threw her arms around Caitlin, he would look at them oddly–almost longingly. When he realized that Caitlin noticed, he would then look away, pretending to be focused on something else.

He didn't speak much with Daisy or Gerald. But he did thank them for so kindly helping him. He said he was a tourist, traveling through the Silver Kingdom. He promised that as soon as he was better, he would "get out of their hair."

He told them that he was from the far south, a land of cold and snow, and had lived there most of his life—which explained his pale skin. He had only recently decided to travel through the Silver Kingdom.

Maggie liked him. Although he was without a doubt a sarcastic person, he was always kind to her and made her laugh. It didn't take long for her to relax around him.

Gerald, on the other hand, thought he was rather strange. Because Gerald had lived in River Town all his life and never traveled beyond its boundaries, his views were very different from Rafe's. He also didn't like the way Rafe's eyes lingered on Caitlin a little longer than they should.

Daisy thought he was funny. She even helped changed his bandages once. Although she, like Gerald, found him strange, she felt he was a good person.

They arrived at Waterfall Haven at night. It was a beautiful place, lush and green. The sound of running water was calming and gave the place a fresh smell.

Gerald wasted no time searching for a place to sleep. It was late and they were tired. He found an inn for them to stay the night.

"I don't mind staying in the cart for the night," Rafe told them. He didn't expect the family to spend their money on him.

"That's not going to happen, dear," Daisy said. She was a very caring woman. Not only did she treat her children with warmth and love, she did the same for everyone. There was no way she would let Rafe stay in the cart.

Gerald paid for their rooms. He shared one with Daisy. Caitlin and Maggie shared one and Rafe had his own room. Caitlin would have liked a room to herself because Maggie displayed no respect for her space or privacy. *Maybe I would have had Rafe's room if he was not traveling with us. Maybe sharing a room was Gerald's way of punishing me.* Caitlin was tired from their journey and had trouble stopping unkind thoughts from barging their way into her head.

Gerald walked to the cart, thinking that he was going to help Rafe to his room. But when he reached the cart, Rafe was already on his feet.

"You are healing fast," he said.

"I am," Rafe said and slowly stretched. "All thanks to your kind family." He told them that he was passing through their small town when the bear attacked him. He admitted that he was lucky to survive.

Caitlin didn't say a word while Rafe was speaking.

And no one said anything about a wolf.

Seeing that Rafe was strong enough to manage, Gerald told him where to find his room and gave him a key. "We are leaving midday tomorrow," he said in parting.

Caitlin wondered if Gerald wanted to leave him here. He didn't invite Rafe to go with them. But then again, Gerald did say he wanted travel companions for safety. If Gerald was hinting that Rafe couldn't come with them, Rafe gave no indication whatsoever.

"Thank you," Rafe said with a smile. "Goodnight, sir."

"He has such good manners," Daisy remarked as he walked into the inn.

Caitlin stared after him and looked away when she realized Gerald was watching her. She didn't want to say goodbye to Rafe. Although he had been sleeping during most of their journey, he still made the trip more enjoyable with his jokes.

Gerald was tired and a bit grumpy. He gave Caitlin her and her sister's room key. Caitlin took their key and carried Rafe's medicine and bandages inside with her.

Maggie followed on her sister's heels, her head hanging, silent, and far from her usual energetic self. Maggie was tired—she had already fallen asleep in the cart next to Rafe and Caitlin had to wake her up when they had reached the inn. She would have carried Maggie to their room if she didn't have to carry Rafe's medicine.

"Aren't you coming?" Daisy asked her husband as they watched their two girls make their way into the inn.

"You go ahead. I want to ask the townspeople if any of them want to travel to Sky Castle," Gerald said. "I'd like to find people to journey with us."

Daisy nodded. "Please don't come to bed too late."

He kissed her on the cheek and watched her follow their daughters into the inn.

Once in their room, Maggie flopped down on their bed, and Caitlin pulled the blanket out from under her sister so that she could throw it over her small body. The little girl drifted off into dreamland. Caitlin wondered if she was dreaming about saving lives as a healer. She had really taken charge when it came to Rafe's health over the past two days. She made sure his bandages were clean and scolded Caitlin when she got the various medicine bottles mixed up.

"You would make a fantastic healer," Caitlin whispered to the sleeping girl. *What a shame that the world was such an unfair place where women didn't have the same opportunities as men.* Maggie would make an outstanding healer because she already had the patience and talent for it. All she needed was the time and the opportunity to learn, to apprentice from someone who had mastered the skills.

Caitlin dimmed the lights. The room was small and worn but much more comfortable than the cart. The windows were cracked and the bed creaked when Maggie rolled over. But Caitlin didn't complain. They were trying to save as much money as possible on their journey. Staying in anything better than this would be too much luxury.

She drew the curtains shut. Maybe tomorrow she

could go explore the town a bit. She liked seeing beautiful places and she liked the freedom of being outside. She didn't have any desire to go swimming, although there was so much water in this town. She would simply explore and maybe get something tasty to eat. Anything would be better than the bread and fruit that they had been eating while traveling. Rafe would agree with her.

*Rafe.* She smiled to herself. *Maybe he would like to go exploring too.* If he was a traveler, he surely enjoyed such things. He had told her about a small town at the outskirts of Water City. He told her that there was so much water in certain parts of this town that the only way to get from house to house was by boat. He clearly had been to so many places in the world, places she had never even heard of.

The thought of water made Caitlin realize just how dirty she was. She hadn't cleaned herself in two days and she had sweated a lot from walking in the sun. Her eyes searched their small room and spied a large wooden tub at the far corner, flanked by two dented tin pails. Caitlin sighed—A *bath is just what I need before bed!*—and started making trips down to the kitchen to fetch some water heated over the inn's great hearth. Three trips total, six pails of water, lukewarm by the time she'd filled the tub.

All the clumping footsteps and the sloshing water did not wake her little sister. Caitlin shrugged off her clothes and climbed into the bath. She lay there, with closed eyes, and soaked in it for a little bit. She then washed and combed her wild hair and scrubbed her dirty nails. When she felt clean, she got out of the bath and dried herself with the rough towel that hung against the wall. The inn provided lavender oil in a small apothecary jar. She soothed some onto her skin.

Then she searched through her clothes. She didn't have much and none of it was at all attractive. So she chose a simple black shirt, with short sleeves, and a wide neckline that hung low over her breast. It hugged her body and was the closest she had to sleepwear. The pants she chose were a bit baggy but they were comfortable and soft.

She looked at herself in the mirror. Her towel-dried hair hung in all directions. Maggie had told her that she had cut her own hair and Caitlin now realized that she had done a poor job. But despite all this, she felt good. She felt clean and more relaxed than she had in a long time. She looked at herself in the mirror and yawned. After two days of traveling her feet hurt and she was tired.

She walked toward the bed, but then her eyes spotted Rafe's medicines in a corner of her room. She had carried it there along with her clothes. Would he need the salve tonight? He needed to apply it three times a day....

Caitlin knew she could easily bring it to him because his room was close to hers. But the idea of knocking on his door made her nervous and she was not sure why. She had never been alone with him before. Would it be different if there was no one else around? Would he be different?

*It's bedtime. He's tired and probably already asleep.* Maybe she should just get into bed and give him the salve tomorrow. Would he even want to see her tonight? Was it appropriate for her to visit his room, all alone, at this hour? *I should just let him rest.*

She paced around a bit. She was overthinking this and making up excuses not to go. She should not have to be scared or nervous about doing something as mundane as taking his medicine to him.

Caitlin walked away from the bed and picked up his salve and bandages. She huffed. If she waited any longer she was going to talk herself out of it. She would show up, give him the medicine, and go to bed. It was really simple.

He was two rooms down the hall and she could be there in a few seconds. Her legs felt a bit numb as she walked to his door. She knocked three times before he opened the door.

The first thing she noticed was his bare chest: he wasn't wearing his shirt. She tried not to stare. She had, after all, seen him without his shirt many times whenever she changed his bandages. And she had found him fully naked back in River Town. He looked in better health now than he did when she'd first seen him in his human form. He had removed the bandages and so she could see that the stitches were healing nicely. He looked clean, like he had also taken a bath.

His hair was dry but sticking up in all directions.

Caitlin's throat felt tight. She was glad he spoke first.

"I was wondering when you would come."

"You knew I would?" she asked as he stepped aside to let her in. Instinctively she moved forward as he closed the door behind her. She tried to look as if she felt comfortable but only succeeded in making herself feel even more awkward.

"I don't blame you. How could you stay away from all this?" he motioned to his shirtless body.

"D-don't flatter yourself," she stuttered as she felt her cheeks getting warm. "I just brought your medicine."

He moved away from the door and she realized that she could open it and run away if she wanted to. Rafe sat down on the bed slowly and carefully—his sides were still hurting.

Caitlin placed the bandages and salve on the bed next to him. Then she regretted doing it. Her arms felt heavy, and for some odd reason, she didn't know what to do with them.

"Relax," he smiled. "I'm not going to bite."

"That's a wise decision," she said.

"Oh yeah?" he raised an eyebrow.

"I bite hard," she warned.

"I doubt that!" he laughed. His laugh was a beautiful sound. She found it contagious and returned his smile. Doing so made some of her nervousness go away and she could breathe again. He was still Rafe—the gorgeous and humorous man who had saved her life.

She watched him as he reached for the salve on the bed and opened the lid. He rubbed it into the scratch marks on his right side before applying some on the stitches. She regretted not helping him but felt too weird to start now. "You heal fast," she observed.

"Inhumanly fast?" he said while still looking at his wounds. He closed the jar and put it aside with the bandages. "Would you like to sit?" he motioned to the bed. There were no chairs in his room.

"I probably should not—it's late." Caitlin said. She glanced at the door, but her feet didn't move.

"You know what I am," he said and got to his feet.

Her heart skipped a beat. "Yes."

He stopped a few feet away from her and observed her the way a cat would a mouse. "Why aren't you afraid?"

"Should I be?" she asked him, maintaining eye contact.

Rafe was the first one to look away. "If your father knew what I was he would try to kill me without thinking twice about it."

"Then we better not tell him," she responded.

Rafe looked into her eyes for a long moment. She wondered if he was trying to figure her out. *He surely must know that if I was going to tell on him, I would have done so by now.... Is he studying me?*

"I've wanted to ask you, but I've not gotten the chance until now.... What happened to the bear?"

Caitlin sagged a little. *Will he hate me for killing one of his kind?* But she remembered how he and the bear fought and how the bear nearly killed him. "I killed her," she said bluntly. There was something about the way he looked at her that made her feel as if he would know if she was lying.

"You and who else?" he asked curiously.

"No one else," she said. "It was just me."

Rafe didn't say anything and she struggled to read his body language. He was inhumanly still—almost as if he was not breathing. His gray eyes looked like thunder clouds.

"It was self-defense, I swear," she confessed.

"How did it make you feel?" he asked. "To take a life?" He came forward and stopped just before their bodies touched. "Powerful? Happy?"

"I was only happy I got away in one piece," she said.

He laughed.

"I don't see what's so funny about it." She looked up at him. He was so tall.

"I don't know what to find funnier," he confessed. "That you, a little farmer girl, killed a dangerous shifter single-handedly." He flicked his hair out of his face. "Or that you're the first human I've ever met who doesn't take pleasure in killing my kind."

"So you're not angry at me?"

"Angry? Why would I be angry? That bear would have killed me if she had the chance!"

"Why would she have killed you?" Caitlin asked as she took a step back. Standing too close made her forget that she should breathe. "Aren't all shifters friends?"

"Why do humans murder each other? Aren't all humans friends?" he asked in return.

His eyes were unlike any she'd ever seen before. She couldn't decide if they reminded her more of ash or thick fog or storm clouds. His pupils were dilated, like those of a predator. His iris was a light gray, almost silver. And around that was a dark gray circle.

His lips were slightly parted. They revealed normal human teeth, no fangs. Caitlin wondered how strong they were. *Oh damn. He probably thinks I'm staring at his lips.*

"So... are you just going to stand there gaping all night?" he drawled.

Her face flushed as she realized how long they've been silent. "I wasn't gaping," she bit back.

"You can thank me later."

"For being gorgeous?" she asked.

"For stopping you before you started to drool all over yourself."

"I'm leaving now," she turned to go but he caught her arm.

"Don't be like that," he said. "I'm just joking."

"I was too," she said with beet-red cheeks. "You're not *that* gorgeous."

"Just a little bit?" he asked.

Her stomach fluttered. He was standing too close to her again. His hand was still on her arm and his eyes refused to let hers go.

Then they heard Maggie scream.

# CHAPTER 15

GERALD WASN'T SURE where to start searching for people in this unfamiliar town. It was late; most people were inside their houses by now. So he went to the only place he knew people wouldn't be sleeping yet—a bar.

He sat down and ordered the cheapest beer on the menu. He had stolen—taken—money from the empty homes in River Town. Everyone was dead so it didn't count as stealing when it no longer belonged to anyone, did it? He was a good and honest man who would never take from another without asking permission first. But he had to keep his family alive and he couldn't do that without money. Their house was burned to the ground, just like their little town.

He had collected enough money from the decimated village to buy a small house. He gave some to Daisy to keep or spend as she saw fit. He kept some in a small pouch hidden under his clothes and hid the rest in their cart. He reckoned it would be best if he didn't keep all their money in one place. This way, if someone tried to rob them, they wouldn't take everything. He wondered if Caitlin took some money too. She was frightfully smart.

Gerald made a face. The beer was not very good, but he got what he paid for. He took two sips and placed it down on the counter before studying his surroundings.

The bar was big but almost empty. Most men were probably tired after a long day's work and probably stayed home with their families.

"Excuse me," Gerald called to the barkeep behind the counter. "I was wondering if you know of anyone who might be planning to travel to Sky Castle?"

"Why do you ask?" the barkeep responded.

"My family and I are heading there. We thought it would be safer to travel in a group." To Gerald's relief the man did not ask why they were going to the castle. If he did, Gerald would not have mentioned the shifters, or what had happened to River Town. He would have made up some story about seeking a good husband for his daughter or trying to find a better job.

"If you had arrived two days earlier you could have gone with a group of men," the barkeep said. "I'm sorry but you are a bit late."

Gerald's heart sank. "Were they transporting fish to the castle?"

"No, unfortunately not," the barkeep said with a sad face and turned away.

There was one other man sitting at the bar. He had been staring into his glass when had Gerald walked in. This man didn't look up at the newcomer and until now he had not spoken. "They are going for our kids," he mumbled.

"Excuse me?" Gerald asked. "It sounded to me as if you said that these men are going to Sky Castle 'for your kids'?"

"They are!" the man slammed his fist down on the bar. It rattled the wood and caused some heads to turn in their direction.

"I don't understand," Gerald said. A part of him wanted to get up and leave. He didn't enjoy the company of drunken men. This man was clearly intoxicated and he was filthy. It looked like he hadn't washed his greasy hair in weeks. His shirt was covered in filth and his pants were torn. Did he have no self-respect?

"Someone has been taking kids..." he said. "Our kids. Our little children..." His voice broke and he started crying.

Maybe it was because of the drinking. Gerald didn't know what to say so he took a gulp of his beer. He looked at the man's pained expression and listened.

"At first it happened slowly..." the man continued. "They took just one: a little girl. Then as time passed, more and more children disappeared."

"Who are 'they'?"

"If I knew that, we wouldn't have this problem,

would we?" the man snapped. He downed his drink like it was a glass of water. Then he wiped his mouth and talked some more. "So the men traveled to Sky Castle to tell the king—"

"Why would this concern the king?" Gerald asked. Surely the king would have better things to do than worry about a child thief.

"Because it's something Magical that's taking them!" the man said and Gerald's blood went cold.

"How do you know that?" Gerald asked.

"Because my little girl told me that she had seen a witch right before she was kidnapped!" The barkeep refilled his glass.

"It's not just kids," another man said. He was sitting at a table with a friend. Both of them were listening to the drunken man ramble. "It's adults too."

His friend joined in: "And it's not just happening in this town. It's happening all over the kingdom!"

Gerald wondered if this was all just some drunken ramblings. Or maybe they were trying to scare him and his family away from their town. He studied them. They all looked tired and sad.

"Why would someone be taking people?" Gerald asked.

"It's the witches!" the man at the bar said. "They want their kingdom back!"

"Screw that!" another said. "We will not go back into slavery!"

Gerald finished his beer. He decided it was time to

go. Everyone was getting worked up about a matter that he didn't want to be involved in. All he wanted was to get his family to Sky Castle safely. He could get them there. He would get them there. His family was his life.

He got to his feet and pushed the chair back into place. He turned to leave this bar and these people.

"Do you have kids?" one drunken man called to his departing back.

Gerald nodded. He was still facing the door.

"Don't let them out of your sight!" he warned. "You never know what creature is waiting to snatch them away in the night."

Gerald pushed the door open and left.

# CHAPTER 16

THE LITTLE GIRL had always been different.

Her mother, Tessa the innkeeper, had a one-night stand with a customer at the inn nine years ago. The man had left and was never to be seen again. But he left her the gift of a baby girl who Tessa named Roxy. He didn't know about this baby, and the innkeeper had no way to contact him to tell him that he had fathered a girl.

When Roxy was born, Tessa knew something was different about her but she couldn't tell what it was. Only when Roxy turned six did Tessa discover what made her daughter different. She found out on the night that Roxy had gotten out of bed for a midnight snack.

Roxy was rummaging through the larder and dropped a jar. The noise woke her mother up. Thinking it was a burglar, Tessa crept down the stairs with a club in her hands so that she could hit the intruder. But when she got to the kitchen, she put the club down after seeing it was Roxy. Her daughter had her nose stuck in the larder—a very long and furry snout.

Roxy's dad was a shifter. At first Tessa was horrified. She had heard the brutal tales of shifters. She had heard of their violence and lack of self-control. But Roxy was still her child. And a mother never abandons her child.

Roxy was a shy child who kept to herself. She didn't have a lot of friends and didn't speak much. She never learned how to fully shift into a fox, but sometimes when she got excited, she would grow a tail that she would wag. Or when she was listening to some distant sound, her ears would turn pointy. But she was harmless. She couldn't even hurt a mouse. And her mother loved her.

Tessa taught Roxy that people feared what was different, what they didn't understand, and that she should keep her *gift* a secret. Roxy was very obedient and lived to please her mother. She never told anyone. Roxy also had never met any other shifters.

"Mommy," Roxy said, interrupting Tessa's thoughts.

Tessa had checked Gerald into the inn. Then she had taken a warm bath and put her night robe on. She was standing in her bedroom now. "Roxy, why are you still awake?" she asked. "I told you to go to bed hours ago!"

"I know," the girl said as she walked into her mother's room. "I couldn't sleep."

Tessa sat down on the bed and patted the mattress. Roxy climbed up and sat next to her. Some nights Roxy would sleep in her bed after a bad dream. But on those nights she came to the room crying. Tonight there weren't any tears, just a worried frown.

"What's bother you, Roxy?"

"There are two men following me," she said to her mother.

Tessa's face went from smiling to scared in an instant. Her daughter had never before said anything like this. "Why would you say that?"

"Because it's true," the girl said. "I saw them when I was at school today. They were watching me through the fence."

"What did they look like?"

"They were big men. One had a scar on his cheek and the other had long hair."

"Were they watching the other kids too?"

Roxy shook her head. "Just me."

"Are you sure you weren't imagining it?" Tessa asked gently. Kids did have wild imaginations. She really hoped that no one was watching her daughter. Why would anyone watch Roxy? She was such a good kid who kept to herself. Her heart was beating so fast and she tried her best to keep her face calm; she was overreacting. No one was after her daughter and no one knew her secret.

"Do you think they know about me?" Roxy asked.

"NO!" Tessa said too loud and too fast. "You didn't tell anyone that you are different, right? Right?"

She looked into her daughter's eyes for the truth, although Roxy never lied. "No, Mama."

"If they don't know, then there is no harm done. I will go and talk to the school tomorrow about these men," she snorted. "Did you tell the teachers?"

The girl shook her head. Her red hair shimmered with the motion. "I thought I should tell you first."

Her mother hugged her tightly to her chest. It was the best feeling in the world to hold her daughter in her arms and to know that she was home and safe. Tessa felt like she could hold her forever but Roxy wiggled in her arms after a while. When she let her go, the little girl jumped off the bed.

"It's time for bed now," Tessa said.

"I just want to eat one cookie!" Roxy said as she ran out of the room and down the stairs before her mother could respond.

Roxy ran to the kitchen and then stuck her hand into the cookie jar. She pulled out a cookie dotted with nuts and berries and was about to take a bite when she smelled something strange.

She sniffed the air—and her little button nose grew into a snout. Something told her that she should know what the scent was, although she hadn't smelled it before.

She put the cookie down and followed her snout. She stopped when she realized that it was coming from one of the guest rooms. Was someone who stayed here as special as she was?

The thought scared and excited her at the same time, and her whiskers twitched as a long, orange tail sprouted from her bottom. She wondered if she might make a new friend. It would be so nice to have someone who understood what it's like to be different.

"There you are," a brutal voice said.

She looked to her right.

"I told you she's a fox," another voice said.

They were the two men from the school. They had followed her home but couldn't be sure that she had Magic until now. Roxy's eyes widened as her fox nose twitched and her fox tail dropped between her legs.

"Grab her, Brutus," the man with the long hair said.

Brutus took a step closer and the girl bolted. She didn't scream—yet. She ran as fast as her little legs could carry her. If the man wasn't blocking her way she would be running to her mother. Instead she ran toward the guest rooms.

In her mind she told herself to stay calm and to run to the room where the smell came from. But she was so scared that she could not focus on the scent and so she could not tell which room it was.

Brutus was on her heels and the man with the scar was right behind him. She would soon be caught. They were much bigger and faster than she was.

Roxy ran down as many halls as she could, hoping to confuse the man. He was right behind her.

Then to her surprise, the other man appeared at the end of the hallway in front of her. She turned left and opened the first door she could find and stumbled into the room. The door slammed into the wall with a loud BANG.

The sound made the girl, who was sleeping in her bed, awaken with fright. She shoved her long brown hair out of her eyes, and for a moment, the two of them just looked at each other.

Then Roxy slammed the door shut and locked it behind her. Brutus started hammering on the door like a mad man.

"What are you doing?" Scarface asked. "You'll wake up the whole inn!"

"It doesn't matter!" Brutus growled. "Let's just get the kid and go!"

"Who are you?" Maggie asked the little girl.

"Help me!" Roxy cried as she moved away from the door. "They want to kidnap me!"

Brutus kicked the door in. At the sight of the two large men standing at their doorway, Maggie screamed.

"We'll take them both!" Scarface said.

Roxy fled to the window. But she couldn't outrun Brutus. He grabbed her arm and pulled her back. She struggled but he put his hand over her face. "Sleep," he said in a hypnotic voice. Roxy went limp and Brutus picked her up, tossing her over his shoulder.

Maggie didn't even make it off the bed before Scarface grabbed her. He put his hand on her forehead. "Sleep," he instructed. Her eyes closed and she too went limp.

The men heard footsteps running toward the room and they knew that they had to get out fast. But if they exited through the door they would surely be caught. So Brutus kicked the window until the glass shattered and they could climb out. The men hurried away from the inn and disappeared into the night.

"Maggie!" Caitlin cried out in panic as she reached the empty room.

Despite his injury, Rafe had kept up with her. He stood behind her in the doorway. The moment he saw the window, he said, "I can track them. But not in this form."

Caitlin turned and looked at him. She knew if the townspeople saw him as a wolf, they would most likely try to kill him. He was already injured, and she did not think it was a good idea for him to run or fight.

Rafe wasn't asking for permission though. He pushed

past her in one fluid motion and jumped through the window. It wasn't two feet that touched down on the ground when he landed, it was four paws.

The gray wolf was big and intimidating. Caitlin had to remind herself that it was Rafe and not some killer animal that was running through the town of Waterfall Haven.

Rafe picked up Maggie's scent instantly. There were three people with her and he could tell that one of them was a lot like him. Rafe took off in the direction they went. He ignored the stinging pain in his side. *It won't be the end of the world if I rip these stitches: Maggie can just redo them. Must rescue Maggie!*

He had to focus on just Maggie's scent. He couldn't lose focus. If he lost focus, he would lose the kid. And who knew what would happen to Maggie if he was unable to save her.

Rafe did not expect Caitlin to keep up. She was a human; humans were slow. But he could hear her feet touch down and lift up and touch down as she sprinted not far behind him. Impressive.

Rafe ran next to one of the many rivers. *There they are!*

They were on a stone bridge crossing the river. There were two men. Each had a limp child in his arms, one of which was Maggie. They were on horseback and on their way out of the town.

*It would be a shame if someone blocked their way,* he thought to himself and he flashed his canines.

140

Horses were no match for Rafe. He sprinted toward the river as he spotted a house with a deck that that jutted over the raging water. He scrambled onto the deck and leaped. His stitches tore, but he didn't notice. He landed with his back paws in the water and his front paws on dry land. Then he sprinted toward the bridge and blocked their path.

He curled his upper lip up to reveal his dangerous, sharp teeth. He saw the fear in the men's eyes. One horse reared and his rider pulled at his reins frantically as he tried to get it under control.

Rafe snorted. *He better not drop that child.*

The other man, the one with a big scar on his cheek, wrapped his left arm around Maggie. He held the reins with that same hand. His horse was more obedient than the other horse, dancing in place, just waiting for the command to run away. Then the man did something that Rafe did not anticipate: he lifted his hand and aimed. A ball of energy flew through the air and hit the wolf in the face.

Rafe squealed and shook his head violently from side to side. At first it hurt. It sent a burning sensation through his lips and cheeks. Then it spread into his nose and he struggled to breathe. Then it reached his eyes and his vision became blurry. The Magic ball had dimmed his senses and numbed his mind. He shook violently.

Brutus couldn't control his horse. It jumped, almost lost balance and almost fell off the bridge. Luckily it regained its balance. Unluckily it took off, and Brutus wasn't a very good rider. He lost his grip on the reins and his horse started sprinting away from the wolf.

"That's the wrong way!" Scarface yelled as Brutus disappeared into the town. Scarface cursed.

The wolf took a shaky step forward, still slightly stunned but still scaring Brutus. He pounced and lashed out blindly, landing with a thump on the bridge. Brutus's horse jumped sideways, its hooves slipping out from under it, and then they came crashing down onto the bridge, right next to the still dazed wolf.

Brutus was lucky to be able to move his leg before his horse could crush it. Brutus held the girl—Maggie —to his chest so that his body would break her fall. She was still fast asleep.

The horse sprang up, leaving Brutus and Maggie where they'd fallen, as Rafe jumped toward it. Brutus rolled under the leaping wolf, still holding Maggie.

Then Brutus looked up and saw two things. He saw a girl running toward the bridge. She was much older than the two they'd nabbed and she looked really, really, really angry. Next he saw that Scarface had gotten control of his horse and had come back for him, and for this Brutus was glad because his own horse had already run off.

"Rafe!" Caitlin called, "Go after the other girl! I've got Maggie!" She laid her eyes on Brutus and took in her little sister beside him. Something inside her snapped. She didn't care that the man was bigger than she was.

She didn't care that he was stronger. *I'll kill you for taking my sister.*

She walked over the bridge with controlled rage. She stopped and looked into his eyes before sprinting toward him.

Brutus shoved Maggie to the side and got to his feet. He took aim, ready to throw a Magic ball, but Caitlin was already upon him. He fired, but she had already grabbed his wrist and moved it away from her face.

The Magic ball hit the bridge and sputtered harmlessly. She punched him in the face as hard as she could. Caitlin didn't know who had taught her how to punch, but whoever did had taught her well.

Brutus stepped back and raised one hand beside his face, taking aim again. Caitlin still had his other hand. She pulled it toward her, and as he pitched forward, she punched him again and then let go of his hand, letting him fall.

She took a step forward and kicked him. But her kick lost most of its impact as he rolled to the right, away from Maggie. Caitlin followed and kicked him again. This time, he grabbed her foot and yanked. She fell to her back. Brutus continued pulling her by her legs. Then he grabbed her hips and pulled again. Her head was next to his hands now. She lashed out blindly. He batted away her hands and then he wrapped one hand around her throat and squeezed.

Her legs kicked out at the air and her arms flailed. She tried to pry his fingers away but his grip was too tight. She tried to hit him in the face but she was too weak to hit hard. Her vision was becoming blurry.

If she didn't break free soon, she was going to pass out.

Rafe had his eyes fixed on Scarface's horse. It was so scared of him. He barely had to twitch and it would start running again. Rafe didn't mind. *I love the hunt. But I don't want that idiot of a rider to fall off and hurt the child.* He snarled once and Scarface battled with his horse for control. Too busy with the reins, he wouldn't have time to throw a Magic ball. And even if he did, he wouldn't be able to aim well with his horse rearing and jumping around.

Rafe shook his head. Luckily the effects of those things didn't last long. Any moment now, he would be as good as new.

Then the horse bolted toward town, and Rafe followed. His senses were still off, but he knew he could catch it. The man's hands went to his saddle knob, holding on, as the horse fled.

*The girl is still asleep in his arms. Whatever spell he put on her was a strong one.*

Rafe jumped easily over a watering well in the middle of the road. He could jump high and far and nothing was going to slow him down.

The horse turned right and ran into a narrow alley. Rafe could barely fit and he heard the sound of stirrups scratching against the brick walls that flanked them.

The horse turned the corner, making another right; this time there was more space. Rafe jumped against the alley wall, launching himself off. In a smooth motion, he was chasing after the horse again.

Rafe thought to himself: *I need a plan. I need to bring down that horse and rider without hurting the little girl. Can I chase the stupid horse until it dies of exhaustion? Probably not.*

Rafe noticed that the stone path they were on led to a fountain. It was round, filled with water and coins. In the middle was a statue of a woman. Rafe also saw that the stones around the fountain looked slippery—especially under a horse's hooves.

The horse was so scared that it didn't slow down. It decided to turn at the last moment. It was a sharp turn. The horse slipped but caught itself. For a moment Rafe thought that the riders would fly off the horse. But the man hung on, dangling off the horse's side, and managed to pull himself up by the saddle horn. The girl was still sleeping in his arms.

And Rafe was still running.

Caitlin squirmed as she battled to breathe, the muscles of her neck hard and taut against Brutus's large, vice-like hands. She could see the focus in his eyes. Those eyes looked down at her. He was eager to watch the life leave her body.

*Well, I don't feel like dying today.* She stuck her right index and middle finger into his eyes sharply. Brutus screamed and let go of her neck to cover his eyes.

Caitlin gasped and got to her feet and then charged at him. She slammed into him, he lost his balance, and both of them fell over the bridge and into the river.

The cold water rushed into Caitlin's nostrils and she realized with a shock that she didn't know how to swim.

# CHAPTER 17

THE RIVER CURRENT was very strong. Caitlin's leg slammed into one of the rocks and the pain made little lights flash across her eyes. She tried kicking to reach the surface, but her leg was weak from the buffeting. Her head bobbed above the water and she gulped in air.

The current forced her down into the streambed, tumbling her helpless body and sending more water into her nose. She bobbed up, snorting and coughing, and went under again. All she saw were bubbles. She had lost sight of Brutus.

Her feet scraped the bottom of the riverbed and she tried to kick herself upward, desperate to breathe again. Her arms flailed uselessly. *How do I not know how to swim? I live next to a river!*

Her head broke through the surface again and she gasped. There was too much water sloshing over her eyes for her to see. She tried blinking and all she saw was a blur. *Oh no... What's that big, dark blur down the river?*

She realized that she was going to hit it, whatever it was. There was no way to avoid the collision. The rough water slammed her into a huge tree trunk that lay halfway over the river.

She tried to lift her arms, tried to find a handhold so she could pull herself up and out. But the river would not allow that. It pinned her cheek against the trunk. She tried to lift her chin up to ease her breathing. Then she heard wood cracking against her ear. The trunk was breaking and she was going to wash away and drown in the river. And she had very little strength left.

Rafe had them. The horse was running toward a dead end. He would corner them there and maybe bite the stupid animal's neck off before it could run any further.

That's when Rafe heard the gasping. He looked toward the river and saw Caitlin. She was pinned against a tree and fighting for her breath. He looked back at the stupid horse. If he didn't catch them now, they would get away.

His wolf ears heard the frantic beating of Caitlin's heart in her chest moments before the tree trunk snapped. Her head disappeared under the water, spurring Rafe into action. He sprinted toward the river, abandoning the chase and letting his quarry go.

When he spotted Caitlin, he tried to get as close to her as possible before jumping into the water and swimming.

He saw that her head was still underwater. He felt her arm touch his leg, felt her reach up and grab a fistful of his fur, and then felt her rigid body relax as she pulled herself up. She wrapped her arms around his neck and gasped for breath.

They both watched the broken tree trunk wash down the river. With her arms still wrapped around his neck, Caitlin kicked into the water as they struggled to swim to the shore. They swam with the current, but sideways. Rafe thought that they might go under again or be slammed against rocks. They made it out faster than he thought they would.

Once they were out of the river, Caitlin threw up. She had swallowed a lot of water. But now was not the time to be embarrassed. "Maggie..." she whispered, forgetting about the pain in her leg, forgetting about everything else. All that mattered was her sister.

So side by side, wolf and girl ran back upstream. They found Maggie on the bridge where Caitlin had left her.

Caitlin flung herself down on the bridge beside Maggie. "What's wrong with her? Why is she still asleep?"

*She's been enchanted by those men,* Rafe tried to say,

but all Caitlin heard were soft growls.

Caitlin touched her sister's face and Maggie's eyes fluttered open. Relieved, Caitlin pulled her to her chest and hugged her for the first time since she was taken. *When did this kid start to mean too much to me?*

Maggie broke the embrace first and then she looked at the wolf. "Rafe," she said as she patted him like he was a dog.

The sound of footsteps approaching made them all turn their attention to the other side of the bridge. There stood a small lady, with gray braided hair and a lot of wrinkles. The wind was blowing, making her skirt look like it was dancing around her.

"Most people are looking for you on the other side of the town," she said to the wolf. "I told them I saw you going that way after a horse and a man with a stolen child."

She came closer and held out a pair of pants that Rafe took in his mouth. "I suggest you shift before they see you."

Rafe disappeared behind a tree. When he came out, he was a human again. Blood seeped from his wound to his pants. Caitlin wondered how badly he was hurt. She knew he would try to cover up the pain with humor or by ignoring it. But he did not look as if he was about to tell a joke. His eyes were weary and he avoided looking at his torn stitches and bloody sides. He was looking at the small, wrinkled woman.

Caitlin looked from Rafe to the lady and she thought

that they didn't know each other. No warm "hello" was spoken. They also didn't embrace the way friends do after not seeing each other for a long time.

"Let's get you two, especially you," staring pointedly at Rafe, "out of sight before they come back."

"My parents..." Caitlin said, and for the first time the old lady looked at her. "They will be worried sick. We need to go back."

"Give it an hour or two for all the commotion to die down," she advised and then looked back at Rafe. "If you get caught now your bravery would have been for nothing."

Rafe followed her first. Maggie clung to Caitlin's arm. The lady's house was behind the one with the big deck from which Rafe jumped. It was the house closest to the bridge.

The old lady had left her door open and they walked in. The smell of herbs welcomed them. There were potted plants everywhere. Tea was boiling on the stove. Caitlin felt as if she was in the middle of a garden and not inside someone's kitchen.

"When I saw you on the bridge, I knew someone was going to get hurt," she said. "So instead of coming to fight, I put on some tea for you." Her smile wrinkled her face even more as she shuffled across the kitchen to close the door.

Caitlin looked at her again. Her muscles were old and saggy. She was more bone and skin than anything else. Caitlin doubted that she was capable of fighting.

"You're welcome to sit," the old lady said and then looked around. "If you can find a place to sit, that is," she cackled. At least, that was the sound she made when she tried to laugh.

Her house was messy. Clothes and rugs lay everywhere. Bugs were crawling on the walls and a large, brown, furry spider was putting the finishing touches to its web in a dark corner. It looked as if the house had not been cleaned in ages.

"My name is Matilda, by the way," she told them.

"I'm Rafe. And this is Caitlin, and Maggie."

Maggie waved sweetly. She didn't look scared like Caitlin thought she would. Maybe she was still foggy from the spell.

"Thank you very much for your help," Rafe continued as she poured the tea.

"Of course," Matilda said. "Us Magic folk must stick together!"

A big window in the adjacent room displayed a great view of the bridge. Caitlin moved toward it so that she would see when the townspeople returned.

Matilda handed Rafe his tea. He took it but didn't drink.

"I know you don't like tea," she rolled her eyes although he had said nothing of the sort. "It's not normal tea. It will help with that," she pointed to his side.

Caitlin looked at Rafe's wounds and her chest felt tight. She did not like it when he got hurt. Had he been anyone else she would not have cared what happened to him.

Matilda poured another cup but with less tea in it and gave it to Caitlin, who thanked her and took a sip. But she fought the urge to spit it out. *Ugh, this is terrible! Like sour cream mixed with water and eggs.* And it was hot so she couldn't drink it quickly without burning her mouth.

But the tea served its purpose. After a few sips Caitlin's leg stopped throbbing. She wondered if it had healed her completely.

Rafe drank his as if it tasted great. He didn't gag or pull faces. He drank sip for sip, as if it was regular tea. Caitlin wondered if he was faking it or if it really tasted different to him. *Maybe Matilda gave me bad tea because I'm not Magical like Rafe.* As Caitlin thought this, she eyed the tea pot. *No, we both drank the same tea.*

Amazingly, Rafe's wounds healed. Although the blood stains remained, his wounds were no longer visible. Not even scars.

"That was amazing!" Rafe exclaimed. "Thank you!"

"You're a witch!" Maggie said. There was no fear in her voice. Only amazement.

"Yes," Matilda said with a smile.

"I have a question, if you don't mind me asking." Caitlin's eyes were fixed on the old lady.

"What is it?"

"How have you not been burned on a stake?"

The old lady and Rafe started laughing like she had

asked the dumbest thing ever. Caitlin looked at them in confusion. She did not like feeling so uninformed and excluded.

"No witch is dumb enough to get burned on a stake!"

Caitlin recalled Rafe saying those exact words to her. She paced around. "So what you are saying is that every witch that has ever been burned was actually just a normal woman?"

Matilda nodded. "It's man's nature to destroy themselves," she said solemnly.

"Maybe it's ours too," Rafe said.

Matilda saw the worry in his eyes. "Maybe we should sit down for this conversation." She walked to the room with the big window and beckoned them to follow her.

This room was smaller than the kitchen and Caitlin decided that it was supposed to be the living room. Matilda's couches and chairs all had paintings and pots sitting on them. She started moving these things to make space for them to sit.

A cat was curled up on one couch looking peaceful until Matilda picked it up and put it on the ground. She sat down where it had lain. The cat looked a little disorientated and stretched after taking its first step. Then it noticed the newcomers and gave a weary *meow*.

"Kitty!" Maggie said.

She let go of Caitlin's hand and walked to the cat. She didn't make any abrupt movements because she didn't want to scare it off.

Caitlin wondered if all witches had cats. This one

wasn't black, like the stereotypical witch-cat. Instead it was white with a brown-ginger back. It looked as if someone had spilled coffee on a white shirt.

The cat allowed Maggie to scratch it. It arched its back in delight and purred softly. Rafe walked past it so that he could take a seat on the couch closest to Matilda. But as he walked past, the cat hissed at him and ran into a different room.

"I'm sorry for scaring the cat away," he said to Matilda. "Animals don't like me very much."

"That's fine," the old lady said. She understood that animals could smell that he was different. "He is a stray that decided to move in with me. So he's a little skittish around strangers."

Caitlin sat down too. She whipped some dirt off the couch, as did Maggie, before sitting down. But it was still dusty and they both sneezed.

"Where are you from, Rafe?" Matilda asked. She could tell from his pale skin that he was not local.

"I'm from Southpaw," he said.

"Well, you are a long way from home." Matilda said. "Why? Usually wolves don't travel very far. And not alone either. Where is your pack?"

"In Southpaw," Rafe said. Caitlin sensed some tension in his voice as he said this. Rafe did not speak a lot about his home and now Caitlin realized that she knew almost nothing about him.

"A lone wolf is an endangered wolf," Matilda warned.

"It wasn't my plan to travel this far," Rafe said. "One

of my friends got... sick."

"Sick? What kind of sickness?" Matilda asked.

"I don't know," Rafe said. "That's what I wanted to find out. He visited family in one of the towns in the Riverlands. He was on his way home when a bear attacked him."

"No normal bear would attack a shifter," Matilda said. Just like her cat, other animals could tell that there was something different about shifters so they feared and avoided them.

"It wasn't a normal bear," Rafe said.

"A shifter? I thought shifters are big on standing together?" Caitlin put in.

"We are," Rafe said. "My friend described the bear as 'crazy.' He said it attacked him without warning. He got away, but the bear bit him."

"Go on," Matilda said as Rafe paused.

"He came home," Rafe said, "and told us the story. We all thought he was going to be fine. His bite wound would heal and life would carry on."

"But..." Matilda said.

"But it didn't," Rafe looked only at her as he was telling the story. "My friend was one of the calmest, kindest men I knew. He was a real softy. The change in him was tremendous after he got bitten. At first, he just seemed a little more irritated with everything and everyone. Then he started getting these bursts of anger and he would slam his fist down on a table or kick a door. The smallest thing would tip him over the edge.

It could be someone talking too loudly or a fly buzzing by his ears."

"What happened?" Matilda asked.

"He lost it," Rafe said. "He went completely mad. It was when he attacked his daughter that a friend ripped his heart out."

"And the body?"

"We burned it," Rafe said.

"What makes you think he was sick?" Matilda asked. "Were there any symptoms?"

"No..." Rafe said.

"Maybe he was just in animal form too long and his animal side took over."

"I've seen that happen before," Rafe said. "This was different." He tried desperately to think of symptoms. "His eyes were very bloodshot."

"I've never heard of a disease like this," Matilda said. "Was he the only one?"

Rafe nodded.

"So you decided to investigate?" Matilda asked.

Rafe nodded again. "I went to the Riverlands but I found nothing. No one knew anything about a disease. Then I found a bear in Caitlin's town...."

"Was it mad too?" Matilda asked.

"Completely insane," he said. "It destroyed her village and killed many humans. It was out of control."

"Where is it now?"

"Out of its misery," Rafe said coldly.

They were silent for a moment, and Caitlin was glad

that he did not tell the witch that she had killed the bear.

"I don't have the answers that you are looking for," Matilda said solemnly. "But I have a good idea where you can find them."

# CHAPTER 18

"SKY CASTLE?!" RAFE exclaimed. "No way! It's filled with humans and there is no Magic. Why would I be looking for a cure to a Magic disease in a non-Magic castle filled with non-Magic morons that want to kill me?"

"My dear Rafe," the witch said while shaking her head. "Do you know your history at all?"

Rafe frowned and waited for the witch to explain her question. She looked at him with a taunting, playful smile that made Caitlin's stomach turn. Did this witch think life was one big game?

"Who built the castle?" Matilda prodded, her eyes glinting in the moonlight shining through the big window. It illuminated her hair and made her look slightly younger. "Who built it centuries ago?"

"Sorcerers..." Rafe realized. He had his back against the window and the moon behind him cast a shadow over his face and made a silver halo around his hair. He looked angelic and out of place in this ugly, filthy, worn-out house. "But it's filled with non-Magic folk now."

"Yes," she nodded. "But that doesn't mean there is no Magic. Our kind built that palace—they designed every corner and every tower. They poured their Magic into the walls and so that castle will never be mundane."

"If only the king new that," Rafe breathed.

"If only," she smiled.

"So why should I go there?" Rafe asked. "What makes you think I'll find answers there?"

"It is where King Leonard lives with all of his healers, knights, and alchemists."

"Are you saying what I think you're saying?"

"It makes sense doesn't it?" she asked. There was a silent mutual understanding between the two of them that made Caitlin feel excluded. "He hates us. If his healers managed to create a disease to kill our kind, it would make killing us easy. Have you ever seen a non-Magic infected with this disease?"

"No," Rafe said.

"So maybe his healers and alchemist made this disease to target us?"

"But that means he made it at the cost of his men's lives," Rafe stated and explained further. "The disease makes us shifters lose control and then we become capable of killing whole villages. Just like that bear did."

"And what better way for him to prove to the people that we are the terrible and bloodthirsty breed he makes us out to be?"

Rafe stared in awe. "You are brilliant."

Matilda smiled. "Thank you." For the first time she turned her attention to Caitlin, who by now was feeling very excluded and irritated. "Another one of non-Magic folk's many problems is that they are very narrow-minded. They see one bad Witch King and think all of us are that way. They turn against anything and anyone who's different from them. They hate the one bad king we had and forgot about the countless good ones. And the fact that they had many dreadful human kings throughout the centuries doesn't even cross their little minds. They can't accept us for being different, so they have to destroy us. It's like they blame us for being born with Magic in our veins. We can't help it. And we can't help that they were born mundane."

*Why is she looking at me? What did I do?* Caitlin wasn't sure why this was aimed at her. *I can't help the way I was born either!* She didn't say anything but gripped the arm on the couch in frustration. Maggie sat quietly next to her, listening to every word as if she was being told a bedtime story.

Matilda pressed the subject: "You non-Magic folk are always trying to harm us."

"That's a bit hypocritical," Caitlin sneered, unable to stay quiet. Her stomach made a knot. She tried not to sound too bitter when she added, "Since you Magic folk have been stealing *our* kids."

She didn't know where the boiling rage came from. Maybe it was because she had her sister sitting so close to her, reminding her how she had almost lost her. Maybe she just needed someone to blame after Brutus washed away.

"It's true," Rafe interjected. "Those two men did have Magic."

Matilda frowned. "Then we are following non-Magic folk's example of killing ourselves." She paused. "This whole time I thought it was non-Magic stealing non-Magic kids," she looked at Maggie.

"I don't think they wanted to steal me," Maggie said. "Or at least they did not plan it."

"What do you mean, child?" Matilda asked.

"There was a little girl who was trying to get away. She ran right into my room. She had pointy ears and funny eyes and a furry tail. They wanted her and just took me along."

"I caught her scent," Rafe said and then pointed out the obvious: "She is a shifter, like me."

A worried frown crept across Matilda's forehead. "So what does this mean? Magic folk are stealing Magic folk's kids?"

"That seems to be the case," Rafe said.

"But that doesn't make any sense," she said. "If it was non-Magic folk catching us and killing us, it would make sense."

"I don't think it's just kids either," Rafe said. "I've overheard several people that adults are also disappearing."

"Magic folk?" she asked.

"I'm not sure."

There was a moment of silence. Matilda was the one who broke it. "Do you think this disease affects only shifters or all Magic folk?"

"I've only seen it affect shifters. The two kidnappers seemed clear minded and fully in control of their actions —and they were Magic folk."

"That's a shame," Matilda said.

Rafe shot her a shocked look.

"It would have been better if they were sick and doing this," Matilda said, "rather than clear-minded and doing this."

Caitlin's blood boiled because this stupid old hag kept ignoring her. She paid more attention to the paintings on the walls than she did to Caitlin. *Am I not a guest? Did she not invite me into the house?*

"I always thought we were a strong race that stuck together," Matilda continued speaking only to Rafe. "We're supposed to help each other in dire situations such as these."

"Thank you for the help," Rafe said weakly and shot a sideways glance at Caitlin.

"Loyalty runs in my family," she said.

"But hospitality obviously doesn't," Caitlin snapped before she could stop herself.

Rafe stared at her but did not speak. She had surprised him with her temper. He hoped she wouldn't take this any further, as a fight with a witch would not end well.

"Whatever is the matter?" the old lady said with an

acid tone.

"You invite me into your house only to treat me like a rug."

The old lady frowned. "You're saying I walked over you?"

"That was a horrible comparison," Rafe giggled under his breath.

Caitlin ignored him. "I meant you brought me in, sat me down, and then pretended I don't exist." The old lady paid him no attention either as Caitlin continued, "You speak only to him, even when I'm the one speaking to you." She knew that Rafe's humor would not prevent an argument, so she cut herself off from saying anything else and just glared at the old lady as if they were the only two people in the room.

"If you're feeling neglected," Matilda said, "why don't you go back out there?" She pointed to the bridge. "I'm sure you will find the villagers who would have happily killed you earlier had I not taken you in."

"At least they'll acknowledge me."

"They'll do more than that, dearie. They'll probably be chanting to you before they burn you."

"That will still be better than drinking your tea."

"Ungrateful wench," the witch sneered. "Get out. Now."

"With pleasure." Caitlin got to her feet and stomped to the door. But right before she could leave the house, she tripped over the rug and fell.

The witch merely laughed.

# CHAPTER 19

"THAT ONE HAS a bad temper," the witch told Rafe as she watched the two sisters leave. "For a moment I thought she was actually going to throw something at me other than her pitiful insults."

"That would have been unfortunate," Rafe said in a placid voice. "I'm sorry for her disrespect."

"How did you meet her?" she asked. The moonlight made the dark room seem almost ghostly.

"She saved my life," Rafe admitted.

The witch raised an eyebrow. "A non-Magic saves a shifter? That is unheard of."

Rafe nodded. Caitlin was not like most non-Magic folk because she did not hate or fear shifters. Rafe wondered if she feared anything. She was very self-confident and had this look that said "don't mess with me." She was the kind of girl that Rafe would trust to have his back in difficult situations.

"Well, don't trust her," the witch warned. "You can't trust anyone who doesn't trust themselves."

"What makes you think she doesn't trust herself?" Rafe asked.

"Her uncertainty," the witch said and then proceeded to explain her perception of Caitlin. "She wanted to speak up earlier because she was frustrated. But she forced the frustration down until it became too much to handle. She couldn't trust herself to have enough self-control to follow through with her original plan."

"She is impulsive," Rafe admitted.

"Impulsive can be dangerous," the witch warned. "Although she saved your life, she is still not our kind. Don't ever forget that."

Rafe nodded and got to his feet. He did not want to speak about Caitlin behind her back. That made him feel as if he was betraying her somehow. He decided that it was time to leave—he did not have anything more to say or to ask of Matilda. "Thank you again for your help."

"I wish I could be of more help," she admitted. "But I might know someone who can help you...."

"Who?" Rafe asked as she suddenly had all of his attention again.

"Another witch," she smiled. "You will find her on the way to the castle by the Sinking Swamp. Everyone calls her Ears."

"Ears?"

"She earned the nickname because somehow she

always manages to hear what is going on in the kingdom. If anyone knows anything about a disease it would be her. And maybe she could enlighten you about the missing people too."

"I'll find her," Rafe said confidently.

"One more thing," the witch said. She got up and walked to the kitchen. There she opened a drawer, scratched through it, and pulled out a small bottle filled with black liquid.

"This is a potion called Blankness," she told him. "It's very rare. Have you heard of it?"

Rafe nodded. "Why are you giving this to me?" He didn't take the bottle, but he looked at it warily.

"You know that girl is trouble. If she tells the wrong people about your secret, you will be killed. And she has a child by her side! You never know what children let slip...."

Rafe took the bottle, cautiously as if it was a snake that would bite him at any moment. He looked at it before stuffing it into his pocket. "I don't know how to use it," he confessed.

"The non-Magic must drink it. You can put it in tea or water. It blends well with any liquid and has no taste," she told him. "Or you could just force it down her throat. She'll go into a blank state where she would just stare in front of her. This potion allows you to give and take memories. But keep in mind that you can't wipe her whole mind—she is too old. You can only take away a few memories—such as all her memories of you. If you tell her to forget about you and your Magic, she will."

"It's that strong?" Rafe asked.

The witch nodded with a smile. "I am excellent at brewing potions. Blankness is the ultimate potion to make non-Magic folk forget all about us. After she drinks it, you will have no time to waste. Talk immediately; command her to forget."

"Can you wipe someone's entire mind with this?" Rafe asked.

"If they are weak-minded, yes." she said. "But it's very risky and most of the time it does not work. You could fry someone's mind, or the effects could wear off. It's much easier to use on children than adults because the older you are the less likely you are to believe what someone tells you."

Rafe did not like the idea of altering someone's mind. He did not want Caitlin to forget him and he hoped it never came to the point where she had to drink this potion. But he conceded that keeping the potion was a good back-up plan if things went horribly wrong. Rafe thanked Matilda again and then left.

Rafe walked back to his room along the stone path. He was shirtless and felt the cold of the night seep into his bones.

The rushing of the waterfalls muffled all other sounds and made the town seem very peaceful. But Rafe knew chaos would break out if people suspected him of being the wolf. He knew it looked suspicious that he was walking around, alone at night, without a shirt. Luckily most people were either indoors or elsewhere searching for the man on horseback.

Rafe reached the inn and saw the innkeeper crying. Her body shook with sobs and she had her arms wrapped around herself as she leaned against the wall. Rafe took a step forward so that he could hug her. A hug would not take away the pain of losing a child, but it would help her to not feel so alone.

Rafe stopped before she saw him, realizing that he was still a stranger to her. Surely she would be frightened if a shirtless man, who she'd seen walking in pain to his room earlier that day, just gave her a hug. He didn't want to scare the woman. So he walked away with a heavy heart.

He decided to climb into his room through the window. If he walked down the hallway there was a chance that he would run into Caitlin or her parents. He did not want to explain to Daisy and Gerald where he had been and he did not want to anger Caitlin even more. She needed time alone to cool down.

Once inside his room, he spotted the orange salve

for his wounds. He was completely healed and Gerald and Daisy would freak out if they saw that. He sighed. He enjoyed traveling with them and they had taken good care of him. He enjoyed their company although he hadn't spoken much during the past two days. He couldn't help being so quiet—the pain medication made his mind foggy. Rafe had been alone for a long time now and hadn't realized how his need for companionship had grown.

He wrapped the bandage around his body. He'd just have to pretend to still be healing on their way to the castle. He hoped he could fake it.

Rafe then sat down on his bed and listened. He could hear Caitlin and Gerald talking in her room....

"What happened?" Gerald asked in his concerned fatherly voice.

"Someone tried to steal Maggie," Caitlin told him. "Two men entered the inn. They found a little girl and chased her."

"Who was the little girl?"

"My daughter," Tessa walked into the room. "She is my daughter, Roxy."

Alone in his room, Rafe could obviously not see the woman's expression, but he could hear the pain in her voice. He shifted uneasily on his bed.

"Do you know why they were after her?" Gerald asked.

"No," the woman said. "But many people have been disappearing."

"So I've heard," Gerald said. "I came back here after

looking for travel companions. That's when Daisy came to me saying that she heard a scream and that you were gone," he continued, looking at Caitlin.

Caitlin swallowed. "The men came in here and grabbed both of the children. They broke the window and ran. I followed them and was lucky enough to get Maggie back."

"You took on two fully grown men by yourself?" Tessa asked. "And still managed to get your sister back?"

Caitlin nodded.

"Daisy told me she didn't know which room was Rafe's. She would have asked him to help search for you while I was away."

"Rafe is still injured. He probably fell asleep early —his medicine must have made him sleep through all the commotion."

Rafe was good at reading people. He could always tell when someone was lying. He could hear their hearts beat slightly faster when they lied. Caitlin lied like a professional. He pictured her green eyes staring into Gerald's eyes. She wouldn't blink. Wouldn't flinch. She'd just look at him, waiting for him to call her a liar. Waiting for him to challenge her.

She also liked fighting. She enjoyed it way too much.

Rafe had to listen intently to her heartbeat. There. He heard it beating just a little bit faster as the lie left her lips. He smiled.

"You don't think he heard anything? Not the window shattering or Maggie screaming?" Gerald said doubtfully.

"No," Caitlin said. "The medicine he is taking does make him very sleepy."

Rafe didn't think Gerald was convinced, but he said nothing more.

Tessa offered Maggie and Caitlin a different room because of their broken window. She also refunded them for the night. She felt too guilty to charge them any money after their horrible ordeal.

Rafe lay on his back and listened as Tessa walked to her room where she cried herself to sleep for losing the person she loved most in the world. Rafe's heart ached for her. He knew that feeling of loss all too well.

# CHAPTER 20

"WILL YOU PLAY with my hair?" Maggie asked sweetly.

"It's bedtime," Caitlin said.

Actually, it was long past bedtime and her body was exhausted. She was so tired that she didn't even care about how dirty she was. She fell down on the bed and just wanted to close her eyes and sleep.

"Please?" Maggie begged. "I'll fall asleep easier that way."

"Fine," Caitlin gave in.

Maggie crawled closer to her older sister who started weaving soothing fingers through her hair.

Caitlin felt how bruised her hand was from the fighting—the pain and stiffness were beginning to set in. She had tried her best to hurt that horrible man. She wished she could have hurt him more.

"Caitlin?" The little girl's voice distracted Caitlin from her violent thoughts.

"Uh-huh?"

"Is Rafe going to have to leave?"

The idea of Rafe leaving made Caitlin's heart ache immediately. She sure didn't want him to leave. She'd gotten attached to him surprisingly quickly. "Why do you ask?"

"Because of what he is..."

"As long as no one knows, he is safe. No one knows..."

"I won't tell anyone," Maggie replied. "Not even Mom and Dad."

"Good." Gerald was the last person who should find out. Caitlin could imagine how his opinion of Rafe would change instantly if he knew the truth. He'd feel betrayed and deceived and scared. She wondered if he would try to kill the wolf. Gerald was not a killer but if he thought his family was in danger, he would do anything to protect them. "They wouldn't understand," Caitlin added.

"Rafe saved us," Maggie yawned. "When we were tied to the stakes, he saved us. Why did he do that?"

"I don't know," Caitlin said honestly.

Minutes later Maggie fell asleep. She had turned her back on her sister so that Caitlin could reach more of her hair. Caitlin brushed her hair to the side and was about to stop, because Maggie had just fallen asleep, when she saw something odd.

At the nape of Maggie's neck was something black. Caitlin leaned forward and moved her sister's hair out of the way to let more moonlight fall on her neck.

Usually her long, thick hair would cover this part of her neck so that the skin there wouldn't be seen. It was a number: 315.

Caitlin frowned. At first, she thought it was painted on but and tried to rub it off with her fingers and some spit. When the numbers stayed, she realized that they had been tattooed there. She felt uneasy and sat up. She went to the bathroom mirror and tried to angle herself so that she could see if she had one too. Why would she have one? And why a number? What did that mean?

She could not see the back of her neck. If she wanted to find out if she had a tattoo, she'd have to ask someone to look. And what if she did? What would she tell them then? And who would she ask? Surely Gerald and Daisy could look, but she didn't want to freak them out. They were already scared enough since their home and everything they loved had been destroyed. Gerald put on a brave face, but Caitlin could tell that he was frightened. He just couldn't admit to his family how much he worried.

Caitlin crawled into a ball beside Maggie. The six-year-old slept peacefully. *She is a tough kid,* Caitlin thought as she closed her eyes. Caitlin wondered if she had been a tough kid too.

That night she had another crazy dream.

She was a kid again, probably twelve years old. She was in a classroom again, but this time it was a different room. This room was much bigger than the one in the other dream and it didn't have any books or desks; it had punching bags and fighting rings instead. There were no candles and the roof was made of glass, letting sunlight stream into the room. There were no windows, and despite the sunlight, she felt cold.

The same students who were in the classroom with the potions were present. They were standing outside of a ring wearing looks of horror on their faces.

Their teacher, Benjamin, was a brutal man. His job was to teach them how to fight, but he enjoyed beating them up more than anything. He didn't see them as children. He didn't see them as human. He hated them.

Everyone watched, too afraid to speak up, as he fought one of the boys. Although the boy was big for his age, he was losing. He managed to stand after two hits and then he collapsed like a bag of bones. He lay groaning on the floor.

Some children gasped. Others muffled their shock by pressing their hands to their mouths. Everyone felt intimidated except one girl. Caitlin was smiling when the boy had fallen.

"Do you find this funny?" the teacher glared at her.

"Highly amusing, actually."

"Would it still be funny if you were the one on the ground?"

"Obviously not. So I'd better stay on my feet then."

The teacher took a step forward. He stood tall and puffed his chest out. His intention was to look tough but to Caitlin he resembled a pigeon who'd gotten his feathers ruffled. He probably had the brains of a pigeon too. His mouth was twisted, making his face look even more brutal. "Why don't you get in here and fight?"

"I thought you'd never ask," Caitlin said, coming forward.

The students made way and she stepped into the ring as the boy on the ground crawled away. No one came to assist him. Most of the kids didn't even look at him. Their eyes were on Caitlin. She did not know if they admired her or thought that she was stupid.

One thing was certain: she was crazy enough to pick a fight. No one ever fought willingly because no one ever won. Not against the teacher. But Caitlin didn't look like she was scared to lose. She had gotten bored from watching and felt excited to be in the ring.

The teacher was twice her size, but she wasn't backing away. She saw him as nothing but a dumb brute. He was strong, stronger than she was, but he was not very fast.

"Are you really going to hit a girl?" she asked him sweetly.

"You're no girl," he said. "You are a monster."

"Then it is unwise of you to fight me. Surrender now and I won't hurt you."

He looked at the little girl. Had he not known better

he would have thought she was harmless. "Are you going to punch me now or hurt me with your words?"

She rolled her eyes to let him think that she wasn't focusing on his every move. She expected the blow. She dodged under it and rammed her shoulder into his stomach.

She heard the breath leave his lungs. It made her way too happy. She hooked his ankle with hers and hoped that he would fall. But she lacked the mass to unbalance him.

He hit her, but this time she was too slow to dodge. His hand smacked her in the mouth. She retreated a few steps and tasted blood. It fueled her.

"I guess you won't be hurting me with your words after all," the teacher snarled. He was all too familiar with Caitlin's insults and snide remarks.

She spat on the ground. "You're going to have to hit a lot harder than that."

He struck air in his next attempt and she moved out of the way when he tried to grab her. She was fast.

"I should have known not to pick a fight with you," she taunted.

"Because I'm the best fighter in the room?"

"Because you're ugly," she retorted. "So you don't have to worry about losing that pretty face." She knew he was a vain man. She was breaking down his ego and hoping that it would cause him to lose focus. That was all she needed. If he lost focus even for a moment, she would win. He was getting angry.

178

"But you have to worry about losing that pretty face, you stupid, dumb, frustrating, dreadful child!" He kicked. This time he got her. She slammed to the ground, rolled, and came to a stop on her side.

She looked up at him from where she lay. "You think I'm pretty?"

He kicked at her again, but this time she was faster. She was on her feet in an instant. She started hitting him, and he blocked her every time, but her small fists did more damage than a normal twelve-year-old's fists could. She got in a lucky shot and he fell. As he fell, she kicked him and his head cracked against the floor. He screamed in agony.

"Don't dent the floor!" Caitlin said.

The other students clapped for her but Caitlin wasn't done. She walked around the man like she was a lioness and he was a helpless deer. He was down on the floor —where he belonged. He wouldn't fight anymore. He couldn't fight anymore.

She kicked him—hard. He rolled over and looked up at her as she kicked again. He groaned in pain and tried to shield himself from the kicks.

"Not so strong now, are you?"

"You'll regret this."

"But aren't you proud of me?" she taunted him. "You wanted me to learn how to fight after all, teacher."

"I never wanted that," he said and looked at her. His face was full of blood and his head was spinning. "I never wanted them to turn you into this."

"Oh yes? Then what should I have been?"

"You should have been a normal kid," he said. "You should have had a normal life. You should have grown up with parents, instead of teachers. You should have grown up with love instead of rage. You should have played games instead of fighting. You should have been a twelve-year-old kid instead of a little monster."

"I'm not that bad," she said as she realized that he was still on the ground and in pain. She had done that —she had hurt him badly. It had been in self-defense at first, but she had enjoyed it too much. She had wanted to hurt him more and more. Instead of helping him up, she turned away and walked out of the fighting ring. "I'm not that bad," she said again.

"But you will be," he whispered with blood dripping from his mouth.

Caitlin woke up next to Maggie. She couldn't sleep for the rest of the night.

# CHAPTER 21

THE MORNING CAME and Caitlin was still lying awake in bed. She was trying to keep her mind blank as she did not want to think about her dream. Then at dawn someone knocked on her door. She immediately got up and opened it.

"Good morning," she whispered to Rafe. "Maggie is still sleeping."

He stepped aside so she could move past him. She closed the door gently behind her so that her sister wouldn't wake up.

"Is something wrong?" she whispered.

"No," he said. "I just couldn't sleep anymore."

"Neither could I," she said.

She saw the dark circles under his eyes and wondered if he too had bad dreams and thoughts that kept him awake. Then she thought it was silly to think that. He probably couldn't sleep because of all the commotion from last night.

"Do you want to go for a walk?" he asked. Then he thought about his question and added, "Despite that fact that we will be walking for the next few days."

She smiled. "I'd love to." Then she looked at the door.

As if Rafe read her mind, he said, "Maggie will be fine. The bad guys are gone, remember?"

She nodded but didn't look convinced so Rafe added, "We will be back before she wakes up."

"Okay," Caitlin said. "We'll probably be leaving earlier than we'd planned to after last night."

"I'll help collect everything we need for the trip," Rafe said.

"I think you should stay in bed," Caitlin agued as they started walking. "You are still wounded, remember?"

"Oh yes," Rafe rolled his eyes. "Does this mean I have to stay in the cart the whole trip?"

"Probably."

He groaned. Then he smiled in a playful manner that made his gray eyes light up. "Will you join me?"

"No."

"I know you want to."

"My dad will kill you."

"I'm a dangerous wolf," he said and smiled with his white teeth. He had a fearless grin on his beautiful face.

"He will most certainly kill you."

"Will you at least consider it?" he continued his teasing.

"No."

"Please?"

"Fine."

"Really?" He sounded truly surprised.

She waited, then said, "No," as he laughed at his hopefulness. The idea of joining him in the cart made her stomach feel funny. A part of her wanted to do it, although she knew she couldn't.

She felt a little light-headed as they walked. "Which way are we going?" she asked, desperate to change the subject.

"You choose."

She chose a road that went in the opposite direction of Matilda's house. She had no desire to see that witch ever again. She was not sure where they were going but she enjoyed the walk. The town was beautiful but smelled of fish in certain areas. The houses were built out of stones and had beautiful flower-filled gardens. Moss covered many walls and lush greenery surrounded them. "Beautiful," she mumbled as she looked around.

"Yes, beautiful," Rafe agreed with his eyes on her and only her.

"Rafe," she said and suddenly looked at him. "Why did you save us from burning?"

"Why do you ask?" he frowned.

"You could have just walked the other way...."

"I could have," he agreed.

"Why didn't you?"

Rafe seemed to think about this for a moment. "You

were a family in need of help, and I was in a position to help."

"But you almost died," she said. "And you got hurt."

"And you came back for me," he said. "I honestly thought you would run away."

"I thought so too," she confessed.

"You're braver than you know," he said.

"Or angrier than I know," she wasn't sure where those words came from.

"Who are you so angry at?" Rafe asked the question to which she had no answer.

She didn't know who was to blame, but she felt like she had this burning fire in her that was just waiting to explode. *Maybe I was born this way... built this way...*

She decided to avoid the question. It would only lead to more questions that she couldn't answer. She focused the conversation back on Rafe. "And you ran after Maggie when they took her...."

"Your sister is adorable," he said. "I would never let anyone hurt her."

"Why does her safety mean anything to you?"

Rafe paused before he answered. That longing look returned, that look in his eyes that she had seen as he watched Maggie hug Caitlin. "She reminds me of someone."

"Someone special?"

"Yes," Rafe said bluntly.

Caitlin knew better than to push him, but she couldn't help herself. She was curious and she didn't know much about him. "A girlfriend maybe?"

Rafe smiled, "You think your six-year-old sister would remind me of a girlfriend?"

"Now that you say it that way..."

He looked at her. "I prefer being alone."

"No one likes to always be alone."

"Am I no one?"

She rolled her eyes. He also had a way of avoiding the things he didn't want to talk about. "Can't you ever be serious?"

"I try not to be," he admitted. "But fine. Sometimes being with someone can be... fun."

"Being with someone?" she pressed. "Like when you are in a relationship?"

"That does have its good parts."

Caitlin couldn't remember whether or not she had been in a romantic relationship before. She tried imagining what it would be like to be committed to someone.

"So what are the best parts than?" she asked. "Of being in a relationship?"

"The beginning," Rafe said without having to think about it.

Caitlin visualized it. "Like when you just meet and make each other nervous?"

"No, long before that," Rafe said.

"Like when you first lay eyes on that special someone and feel the butterflies?" she asked as her cheeks reddened.

"No, even before that," Rafe said again.

"Before you *meet* them?"

"Yes." Rafe smiled and paused for effect. "In other words, when you are single."

She glared at him. "You are most certainly sitting alone in the back of the cart the whole way."

He laughed. It was such a beautiful sound that she would always recognize anywhere. When he stopped his face was serious and his voice was soft. "I doubt that."

She looked at him and was aware of how hot her face had become. "We should start walking back," she said.

They turned around and walked back on the path they'd taken.

"So have you ever done this before?" she asked him.

"Done what?"

"Traveled with a bunch of non-Magic folk."

"No," he confessed. "I've actually not traveled that much. Wolves like staying where it's cold. I just know something about the world because I like to observe folks closely and I am able to learn new things quickly."

"Do you regret leaving home then?"

He shook his head. "There's nothing left there for me."

"But your family must miss you terribly."

Rafe's eyes went cold and he diverted his gaze. She saw the muscles in his jaw tense.

"Did I say something wrong?" she asked.

"I don't want to talk about my family," he said in a clipped voice.

186

"Why not? You know all about mine."

"That's different."

"How is it different?" she pressed and saw the irritation in his eyes.

"It just is."

"So it's alright if you want to get to know me, but it's not alright for me to get to know you?"

"I don't know you," he said coldly and stopped walking.

"Well," she said. "Ask me anything you want to know about me."

"How old were you when your father taught you that Magic is bad and that all Magical beings deserve to be murdered?"

"I don't know," she said honestly.

"Probably young," he said. "Just look at how young Maggie—"

"Maggie does not wish you, or anyone else, harm," Caitlin interrupted. "Why are you acting like you hate us?"

"I'm not the hater," he sneered.

"And I am?"

"I'm sorry. I didn't mean to aim that at you," he said a little gentler.

"Maybe I am not the angry one after all," she said.

"Maybe not. I doubt you have anything to be angry about."

"And you do?" she asked without bothering to hide her irritation.

Rafe didn't answer as they'd arrived at the inn. He brushed past her and went to his room without saying another word.

# CHAPTER 22

DYLAN ARCHER HAD grown up. He was a hunter, just like his dad. Only, he was much better than his dad. He was strong, and fast and agile. He could fight, and fight well, with any weapon that was given to him. If he wasn't given a weapon, he would find one, or make one, or be one.

It was after dark when he walked into a bar with his father by his side. He did what he always did when he walked into a strange place: he observed.

He saw three bartenders: two women and one man. Most seats at the bar counter were taken. One lady sat alone by a table close to the door, sipping her drink while her fluffy dog lay obediently by her feet. People were talking, drinking, and laughing excessively.

He noticed a few heads turn as he and his father entered. People always stared at them whenever they appeared in their professional attire. From their leather coats and all of the weapons they carried on them, it was easy to tell that they were hunters.

They had just arrived in the town of Farmbell. Although they'd left most of their weapons in their room at the inn, Dylan carried his bow and arrows and Liam carried his sword. A sword had always been his father's favorite weapon. Dylan used to watch his father practice when he was a boy. He always thought his father was brilliant and that he would have made a fantastic knight. Of course, only a child would think that being a knight was a dangerous but brave thing to do. Now that Dylan was an adult, he knew most knights would run away if they had to fight the things he and his father routinely fought.

As always, Dylan ignored their stares. He walked to the bar and took a seat. The bar lady gave him a smile as she asked him what he wanted to drink. He and his father both ordered whisky.

He noticed the bar lady study him. She first took in his bow, his athletic body, then his face, and even his hands. When she realized that he noticed her staring at him, she blushed and turned away. Dylan couldn't help but smile. It was nice being admired.

"She's pretty," his father said to him. "But she's not the reason we are here."

"Work first, fun later," Dylan said and took a sip of whisky. But his father noticed his eyes lingering on her a little too long. He had only said what his father wanted to hear.

"I mean it, Dylan. I need you sharp and focused."

"Yes, father." He didn't want a pretty girl to get caught up in his life anyway. He didn't have the time to put in all of the effort that a woman would need. He also didn't want a woman living the dangerous life that he lived. Not after what happened to his mother.

"You folks are not from around here," said the man who was sitting next to Liam. He looked drunk and had some beer dripping off his beard.

"Clearly not," Dylan responded.

"What's your business here then?"

"We're hunting," Liam said.

With Liam's attention diverted, Dylan winked at the bar lady. She blushed and said something to her friend. The friend looked at Dylan's face and then they both giggled.

"Aren't you going to let me in on the joke?" he asked the girl.

She was really pretty. She had long, red hair that shimmered like a newly hammered copper kettle. Her brown eyes reminded him of chocolate and her skin was beautifully pale like the moon. She had freckles on her nose. "No," the girl smiled sweetly. She walked to him. Her blouse hung low over her breasts as she leaned over the bar to take Dylan's glass. "Would you like another?" she asked.

"I shouldn't," he said. "We've got work to do."

"It's after hours. I'm sure work can wait until tomorrow."

The other bar lady walked past him toward the table by the door. She carried a brew on a tray and thumped it on the heavy wood table in front of the customer. Dylan's back was to the door, but he could hear the little dog growl at her as she passed by.

The man on Dylan's left was talking too much to drink his beer. It stood there on the counter untouched. "What is he drinking?" Dylan asked her.

"Our famous draft beer," she said.

Dylan smiled at her and she blushed again. "I'll take one of those."

She obediently got him one, and when no one was looking, he swapped it with the one that the man hadn't touched. He drank it slowly.

"This man here was just telling me where to hunt foxes," Liam said to Dylan.

Although Liam's voice was calm and gentle Dylan knew his father very well. He was disappointed. Hunting wolves was much more exciting than hunting foxes. Dylan could also tell his dad was irritated with the moron for not realizing what they were.

The man rambled on while Liam pretended to listen. At least this idiot made his father blend in as well as he possibly could. He made Liam look like any other normal man who came to the bar to drink after a long day's work. Liam could just nod or occasionally say "yes," and the man would keep talking. Great. This way, he didn't need to focus on the conversation. He could focus on what was going on all around him.

The red-haired bar lady kept staring at Dylan as he drank his beer. She had to admit that he was pretty, much prettier than most men around here. He had tanned skin that set off the bluest eyes she had ever seen. His blond hair was dirty, but she didn't mind. It was a sign that he had been working. He also had a lot of scars. She knew how he'd gotten them. From the way he talked, walked, and carried his bow, anyone could tell he was a hunter.

"Are you just going to stare at me the whole night?" Dylan asked.

"I would like to, if you don't mind." She smiled sweetly.

"I don't mind at all. As long as you talk to me while doing it."

She played with her hair and bit her lip. "What do you want to talk about?"

"You." His slow smile reached his blue eyes.

"There's not much to say...." she said innocently.

"That can't be true... because you are stunning."

She shifted her weight nervously. "I'm Clarissa."

She waved her hand awkwardly and Dylan wondered if she wished she was more elegant. He gently caught her hand in the air and leaned over to kiss it. It was a smooth and soft motion. Her face went as red as her hair.

"It's a pleasure to meet you, Clarissa," he said as he held both her hand and her eyes.

"The p-pleasure is mine. Have you ever been to Farmbell before?"

"It's our first time here."

"Will you be staying long?"

"I doubt it," he said, finishing his beer and setting his tankard down. "I never stay too long in one place."

"That's a shame," she said leaning slowly in front of him to clear the counter.

The man next to Dylan remembered that he had a beer. He downed it in front of his friends and received a pat on the back.

"A shame you say?" Dylan said. "How come?"

"Farmbell can be a fun place."

"I'm sure you could make it fun."

"How can I make it fun?" she asked with glinting eyes.

"You could show me around...."

"What places are you interested in seeing?" She played with her skirt.

"There's a quiet little street behind the bar..." he hinted.

"Then maybe you should find your way to it." Her eyes met his. She smiled. He smiled back.

Then she had to move on to another customer. Dylan got up and accidently knocked his chair over. It was a clumsy move that could easily be mistaken for a drunken one.

Liam grabbed his arm. "Where are you going?"

"To the back of the bar," Dylan shrugged his arm off.

"We're working, Dylan," his father reminded him.

"I know," Dylan said and walked toward the door. Out of the corner of his eye, he saw the man who had been sitting next to him stumble and fall.

He walked past the little white dog that was sleeping now. A man had joined its mistress who paid him no mind and continued to nurse her drink.

Dylan walked out of the bar and turned left sharply. He walked to the little street behind the bar and found a door that led back into the bar. Dylan leaned against the wall and positioned himself so that he could watch the backdoor. The street was dark and lonely.

After waiting five minutes, he wondered if he had been stood up. To his relief, the door opened and the pretty red-haired girl walked out and closed the door behind her.

"I was beginning to think that you weren't coming," he said.

She walked up to him with her hands behind her back. "I'm here now."

She stopped so close to him that he could feel her breath on his face. She was tall and didn't need to stand on her toes to kiss him. The kiss caught him by surprise and he stepped backward. His back touched the cold stone of the wall. She followed him easily, leaned in, and kissed him harder.

His hands went to her small waist and he pulled her in. She gasped as if surprised by his sudden movement. He moved quickly, one hand grasping her lower back while the other catching hold of both her wrists.

"NO!" she cried and tried to pull away, but he was stronger.

"You're a sneaky little fox, aren't you?" he smiled.

She pulled against him again. But he found it easy to restrain her.

"Stop fighting," he said, "and you'll make this a whole lot easier."

He allowed her to pull one arm free and as he expected, she swung the knife that she had been hiding behind her back toward his face. He caught her hand mid-swing and turned her so that her back slammed against the wall. His hand gripped hers and forced it upward, stopping only when the knife she held pressed against her own neck, releasing one tiny droplet of blood. She tried to put as much force as possible against his arm.

*Stupid girl! Now, I'll have to push back.* If she stopped pushing, then his hand would move forward and the knife would slice through her throat. *And whose fault would that be?*

He dropped her other hand and let his arm fall lazily to his side. She used her free hand to dig her nails into the arm that still held her and tried to push it away. She drew in a deep and shaky breath.

"Don't scream," he warned her with a voice as cold as ice.

"I w-won't," she said and he believed her. "How did you know?"

"I wasn't sure," he admitted. "Not until I saw you come at me with a knife."

She glared.

Dylan now knew her nervousness inside the bar

wasn't because she admired him. It was because she was scared of him. "And you did poison my drink..."

"Oops," she said, while still leaning against the knife.

"And your bar lady friend is a shifter too," he continued.

Clarissa's eyes widened in horror, confirming that he had guessed right the second time too. He was good at guessing games.

"I saw the sweet little doggy growl at her. Animals know what unnatural creatures you are. They always betray your secret."

She hissed at him. "You're doing this to me because of the way I was born?"

"I'm doing this to protect innocent human lives."

She was shaking but trying her best to put on a brave face. He pushed the knife a little harder and it drew one, two, three bigger drops of blood. Usually they'd start crying by now. Dylan was impressed.

"Tell me where I can find the rest of your kind," he demanded.

"If I tell you, you'll kill me anyway."

"Yes," he admitted. "But I'll kill you quickly. If you don't tell me, I will hurt you first. Slowly."

She believed him. He had the ice-cold eyes of a killer and the strong, unwavering hands of a man who had taken many lives. She had no choice. "They are at the edge of the woods."

He wanted to dig the knife further into her neck in frustration. But if he did that, he would kill her. So instead he slammed her free hand against the wall, next to her face. She winced like he knew she would. "Don't lie to me."

"Then I won't say anything," she said.

The backdoor slammed open, hitting Dylan hard, and he only just managed to move the knife away from Clarissa's throat.

She kicked his leg and pulled free. The woman who'd opened the door was about to run back inside but Dylan grabbed her arm and yanked her out of the doorway, easily throwing her to the ground. He couldn't let them go back inside to a bar full of witnesses.

The other girl hit Dylan in the face, but she wasn't very good at it. The blow didn't hurt—it only frustrated him more.

"Run!" Clarissa screamed at her friend.

Dylan sighed as he watched them take off. He could catch them easily. But his father would most likely torture them both until one of them talked. And he wasn't in the mood to hear them crying.

He took his bow and drew an arrow from the quiver strapped across his back. They were already a good distance away. Dylan didn't mind. He never missed.

He shot twice and watched both bodies drop. He left them there in the street, for the rats to eat, and walked back into the bar to fetch his dad.

"Did you run into any trouble?" Liam asked.

"Nothing I couldn't handle. Did you find any work for us?"

Liam nodded. "I heard a story about a witch that lives in the Sinking Swamp."

"That's far away," Dylan said. "Let's stay a little longer. I have a feeling that there is a family of foxes somewhere around here just dying to meet us."

# CHAPTER 23

RAFE FELT A little guilty for being mean to Caitlin. She had only wanted to get to know him better and couldn't understand why he'd become angry. The truth was that this happened whenever someone wanted to know something about his family. He was simply not ready to talk about them. He might never be ready.

He didn't have anything to pack so he walked to the nearest shop and bought himself some clothes. Then he went to lie down in the cart and pretended to still be wounded. It was terribly frustrating to lie there and watch everyone work. Usually he would have helped and done the work faster than any of them could.

Even little Maggie helped them to carry their things to the cart. A six-year-old did more than he was doing. Lying down in this cart for even five minutes was hard for him. He couldn't imagine what it would feel like if he had to continue this ruse for days.

Daisy put some fruit and bread into the cart next to him. He eyed it warily but didn't say anything.

Daisy saw his disgust and laughed. "Rafe, there is a lot of water here and we will catch fish for dinner tonight. You won't have to survive on just fruit and bread."

"Can I go buy some steak?" he asked shyly. "Just in case the fish don't feel like dying today."

"No," Daisy laughed. "It will go to waste."

He stared at the butcher's shop longingly but he listened to Daisy as if she was his own mother. Still, the smell of meat filled his nostrils and made his stomach growl.

"You look like a puppy that got kicked out of the house," Caitlin remarked. Her voice made him jump since he hadn't realized she was there.

"And how does that look?" he asked.

"It's a sad longing look."

"No, it's a hungry look," he corrected her.

She tossed him an apple, which he caught and tossed back. "I prefer not to eat my food's food," he explained.

"Okay. Suit yourself," she said and took a large bite. The apple was tart, just the way she liked it. When she finished eating, she walked to Penny and placed the apple core on her palm, extending her hand so that the horse could eat. But Penny turned her head away.

Maggie took the apple core from her sister and

offered it to the horse. This time the horse took it and ate it. Maggie giggled.

"Well, she doesn't like me," Caitlin said. Then she fell in step with Gerald. "Can't we maybe buy some more horses? They will allow us to travel much faster.... I took some money from River Town when we left," she confessed. "So I can pay for them."

"That's kind of you," Gerald said. "But a father should not be taking his child's money. It's my job to provide for you while I still can. Then one day when I am old, it will be your turn to provide for me."

"Horses are expensive," she pressed. Then she looked at his hair and pointed. "What is that?"

"What's what?" he asked.

"It's a gray hair!" she exclaimed in mock horror.

"Nonsense!" he rolled his eyes. Then he added with a twinkle. "You're not paying for the horses."

"Fine," she laughed. "I'll return the favor one day."

"The favor?" Gerald asked, his brows wrinkling. "It's not a favor. It's my duty as a father to provide for you."

"A horse is a luxury," she said.

"And it's fun for me as your father to spoil you."

She smiled at him and was glad that he was in her life. The man had a good heart and she knew he would give her anything and everything that he could.

"You're such a great person," she told him.

"That's good to hear," he said. "I've heard that girls search for boys that are much like their fathers—to marry, that is."

"Are we back to the marriage talk?" she said with a groan. Her mood immediately changed and she forgot that a moment ago she was admiring her father.

"I don't know why it bothers you so much," he said. "I know you aren't the most affectionate person, but you are beautiful."

"So you're saying that I'll catch a man with my looks and then drive him away with my coldness?"

Her father ignored her snide remark. "You aren't going to be young and beautiful forever, Caitlin."

"I know that."

"I just want what is best for you."

"That, and a man that can give me the whole world," she rolled her eyes.

"No," her father said. "I want a man to treat you like you *are* his whole world."

That touched something in her heart and her irritation melted away. She looked at her father with a warm look. He had nothing but love in his heart for her. "I'm just not ready yet."

"You're never ready," her father said. "I know that you don't want any advice on love from your old man...."

"But?" she smiled.

"But," he laughed. "But I am smarter than you think. And I can read men better than you can. I can tell what their intentions are."

"Is this about Rafe?" she asked.

"I see the way you look at him," her father said. "You look at him wide-eyed and hopeful."

Caitlin didn't bother denying it. During the past few days, she did stare at Rafe from time to time. She always looked away immediately whenever he noticed.

"And he looks at you the way a wolf looks at a lamb."

Her heart skipped a beat. That was just a saying –her father had no idea that Rafe was a wolf.

"I know you can't choose what you feel," he continued. "But at least try to resist falling in love with him."

"Why? What's the worst that could happen?"

"I don't know what the worst part will be," Gerald said. "But I can tell you what will eventually happen."

"Okay..."

"You will fall in love and then he will leave."

"You can't know that," she said.

"Caitlin, I can see it in his eyes. I can hear it in his voice. He doesn't have a bad heart, but he will leave you nonetheless."

The idea of Rafe leaving made Caitlin sick. She stumbled but didn't fall. Her mind was racing and she decided that her father was wrong–Rafe would not leave her.

Gerald watched her closely and then laughed bitterly.

"What?" she asked.

"Here I was, hoping to convince you to consider marriage," he said. "But now I find myself trying to talk you out of love–I hadn't realized how far you had already fallen and how fast."

Caitlin didn't say anything. Until now she hadn't

admitted her feelings to herself. It was strange to fall in love for the first time. And it was scary to wonder if Rafe felt the same way.

"My baby girl," he sighed. "Nothing can break a woman's heart as badly as a first love."

"I won't get it broken," she said.

Then Maggie joined them and they changed topics. She was as energetic and talkative as always.

Rafe looked up at the blue sky from the back of the cart. With his wolf-like ears he had heard everything Gerald had said. "He is a wise old man," Rafe whispered to the wind.

# CHAPTER 24

THEY TRAVELED UNTIL sunset and then set up camp by one of the rivers where the current wasn't too strong and they could fish. Wildflowers grew between the long green grasses and the branches of willow trees swayed in the wind. Caitlin paused to breathe in the peace and beauty of the place.

Humming, Maggie went digging for worms while Gerald unpacked his fishing rod and other gear from their cart. It didn't take long for Maggie to return with a cupful of worms for baiting the hooks. Gerald was soon tossing his line into the water. Having spent his entire life near rivers, he was an expert fisherman, able to cast his line into the smallest target.

Meanwhile, Daisy made a fire. This was difficult because the sticks were wet and did not burn easily. She also had to use some green leaves to get the fire going and they sent up clouds of smoke. Luckily

Gerald found a dead tree and cut it down so that they could use the wood for fire. He then returned to his fishing rods and waited for the fish to bite.

Daisy prepared a salad from the little bit of vegetables they had. Rafe sniffed at the air around camp and found the smell of raw fish more appetizing than the smell of green peppers in the salad.

Caitlin made their beds on the ground beside the cart and near the fire. She used the wool blankets and fur coats that they had found in their village. She did not make Rafe's bed as she assumed he would sleep in the cart. He sat there still, watching everyone busy at work and looking very bored. Finished with her task, Caitlin rose and walked to Penny, leading her to a tree and tying her halter to a nearby bush so that she could graze but not run away.

Still humming softly, Maggie went to Rafe and pretended to help him with his wounds. She ended up throwing out the medicine that Rafe would have drunk if he were still in pain. He appreciated the effort that the little girl went through to keep his secret but he thought it a waste to throw out the medicine.

After Maggie finished, Rafe decided he couldn't lie still anymore. So when no one was looking he stretched and then got to his feet and started walking toward the river. He had taken five steps before his pace slowed —he'd nearly forgotten to feign being injured still.

"Do you mind if I sit?" he asked Gerald when he arrived at the riverbank.

"Not at all. I brought another fishing rod if you would like to fish as well. It's kept in the front of the cart."

Gerald started to walk back to the cart but Rafe stopped him with a smile. "I can get it. My wounds will heal faster if I move more."

This time Rafe remembered to walk slowly and carefully, as if he was on the mend but still in pain. He returned to Gerald with the rod, baited the hook, and cast it expertly into the water.

"Do you enjoy fishing?" Gerald asked as Rafe sat down beside him.

"Not really," Rafe said honestly.

"Well you clearly know how," Gerald observed. "Who taught you?"

Rafe did his best to keep a neutral face. "My father did."

"He taught you well," Gerald said. "You don't speak much about your family."

"There's not much to say," Rafe said and tried to change the topic by leading Gerald to talk about his own family. "Your family is lovely."

"I know," Gerald said. But he changed the subject too because he was worried that talking about his family would lead to talking about Caitlin. And he did not want to talk to Rafe about his daughter. "How long will you be traveling with us?"

Rafe wondered if he was overstaying his welcome. He didn't intend to do that, but it was also safer for them to travel with more people. "I actually decided that I wanted to go to the castle too. And if you don't mind, I'd like to continue to travel with you. It's safer in a group."

Gerald's face went a bit paler. "Why are you going to the castle?"

"I think it might be the ideal place to look for a job," Rafe lied.

"Isn't there work back in Southpaw for you?"

"Nothing that interests me."

"What, if I may ask, does interest you?" Gerald asked with an edge to his voice.

Then a fish bit the hook. Rafe was on his feet immediately, jerking his rod backward in one strong, quick motion. The fish flew out of the water in an arc and landed on the muddy bank. It was a big one. He smiled as he trapped it beneath his palm and then tossed it into a basket.

"Nice catch," Gerald said. He didn't mean to sound gruff, but Rafe had jumped up awfully fast for a wounded man. *How are his wounds healing so quickly?* Gerald wondered. He looked at Rafe's shirt and wished that he could see through the material.

"Thank you," Rafe said. He heard the stiffness in Gerald's voice and wished that Gerald had caught the fish instead.

"Maybe you should clean it, if you don't mind." Gerald said. "Maggie will be hungry so if we don't catch anything else, we can cook that one early."

Rafe nodded. He didn't have a taste for fish, but it was still much better than just the green stuff. He preferred red meat and regretted not buying steak earlier.

Gerald rubbed his neck and something caught Rafe's eye. A small tattoo peeped just under the hairline at the nape of Gerald's neck. Rafe didn't have time for a closer look, but he swore it was a number. "Do you like tattoos?" Rafe asked.

"What?" Gerald was caught off guard with the question. "No, no, I don't like them at all."

Then there was an uncomfortable silence for a few minutes. Rafe decided to break the silence with the thoughts that were swirling around in his mind. "I have no intention of hurting your daughter."

"Excuse me?" Gerald said, wondering if he had heard the young man correctly.

"I have no intention of hurting your daughter," Rafe said again. "I can see it in your eyes—that you worry about me hurting her."

"Young man, if I thought you would *intentionally* hurt my daughter, you would not be sitting here now," Gerald said.

Another fish bit and this time it was Gerald who caught it. He pulled it in and smiled when he saw how big it was.

"Wow!" Rafe exclaimed. "It's huge!"

Gerald pulled the fish farther up the riverbank and then cut the line.

"I'll clean it," Rafe offered.

"Thank you," Gerald said and then he took the fishing rods back to the cart.

Caitlin walked to the river to join Rafe. "That's disgusting," she said as she watched him gutting the fish.

"Don't be such a girly-girl," he teased and grinned at her with his cloud-white teeth. "But wasn't it you who went digging for worms?"

"No, you know perfectly well that was Maggie. And I don't really feel like helping you with that anyway. So... I think I shall go sit by the fire."

"Hey!" Rafe called her back to him. "I'm cold, I'm hungry, and I smell like a fish."

"So?"

"So, I think I need a compliment to make me feel better."

"Sure. You..." she paused and grinned, "have an excellent sense of smell."

It was his turn to glare. The glaring turned into a goofy smile the moment she turned her back on him and walked to the fire.

Maggie was drawing princesses in the sand while she waited for them to prepare the food.

They had wooden cups with them and Caitlin scooped water from the flowing river for them to drink. She brought everyone their drinks instead of putting the cups down by the fire. When she brought Rafe his drink, she accidentally spilled it. He moved aside just in time to avoid being splashed.

"That was your fault," she told him.

"How was that MY fault?"

"You make me nervous."

He looked into her eyes and smiled warmly. His smile was intoxicating. She could have stared at the perfect curves of his lips for much longer but dinner was ready. She joined her family as they sat around the fire to eat.

The fish was delicious. Even Rafe was licking his fingers.

Gerald smiled. "As you get older in life you realize that all that really matters is family."

"It's a shame most people only realize that when they are older," Rafe said.

"Is your family close?" Daisy asked lightheartedly. "Do you have a good relationship with them?"

Rafe swallowed and nodded. He expected them to ask questions now that he wasn't asleep in the cart the whole time. No family would feel totally comfortable traveling with a man they knew nothing about. But he didn't want to talk about it and they didn't ask anymore.

That night everyone was tired after a long day of walking. Everyone fell asleep fast except for Rafe who had been lying down the whole day. He tossed and turned before he finally got up and walked down to the river.

Caitlin watched him from where she lay next to

the fire. The moonlight illuminated his pale skin. His wavy, dark hair shone like black polish. She decided to join him by the water.

"You're up," he greeted her with surprise.

"Yeah, I don't really sleep a lot." She sat down in the long grass.

"Why is that?"

"I have a lot of bad dreams."

"As do I," Rafe mumbled.

She wanted to ask. She wanted to pry. But the more she pushed him to open up, the more he shut her out. It was frustrating but alluring at the same time.

"So you can't swim," Rafe said, changing the subject. "How come you've never learned? It's very unusual for someone who grew up in the Riverlands to not know how to swim."

She shrugged. "I don't know."

"I didn't even know your town existed," Rafe confessed, changing topics.

"Yeah?"

He nodded. "It's really small and far from everything. It was pure chance that I found it while I was looking for the bears."

"I'm glad you did find it."

"You should be. Otherwise, you would probably never have found a swim teacher," he said playfully, back on topic.

"A swim teacher?"

"Me." His white teeth glinted in the moonlight and

Caitlin thought they looked sharper than usual.

"Rafe, are you a werewolf?" she asked and then bit her lip. It sounded really lame when she asked it like that.

Rafe laughed. "Don't you know anything about Magical creatures?"

"I guess not..."

"Werewolves are slaves to the moon and they can only turn during the full moon. I am a shifter. I can shift whenever I please."

"Is it painful?"

"No."

"Dangerous?"

"Only if I stay an animal for too long. The longer I stay an animal, the more animal I become."

"Oh."

Rafe clasped his hands together and looked at the water. "So, swimming lessons..."

Caitlin looked at the flowing river. She couldn't understand why, but she really did not want to go swimming. So she tried to keep talking as much as possible. "Why should you be the one to teach me?"

"Because you have no other options. Besides, swimming is fun."

"How did you learn?"

Rafe looked at the river as he spoke. "My father taught me. During the summer months, there is a lot of water in Southpaw. We had a huge lake by our house. All the kids were required to learn how to swim so that they would know what to do if they fell in by accident."

"All of the kids?"

"Yes. My younger sister and my older sister and all my cousins."

"Did all of you live together then?"

He nodded. "Wolves form packs, remember?"

"So all of them are like you?"

He smiled. "Of course."

"If it's so much safer in a pack, why did they let you leave alone when you went looking for a bear?"

"I've been alone for a long time," Rafe said. The sadness crept back into his eyes.

She tilted her head and looked at him a bit puzzled. She wanted him to say more.

"All of the water freezes in the cold months," Rafe continued. "Have you ever walked on a frozen lake?"

"Not that I can remember."

"My family and I used to ice-skate on the lake by our home."

"Did your father teach you how to skate too?"

"No," Rafe laughed. "My father only taught me the skills he thought I needed to be the man he wanted me to be."

"I'm sure you didn't disappoint him," she meant the words kindly. She thought he'd take it as a compliment, but he didn't look happy at all. "Did I say something wrong?"

"No," he said. Then to her surprise he explained. "I

did disappoint him."

"By doing what?"

"I don't think it was really anything I did. It was more who I am."

"Tell me..."

"I'm a very free-spirited wolf, Caitlin," he explained with a half-smile. "I don't like people telling me what to do and I don't like being forced to do anything. I come and go as I please. For a wolf, this isn't... appropriate behavior," he sighed. "My dad always wanted me to stay home and to learn and grow so that one day I would become the leader of our wolf pack."

"Isn't that a great honor?" she asked.

"It is," he nodded. "But an honor and responsibility I didn't want."

"How come?"

"It was too much responsibility. And I didn't want to spend my life making sacrifices for others and devising plans to protect them."

Caitlin edged a little closer to him as he talked.

"I was just a kid the first time my father told me his plans for me. We got into a huge fight. Both of us said things we shouldn't have. I ended up storming out of the house and into the snow. The lake was frozen, but I didn't realize how thin the ice was."

"Oh no." Caitlin breathed as she predicted what was going to happen in this story.

"I fell through. It happened so fast.... I couldn't think... couldn't breathe... The water was so cold that

216

it felt like millions of little needles were stabbing my skin."

Caitlin grimaced. "Did your father save you?"

Rafe shook his head. "No, he didn't know I'd fallen in. It was just luck that I got myself out. I managed to stumble back to the house. I thought I'd freeze to death."

"What did your father say? He must have been worried."

Rafe pictured his father. The man had no time for disobedience. "Actually he told me that if I ever left again, I wouldn't be welcomed back."

"I'm sure he didn't mean it."

"Oh, he meant it. I never saw it as walking out on my family when I left a few years later. I saw it as just taking a really long break from them."

"Have you seen them since you left again?"

Rafe swallowed. "Yes."

"And did the rest of the family welcome you back?"

Rafe pulled his arms to his chest, crossing them over his heart as if he was protecting it. "No," he said with the saddest voice she had ever heard. He swallowed and struggled to get the next words out. "They were all dead."

Caitlin stared at him in horror. *What? ALL of them?* Caitlin twitched in the grass. She was dying to ask Rafe what had happened, but she stopped herself. He looked like he was on the verge of tears. She reached out to touch him but he pulled away. He blinked his eyes but they were still shiny.

"I've never told anyone that," he said.

Caitlin remained silent. There was nothing left for her to say. He was hurting, had probably been hurting for years. And there was nothing she could do to ease his pain.

"Don't look so sad," Rafe told her.

"But you are hurting," she said. "If you're hurting, I'm hurting." She meant those words. She could feel his pain in her heart as if it were her own. It was not a burning fire but a burning coldness.

She leaned closer to Rafe and rested her head on his shoulder. He didn't allow tears to roll down his face. He had excelled at learning how not to cry when he was a kid. No matter how much he and his father fought, the old wolf had never seen him cry. Not since he was a toddler.

He often wondered if the tears that didn't fall from his eyes were the tears that were drowning his heart. The reason that he lay awake most nights was because he knew that if he slept, he'd go back there, back to their mansion in Southpaw. He did not want to go there anymore.

Caitlin was sweet. She felt warm and soft against his shoulder. And on any other night, he would have wrapped his arm around her. But tonight he felt alone. He didn't want her with him at this moment. He didn't want anyone nearby.

He had walked out on his family. He had chosen to

leave. And when he returned, they were all dead. In his mind he could still see the corpses that decorated their once lively mansion.

He deserved to be alone.

He got up and Caitlin, who had been leaning on him, had to reach out her arms so that she didn't fall over. She sat up and looked after him. "Where are you going?" she asked, startled.

"To bed," he said coldly. He didn't wish her a good night. He didn't flash his killer smile. He just turned and walked away with his head hanging.

Rafe crawled under the blankets and watched Caitlin lie down beside her sister. He realized that she had given him the warmest blanket when she had made the beds earlier that day. Rafe grimaced. She was not the first beautiful young woman who thought that she could melt his icy heart.

# CHAPTER 25

CAITLIN DIDN'T REMEMBER much of the dream she had that night. It came back to her in flashes. She was tied to a table and there were people all around her. They were talking about her as if she wasn't there. They were talking about how great she could be.

But they had also hurt her. She felt their needles in her skin, and they wouldn't let her go no matter how much she pleaded. She screamed and cried and cursed, but no one cared.

She woke abruptly and sat up. Her body was sweaty and shaky.

"Did you have a bad dream?" Daisy asked.

Caitlin looked to her left. Daisy and Gerald had already packed their beds and started to make breakfast. Daisy was looking at her with a concerned motherly face.

She nodded.

"You were talking in your sleep," Daisy said.

"What did I say?" Caitlin got up slowly and stretched.

"You were mumbling," Daisy said. "So I couldn't make out anything."

"Oh."

"Do you want to talk about the dream?"

Caitlin shook her head. She most certainly didn't want to share any of her dreams. "No, I don't remember much of it anyway."

Rafe was back to his usual joking self that morning. He didn't mention their conversation last night and she didn't bring his family up. He looked happy again, but she knew the pain was eating him from the inside out. She pitied him but at the same time she felt special that he chose to tell her. She knew it wasn't easy for him to open up and yet he trusted her enough to tell her about his biggest heartache.

She wondered how she would feel if her family was dead. Would she miss them or miss having people who cared about her? No, they did more than care: they loved her. *But do I love them?* Caitlin turned her attention to Maggie and gently nudged her awake. The little girl groaned once, rolled over, and then sat up. Her hair hungover her face as she stretched. *These people are my family. I should love them. Everyone loves their family.*

They ate breakfast together and started walking again. Rafe lay in the back of the cart and looked bored while Maggie danced around Penny who was very patient and calm.

"You're going to wear yourself out," Gerald warned her.

"Then I'll just ride on the cart with Rafe," she said and left Penny's side to hunt for flowers.

They traveled in silence for a long time. Every once in a while the silence was interrupted by Maggie telling Rafe about her flowers. He listened like flowers were what made his world go round.

They ate fruit and bread for lunch, as they walked.

Three days later, they reached the next little town.

"This is Water Spark," Gerald told them. "It is the last town in the Riverlands that we will be passing through."

Caitlin was grateful when they arrived at an inn. The soft bed was going to be so much nicer than the ground she had been sleeping on. She couldn't wait to rest her head against a soft, welcoming pillow. But there were things to be done before that could happen.

Gerald told them that he was going to look for more

horses so that they could travel faster. Rafe wanted to go with him, but since he was still pretending to be in pain, he told them that he would go to his room and bathe instead.

"Can we go buy a new dress?" Maggie asked Daisy.

"You have plenty of dresses," her mother said. "It's your sister who needs some woman-like clothes."

"Please?"

Daisy gave in without putting up much of a fight. Maggie had been such a good girl these past few days. She was a pleasant travel companion. She helped as much as possible and hardly ever complained. Maggie deserved a treat.

Caitlin politely declined their invitation to go shopping and went to her room. She didn't want to walk around much more because her feet hurt. She also didn't think she'd enjoy shopping.

She trudged up to her room, took a bath, and felt warm and relaxed afterward. But she no longer wanted to sleep. She sat on her bed with nothing to do. She waited for a little while, hoping that Rafe would come to her. He didn't.

Caitlin didn't have a lot of patience. She decided to go to him. She resolved not to act nervous—they were friends after all.

He found her standing awkwardly in the hall as he opened his door. He was shirtless again and her heart skipped a beat. He invited her inside and she watched him wrap the bandage around himself.

"Are you still pretending to be in pain?" she teased.

"Did you come here to pretend to be my healer?"

"No," she snapped at him and paced around.

Rafe was different around her when they were alone. He was more intense. And although he was always making jokes, she knew he had a serious side that he didn't let many people see.

"Then why are you here?" he asked. His voice wasn't unwelcoming. It was teasing.

"Do I need a reason to visit you?"

He had finished bandaging himself and was now pulling on a shirt to cover his beautiful body. She wanted him to remove his shirt again but said no such thing.

"No," he smiled. "But I think you came here to ask me something."

"What did I come to ask you?"

"To teach you how to swim of course!"

"Not that again." She rolled her eyes. "Why are you pressuring me?"

"Why are you so scared?"

"I'm not scared," she lied. She was scared. After falling into the river at Waterfall Haven, how could she not be? It was terrible not being able to breathe, having water rush into her nose and mouth. She hated the water pushing her whole body around. She hated losing control. She had no desire to ever be in that position again.

Rafe walked closer to her but she refused to retreat. Although she was tall, he still looked down at her. He loved the way she got nervous when he was standing too close. He loved it even more when she tried to hide it.

"Caitlin, you do know that as a shifter I have extraordinary hearing abilities, right?" he murmured softly, his breath brushing the top of her head.

"Yes..." she whispered. She tilted her head up and her green eyes locked with his gray ones.

"Did you know that I can hear your heart beating?" He leaned forward so that their faces were only inches apart.

"I didn't know...."

"This means I can hear your heart speed up. Or slow down. I can hear when you lie."

Her heart beat even faster. "I've been told I'm a good liar."

"Oh, one of the best I have ever met," Rafe murmured.

For a moment she thought that he would kiss her. But he did not. Instead he stepped around her and opened the door. She felt her stomach sink and tried to regulate her breathing. Did he know that she had been holding her breath?

He walked around her and was outside first. She forgot all about her sore feet and hurried after him, falling into step beside him.

"Where are we going?" she asked.

"There is a dam just outside the town. It's not as big as the one that the town is built around, but it is more private. You'll be able to focus better there."

"Oh, the swimming... Do we really have to do this now?" she asked.

"If you keep avoiding what you fear, you'll never face it," Rafe said.

"You're so wise," she said, imitating his school-marmish tone.

The walk was more silent than Caitlin wanted it to be. She wanted Rafe to talk to her. She wanted Rafe to be more interested in her. She wanted to talk to him. But she didn't know what to say. Her mind went blank.

They reached the dam. It was bigger than she thought it would be and water lilies floated everywhere. Maggie would have loved them.

"Now what?" she asked Rafe as she looked at the water.

"Now you swim," he said.

Before she could stop him, he picked her up and threw her into the dam. She fell into the water with one big splash. She instantly panicked. Her legs kicked out and her arms splashed around. There was water everywhere! It got into her ears and eyes and mouth.

She managed to get her head above the water. "Help!" she cried before her head went under again. She kicked, felt the muddy bottom, and her head was above the water again. She gulped in air greedily. "What do I do? What do I do?" she cried, panicking and gasping.

"You can try standing," Rafe said in a calm voice.

It took a moment for the words to sink in. Then she put her feet down in the mud and stood up. The water reached her shoulders and a tiny blue frog sat atop her head. It croaked once before jumping and landing onto a lily pad. Caitlin was panting as she glared up at Rafe.

He couldn't hold his laughter back anymore. He laughed so that that his stomach hurt and his eyes watered. Caitlin was angry. Her face grew hotter and hotter despite the cool wetness of the water. There was nothing funny about this!

"How dare you scare me like that!" she cried.

"How dare you get scared like that?" he managed to choke out between whoops of laughter.

She splashed him and he jumped in. Then all of her anger disappeared and she started laughing at her own silliness.

Rafe's eyes sparkled as he plucked a white lily flower from its green pad and held it out to her. She rolled her eyes but accepted it. Both of them glowed with happiness. Both felt like the world revolved only around them and their problems drowned in the river. Their sadness washed away for that moment, all but forgotten.

A waterfowl took flight from the grasses on the other side of the dam. Neither of them saw the assassin hiding there.

# CHAPTER 26

HE WAS KNOWN as Black Blade.

He had been trained since the age of seven to become the killer he was today. He had been trained by the best men in the Silver Kingdom and he had become a better fighter than all of them.

His services were in high demand and only the wealthiest people in the kingdom could afford him. He had never let any of them down. If they wanted someone dead, he would see to it, bringing them that person's head as proof.

He possessed no Magical powers, but he didn't need them. He could kill any Magical being or any human as long as the price was high enough.

And his price was high.

He didn't know the man who paid him to kill the girl. He didn't need to know him. He didn't need to know why a girl so young had to die. All that mattered was that he had the money. The pocket on the inside of his coat felt heavy because it was filled with gold. This made him smile.

The man who bought his services didn't even provide his real name. He only told him where to leave the girl's head. Black Blade wondered if the man was worried that he would get caught and inform on him. If so, the man was a fool. He would never get caught. And if he somehow got caught and his captors tortured him, he would never give up his employer. He wouldn't do that no matter the amount of pain.

He touched the gold in his pocket. But maybe for the right price...

He hadn't grown up with honor. He had no dignity and no loyalties. He lived his life doing what was best for him and him alone.

Because he was an assassin, he was feared and didn't have any friends. No one loved him or cared for him. He didn't mind. It was their loss, not his.

Now he lay on his stomach in the grass, looking toward the water where the girl was swimming. She matched the description that his employer had given him, but his employer had said she was traveling with a family. The family consisted of a father, a mother, and a little girl. His employer hadn't said anything about another man.

Black Blade didn't mind killing the man if that meant that he would get the job done and kill the girl. This was the perfect place for the kill, far away from everyone else.

He just had to confirm that it was her. That she was Caitlin Wilde, his target. He didn't want to kill the wrong girl: he would lose time and have to start the search all over again. So he waited patiently for confirmation, waited for the young man to say her name. Unfortunately, the two of them were too busy acting like kids. They were laughing and splashing around like two idiots.

Love struck idiots.

Black Blade tilted his head to the side. He saw the way the young man looked at the girl. He looked at her with a fire burning in his eyes. It was a fun and intense and hungry look at the same time. It was the way Black Blade would look at a hunk of roasting meat.

And then there was the way she looked at him. She looked at him all innocent and wide-eyed. She stared at him often like they were the only two people on the planet. Black Blade wondered if any woman would ever look at him like that. *But do I even want a woman to look at me like that?*

The girl learned to swim quickly. It only took her a few tries before she succeeded. He wondered how she would react if he grabbed that hair of hers and forced her head under the water. *Why is her hair so short anyway? It would be much easier to grab if it were longer.*

Black Blade looked at the man again and wondered if the man would defend her when he attacked. If so, then the man would only die alongside her. The wise thing to do was to run fast and far, and Black Blade would let him go. He was only paid for the girl and he hated doing more than what he got paid to do.

Black Blade stood up in the grass, startling a water-fowl into flight.

They were done swimming. They got out of the water and they were both walking away with their backs turned to him. His knife was in his hand. He held it calmly by his side. From where he stood, he could throw the knife right into the back of her head.

He just had to know if she was the right girl. "Caitlin Wilde," he said.

She turned around to see who had called her. This confirmed that she was his target. She hadn't even turned the whole way, hadn't even seen him, before the blade slashed through the air.

He threw it perfectly, as always. Black Blade had been doing this for so long that it felt like slow-motion. He knew that if bystanders had witnessed it, they would have experienced it differently. They would feel like everything was happening too fast. They would not have been able to focus on the flying knife until it was stopped by Caitlin's head.

A smile spread across his lips as the knife neared her head. Then, just before contact, something unex-pected happened. The man reached out and grabbed the knife by its hilt with unnaturally fast reflexes. He stopped it mid-flight before it touched her. For a second, she gaped at it as if she had trouble processing what had happened.

Rafe lowered the knife and looked at the assassin.

"I've never seen anyone with reflexes like that," Black Blade said.

"You haven't seen anything yet," Rafe sneered.

"Don't get brave now that I've given you a weapon."

"I don't need it," Rafe said and handed the knife to Caitlin.

"How ungrateful," Black Blade sneered. Then he realized that the man had said "I don't *need* it" instead of "I don't *want* it."

Caitlin held the knife awkwardly. This irritated the assassin like a fly would irritate a horse. Girls just didn't know how to use weapons. "Would you like me to show you how to use that?" he offered her.

"How?" she asked.

"Come here and I'll show you," he said.

"So you'll try to kill me again?"

"No," he said. "Trying means I might fail. I'm *going* to kill you."

"I don't really feel up for it," she sounded bored. "Can't you come back another day? I've had enough lessons today."

He was at a loss for words. No one had ever insulted him like this before. Usually people trembled at the sight of him. "Will you feel like dying on another day?"

"Probably not. But maybe you'll get lucky."

"I don't believe in luck," he said and threw the second

knife. His eyes widened with amazement as the man caught it easily again.

The girl stepped back in shock. "Will you stop doing that?" she said. At least she didn't look bored anymore.

"I'll stop when I get it right!" Black Blade snapped. He reached into his pocket and then groaned as he realized he didn't have any more knives to throw. He had only brought two. Usually he only needed one.

"Is there a problem?" Rafe asked lazily. "Would you like me to throw this one back to you?"

"If you would be so kind," Black Blade responded.

Rafe considered throwing it into the assassin's face but he wasn't a very good knife thrower. He might actually miss, or the assassin might duck. So he handed both knives to Caitlin.

The assassin looked at her bored expression and imagined smacking it off her face. Then he looked at the young man, who was just taunting him. Anger boiled in his blood. "Do you not know who I am?!" he managed to choke out.

"Black Blade," Rafe said.

Black Blade looked confused. "How did you know?" He was disguised as a peasant.

Rafe looked at the black blades that Caitlin held. "Lucky guess?"

"If you've heard of me, you'll know how good I am at killing."

"So far, all you've been good at is talking, and your conversation hasn't exactly been riveting," Caitlin pointed out. "Why are you trying to kill me? What did I ever do to you?"

"It's not personal," he said through gritted teeth.

"So someone paid you," Rafe said. "Do you mind telling us who?"

"Of course I mind!" Black Blade yelled, losing his temper and making Caitlin giggle. "I have been paid to kill, not to speak!"

"Can I pay you to speak?" Rafe offered.

Black Blade thought about this for a moment. "You can't afford me."

"Consider my sparing your life your payment," Rafe said. He knew the assassin was a good fighter. He hoped Caitlin knew how to use those blades. She looked way too bored as she swished them around absent-mindedly.

The assassin had two swords strapped to his back. He reached for them and smiled. "Enough talking."

"Good. I thought you'd never shut up," Rafe said.

"Let's get down to business then." Black Blade took a step forward. He was ready for this. He couldn't wait. He was so excited! He could picture the whole fight in his mind. He could picture slicing the young man into bits. He could already hear his screams. He was ready for blood. He was ready for resistance. He was ready for a little bit of a challenge. He was ready for everything—except what followed.

Rafe took his shirt off.

"What are you doing?" Black Blade cried in surprise.

"It's not what you think," Rafe said. His hand went to his belt.

"Please stop," Black Blade begged. "I don't think I can fight a naked man."

"That's disappointing," Rafe said as his belt fell to the ground.

The assassin decided to strike before the man took his pants off. He ran forward and jumped. To his surprise the girl rammed into him, and instead of kicking his big feet into the man's chest he found himself on the ground.

He wasn't sure how that had happened. People rarely caught him by surprise. He jumped to his feet. Both of his swords were still in his hands. He swung fast—very fast. How did she manage to duck? The sword only just missed her throat.

Caitlin still held his two knives, but they were small and used for throwing. She was standing too close to throw them and yet they were too small to ward off his swords. She'd have to get close if she wanted to stab him. But getting close would be really hard if he kept swinging his swords like a skilled madman.

He swung the sword again and she bent forward. It scraped the air above her back. Her hand shot forward with the knives in them, but he was already turning around following the momentum of his swords. He twirled with the grace of a dancer and moved with the quick cunning of a snake. He swung his swords toward the young man. But when he looked at the spot where Rafe had been standing, he was surprised. There was a wolf instead of a human.

The wolf was very big, and he had anticipated a man, not a wolf, to attack. The wolf jumped forward with his mouth wide open. But he didn't latch his jaw onto the assassin's arm. Instead he knocked the man over.

Black Blade didn't fall to the ground the way most people would have. When he realized he was falling he let himself fall so that he could use the momentum to roll. He rolled over backward and onto his haunches.

Rafe spun around and charged but the swords were already aimed at him. Rafe realized that he would run into them so he jumped up instead. He landed as the assassin slashed out toward Caitlin who then slipped to the side.

Black Blade had an enemy on either side of him. He couldn't watch his back, so he spun between the two of them. He tried not to take his eyes off either of them for too long. He was like a whirlwind—slashing side to side.

"How did a farm girl learn to fight this well?" he asked.

Caitlin hadn't realized it until now. But she was actually fighting pretty well. She wasn't hurt yet and she wasn't scared. "I don't fight well," she retorted. "You just fight badly." But the talking had distracted her and he kicked her in the stomach. The air left her lungs and she stepped back instinctively.

This was his chance. Black Blade stepped forward, swinging. He turned his back on the wolf–and Rafe pounced. The assassin fell on his face, lost his grip on his swords, and choked down a mouthful of dirt. Rafe was standing over him, with a paw on either side of him.

Black Blade only realized how big the wolf truly was when he turned and stared at the long white canines. Rafe opened his mouth to bite the assassin's face, but Black Blade was faster. He found the hilt of a sword, gripped it, and pulled it forward. The hard backside of the hilt collided with Rafe's teeth.

The wolf yelped and threw his head up in the air to shake away the pain. But this exposed his neck. The sword was long and the wolf was too close so it would be hard to slash. But he could do it–if it wasn't for Caitlin.

Caitlin stepped forward, onto the assassin's hand, grinding it into the ground. Black Blade cried out and let go of one sword. He tried to swing the other one at her, but she was expecting it. She kicked out with her foot, knocking his wrist aside. She kicked so hard that he released his grip on the sword.

Then with all his might, he pulled his other hand out from under her foot. She lost her balance but managed to stay upright. Black Blade tried to reach for his sword, but the wolf blocked him. Blood dripped from Rafe's mouth where the assassin had hit him.

Caitlin kicked his other sword out of reach, and he scrambled to his feet. He didn't have any weapons now, just his fists. And his fists wouldn't do him any good against a wolf. But he still had his legs.

Black Blade started sprinting toward the nearest tree, Rafe on his heels. The wolf was opening his mouth to bite when the man reached up for a low hanging branch. He lifted himself and used the motion to swing himself up onto the branch.

Rafe doubled back and Black Blade swung downward in a full circle. This time, he kicked Rafe in the face before coming to a stop atop the branch again.

Rafe was angry now. He snarled and jumped up. His teeth latched onto the branch, and for a moment, he just hung there. Black Blade was about to kick him in the face again, but when he heard the branch crack, he decided to climb to a higher branch.

Caitlin looked at the knife she was holding in her right hand. She touched the blade. Somehow she remembered how to hold it.... It felt right, no longer awkward. *All I have to do is flick my wrist. Easy-peasy.* She looked at the assassin again. The higher he climbed up the tree, the harder it would be to hit him. She didn't have to think about what she wanted to do. She flicked her wrist.

The knife came to a stop in the tree trunk beside Black Blade's head. He pulled it from the bark. She was stupid to have handed it back to him so nicely. She should have thrown rocks at him instead. Now she has given him back his weapon.

He pulled himself onto the next branch and looked down at her. She was in the open. He was very fast. The knife flew through the air. He was so fast the wolf didn't have time to jump in front of it. The assassin could see in the wolf's eyes that he would take a knife in the heart for the girl. He imagined failure creeping in the shifter's eyes when the blade killed her in front of him.

Then the impossible happened.

Caitlin knew she shouldn't have thrown the blade the moment she missed. She watched him intently and was ready when he threw it. Her hand snatched out and closed around the knife before it hit her face. Unfortunately, she had grabbed the blade and her hand started to bleed.

Rafe stared in amazement as she dropped the knife to the floor. Black Blade stared in horror.

"Are you a shifter as well?" the assassin asked.

"No," she responded.

"Then what are you? No non-Magic has reflexes like yours."

She didn't answer him.

At that moment Black Blade decided that she wasn't worth the money. He needed much more money to kill her than he had been paid. He would go back to his stupid employer to demand double. Or maybe he would just kill him.

He brought his fingers to his mouth and whistled.

Obediently, his only friend in the world came to get him. A white Arabian mare bolted through the trees straight toward him and Black Blade jumped onto her back. She didn't stop or slow down. He kicked her in the sides to run faster.

"No, Rafe!"

The wolf was about to chase him. Rafe looked at Caitlin and then at the sprinting horse. He whimpered like a little child forced to abide by rules he so badly wanted to break.

"No," she said again. "I don't want you to go fight by yourself." If she could keep up with him, then she'd go with him. But the assassin was a really good fighter and she didn't want to take the chance of Rafe losing.

Rafe looked at the swords lying on the grass. He should have gone. He should have chased the unarmed man down while he'd had the chance. He could have caught that horse and killed them both.

He shifted back to human form while Caitlin averted her eyes to give him privacy. He put his clothes on again. "Why is someone trying to kill you?" he asked.

"I don't know."

"Can you think of anyone who would want you dead?"

"No..." her voice was barely above a whisper.

"How did you catch that knife so fast?"

"I don't know," she said again.

"That assassin asks a lot of money to do his job," Rafe continued. "Whoever paid him paid him well. Someone really wants you dead."

"Do you think he will come back?"

"Yes. A man like that is serious about what he does. His reputation is everything to him. He is not the kind of man who can tolerate defeat. He will come back, and he will be better prepared next time."

# CHAPTER 27

THEY WALKED BACK to the inn and found Maggie in the garden smelling the flowers. She wore a blue dress that fell to the floor in waves. It had short sleeves and a puffy skirt. She had her long hair braided back so it didn't fall into her face. She wore brand new sandals.

She was lost in her thoughts. She was daydreaming, pretending to be a lady in the castle, choosing flowers for decorating the tables at a party. She looked up, spotted them, and ran over to hug Caitlin.

"The flowers here are more beautiful than any flowers back home!" she told Caitlin.

"I'm glad you are having so much fun," Caitlin said, returning the hug briefly with one arm.

"You look like a princess," Rafe told the smiling child.

She turned toward him and curtsied. "Thank you, good

sir." Then she frowned and said, "Why is your lip bleeding?"

Caitlin was about to interrupt with a story, but she couldn't think fast enough.

"Your sister kissed me a little too hard," Rafe told her.

The little girl gasped and looked from Caitlin to Rafe. "That's not how a kiss is supposed to work!" she said as if she had kissed many boys before.

"How would you know how kissing works?" Caitlin asked.

"Because I've kissed someone before," she told her older sister.

"Really?"

Maggie nodded. "It was in the beginning of the year. He was a good friend, so I kissed him on the cheek."

"A cheek kiss is not a proper kiss," Caitlin laughed.

"Well, at least his cheek did not bleed," she talked back.

Now it was Rafe and Maggie's turn to laugh.

"And what happened to your hand?" Maggie asked her sister.

Rafe had torn his bandage when he shifted and then used some of the pieces to wrap Caitlin's bleeding hand. "She hit me when I told her she's a bad kisser," he said with a wink.

"Caitlin!" Maggie exclaimed, the joke sailing right over her head. "That's not nice!"

"It's also not nice to call someone a bad kisser!" her

older sister defended herself.

"It's alright." Rafe looked at Caitlin. "You just need to practice more."

Caitlin blushed, more from fury than amusement.

"There you are," Daisy spotted them. "I was wondering where you were." Then she saw Caitlin's hand.

Since Daisy was no six-year-old girl, she would never believe that Caitlin had cut her hand while hitting Rafe. *It would also be best to leave a kiss—that didn't happen —out of the conversation,* thought Caitlin to herself. So aloud she said, "We went for a walk and I fell and cut it on the rocks."

Daisy believed the lie and didn't probe any further. Caitlin's heart didn't beat much louder when she lied this time and Rafe wondered if she felt any guilt at all.

That night they went out to a nice dinner. This was something the family didn't do very often because it was expensive. Gerald thought they deserved it after having traveled so hard and far.

Caitlin felt uneasy the whole time. She couldn't help but look around nervously at the strangers in the pub and on the streets. She kept expecting one of them to jump out to try to kill her.

Rafe sensed her uneasiness and stayed by her side for as long as possible. He could protect her better than anyone, and she knew it. She liked his presence. She also liked the way he looked at her—like she was a precious thing that he had to protect.

She studied him at dinner. But Rafe rarely looked

at her. He had a completely different focus for his attention. In Water Spark, he had heard rumors of people disappearing. So now he was eavesdropping on all the nearby conversations. Like Caitlin, he was anxious and couldn't wait to reach the next town. There he would search for Ears, the witch who hears everything.

And so their evening progressed, with both Caitlin and Rafe on edge; Maggie in her usual cheerful and talkative self; and Gerald in full planning mode, with Daisy providing guidance and support. They were all tired when they finally returned to the inn.

But later that night, Caitlin's sleep was troubled by another nightmare.

She dreamed she was sitting against a wall. She had a pile of books in front of her. None of them were nice stories or the kind of books you would expect a thirteen-year-old to read. They were all educational books about the kingdom.

"Are you still studying?" a boy asked. His name was Eddy. He was short and fat, with round cheeks and stubby feet. He was well liked by the other kids but not a favorite of the teachers.

"I enjoy it," Caitlin lied. The truth was she had no

friends. So if she didn't study or train, then she wouldn't have anything to do. She got bored really fast with most things, but at least reading kept her mind occupied.

"You must have the map of the whole kingdom memorized by now," Eddy said.

"We all should," she winked. If he had been any other kid, she would have ignored him and kept her face in her book. But most kids here didn't talk to her, and Eddy was always kind.

He sat down next to her and looked at the map with curiosity, as if he hadn't seen it a million times before. "Have you figured out where in the kingdom we are?

"You're not supposed to be asking a question like that," she said, when in truth she had been trying to figure it out for a long time.

"I can't help it," Eddy confessed. "We've never gone beyond these walls. The adults try so desperately to keep the outside world a secret from us."

"Or they're trying to keep us a secret from the outside world," Caitlin said.

"What do you mean?" Eddy asked.

"We're different," Caitlin said. "We can do things that these adults can't."

"Yes," Eddy admitted. "But that's why they are studying us, isn't it?"

"I guess so..." she said. Then she sighed and closed her book. When she spoke again her voice was soft, with a whiny note to it. "I hate this life."

"Why?" Eddy gaped at her. They lived similar lives,

but he did not hate this life like she did. But it was a confusing life. He grew up without a family and surrounded by alchemists who documented his every move and teachers who taught him skills that would only be useful to warriors. He explained to her why he didn't understand why she, of all people, would hate this life. "You are so good at it! You're always top of the class."

"But everyone is scared of me," she said softly. Caitlin wasn't the most social person, but she had a powerful need for a friend. For someone who was like her. But there was no one like that here. She was the outsider. The loner. The weirdo.

"Well... you do have a bit of a temper," he told her as gently as he could.

She smiled as there was no denying it. Her eyes skimmed the walls as she asked, "Have you ever thought about running away?"

Eddy shook his head. "No, where would I go? And besides, it's impossible to get out of here."

"But kids do disappear," Caitlin pointed out. "Every year there are fewer and fewer of us. And the teachers never give us an explanation."

"And you think they're running away?"

She nodded. Her eyes were hopeful, like those of a kid much younger than her. "There must be a way out of here—the teachers come and go as they please."

"Wherever the way out is, they have hidden it really well."

"I don't think so," she argued. "It must be in one of the restricted areas that the patronizers guard."

"If the patronizers guard it, I don't want to go there." Eddy said, not bothering to hide the fear in his voice.

Patronizers were beastly, brainless things. They were all very tall and skinny. They wore red hoods that fell over their pale faces. Sometimes when they looked up you could see their yellow eyes. They had knives or swords instead of fingers and they were very fast. They were the guards in that dreadful, cold, dark place.

Caitlin had tried to find out about them, searching the stacks in the library many times, but she found no books that even mentioned their names. She had no idea how these beings came to exist. All she knew was that you should never cross them.

"I don't think the kids are escaping," Eddy admitted in a scared whisper.

"Then what's happening to them?" Caitlin asked. She felt her heart sink. If they weren't escaping, how was she ever going to?

"They're dying."

"Why would they be dying?" Caitlin asked with a horror-filled voice. That was not the answer she wanted to hear.

"I overheard a conversation that I should not have heard," he confessed. "So if I tell you then you can't tell anyone."

She nodded fast. She had very little patience and

she wanted to hear what he had to say immediately. She was not lying when she agreed not to tell anyone —as she had no one to tell.

"I heard a teacher talking with one of the alchemists," he said. "You know, those alchemists that always do our checkups? The ones that draw blood and inspect us?"

She nodded again.

"Well, he asked the teacher how the kids were performing. She told him that the younger we were, the better. When we are young, we are obedient and healthy. But the older we got, the worse we performed. She said the bodies of the older kids couldn't handle the change. The older we got, the *sicker* we got."

"I have seen some sick kids," she admitted. She'd seen a few actually. At first it started as headaches or muscle pain. But it would get worse and worse. Caitlin once saw a girl throwing up blood in the girls' bathroom. Now that she thought about it, she never saw that girl again. Caitlin wrapped her arms around herself. She hasn't been feeling sick.

"The alchemist said that the older we get, the harder it is for our bodies to adapt. She said that most of us won't make it to the age of sixteen."

Caitlin woke up, sweaty, next to her sister. She sat up and reached for the cup of water on the bedside table.

These dreams scared her. There was something about them that made them different from normal dreams. She could not put her finger on what it was that made them feel real. More like a memory and not a dream.

She drank the cool water and tried her best to relax. She replayed the things Eddy had told her in her dream. But none of it made sense. Yet.

# CHAPTER 28

THE NEXT MORNING Gerald had a surprise for his family and Rafe. After they had all gotten up, gotten dressed, and packed their belongings into the cart, Gerald led them to the stables where three horses were waiting.

The three horses weren't as big and strong as Penny. They weren't built for pulling carts or carriages. They had thinner, faster legs and leaner bodies. They had Arabian blood in them, which meant they had good endurance.

Although the cart would still slow them down, traveling on horseback would make their journey faster and much more comfortable.

"Wow!" Maggie was the first to react. She ran to the horses, making happy, squealing sounds. Luckily none of them spooked.

251

"Careful, Maggie!" Gerald warned. "You don't want to startle them."

She silenced her squeals and slowed her movements and then started petting them. One horse was dark brown with a white star on his forehead. Maggie petted him first and let him sniff her hand. But when the horse realized that she did not have any food, it lost interest.

"This is awesome!" Caitlin exclaimed. "Thank you so much!" Not an affectionate person, she didn't hug her father; she just smiled at him. Then she walked to Maggie and held out her hand.

The second horse was a dun—he was the color of sand—and wore long black socks. He sniffed Caitlin's hand with his ears pricked forward. His lips rubbed over her skin and when he realized she had no treats, he lost interest as well.

"I didn't expect you to get me a horse," Rafe said. He didn't smile as he warily eyed the gray creature from a distance. "I would have been fine sitting in the cart."

"Nonsense," Gerald said. "You've been healing fast. I think you'll do fine riding. Besides, Daisy will steer the cart while Maggie sits in the back. She's too small to ride a horse by herself."

"Hey!" Maggie objected. "That's not true!"

Gerald didn't bother arguing with his six-year-old. She focused her attention back on the horses and petted all of them.

"What are their names?" Maggie asked.

"The previous owner didn't say," Gerald admitted.

He gave Caitlin and Rafe each a bridle and pointed to their saddles. He then walked to the dark brown horse.

"This one is Star," Maggie decided. "Because he has a star on his forehead."

"That's a fine name," Gerald said.

Caitlin walked to her horse, the dun. He was well trained and didn't pull his head away when she put the bridle on.

"What are you going to name yours?" Maggie asked. But before Caitlin could answer, she volunteered, "You should name him Prince. He looks like he is dressed for a ball with those socks."

Caitlin smiled. "Prince is perfect."

"Aren't you going to saddle yours?" Gerald asked Rafe who stood frozen. "Do you know how?"

"I do," Rafe said tightly and slowly walked toward his horse.

The gray mare caught his scent and then backed up nervously into the corner of her stable. When Rafe entered, she shied away from him. He tried to soothe her with a calming voice but it wasn't working. When he finally grabbed her nose, she tried to pull free and bolt. If he wasn't as strong as he was, she would have succeeded. He put the bridle on forcefully.

Gerald didn't look pleased. "I should take her back! I paid for well-trained and calm horses."

"It's fine," Rafe said. He knew no horse was going to

be calm around him. But Gerald wasn't convinced, so Rafe added, "I will enjoy training her and earning her trust."

"She needs a name!" Maggie pointed out.

"You are good with giving names," Rafe said. "Do you have any ideas?"

"Misty," Maggie didn't need to think about it. "She looks like a cloud of mist."

Rafe nodded in agreement.

Caitlin and Gerald saddled Star and Prince easily. But Misty paced around nervously as Rafe put the saddle on. When he opened the stable door to lead her out, she tried to bolt again.

"The horses are lovely!" Daisy exclaimed. She was sitting on the cart and Penny was ready to go.

Maggie wanted to ride on horseback too, so Caitlin helped her up onto Prince's back. She didn't weigh much and the gelding carried the two of them easily.

Caitlin couldn't remember if she had ever ridden before. Her slight awkwardness told her that she had very limited experience but that she knew she would learn quickly.

From time to time, Caitlin let Maggie take the reins. They would trot for short periods, but it rattled them and bounced them around so much that Caitlin thought both of them would fall off. Luckily they did not.

Maggie laughed even more than usual. She talked to Prince as if he was a person and petted his neck as they rode. She sang songs and started to braid his dun-colored mane as they rode.

Gerald didn't talk much but he kept looking at his two beautiful daughters. Seeing his children happy made Gerald feel good.

Rafe was silent much of the time. Misty's coat broke out in a sweat and she pranced around like a horse that was stressed out of her mind. He tried to keep calm and tried not to look too annoyed.

They traveled for three days before they reached the next town. It was a small town where nothing ever happened. But Rafe was very excited because it was close to the Sinking Swamp, home of the witch he was seeking.

The first night he couldn't wait to get away from the family and venture into the swamp. He wasn't sure how he would find the witch they called Ears, but find her he would.

Caitlin could sense his uneasiness. He was distant and quiet. He didn't crack as many jokes as he usually did.

That night when everyone went to bed Caitlin lay awake fully dressed. She had left her room door slightly ajar, hoping that he would come to her. She listened and heard his door creak open and then heard him walk past her room.

She got up. "Hey!" she whispered as she poked her head outside her door. "Where are you going?"

Rafe turned around. "There is someone I need to find."

Caitlin stepped out, closed her room door, and walked toward him. "Who are we looking for?"

"'We' aren't looking for anyone," Rafe said. "This involves Magic. So I need to do it alone."

"Oh come on," Caitlin sighed.

"You saw how Matilda treated you," Rafe said. "The witch I am searching for will be no different."

Caitlin crossed her arms and Rafe admitted to himself that he liked her stubbornness. He had always liked strong women.

"Why are you looking for her?"

"Matilda said she might know something about the missing children...."

Caitlin wondered what else Matilda had said after she had left. She thought about those two men who had tried to take Maggie. She thought of Roxy too: *What happened to that poor child?* "I want to come," Caitlin insisted.

Rafe seemed to consider it for a moment. He didn't like arguing. "She's not going to like a non-Magic knowing about our business. And you might start another fight."

"I won't," she glared. "I hardly ever start fights."

"You're starting one now."

"This isn't a fight."

"Yet."

"I promise I'll be nice," she said with crossed arms.

"I'll be walking," he said, "or running as a wolf. You can't keep up."

"I have a horse."

"That's scared of me. So it can't come."

"But I can."

"Have you not heard a word I've said?" Rafe realized he was raising his voice. He took a deep breath and spoke softer. "Caitlin, just sit this one out."

"No."

"Please?"

"NO."

"You are the most stubborn person I know!" he said and stomped away like a child throwing a tantrum.

Ha, I win! Caitlin smiled. She followed him outside.

The stars winked at them and the moon illuminated the path leading out of the small town. The cool breeze ran its fingers through Caitlin's hair. The grasses and leaves made soft shushing noises as their footsteps padded on the gravel path. They heard owls hooting, crickets singing, and the distant chattering of the townspeople. The chattering faded into nothingness as they left the little town behind.

"How do you know where to go?" Caitlin asked.

Rafe had been silent for a while. His annoyance with her dimmed with the chattering. "I found a map in one of the shops close to the inn."

Caitlin wondered how he even had time to go there but she didn't ask. She sensed that he was calm now and she fell in step beside him. "How far is it?"

"If the map is right, then it's not far at all. The swamp is just outside the town. It's famous."

"For what?"

"Killing people."

"Oh," that wasn't the answer she had been hoping for, but it didn't scare her either. Nothing bad was going to happen as long as Rafe was around.

"Do you feel like turning back now?" Rafe asked, eying her.

"Why do you want me gone so badly?" she asked. "Haven't I proven that I can take care of myself?"

Rafe thought back to how she had fought the assassin. She had surprised him. He wondered where she had learned to fight like that.

"It's not personal," he said honestly. "I just need the witch to *want* to help me. Bringing a non-Magic to her house isn't a great way to gain her trust."

Caitlin's irritation faded when she realized that what Rafe was saying was true. But she didn't want to turn back and she didn't want to be left out. She asked, "What are you hoping to learn from her?"

"I want to know what exactly she knows about this disease that's killing my kind. I need to find a cure."

"What makes you think there's a cure?"

"I'm trying to be optimistic," he said. "And I want to talk to her about the Magic kids that are disappearing."

"Do you think there could be some connection? Between the kids and the disease?" she asked evenly.

"What's on your mind?" He stopped walking to face her and read her features. The way she had lifted her brow when she had asked her question told him that she already had a theory.

"Roxy," Caitlin said. "She was a shifter. She was taken by Magic folk. I was wondering if maybe they were using shifter kids to look for a cure."

"What put that thought into your head?" Rafe asked with horror in his voice.

Caitlin shrugged. She had no idea where the idea had come from. Maybe it was because of the strange dreams she was having. Maybe her mind was darker and more twisted than she knew. "It makes sense, doesn't it? So far, it doesn't seem like any non-Magic people have disappeared without a trace."

Rafe thought about it. "It does make sense. But Matilda told me to look for answers in the palace. There's no way my kind would be anywhere near the king unless they are prisoners."

They resumed walking side by side in silence. Caitlin looked at him and thought about what he said. He wanted to find a cure and help his kind. He was a good man.

"Your turn," he said, breaking their silence.

"What?"

"What are you hoping to learn?" he asked and saw her eyes look away, as if she didn't want him to see what she was thinking, feeling.

"What do you mean? I'm just here to keep you company." She tried to sound casual and unconcerned, as if she was just out for a moonlit stroll.

Rafe stopped suddenly and turned to her. His movement was quick and swift and caught her off guard. "You know it's easier for me to get what I want if I go alone. Yet you won't let me. That makes me think this is more about you than about me."

She forced herself to look into his eyes. "You've got it wrong. I just don't want you to go out alone. And I don't want to be left at the inn. Not after all we've been through."

Rafe stepped closer so that they were inches apart. She looked up at him while her arms dangled at her sides and felt heavy.

"Caitlin," he said softly. "You're a good liar."

Her face went blank.

"But you can't lie to me," he said and then started walking again. He could hear the frantic beating of her heart. He did not know what hidden motives she had but decided that if he was patient, he would find out.

They walked in silence for a little while. He started thinking that she was not going to speak again. Then she opened her mouth. "I have trouble remembering," she said at last, her voice small and hollow.

"Like, memory loss?" he asked her. "What don't you remember?"

"Everything..."

But before she had time to explain herself, a scream shattered the darkness.

# CHAPTER 29

THE SCREAM WAS more angry than scared. Rafe and Caitlin immediately ran toward it. Caitlin pulled out the single black dagger that she had been hiding in her jacket, one of Black Blade's two daggers.

They stopped running when they reached the swamp and Rafe tensed beside her. This was the place he had been searching for.

It was not the kind of lush green swamp filled with trees and birds that Caitlin had imagined. It was ugly and dead. The trees had no leaves. Their dead branches reached into the air as if throwing their arms up for help while their trunks sunk away in the mud. There was so much dark, sticky mud everywhere. The grass was brown and mushy and rotten, with patches that looked like spongy stepping stones. Rafe wondered if he could walk on those spongy patches of grass, or if he would sink and keep on sinking until the swamp swallowed him whole. And the water—was it even water? It was thick and black, so black it reflected everything at once and yet nothing at all.

Caitlin took the first step. Rafe reached out to pull her back, but he was too late. Her foot was on a spongy brown patch. She put some of her weight onto it and gradually more. Then she shifted all her weight onto that foot. "Well, I'm not sinking," she smiled and hopped onto the next grass patch.

Rafe was still hesitant because he knew he was heavier than her. He took his first step. The grass squelched under her feet and made sucking noises. He was relieved that he wasn't sinking. He didn't know if he should smile for having the nerve to move forward or cringe because he still had far to go. Then he looked up and saw Caitlin far ahead of him. *Does anything ever scare her?*

They continued to jump from one grassy patch to the next and the next, making their way through the swamp with Caitlin leading the way.

At long last, they saw a cottage in the distance. It stood alone, deep in the middle of the swamp. *It has to belong to Ears. Is the witch in danger? Why else would she be living way out here? And shouldn't a witch be able to protect herself?* Rafe wondered before he caught the scent. "Caitlin!" he yelled. "Watch out! There are shifters here!"

The words had barely left his lips when the shifters

spotted them. There were two, both cougars. And both stark-raving mad. They were prowling beside the witch's cottage.

The first cougar charged Caitlin, who was nearest, its paws sinking in the muck with every step. Caitlin did not have a lot of time to think and almost froze in her tracks. Then she realized that they were running too fast to sink in the mud, but if their speed broke...

She looked around but couldn't spot any way to evade them. The patches of grass were a slow way of moving but they were her *only* way of moving.

Rafe didn't need to look at her face to see her worry. If he shifted, he wasn't sure how he was going to stay on the grass either. But he thought that he might be quicker in his human form. Time was running out.

The first cougar had mud all over its fur. The mud splattered up into its face and eyes as it charged. But none of this registered: it was clearly crazed and out of control. It neared Caitlin and then gathered up its haunches and leaped.

Caitlin tried to dodge it, but a claw hooked her shoulder and latched on. The cougar tumbled into the black water, dragging Caitlin with it.

Rafe watched in fear as both of their heads went under. He jumped from grassy patch to grassy patch as fast as he could and resisted the urge to jump into the water after Caitlin. He would be of no use to her dead.

Amazingly her head appeared above the surface.

She rubbed the black water out of her eyes and started swimming toward the grassy bank. The cougar struggled to get its head above the water.

Rafe was there in an instant to pull her from the water. She was dirty, but he didn't care. He was about to grab her hand and drag her behind him as he ran, but she pulled her hand free before he could take off.

"What's the matter with it?" she asked.

Rafe looked back at the cougar. The cat was biting the air ferociously while hissing at them. It was trying to swim, trying to get out. But it was sinking in that spot.

Rafe watched its head go under and shuddered. Whether or not the creature was mad, it was one less shifter. One more death among that misbegotten race.

"I didn't struggle to swim to the shore," Caitlin said.

"I don't know what just happened," Rafe said. "But I do know we need to get away from the second cougar."

Caitlin hadn't realized how close the next one was.

"When it charges us, we need to duck down and then shove it up and over, toward the water," Rafe instructed. "Hopefully our timing will be perfect."

"Hopefully?" she asked, not liking the sound of the word.

"Do you have a better idea?" Rafe asked.

She looked at the knife that was still in her hand. "I could use this."

"And throw your only weapon into the swamp?" he asked.

"Your lack of faith in me is disturbing," she said as she readied the weapon. Her hands were trembling and she wasn't focusing. The knife flew through the air and missed the cougar. She watched as it fell harmlessly on one of the grass patches.

The cougar jumped.

Rafe grabbed Caitlin's shoulders and yanked her down just in time. The cougar went soaring over them and landed with its back paws in the mud. It was stuck. The cougar slashed at the air with its front claws and tried to pull its hind paws free.

"You missed," Rafe pointed out.

"Can't you say something useful?" Caitlin snapped in frustration.

"Shut up and run."

Caitlin took off. She picked up her knife as they ran toward the cottage. Rafe was surprised at how agile and fast she was. She really wasn't an ordinary farmer's daughter.

He could hear the cougar going berserk in the swamp. He hoped it would sink deeper. He didn't dare look back to see how much of its hind legs were gone. He didn't want to waste time or break his speed by looking back in curiosity. If he had, he would have seen the front legs of the cougar clawing at the grass. He would have seen the crazy animal digging its claws into the sod and pulling with all its might. He would have seen the cougar's teeth gnashing in anger and frustration. Then it broke free.

Caitlin was near the front steps of the cottage, leading up to a big porch. She wondered how it wasn't sinking in the swamp. She spotted a log to her right, drifting in the water, and more mud to her left. She paused at the steps and looked back. How was Rafe so much slower than her?

She saw the cougar at his heels. Then Rafe reached Caitlin and jumped in front of her so that he could face the cougar. The cougar slowed its charge.

"Caitlin, back up into the house," he ordered.

She walked backward and got on the first step to the porch. Her wary eyes kept watch of the cougar and Rafe's tense back.

Then something unexpected happened. The log to Caitlin's right came alive!

Rafe jumped back. In the process he knocked Caitlin over, and both of them fell onto the porch. They sat up in time to see that the log was an alligator.

The cougar went straight into the water after it. The alligator snapped its jaws open, sunk its teeth into the cougar, locked its mouth, and dragged it under the black water.

Neither of them had time to recover before they heard a voice coming from behind them.

"Welcome to my home."

# CHAPTER 30

NEITHER OF THEM greeted the witch. They were too focused on the alligator as it crunched the shifter's bones.

"Never you mind my dear Ali," she said to them. "He's quite harmless."

"Sure, sounds like it," Rafe said sarcastically.

More bones crunched.

"He's just not used to visitors," the witch said. "We don't get many."

"Have you ever thought that you don't get many visitors because he may be eating them all?" Rafe asked.

The witch laughed but didn't answer. Caitlin finally looked at her. She wore an apron and had an oddly young face framed with gray hair. She had thin, twig-like lips, and big rabbit-like eyes.

She looked down at Caitlin. "You look terrible, my dear."

"The swamp tried to eat me," Caitlin said and got to her feet.

"Nonsense," the witch crossed her arms. "There is no swamp."

Caitlin frowned as she turned to face the swamp behind her. To her surprise, green meadows had replaced the mud. Flowers and trees had replaced the black water and fresh, sweet air had replaced the fowl stench.

"It was all an illusion?" Rafe asked.

The witch smiled. "You're a smart one."

"But how?" Rafe asked in awe.

"The flowers in the meadow... I give them some water filled with a potion every so often. The scent they carry into the air causes the swamp hallucination."

"But the cougar..." Caitlin said and walked to the edge of the porch. Its body lay there, but it wasn't eaten. It was whole and didn't have a single scratch on it. It had not been eaten by an alligator but it was not breathing either.

"If you're mind believes that something is real," the witch said, "then it is real."

"So what kills them?" Rafe asked. "The idea of dying?"

The witch nodded. "They are convinced they are dying so their bodies shut down. The illusion wears off once you are in the house. I've got flowers here that counteract the hallucination. And the illusions don't work on me because I created them. I am a master of illusions." She then executed a graceful bow.

"Why did the other cougar sink," Caitlin asked her, "and I didn't?"

"The illusion works like this: you can only make it through the swamp if you have good intentions."

"Brilliant," Rafe said.

"Thank you," she smiled. "Unfortunately, it's killed many sick shifters."

"You know about the disease?" Rafe asked.

"Of course I do! They don't call me Ears for nothing!" She clasped her hands together. "Let's go inside."

Rafe followed first, with Caitlin trailing him. She immediately liked Ears more than Matilda. This witch was warmer and kinder. She hadn't mentioned anything about Caitlin being non-Magic, so Caitlin decided not to say anything. The last thing she wanted was an argument.

"You've come a long way," Ears said and looked Rafe up and down. "Pale skin, a shifter, and quite handsome," she observed. "You must be from Southpaw."

Rafe nodded.

Then she turned to Caitlin. She looked at her from side to side and then from head to toe. Absently, she touched Caitlin's arm with her finger as if in thought. "But you... you're a difficult one."

Caitlin stood awkwardly and remained silent. At least this witch wasn't excluding her like the previous one did.

"She's from—"

"No! Don't tell me!" the witch shushed Rafe. She looked at Caitlin a moment longer. "I'd say you're from Sky Castle."

Rafe chuckled.

"Don't laugh," Ears said. "Just look at her. She's built like a warrior, moves and stands like one. She's clearly been trained in their ways."

Caitlin didn't know what to say. She didn't like the words "their ways," although Ears didn't say it with malice. Caitlin decided to correct her. "I'm from River Town."

"I've never heard of it," the witch said.

"It's in the Riverlands," Caitlin supplied.

"There's no way that you are from the Riverlands," the witch said. "Tell me where you are really from?"

Caitlin stood still and cleared her throat. "That's why I am here," she confessed. "I don't know."

The witch tilted her head. "We need something to drink for this conversation."

Rafe and Caitlin sat down by the kitchen table while Ears took out some cups that she set in front of them. Then she sat down, instead of getting them drinks. Rafe frowned, looking at the empty cups, but didn't say anything.

"I can't get drinks if I don't know what for," she explained as if she had read his mind. "She could have memory loss, or maybe she hit her head."

"I really don't know," Caitlin admitted in a low voice.

"Then what *do* you know?" the witch asked with kind eyes.

"Nothing... I woke up one day with no idea who I am. I didn't know who I was, and I didn't know my own family."

"That's... unheard of." Ears frowned. "When was this?"

"A week and a half ago."

"Have you remembered anything since then?"

"No." Caitlin shook her head. "It's like my mind was wiped blank."

"Have you heard of a potion called Blankness?" Rafe spoke up. There was an edge to his voice that Caitlin didn't understand.

"Have I heard of a potion called Blankness?" the witch mimicked with a laugh. "My dear boy, I am witch. Of course I've heard of it!"

"This sounds like something that potion could do..."

The witch shook her head. "Firstly, that potion is nearly impossible to come by. Few witches know how to make it. I don't even know how to make it."

Caitlin studied Rafe's face. He looked calm yet intrigued. Almost entranced by the witch.

"It's also very dangerous. If you give too little of that potion, the person can start remembering again. But if you give too much, their minds turn into those of babies. They forget how to walk and talk and take care of themselves. It is impossible to completely erase all the memories of someone her age. If it was used

272

on her, it could only have been used to take away specific memories, like making her forget a certain person, place, or event."

"Then what could have caused my memory loss?" Caitlin asked.

The witch got up and started making something to drink. She added water and herbs and all kinds of weird stuff. The drink looked gross when she put it in front of Caitlin.

"Go on... It tastes better than it looks," she prodded with a kind smile.

"What is it?" Caitlin asked. She remembered the horrible taste of the tea Matilda had given her and hoped that this didn't taste like that.

"It's a memory potion, my own brew," Ears said. "It might help."

Caitlin drank it. "It tastes like mint," she smiled.

"It should work really fast," the witch said.

Caitlin drank it all, but she felt no change. She searched her mind but there was nothing to be found. Her face fell. It didn't work.

"This is very odd," the witch said. "Unlike anything I've ever seen."

"What could it be?" Rafe asked.

"Whatever it is, no potion or witch did this to you," she tilted her head.

"So there is nothing you can do to help?" Rafe asked. He sounded worried and Caitlin wished that she had told him sooner about her memory loss. They were friends and friends trusted each other with their secrets and worries.

Ears shook her head. "You'll have to help yourself."

"How?" Caitlin asked.

"*Will* your mind to remember. The mind is a powerful tool. Use it."

"Are you saying I don't want to remember?" Caitlin asked.

"I'm saying you don't want it bad enough."

Caitlin remembered what Gerald had said about the mind blocking some memories out because they were too traumatic. But surely, all of her memories can't be bad.

"Does your family also have problems remembering?" Rafe asked.

"No, it's just me. They talk to me like I've been with them my whole life. Like everything is normal."

"Then don't turn to them for answers," Ears said.

"So who should I turn to? If my family doesn't know anything, and my memories are blank, I have no one, nowhere to turn to."

Ears smiled. "Turn to your dreams."

# CHAPTER 31

HER DREAMS. CAITLIN tried her best not to cringe at the idea. She didn't have dreams; she had nightmares. She hated every single one of them.

"Why do you say that?" she asked, trying to keep her voice as placid as possible.

"Because your past might be stuck in your sub-conscious. Have you had any strange dreams lately?"

Rafe saw the confused and worried look on Caitlin's face. He remembered how she had told him that she couldn't sleep. Suddenly a lot of things made sense to him. Why she never talked about herself. Why she never answered his questions. It was all because she couldn't remember anything.

A little part inside of Rafe was slightly hurt and, even more so, disappointed. He had opened up to her. He had told her about his family. But she hadn't told him about her missing memories.

"I've had nightmares," she confessed.

"What were they like?" Ears asked.

"Not like normal dreams," she said. "More like déjà vu. And I am younger in all of them too."

"Can you remember them clearly?" Ears asked. "Like they were real and not just a dream?"

Caitlin nodded. Every time she dreamed, it felt too real. She saw too many details and too many things that couldn't have been made up.

"Tell us about them," Ears said.

Thinking about the dark nightmares made Caitlin shudder. How could she explain to them that in her dreams she poisons other kids and beats up teachers? How can she tell them that people say stuff about her in her dreams that she doesn't even understand. "I'd rather not."

For three full heartbeats, Rafe and the witch just stared at her. Rafe wanted to push her to talk the way she always pushed him.

Ears beat him to responding first. "Alright," the witch said. She got up and scratched around her cupboard. Her house was as untidy as Matilda's. Caitlin was surprised that it didn't take her longer to find what she was digging for.

The witch pulled out a dream catcher. It had a spiral in the middle and was woven with grass from the meadow. Rocks, beads, and feathers hung from little strings. "This will catch your dreams and help you dream even more. Sleep with it over the top of your bed or under a pillow."

"Your solution is to increase my nightmares?"

"No. My solution is to bring back memories," Ears said. "There are truths hidden in your dreams."

She held out the dream catcher but Caitlin didn't take it. If her past was hidden in those dreams, then maybe she didn't want to remember.

"You don't want it?" Ears sounded truly surprised.

"She's just in a state of awe," Rafe said, taking the dream catcher. He tucked it in his pocket. "She's not used to witches being so kind and generous."

Ears didn't look convinced, so Rafe added, "Thank you."

She turned her attention away from Caitlin and focused on Rafe instead. "Why are *you* here?"

"I want to talk to you about this disease," Rafe said. "I'm sure you've heard of it. The one that's plaguing the shifters."

"The infection rates are rising every day," she said. "The locals call it Craybies, the crazy disease."

"What do you know about it?"

"I know that about a month ago, a shifter was taken by the king's men. He was hidden away somewhere in the castle. When he broke free, he was stark-raving mad."

"He got out of the castle? Alive?"

She nodded, "He got out, or he was let go."

Rafe shuddered.

"When he came out, he was nothing like the once sane man who had been dragged into the castle," Ears said with sorrow in her voice. "And every shifter that he bit went mad too. The disease is spreading fast. If it continues at this rate, there will be no sane shifters left."

"And it only affects the shifters?" Rafe asked.

"Yes. All the other non-Magic folk that have been bitten didn't get infected."

"So its origin is at the castle," Rafe said as he thought back to what Matilda had told him. "That's where the king and his alchemists are."

"And also your only hope of finding a cure," Ears said. "I believe the king created this disease to strike fear into the people's hearts. So that they could see how bad Magic truly is. How dangerous we are. He won't care that some human lives are lost. It doesn't matter as long as the shifters die."

"But why target only the shifters?" Rafe asked.

"I don't think he is," she said. "I've heard rumors that this disease is only the beginning."

"The beginning of what?' Rafe asked.

"The beginning of our end. The end of all who have Magic," Ears said gravely. "He knows there is still a lot of us left and he wants us all dead."

"But all Magic folk are in hiding. And they can't tell us apart from the non-Magic," Rafe said.

"For now," Ears said. "But he is cunning. He wants us gone. I think if we don't make a stand soon, we will all die."

"How would he wipe all of us out?" Rafe asked. He showed no outward sign of fear and was glad that they couldn't hear his heart hammering.

Ears paused before she told them, "He is creating a weapon."

"Creating?" Caitlin asked.

"A weapon for himself," Ears explained. "An unstoppable monster that is going to wipe out all Magic folk for good. It's rumored to be hidden in the castle."

"It's a living thing?" Caitlin asked. "Not like a sword?"

"More like a beast," Ears said. "Some locals have heard its angered screams. It's trained to hate us Magic folk."

"But has anyone seen it?" Caitlin asked. When Ears didn't answer, she knew that no one had. Maybe they were just stories made up to scare the people.

Rafe was thinking the same thing. "It's just a rumor, right?" he asked. "There are plenty of rumours. I once heard he had a hell horse locked up there as well."

"What's a hell horse?" Caitlin asked.

Ears turned to her. "They are vicious creatures with the body of a horse but the mind of a predator. They have teeth like knives and hooves of iron. They say their red eyes can see your fear. They are unruly, violent, temperamental creatures."

"When King Leonard was preparing his army to fight the Witch King," Rafe told her, "he sent his men to try to tame some of these creatures. But all the men died."

It was Ears turn to speak again. "Hell horses harm everyone and everything except their own kind, or the few they choose to love."

"I've never seen one," Rafe said. "They stay away from civilization and hide in the darkest places they can find—places where most humans would lose their minds."

"But if these animals are so unruly, how did he get one? And what does he do with it?"

"He has a stallion that had been kicked out of its herd," Ears explained. "It was much easier to catch without the protection of a family. "

"And what does he want to do with it?" Rafe asked Caitlin's question again. He was curious but not convinced that there was an actual hell horse living in the castle.

It was not Ears who answered. "The weapon," Caitlin said. "It's this creature."

Ears smiled. "That's surely a possibility. If he can conquer a hell horse and bend it to his will.... Magic folk would struggle to fight it."

"But hell horses can be killed," Rafe said.

"We don't know what they are doing to it," Ears said. "Or to the kids that have gone missing."

"I've met two of the kidnappers. They had Magic," Rafe said with a puzzled look on his face.

"They must have switched sides. Maybe in exchange for their help, the king spared their lives," the witch answered.

"I don't think they'd just switch sides," Rafe argued. "And I don't think the king wants Magic folk working for him either."

"You don't think Magic folk will switch sides," Ears said. "But you think a little non-Magic girl will."

Rafe looked at Caitlin and was silent for a moment. "Yes," he said. "She saved my life. She's different."

"I'm glad you can tell," the witch said. She left it at that and turned back to Caitlin. "Tell me about that knife," she said as she stared at Caitlin's lap.

Caitlin realized she had put it there where it now felt heavy–despite the fact that it was light as a feather and easy to wield. "It's not mine," she said.

"I know that knife," Ears said. "It belongs to Black Blade, the assassin."

"So he's that famous?" Caitlin sighed. Everyone seemed to know who he was and what he did for a living.

Ears nodded. "Who would send an assassin after a harmless girl from River Town?" Ears asked but didn't expect an answer. "Unless you're not harmless or not from River Town."

In her heart Caitlin knew she would have to try to remember her past. There must be a lot to it.

"Can you think of anyone who would want you dead?" Ears asked her.

Caitlin shook her head. She didn't even know a lot of people.

"I can," Rafe said to her surprise.

"Who?" she asked.

"That old guy that had you tied to the stake."

"Campbell?" Caitlin remembered. "He was the town leader."

"Well, he wanted you dead really bad," Rafe said. "He was prepared to fight me to get to you."

Caitlin searched her memories. What Rafe was saying was true. That man despised her. He had made it perfectly clear.

"He said some really weird things to me," Caitlin admitted as she remembered all the things Campbell had said. "And he's still alive. He escaped the town on horseback."

"Can you remember anything about him?" Ears asked. "Is there anything you can tell me that would be useful?"

"I honestly don't remember," Caitlin confessed. "What should I do now?"

"Be prepared for him to try and have you killed—again," Ears said. "So try to find out who he is and where he lives. Then you can talk to him."

"Talk to him..." Caitlin repeated. Talking to someone who wanted to kill her didn't sound like such a great idea.

"Good idea. Maybe we can squeeze the truth out of Black Blade," Rafe said, agreeing with Ears.

"We're close to Sky Castle," Caitlin said. "If that's where Campbell escaped to, then that's where Black Blade probably is right now. He tracked me here, so he's probably guessed where we're going.... Maybe he's already waiting for us and his next attack will be there."

"I think it will," Ears agreed. "But be careful. There are lots of shifters infected with Craybies around the castle." She looked at Rafe. "It only takes one bite for you to go crazy. You might wind up losing your mind and killing your friend here before Black Blade even finds you."

# CHAPTER 32

BLACK BLADE WAS irritated. The ride to the castle was a long and slow ride. It took him much longer than it usually did to get there because Jasmine threw a shoe. He had just gotten it fixed before leaving the town when she threw another one. He had to return to town to have all of her shoes replaced.

Of course, he wasn't irritated at his precious mare. She was stunning and fast and loyal and smart. He was irritated at the idiot who'd hired him. That old gray guy should have told him that it wasn't a normal job. He should have warned him that killing her would be challenging. He also should have paid more.

The ride up the Whispering Mountains was always a hard one. One of the reasons Sky Castle was so difficult to attack was because of its location. There was only one road leading up to it. The mountains were dotted with large boulders, some of which would fall and block the road.

Jasmine grew tired from all the uphill climbing. Although she was very fit, and an endurance horse, she had been traveling for days now. Black Blade often walked beside her so that she didn't have to carry him up the mountain.

She turned her eyes toward him. Those big, big eyes made his heart melt. Then she nudged him with her nose. "I don't have any more water left," he confessed and patted her neck. "But we're almost there. Then you can drink as much as you want."

When they neared the castle, he mounted her again and he rode inside. He found her a good stable with water and food. He told the stable boy to "bugger off" when the child offered to groom and clean her. He didn't like other people taking care of his horse. He could do it himself. After Jasmine was settled, he retraced his path and went to the gardens where he knew he would find the old man.

The old man was talking to a group of ladies when he spotted the assassin. His face went blank as he made his way to Black Blade. "What are you doing here?" the old man growled.

"We need to talk," Black Blade said, meeting his eyes. The assassin wore normal clothes and not his usual head-to-toe black. He looked like a traveling merchant. If he had any weapons on him, then they were hidden—weapons would only draw unwanted attention.

"Fine," the old man said. "But not here." His face turned white.

Black Blade followed him deeper into the castle. Sky Castle was big and majestic with countless passageways and rooms. They reached a room that was bolted shut. Campbell unlocked it with a key he carried in his belt pouch. After they entered, he immediately closed the door behind them and locked it.

"I don't see her head," he said, getting straight to business.

"I don't have her head," Black Blade said and leaned against the wall. His eyes were fixed on the gray-haired man.

"Then where is it?" Campbell asked, thinking that the assassin didn't want to carry a decapitated head in a bag dripping blood around the castle.

"Attached to her neck," Black Blade said. He didn't bother to hide the irritation from his voice.

It took a moment for the words to sink into Campbell's mind. "She's still alive?"

Black Blade nodded.

"You failed me," Campbell sneered.

"Watch your tongue, old man!" the assassin hissed and stood up straight. "You didn't tell me what I was up against."

"So one little girl was too much for the great Black Blade?" Campbell scoffed.

"She's clearly not a normal girl!" Black Blade said. "She's... different."

Black Blade didn't think it was possible for the man's face to get paler, but it did. He swallowed nervously. "How is she different?" Campbell asked. "What did she do?"

"She fought me. She fights like she has been trained, and trained well."

"So she's starting to remember," Campbell said almost to himself.

"What?" Black Blade asked. He was confused.

"She can't remember! We can't let her!" The man's face went from snow-white to beet-red. "We can't let her remember who she is or what she is."

"What exactly is she?" Black Blade asked.

Campbell evaded the assassin with a volley of his own questions. "How did she get away? How could you let her get away?! How could one little girl fight you off?"

Black Blade's face went red. "She had a shifter-wolf at her side," he said, defending himself.

"So?" Campbell asked. "Why didn't you kill it too?"

"I was only paid to kill one," Black Blade said. He would never admit that they had beaten him in a fight. Never.

"And yet that 'one' still lives!" Campbell snapped. He couldn't remember the last time he was so angry at someone. He thought this assassin was the best. Everyone told him that this assassin could get any job done. So he paid him well and expected to get the girl's head in return.

"Double the money," Black Blade said, "and I will kill them both."

Campbell laughed. "Do you really think that I would use your services again? You've proven yourself useless."

Black Blade considered gutting him then and there. But if he killed an employer it would be bad for business. Although he would enjoy it...

"You won't find anyone who can do a job as good as I can." He tried to sound as sure of himself as he possibly could.

"Then I'm doomed," the old man growled. "Where is she now?"

"She is on her way to the castle," Black Blade said and instantly regretted it. He shouldn't be giving this man any information. At least, not without a fee.

Campbell smiled. "She's coming straight to me then."

"She's dangerous," Black Blade said. "You still need me."

Campbell looked at him. "You had your chance."

"The wolf will eat you before you kill her."

"Not if I expose the wolf for what he is. Stupid shifter. He should know that none of his kind can survive in this castle."

"You're making a huge mistake," Black Blade was frustrated. How dare this man refuse his services!

"The only mistake I have made so far is hiring you."

Black Blade stormed out of the room. *How dare that old man insult me? I'll kill the girl when she gets here. I'll prove to him that I can do it. And wouldn't he just hate it if I beat him to it. I'm the best killer in the kingdom—in all the kingdoms!*

By the time Black Blade reached the stables his anger had faded. He was smiling, greedily thinking of the extra fee he would extract from the old man.

# CHAPTER 33

DYLAN HAD WASHED the blood off his hands in a small creek. They had left the little town and were on their way to Water Spark, the town closest to the Sinking Swamp.

On their way there, they encountered another shifter. This one begged Liam to spare its life, insisting that it wasn't mad like the rest of its kind. But these words did not stay the hands of the hunters.

Dylan gutted the shifter when it tried to run. The foul creature died at his hands, like many others had and many more would.

Dylan thought about what he and his dad had experienced this past month: more shifter attacks than usual. Something was wrong. Why would they expose themselves? "Do you think it's true?" Dylan asked his dad when he returned from a water trough to wash his hands.

"Do I think what is true?" Liam asked.

Dylan took a seat beside his dad. They were staying at a cozy inn. It was nice but the town was small and uneventful. They wouldn't stay long. They just had to find the witch. "That the shifters are getting sick," Dylan said. "All those stories we hear about a disease that drives them mad."

"That is nonsense," Liam said. "It's a lie conjured up by the idiots who support Magic." He motioned for his son to be quiet so he could better listen to the conversations around him. He was listening for gossip and rumors about Magic or shifters nearby. He was looking for something to kill.

"I'm not so sure about that," Dylan said hesitantly.

"What are you saying?" Liam said, annoyed at the interruption of his task.

"I'm saying that some of them are wilder than others. But some look like they are more in control." Dylan had seen so many shifters over the years. He had learned their ways. He found most of them to be sly and cunning. None of them ever just revealed what they were.

"None of them are in control," Liam spat. "They are all monsters who would rip us apart without thinking twice about it. Never forget that."

"But what if something is making them that way?" Dylan knew better than to press the subject with his

291

dad. Once his father had made up his mind, there was no changing it. But he continued to argue his point this time because he couldn't deny that feeling that something was somehow... off.

"That kind of thinking will get you killed," Liam said under his breath.

"I won't get killed." Dylan sounded sure of himself.

"That's what many of the hunters say. And many die every year."

Dylan knew this was true. Every year some of them died tragic deaths. He wondered if he too was going to die because of his job one day. Then he pushed the thought aside and decided to change the subject.

"Have you heard anything from Aunt Lillian?"

When he grew up, he saw his aunt Lillian everyday. She'd helped raise him after his mother had died. But as he got older, she went away on longer hunts and came back for shorter visits. He had gone hunting with her before and he had to admit that she was very good at her job. Perhaps she was so good at it because she loved it.

"She's out west," Liam said.

"So she's not planning on hunting with us any time soon," Dylan sighed.

Liam hunted out of hatred and revenge while Lillian Hunter out of passion. Killing shifters was her favorite thing to do.

"I'm sure she's got her hands full," Liam said to his son. Then he stood up. "Are you ready to leave?"

"We're going hunting already? We just got here!" Dylan was tired. They had been traveling for days and his muscles hurt. He didn't feel like going anywhere and he didn't feel like fighting.

"We still have some daylight left," Liam said.

"Can't we go tomorrow?"

"Absolutely not." Liam looked at his son and taunted him: "Are you scared?"

"I run toward what I fear," Dylan recited.

His dad smiled. "What's the problem then?"

Dylan sighed. The problem was that he was tired. But he couldn't say that. So instead he said, "We've never fought a witch before. I think we should do some research first. To make sure there are no surprises."

"It's one witch," Liam said in a bored voice. "We've taken out families of shifters. We can do this."

Dylan got to his feet and felt like an old man. He knew he was not going to win the argument with his father. He had an idea: "Let's take the horses."

"Alright," Liam agreed as he geared up.

Together they went to the stables and saddled their horses. Their horses were big and strong so that they could carry the weight of a grown man, plus his food and water and weapons. They were muscular and fit from all the traveling and load-bearing.

Dylan saddled his horse and mounted before his dad. He waited for Liam to do the same and then they rode off. They galloped away from town and then slowed down as they entered the swamp.

"This place is horrible," Dylan said. His eyes lingered on the black water. It reminded him of oil. He didn't want to walk through it.

"We should not take the horses through." Liam said to Dylan's disappointment. "I'm sure they will sink."

"And we won't?" Dylan asked. "Just look at this place! This story you heard about a witch must have been an old wives' tale."

"You think I fell for some cheap gossip?" Liam growled. He hated when his son thought he was gullible or was making a mistake. "But fine, we'll take the horses if you feel that strongly about it.

Dylan knew his dad was annoyed with him and decided to avoid answering the baited question. Anyway, Liam gave in on riding the horses into the swamp. So he quickly changed the topic. "Just look at this place! No one could possibly live in that house. It's too far from town and surrounded by a death trap." He swept his arm in a wide arc in front of him, taking in the almost impenetrable swamplands and the tiny cottage in the distance.

Liam looked at the little house in the middle of the swamp. His son had a point. The swamp was dark and deadly, even in daylight. There were little patches of grass that might support his and his horse's combined weight—*might*. The idea of sinking into the swamp was not appealing.

"Let's turn back now, before we go any farther and can't retreat," Dylan said with a hopeful voice. "There's no point in going hunting if both of us drown."

His father was considering it. Dylan could tell from his blank face and still body. His eyes stared in front of him at nothing.

"That house must be abandoned and sinking already. There is nothing here to hunt," Dylan continued.

A twig snapped behind them, but it didn't make them jump. It only made them more aware of their surroundings.

"You're wrong," Liam said, motioning them forward.

But both horses started prancing around nervously. Dylan's horse arched its neck, and as he pulled at the bit, it lashed out with a front leg, desperate to run away.

"What is it?" Dylan asked.

The words had barely left his lips when the cougar pounced. It had been sitting in the tree above them. They never expected to be attacked from that direction.

The wild cat jumped onto Liam's horse, causing both Liam and his horse to fall to the ground. It was just plain luck that the horse didn't fall on top of Liam.

Dylan tried to calm his own panicking horse but it was too scared to listen. Adrenaline took over as it fled—with Dylan hanging on for dear life—into the swamp. Its hooves sank into a deep mud hole and Dylan lost his balance, falling forward onto his horse's neck. Then he wrapped one hand around its neck and tangled his other hand into its mane, desperate not to fall off. The horse splashed trough the water and plowed through the mud, its breath ragged and its eyes wild.

Dylan pushed himself back into the saddle. The horse couldn't run very fast in the uneven mud, but it was a very bumpy ride. He reached for the reins that were flapping around the horse's neck, got a good grip on them, and pulled. The horse resisted him, tossing its head up and down and side to side, fighting for control of its bit. Dylan lifted out of the saddle and touched down again. If he couldn't pull the horse to a stop, he would have to turn it in order to bleed off some of its speed. So he leaned forward, grabbed the part of the left rein closest to the bit, and pulled.

It worked. The horse's head turned and its gait started to slow as it veered to the left. But it was still running scared and didn't watch where it was stepping. Its front hoof sank deep into the mud and it stumbled, launching Dylan over its neck and into the black water. The horse didn't fall. It regained its balance and ran away, leaving its rider in the dark water.

Dylan's head broke the surface and he coughed up black water. He cursed under his breath before realizing that he was almost at the little cottage. His horse had run straight for it and then dumped him right in front of it—well, almost right in front of it.

Dylan started swimming for the front porch and then saw a log floating toward him. It took him a moment to realize that it was an alligator. He started to reach for the knife at his belt but then realized how close he had to let the alligator come to him for him to be able to stab it. So instead he swam toward the porch as fast as he could.

He was almost there. So close. His hand reached out and, just before he could touch the lowest step, he felt a pain in his leg. The alligator had him. He screamed and went for his knife.

If this creature dragged him under the water, he would surely drown. He did not want to die—he wasn't ready to die. He stabbed his knife into the alligator's head, burying it into the reptile's skull right between the eyes, where it stuck straight up. When the alligator's jaws opened to release his leg, Dylan kicked it in the face, dislodging his knife. Apparently, alligator skulls are thick and virtually impenetrable.

Dylan angled himself toward the porch and started kicking frantically for shore. But it didn't feel like he was moving. It felt like he was sinking. His movements slowed as he began to despair. He could not reach it. Any moment now his head would go under and the swamp would swallow him whole, or the alligator would come back to finish what it had started.

To his surprise and relief, he felt someone's hand grasp his. This someone pulled and pulled until Dylan rolled onto the porch. He gasped for breath as the hand let him go. He then reached down for the leg that the alligator had bitten. He expected a lot of blood and even more pain. Then as he breathed in the scent of the flowers on the porch his mind cleared. "I thought that thing had ripped my leg off," he said, staring at his foot in amazement.

"What thing?"

He turned to the woman who had saved his life. She didn't look very witch-like as she smiled down at him.

As Dylan stood up, he found himself shaking. He managed to regain control of his body, with the exception of his hands which he then clenched to hide their trembling. He looked back to where the alligator should have been. Instead he found grass and flowers. The black water was now a beautiful meadow. Dylan was enchanted, but only for a few seconds. Then he shook himself. The witch was messing with his head.

He quickly assessed his situation. He had lost one knife in the swamp. His sword and arrows were strapped to his horse that had run away. He only had one weapon left—a dagger. He drew it.

The witch raised her eyebrow. She looked more curious than scared. "Is that any way to treat some-one who just saved your life?"

"You're a witch!" he spat.

"And you are a hunter," she said, looking more intrigued than scared. "If I am guessing correctly, you're Dylan Archer."

Dylan's face went a little whiter and he gripped his dagger a little tighter. "How do you know who I am?"

"I have ears everywhere," she said slyly before chuckling over her own pun. "I have heard countless stories of you being a cold-blooded murderer."

"Those are lies," he spat. "I only kill those that kill."

She tilted her head to the side. "That's what your father would like you to believe, isn't it?"

"You don't know a thing about my father," Dylan snarled. He was slowly getting angry. Who was this witch to talk to him about his family?

"Liam Archer," she said his father's name calmly. "The man whose wife got brutally killed and who has been blaming it on every single shifter that's ever lived." She pulled a vial from her pocket.

"What's that?" he asked. He looked at it as if it might explode.

"Poison," she responded calmly.

He wondered if she was going to throw it into his face. How else would she get him to drink it? But instead of bringing it to him she walked to her flowers and deposited a drop into each pot.

"I'm not going to kill you," she said. "I'm glad you are here."

"You know who I am and what I do," Dylan said. "So you know why I'm here—to kill you. Why would you be glad?"

She smiled.

He watched the flowers die: they crumpled up and withered away into lifeless brown sticks. Whatever poison she had given them was really strong.

"Come inside. We should talk."

She turned her back on him. No one has ever done that. Was she not scared that he would kill her? He could easily stab her in the back. But instead of attacking, he found himself following her inside. He followed slowly and cautiously and his eyes lingered on her back.

The cottage was filled with flowers. They were all different shapes and sizes and colors, and they made the place look nice. He watched as she slowly poisoned them too.

"Yesterday I met a girl," the witch told him. "I could sense there was something different about her, but I couldn't tell what. She came looking for answers that I didn't realize I had because I didn't realize who she was."

"Why are you telling me this?" Dylan asked. Usually he didn't talk to the Magic folk before killing them. He only spoke when he wanted them to tell him where their packs were. Usually he completed the job quickly.

"It's important that you know," the witch said. "This girl can be the end of everything."

"You're just buying time before I kill you."

"Does it look like I am trying to run?"

He just stood there and looked at her. She was far too calm. There was no fear in her eyes and her hands weren't shaking.

"This girl is on her way to Sky Castle. You'll meet her there."

"I'm not going to the castle," Dylan said.

"You'll soon receive an invitation from the king. He is in need of your services."

"He wants to commission me to kill shifters?"

She nodded. "They've been going mad and killing many of his people ever since the disease started."

"So this disease... It's real?" Dylan didn't think he was supposed to believe a witch, but he couldn't help but hear the truth in her words.

She nodded again. "It's wiping them out and they are killing many non-Magic folk because of it."

"Why are you telling me this?" Dylan asked.

"This girl—I feel I should at least give her a chance. She has had a very hard life and I try to think that everyone has a piece of good inside of them. With her memories gone, maybe she could start a new life. A good life. Maybe she will never remember who she was or what she is supposed to do."

"What's she supposed to do?"

"If I tell you, you'd kill her immediately without giving her a chance to change her future." The witch thought about the wolf and how he trusted the girl. If he thought she could change, then maybe there was hope for her after all. "I don't believe in killing anyone without giving them a chance to be better," the witch said to him. "But if this girl finds out who she is, and if she snaps, then I need you to kill her."

"What?" Dylan was so confused. It was the first time one of the Magic folk asked something like this of him.

"You will find her in Sky Castle. She goes by the name of Caitlin Wilde," the witch said. "Keep a close eye on her."

"I'm not going to do what a witch tells me to do," Dylan said.

"Then why haven't you attacked me yet?" she asked him and looked at the knife in his hand. "Is it because a part of you believes me?"

"I don't know this girl," Dylan said. "And I've never even heard of her, never heard rumors of a girl being a threat to anyone or anything."

"By the time you hear of her being a threat, it will be too late," the witch said. "The castle isn't a good place for her. You should take her away."

"What? You're crazy."

"If she's good, if she's got a good heart, you should take her away." Ears paused. "I can see in your eyes that you want to leave your hunting days behind you. You never wanted this life."

"But it's the only life I've got."

"You're always one decision away from a completely different life," she said. "You just have to want it badly enough."

"If I quit my job, many innocent people will be killed by your kind!"

"My kind?" she laughed. "You're the ones slaughtering us!"

"It's self-defense," he argued.

"You have a knife in your hand; I have no weapons," she pointed out. "You came to my house to kill me. That's not self-defense. That's murder."

"If you feel this way about me," he said. "Why ask me to go help the girl?"

"Because," she said, looking directly into his eyes,

"I sense something good in you. And I think that good part might be what saves her."

"But?" he prodded.

"But, you have also been twisted by your father and his beliefs. He's turned you into enough of a monster that should the girl become a threat, I know you'd be able to put an end to her."

"You're asking me to befriend a stranger who I might eventually need to kill?" He gaped. "That's not friendship. It's being disloyal, it's a betrayal, and it's not right."

"Sometimes to do the right thing, one must forget loyalty," she said.

"This is the talk of an old witch!" he said. "Of course, you know nothing about loyalty."

She tilted her head to the side and then poisoned some more flowers. *Why would she possibly be killing her garden?* Dylan wondered.

"Why haven't you attacked me yet?" she asked again. "Your father would have wanted you to butcher me the moment I pulled you onto the porch."

"I wasn't sure if you were the witch," he lied.

"Nonsense!" she said. "You were second-guessing yourself as you have done many times before. Deep down, you know that what you are doing is wrong. You know I'm not the bad one here."

"You're a murderer!"

"And you're not?"

"I'm going to kill you," he said and took a step

303

forward, "and everyone like you."

"If that's what you think," she said sadly, "then you should just kill the girl immediately. You can't save her, or anyone, if your heart's so twisted."

"Enough," he said as he watched the last flower die.

At that moment, his dad burst through the door with his sword in his hand. Blood stained one of his shoulders. "Where's the witch?" he cried.

Dylan looked back toward the witch, but she had disappeared. How had she disappeared?

And to make matters worse, the house started sinking.

Ears watched them panic as they breathed in the scent of the flowers. She studied Dylan. Maybe she had made a mistake to tell him about Caitlin. He had a lot of hate in his heart. He hated monsters, the shifters and the Magic folk he and his father hunted. She wondered when and if he would realize that he had turned into the very thing he hated. He had turned into a monster.

These non-Magic people would never understand that Magic didn't make you a monster. *Your choices are what define you, Dylan. Think carefully and choose wisely,* the witch thought silently as she continued to watch father and son.

She hadn't told Dylan a lot. She, of course, would never tell him about Rafe. She wouldn't want the handsome young wolf, or any shifter, killed.

But something had to be done about Caitlin. She needed someone who was mentally strong to be there for her. She would need someone to help her when she found out who she was.

Ears didn't think Rafe was this person.

Ears knew Caitlin would find the answers she was looking for in the castle. She just hoped that the girl had as good a heart as Rafe thought she had and that she was capable of making the right choices.

Ears sat down comfortably as she watched her illusion play out. The two men thought her house was sinking. She watched them scuttle from the house and make their way out of the swamp. And a small part of her heart wished that they had drowned in it.

# CHAPTER 34

"YOU REALLY AREN'T good with animals," Gerald said to Rafe.

He didn't say it in a mean way. He said it casually, but Caitlin could tell from the way his lip curled back, that he wasn't impressed.

Misty had just tried to buck Rafe off again. Luckily he hadn't fallen. Caitlin knew the horse would have run away if he had fallen and maybe they wouldn't have been able to catch her again. That would have been a mess. None of the other horses would want Rafe on their backs either and his weight would slow down the cart if he rode on it.

"I try my best to be likeable," Rafe said to Gerald. "But she's a stubborn one."

The mare snorted as if she understood him. Gerald had offered to switch horses with Rafe but Rafe didn't want to. At first Gerald had thought he had just bought a wild horse. But as time went by, he noticed that Rafe put all the horses on edge. Gerald didn't know what the horses were sensing about Rafe that he couldn't, but he knew he didn't like it.

"It's going to be a slow trip up the mountain with Penny pulling our cart," Daisy observed the huge mountain and its only road. "Should we leave the cart?"

Gerald thought about this for a moment. "I think we should take it with us. It's the easiest way to get our things up there. It might be slower but at least we will have all of our belongings."

They started up the mountain. Boulders were everywhere, on either side of the road, and Caitlin wondered how the people who built this passageway did it. Then the road climbed; it went up and up as if there was no end. One side of the road was a sheer wall of rock; the other side was just as sheer but went straight down. If you fell, you would die. There were sharp, switchback turns every so often, usually around a large boulder that the builders probably hadn't even tried to move.

"Have you ever been to the castle?" Gerald asked Rafe.

"I have not. But I hear it's impressive." If Rafe was nervous about going to a place where he would instantly be killed if people found out what he was, then he didn't show it. He had his usual, beautiful smile on his face. As the sun shone down on his pale skin, Caitlin wondered if he would burn or if he might actually get some color. She had tried to ride next to him, but Prince wanted to keep his distance from Rafe. She didn't force her horse any closer than it wanted to go.

Maggie was so excited. She rode with Gerald and laughed every so often. "How will it work when we arrive?" the six-year-old asked. "Will they welcome us?"

"We'll go to talk to the king's advisor and right hand, Lady Katherine Black, about what happened in River Town. We will tell her why we are seeking refuge," Gerald said. He had one arm wrapped around his daughter's waist and his other hand on the reins. She was small enough that, when she sat in front of him, both of them could still ride comfortably.

"Why don't we go straight to the king?"

"Our king is too busy with more important matters. He doesn't have time to listen to our problems," Gerald explained.

"Is Lady Katherine going to help us?" Maggie asked as she played with Star's mane.

"She will listen to our problems and help find a solution. If we are lucky, we get to stay in the castle. Would you like that?"

"Yes! That would be amazing!"

Gerald made Star walk slowly so that they could stay beside the cart that Penny was pulling. Misty led the way, always walking at a fast clip with Rafe on her back, as if she wanted to run away from him. Prince, with Caitlin in control of the reins, easily kept pace with Misty and Rafe.

"Are you alright?" Caitlin asked Rafe.

"I'm not going to go with you guys to talk to Lady Katherine Black," Rafe said in a low voice. They were out of earshot.

"Why not?" Caitlin asked.

"Well firstly, I'm not from your town, and I don't have a story to tell her." His eyes were fixed on the road ahead of him. Usually he looked at Caitlin when he spoke to her. "And secondly, I don't want to be around someone like *that*."

"Someone like what?" Caitlin asked as she sensed the disgust in his voice.

"Someone who is a dark, malicious sadist. She's evil. She's the king's advisor and his right hand. She's ordered many of us shifters killed. She helps him rule the Silver kingdom. She whispers in his ear what horrible things he should do. She's cunning and makes up plans of her own to punish my kind. I think she's the only person who hates us more than the king does."

Caitlin swallowed. "Maybe you shouldn't come with us at all."

Rafe's eyes found hers. "I'm not going to run away, Caitlin."

Her heart tightened. He was going into the most dangerous place in the kingdom, the most dangerous place for him. If he got hurt, she would get hurt as well. What would she do then? What could she do? She was emotionally attached to Rafe. She didn't want anything bad to ever happen to him.

"I'm not telling you to run away," she said. Truthfully, she didn't want him to ever leave. "But can you please sit this one out?"

"Both witches told me that I would find the answers that I need there, in Sky Castle," he said. He thought about the disease and how terrible it would be if he got it. He didn't want to get something like that. He'd rather kill himself.

"I know," Caitlin sighed. "I just don't want you to get hurt."

"I don't want you to get hurt either," Rafe said and finally met her eyes.

She thought about the assassin and wondered when he would find her again. What if he came to her when she was sleeping? "I won't," she said. "I can protect myself."

Rafe didn't argue. She was capable of fighting, but he did not want to talk about that. Rafe changed the subject. "Do you want to talk about what you told Ears?"

Caitlin took a deep breath. She knew the subject about her memories would come up some time. It still wasn't an easy topic. "What about it?"

"Maybe we should start with your dreams."

"I really don't want to talk about that," she said tightly.

"Why not?"

"They're frightening—Rafe, what if I am not a good person?"

"That depends on what your definition of good is," Rafe said. "Some people think I am a bad guy, remember?"

"You're not bad," she said quickly.

"Everyone has a little bad in them," Rafe admitted. "But yes, I try to be a good man."

She smiled at him. He was a good man—probably the best one that she knew. And he was smart. Maybe he could help her figure out her past.

"What do you think could have happened to make me forget EVERTHING? I can't even remember my own family. And they're never in my dreams."

Rafe swallowed. "Have you noticed their tattoos?"

"You're very observant," she remarked. "Yes, I have seen the numbers at the back of their necks. I don't know what they are."

"You don't have one," Rafe said. "I checked."

"How do I know where in the castle to find answers?" she asked him after a pause.

"The answers will probably find you," Rafe said. "When Black Blade returns, I will be ready, by your side, and we'll get him. Then we'll get him to talk."

"How will we get him to talk?" she asked with a tight throat. She wondered how much they would have to hurt such a man before he told them anything. The idea of hurting someone made her feel nothing.

Rafe looked at her with cold eyes but didn't say anything. She had an idea that he was better when it came to inflicting pain than she was, although he did not enjoy it.

"Thank you for helping me with this," she said. "I don't know what I'd do without you."

"I'll always be there to help you," he smiled at her.

She found comfort in his presence and felt warmth in his smile. If he was always with her, then she would always feel happy.

Sky Castle came into view as they rounded the next switchback. It was built high atop the mountain with a view of the surrounding cliffs. Only one road led to it, so it could only be attacked from that one direction. It was a strong fortress, built from the boulders of the mountain. A high wall surrounded it. A heavy iron gate barred unwanted entry. *Easy to defend and almost impossible to breach*, Caitlin thought to herself. But it was also beautiful. If you looked at it from certain angles, it looked like it was floating in the sky. Its towers stretched so high that some of them were obscured by clouds. It looked like something out of one of Maggie's fairy tales.

"Wow!" Maggie exclaimed. "Look at the wild dogs!"

The Wilde family and Rafe turned their heads in unison to see where she was pointing. A pack of dogs glared at them from nearby. Saliva dripped from their mouths and low growling sounds came from their throats.

"Those aren't dogs!" Rafe warned the family. "Run!"

There were at least seven of them. Caitlin knew they were shifters even before Rafe told them. They were all stark-raving mad. They emerged from behind the giant boulders one by one, snarling at the humans.

"Our horses can outrun them," Caitlin said to Rafe. She gripped the reins as her horse pranced nervously.

"But the cart can't."

Caitlin was amazed at how Rafe was always thinking about her family's safety. He thought about them long before she did. They looked back at Daisy who gripped the reins like her life depended on it. Her face was pale.

Star was the first horse that spooked. He flew back onto his hind legs. Maggie squealed and Gerald tightened his arm around her. The horse touched down and Gerald had to pull back hard on the reins for it to obey. It threw its head from side to side in an unruly manner.

Then wild dogs attacked. They streamed down from the rocks like insects. Their teeth were showing and horrible growling sounds escaped their throats.

Penny spooked next. She couldn't turn around to run downhill, as the cart wouldn't allow it, so she sprinted forward and up the mountain. Her huge hooves dug into the stones as she pulled the cart with all of her might. Daisy tried to steer her straight but Penny was panicking. Then one of the cart's wheels hit a rock and the cart tilted to its side and rolled forward, tilted like that, for a moment before falling completely on its side and crashing to a hard stop. Penny broke free and ran off with one of the dogs chasing her.

Daisy fell off the cart and cried out as she landed on her side. She scrambled to her feet and then bent down by the cart—as if it could shield her against the attacking dogs.

"Gerald, I'll help Daisy. Just take Maggie and run!" Rafe ordered. "You two can make it to the castle."

Gerald didn't want to leave his family but he could do nothing to help them. The only thing he could do was get his younger daughter to safety. He kicked his heels into the horse's side. Star started running toward the castle. Two dogs followed him closely.

Rafe urged Misty toward Daisy. The horse resisted but Rafe was forceful and she submitted. Once they reached Daisy, he jumped off swiftly. "Get on!" he ordered.

Daisy was a good and a kind woman. She wasn't brave or stubborn and didn't resist the offer. She was good at following orders. Misty pranced nervously around but Rafe pushed Daisy into the saddle. She sat down clumsily and reached for the reins.

"Ride to the castle and don't look back." He turned Misty to face the castle and she started running the moment he let go of the reins. One dog followed them.

Rafe saw a dog charge at him. He had no weapons with him. So he picked up a stone and threw it at the dog's face as it jumped toward him, temporarily deflecting its attack.

Rafe was in a quandary. There were three dogs and

he knew he couldn't fight them in human form. But he also knew that if he shifted here and someone saw him, he would be killed. But then if he got bitten by a dog, he would get infected.

"Rafe!" Caitlin called and interrupted his indecision with an order: "Get on my horse! Now!"

Another dog jumped at him and he dodged just in the nick of time. The three were surrounding him, boxing him in, saliva dripping from their open mouths.

Caitlin tried to urge her horse forward, but he didn't want to. He reared again and she barely managed to stay on top.

Rafe glanced at the three dogs and then he bolted. He skidded past one and made his way toward Caitlin and her horse. He was tall enough to swing his leg over easily and lucky enough to not be bitten as a dog's jaw snapped shut inches away from his leg.

Prince took off, as Rafe's bottom touched its back and he wrapped his arms around Caitlin. The castle entrance was so close, but the dogs that had been chasing her family were in front of it. There were dogs behind them and dogs in front of them, a sheer drop on one side and the castle wall on the other side. They were boxed in.

Then arrows rained down from the castle wall. The castle guards came to their rescue, startling the dogs. They were doing a great job keeping the dogs at bay until a stray arrow hit the ground next to Prince and spooked the horse even more. Prince swerved left.

Caitlin grabbed a fistful of mane. She lost control of the horse. It was running next to the castle wall–rushing headlong for the cliff. Then the road ran out and Prince slowed. Huge rocks blocked its path.

The dogs resumed their charge, leaping over the rocks gracefully. Rafe and Caitlin knew that the dogs would soon be upon them.

Prince's hooves slipped over the loose gravel. But he kept his balance as he moved forward. More arrows flew down around them, spooking the horse even more. Prince stumbled again, and this time Rafe slipped to the left.

He knew he was going to fall even before he hit the ground. He let go of Caitlin, not wanting to pull her with him. Rafe hit the ground hard and when he got to his feet, he saw that Caitlin had also fallen. He rushed to her side. To their left was the castle wall. To their right were more rocks. In front of them were the dogs and behind them was a cliff. Still boxed in.

Caitlin looked down the cliff. It was so high. If they were to fall, they'd die. Rafe stood in front of her and she looked at the dogs from over his shoulder. The number of dogs had dwindled. The archers had killed most of them and more arrows were finding their targets. She watched the men stand on the walls as they pulled their bowstrings back and fired their arrows. They had good aim.

"Don't shift," she whispered into Rafe's ear. She thought he might shift in self-defense but that would only result in the archers shooting at him too.

"I wasn't planning to," he said.

One of the dogs met Caitlin's eyes. She realized that it was going to jump at them. Actually, it was going to jump at Rafe who shielded her. It was going to sink its teeth into him and infect him. As a result, he was going to die.

She couldn't let that happen. So when the wild dog jumped, she was ready. She shoved Rafe to the side and let the crazy animal sink its teeth into her shoulder.

# CHAPTER 35

RAFE HIT THE rocks and broke his fall with his hands. He looked up and saw the dog with its mouth on Caitlin's shoulder. Suddenly, he saw the dog fall to the ground, an arrow buried in its neck and a look of shock in its eyes—as if it hadn't realized that it could in fact die.

Caitlin's shoulder hurt like hell, which made her mad, almost as mad as the mad dogs they'd just fought off. She hated the feeling of pain, the feeling of weakness. She was about to kick the dog but when she looked at it, she saw that it had become a human boy. He looked no older than sixteen. His eyes were open and staring at her. His hands were reaching for her as if he wanted her help. Then his body lay still.

Rafe sat back with a look of horror on his face. For once he was quiet. No jokes came from his mouth, no sarcastic smile on his lips.

"Rafe," she put one bloodied hand on his shoulder and held her injured shoulder with the other. She understood that it was hard for him to see another of his kind get hurt or die.

It was difficult for her too because she didn't know how to comfort him. He always made her feel better. But how could she return the favor? He had a way of shutting down when he was hurting. He showed no emotions and pushed people away. It was as if he thought no one could understand or share his pain.

She saw his eyes grow cold and his face go blank as he watched the other corpses transform into men and women and kids. They all had similar features—they were a family.

She remembered that Rafe had told her that his family died. Did something like this happen? Were these deaths triggering memories that he wanted to forget?

She studied his stony expression and then reached to touch his hand. But he shrugged her hand off. "Let's get back to the castle," he said as he got to his feet. "You need a healer."

"It's not that bad," Caitlin lied. She was starting to feel a little light-headed from the loss of blood as she stood up.

Side by side, they walked together in silence to the castle's big gates. Caitlin wanted to take Rafe's hand in hers. But he was so cold she didn't dare to get closer to him than she already was.

They walked into the castle and Rafe had to bite back the urge to rip the archers apart. He knew that the wild dogs were sick. He knew they were going to kill him and Caitlin. He knew they had to die. But he couldn't accept their deaths—their *murders*—at the hands of the people who hated them, people who kill just for fun. He wondered if the archers enjoyed shooting them from high up on the wall. They shot from a point of safety and advantage—the wild dogs couldn't fight back.

Once they were inside the castle, he walked away. Caitlin didn't know where he was going. He stormed past the guards and past the archers and disappeared into the castle.

Caitlin's heart ached for her friend. She had this longing feeling deep down inside that consumed her. She wanted, needed, to be with him and would have followed him, but she heard Maggie crying her name. Then she felt little arms squeezing her waist.

"I thought they got you!" Maggie wailed. Tears were running down her face.

Caitlin scooped her up and hugged her back. "As you can see, I'm fine," she said gently.

"Your shoulder isn't!" her little sister pointed out.

Caitlin looked at the blood on her shoulder. She set Maggie down as she felt a little light-headed. She was glad that the wild dog had bitten her instead of Rafe. She would heal. She was non-Magic and couldn't get infected. She'd get better.

Gerald and Daisy came toward her. They wrapped their arms around both girls in one big family hug. Although Caitlin didn't hug any of them back, she decided that it wasn't so bad to have their caring arms wrapped around her after all.

Her shoulder had been cleaned and bandaged. She tried to keep it as motionless as possible as they were escorted into the throne room by the guards.

Maggie had been holding Caitlin's hand when the healer had attended to her wounds and she still hadn't let go. Caitlin didn't pull her hand free. She realized that although the contact didn't really comfort her, it comforted her sister.

The throne room's doors were big and heavy. They were made of wood and had detailed carvings in them. Caitlin's eyes roamed over the doors and realized that the carvings depicted King Leonard overthrowing the Witch King. Then she let her gaze rest on the guards on either side of the doors. They stood perfectly still and expressionless and reminded her of statues.

The Wilde family walked through the entrance together and found themselves inside a long, rectangular room. A chandelier hung from the roof. The floor was made of a beautiful gray stone. At the end on the room was a silver throne. It was huge and made out of real silver. To the throne's right was a smaller silver chair. It had jewels embedded in it that shimmered. Caitlin wondered if they were diamonds and how much that chair was worth.

In the jeweled chair sat a lady, tall and slim, powerful and intimidating. She wore rings on her fingers and pearls around her neck. Her dress was black with a blue shimmer to it. Her long black hair reached her tiny waist.

"Lady Katherine," the guard said. "May I present to you the Wilde family. They are here from—" he paused.

"River Town," Gerald helped him then shifted his eyes to the king's advisor and added, "Milady."

Lady Katherine Black, the king's right hand and advisor, tensed. For a moment she stared at them as if she knew something they didn't.

"Leave us," she told the guards.

They exchanged wary glances but didn't object. Usually someone as important as Lady Katherine wouldn't ask to be left alone and unprotected. But they didn't dare to question her command, so they turned around and started walking.

"And close the doors behind you," she added.

They did as she asked and the heavy doors creaked shut. The Wilde family was alone with her and the world suddenly felt much smaller.

For a moment, all was silent and then Gerald took a

322

step forward and bowed. "Milady, my name is Gerald Wilde. I have brought my family here to seek refuge." His voice didn't shake although he was nervous. Caitlin felt proud of him: it took a lot of courage to come and talk to this woman.

Katherine observed them all but her eyes lingered on Caitlin before she spoke. "I've heard about your town. And I have been expecting you."

Caitlin's blood ran cold. The only person, other than her family and Rafe, who escaped the town alive, was Nicolas Campbell. Had he been here in the castle telling the king's advisor about them? Surely not, because if he had, she would have had them killed instantly—association with Magic. Maybe Campbell thought the assassin was going to kill her before the Wildes ever reached Sky Castle. That was probably it.

Caitlin wondered if he was still in the castle somewhere. She wanted to ask, but knew she wasn't in any position to ask Lady Katherine any questions. So instead she listened as Katherine asked Gerald to give her the detailed story of what had happened. He told it as best he could but left out the part where they were tied to the stakes, about to be burned for their association with Magic.

"River Town was small and not many people know about it," Katherine said. "You will not tell anyone where you are from. I don't want the people to be frightened, or to know that the shifters destroyed a whole town. You are welcome to stay in the castle. I will arrange a job for you, and everyone will be safe. As for the shifters, I will hire the best hunters to kill them."

"Thank you kindly, Milady," Gerald said.

Caitlin felt guilt tug at her heart. Lady Katherine was going to send hunters to kill the shifters. Maybe she should have said something, but if she had she would have been in a lot of trouble for defending them.

She thought about Rafe. He was so stable and so brave. He had saved her family's lives and placed her life above his own. He was proof that all shifters weren't bad.

She wondered whether the hunters would only kill the sick shifters. It was wishful thinking but maybe the healthy ones could get away.

As she turned around to exit the throne room, Caitlin suddenly felt light-headed. The room started swirling. Sweat broke out on her brow. There was a ringing in her ears that made everything worse. She took an off-balance step but managed to catch herself before she could fall.

Lady Katherine said something, but she couldn't hear and couldn't focus. Is she talking to me? Caitlin's hands went to her injured shoulder. It was burning as if on fire. She tried to push the pain aside but it was overwhelming.

Her family and Lady Katherine watched as Caitlin sank to her knees and then fell to the floor. It sounded like she wanted to scream but was in too much pain to get it out.

"Caitlin!" Gerald's voice was full of worry. He reached for her but she kicked his hand away and started squirming around on the floor.

"It's that bite!" Daisy said. "It's making her sick! It's her shoulder! There, where that shifter dog sank his teeth in."

Lady Katherine was standing now. She looked down at them with big, worried eyes. Then she called for the guards.

"I've never heard of a human becoming sick of a bite," she told Gerald and Daisy. "I will have her escorted to a private room where our healers will examine her."

"Can't she stay with us?" Daisy asked, worried. Then she realized how she had spoken to the king's right hand. She added, "Please, Milady. My children are my world. I need to be with her to look after her and make sure that she will be alright."

"Our trustworthy healers will make sure of that," Katherine assured her with stern eyes. Everyone could hear from her tone of voice that her decision was final.

The guards came into the room. The Wilde family watched helplessly as they picked Caitlin up from the floor and carried her away to another room where she would be alone, confused and hurt.

Lady Katherine dismissed them and then also left the throne room. She didn't have anything more to say to the family. They weren't a priority and what they wanted for their elder daughter wasn't her concern.

The safety of her people was what concerned her.

She immediately met with a healer who was standing inside the room where Caitlin was taken. The room was small and private. Caitlin was strapped to a narrow bed.

"Healer Dan," Katherine said in her placid voice.

The middle-aged man turned around and faced her. He was attractive and intelligent too. "Yes, Milady?"

"Why is she strapped to the bed?" Katherine eyes lingered on the girl who was straining against her bonds. Her head swished from side to side. She was sweating like she had just run for miles. Her wet hair clung to her face and drops of saliva sprayed from her mouth every time she exhaled.

"She's strapped to the bed to keep her from harming herself and others. She seems to have lost all control—like she has gone crazy."

"Crazy?" Katherine repeated. "A shifter that had Craybies bit her. Is it possible that she has the disease?"

"I've never heard of a non-Magic, like this girl, getting it," he answered.

Katherine could see that he was unsure and confused and that he didn't like feeling this way. But she had a lot of confidence in him. She believed he could figure out what was going on faster than any other healer could.

"I will do everything in my power to find out why this is happening and I will try to help her," Healer Dan said.

Katherine frowned. "If non-Magic folk can get this disease, it would be catastrophic."

Healer Dan nodded. "I know."

That night the whole Wilde family had trouble sleeping.

Maggie cried and swore she wouldn't sleep until Caitlin returned. She didn't run around, she didn't laugh, and she didn't talk as much as she usually would. It felt as if a piece of her heart was missing. She didn't understand why her favorite person in the world had been taken from her.

Maggie considered herself a good healer. She could take care of her sister like she took care of Rafe. She would sit with her all night if that was what it took for Caitlin to get better. She would bring her lots of water and put a wet cloth to put on her head to decrease the fever.

The new house assigned to the Wilde family was pretty, and Maggie would have loved to have had Caitlin to share it with her. But for the entire night, she cried to her mother.

Hearing her daughter sob made Daisy's heart ache. How could she explain to Maggie that there was nothing more she could do? Lady Katherine had given the order and they had to obey. That was simply the way the world worked.

Gerald sat outside the house. His head was hanging and his shoulders were drooping. His heart felt heavy. There wasn't a worse feeling in the world than the feeling of not being able to help your own child. He listened to Maggie cry. He listened to Daisy try to soothe her. And he thought about those terrible shifters and how much he hated them. *They did this. They hurt my little girl. Why did they have to do that? The crazy animals just attacked them without reason!* He couldn't wait for the hunters to come. He hoped they were as good as he was told.

"Gerald?"

Gerald looked up into a face he hadn't seen all day. Rafe was looking at him like he knew something was wrong.

"Where have you been?" Gerald snapped.

"I've been exploring," Rafe confessed. "And I didn't know which house they gave you, so it took me some time to find you."

Rafe actually just needed time alone. He had sat by himself for a long time to make peace with the deaths of the wild dogs. Then he had sniffed out the Wilde family.

Gerald shrugged. "We don't have a spare room. You can sleep on the couch."

"That's very kind of you," Rafe said. "But I've been

staying with you for long enough now. I don't want to take advantage of your hospitality."

Gerald looked up at him with cold eyes. Rafe thought the man would be happy if he left but now Gerald simply looked angry.

"You are leaving?" Gerald growled.

"What? No!" Rafe said quickly. "I was just going to get my own place so that you don't have to take care of me."

"Oh," Gerald said as his shoulders slumped again. The anger disappeared as fast as it had appeared.

"I came to say goodnight to everyone," Rafe said sweetly. He looked down at the man but hardly recognized him. He looked broken and defeated—a look Rafe had never seen on him before.

"What's wrong?" Rafe asked and sat down beside him. He rested his elbows on his knees and kept his eyes on the older man.

"They took her," Gerald said with tears in his eyes.

"Who took who?" Rafe asked.

Slowly Gerald told Rafe what had happened. Rafe listened in silence. His nails bit into his arms when he crossed them. His eyes were weary and his heart filled with sorrow.

If Lady Katherine thought Caitlin posed a threat to her people, she would kill her without thinking twice about it. She hated anything to do with Magic.

Rafe's chest felt too tight to speak as he was overwhelmed with guilt. *He* was the target of that wild dog.

That dog was going to kill him. It should have been him, not her. Why did Caitlin have to save his life? He was supposed to protect her, not the other way around.

Rafe didn't know if he could forgive himself if Katherine's men killed her. What had he been thinking when he befriended a non-Magic human girl? He should have known that their friendship would only place her life in danger. He should have left the moment his wounds had healed.

Rafe couldn't look into Gerald's eyes. How was he supposed to speak to the loving father of the girl he'd failed to protect? He got up and was about to leave when Maggie spotted him.

"Rafe!" she cried and ran to him. She was still sobbing and he picked her up. She pressed her head into his shoulder and he felt her warm tears through his clothes.

Daisy had followed Maggie from her room and stopped when she saw Rafe. She was glad that he had returned. Although they had not known him very long, she saw him as a part of the family. He belonged with them.

"I can't get her to sleep," Daisy stated and leaned against the wall. She was so tired that dark circles shadowed her eyes and her body felt weak.

"I can't sleep without Caitlin beside me," Maggie explained to Rafe.

Rafe understood her feelings better than most people

could. He knew what it was like to miss someone with every piece of your heart. Rafe hugged her tightly and carried her to bed. She lay in his arms and cried her heart out. Daisy thought the kid would be up the whole night.

Rafe held her hand and sang her a lullaby. His throat was tight and he was mumbling more than singing. Daisy couldn't make out the words, or the melody—he was off-key. Amazingly Maggie fell asleep in Rafe arms not long after he began singing.

Rafe decided to stay with them for the night.

The next morning Lady Katherine stood in the room where Caitlin was being held and studied the girl sleeping peacefully.

"Good morning," she said to Healer Dan. She had heard him enter the room but didn't turn around to face him.

"It's a good morning indeed," Healer Dan said cheerfully. "She is healed."

"What?" Katherine asked with shock in her voice. She didn't mean to blurt out the word in such an unladylike way. "How is this possible?"

"Her body fought off the infection," Healer Dan said. "She didn't need any help from me."

Katherine stared at the girl in disbelief. She's the first non-Magic to get the disease and the first person ever to survive it. "So, she poses no threat?"

"She poses no threat at all." Then his expression changed from happy to cautious. "What would you have me do with her?"

Lady Katherine hesitated. "Send her back to her family. I'm sure they're anxious to see her."

Lady Katherine looked back at the sleeping girl one last time before she walked away. She didn't know why, but she felt uneasy and confused.

# CHAPTER 36

CAITLIN WOKE UP and touched her head. It hurt a little bit. She squeezed her eyes shut and then opened them again. Then she sat up with a groan.

"Good morning, Miss Wilde," an unfamiliar voice said. It sounded way too cheerful—and Caitlin was in no mood for that.

A dark-haired man stood beside her bed. He was tall and smiling. He was the only other person in the room with her.

She shifted her weight on the bed. The mattress was thin—she could feel the wood slats underneath it—and she didn't have a pillow or a blanket. There were leather straps at each side of the bed. They looked as if they were intended to bind wrists and ankles. She didn't like them and immediately felt uncomfortable.

"Go away," she snapped at the man.

He raised his eyebrows and his smile vanished. He spoke to her in a controlled voice although she had a feeling he was itching to snap at her.

"I am Healer Dan. I was the one who checked on you after that terrible shifter bit you."

"I'm fine now," she glared at him. If he was expecting her to thank him, he was going to end up disappointed. She didn't like him one bit. She didn't like this room either. It was too small and she felt like she was locked up. She wanted to get out and get away. The door was open....

"Yes, amazingly you are fine," the healer agreed with her but didn't sound pleased.

She swung her feet off the bed and sat there for a moment, feet dangling, to get her bearings. She was still a bit groggy but didn't feel sick. Her shoulder was all wrapped up. It felt stiff but it wasn't burning anymore.

"I have never heard of a non-Magic getting infected by this disease," the healer said. His voice was heavy with meaning.

"Are you saying I'm Magic folk?" she spat at him.

He knew that accusing someone of being Magical was a serious charge. He forced a smile on his lips. "No, I'm just stating that you are... different."

"Whatever," she slid off the bed and got to her feet.

"I have a few questions for you, Miss Wilde, if you don't mind me asking," the healer said politely.

"I do mind you asking," she said as rudely as possible

before stomping to the door. The healer called after her but she ignored him.

Caitlin didn't want to see his stupid face or answer his stupid questions. She refused to be a patient of his and wanted to get as far away as possible.

She didn't know where in the castle she was or where she was going. She didn't mind the darkness. It was the unfamiliarity that made her jump at every shadow and sound. She walked fast and looked behind her every now and then, expecting someone to come after her.

She saw sunlight and ran toward it. It welcomed her warmly but hurt her eyes. She must have been in the dark too long. She squeezed her eyes shut and when she opened them again, she studied her surroundings. She was outside, in a courtyard. The flowers made the air smell sweet and made the garden look safe and pretty. The courtyard was isolated and looked like the perfect place to hide. In the middle was a fountain built of beautiful stones that glittered as they caught the sunlight. White stone paths radiated outward from it. In the middle of the fountain was a stone dancer. Her arms were in the air and her head was thrown back. Water flowed from her head as if it was her hair.

A young man was sitting on the wall at the edge of the fountain. He had a strong back and muscular arms. His skin was tanned and had a healthy glow. His blond hair shone in the sunlight. A bow and a quiver of arrows hung over his back. He was wearing leather clothes—clothes that she had never seen anyone wear before. He had his back turned to her. She imagined his face to be pretty. She watched him throw a coin into the water and wondered what he'd wished for.

Usually she would turn away. Caitlin didn't like talking to strangers and she didn't like making friends. But something about this man was familiar....

"What are you wishing for?" she asked.

Her voice made him jump to his feet and spin around. He had a handsome face. His pink lips were parted to reveal even, white teeth. His ocean-blue eyes fixed on her green ones. "You scared me," he laughed. "Not many people manage to do that." His laugh was low and surprisingly musical and made Caitlin's lips twitch into a smile.

Then she frowned. "I've been told I'm different from most people. But I don't know if it's a good thing."

"Being different can be hard," the man said and sat down again. He clearly didn't view women as a threat.

"How would you know?" she asked in confusion.

He tilted his head to the side. It was very rare that someone didn't know that he was a hunter. "Because most people I meet say I'm different too."

She walked closer to him. She could now see her reflection quivering and blurred in the water. Although she couldn't see herself clearly, she knew that she looked tired and that her hair was a mess. She tried shrugging her shoulders and noticed that they ached.

She started fidgeting and realized that she was feeling very self-conscious. So she turned away from her reflection and focused on the beautiful young man instead.

"So do you wish to be like most people then?" she asked as she eyed the many coins glinting under the water.

"Something like that. But not quite." He wanted an easier life. He wanted a good life. He wanted a life where he could do what he wanted to do instead of having to save everyone all the time. "I wouldn't want to be like most people."

"Why is that?" she asked.

"It would be boring," he shrugged. "Most people stay in one place their whole lives. They never live or learn. They just exist."

Caitlin thought about River Town and how boring and uneventful Maggie told her it was. Was she one of those people? She didn't want to be. "What would you like to be then?"

His blue eyes were on the shimmering water as he gave her a one-word answer: "Free."

She looked at the man. There was something about him that made her feel nervous but safe at the same time. He made her feel calm and controlled where Rafe made her feel rebellious and exhilarated.

"So be free then," she said as if it was that simple.

"It's not that easy," he sighed.

"Why not?"

The young man wondered if he should explain to her how complicated his life was. Would she even understand? "My job is... time-consuming," he ended up saying.

"So quit," she said and studied his face. He had a beautiful jawline. Every time he gritted his teeth, the muscles in his jaw bulged.

"It's not that simple," he sighed. "My job keeps people alive. I save lives. If I quit my job, people will die."

She tilted her head to the side. "Maybe I'm way off here... But you shouldn't be doing a job that makes you unhappy. Your unhappiness will slowly kill you."

"I'm not that unhappy," he said. But he knew it wasn't true. Day after day, he felt the unhappiness eat away at him. "My job is fulfilling in many ways," he argued, more to himself than to her.

Caitlin looked at him. She probably wasn't the best person to give life advice. And this man was a stranger! Yet they were talking about very personal things as if they trusted each other. "That's good," she said weakly, unable to think of anything else to say.

He smiled. "You don't know who I am, do you?"

"Should I?" she asked and sat down next to him. The stones were slowly warming up under the heat of the sun.

"Most people do," he said, smiling again. "Who are you?"

"Caitlin Wilde." *Not that there's much more I can really*

*tell you about myself,* she thought to herself.

For a moment he seemed to freeze up and he looked at her strangely. His look was a mixture of puzzlement and anxiety. She wondered if maybe they did know each other. When he didn't speak, she asked, "So what about you? Who are you?"

"Dylan Archer," he said with a slight bow of his head.

Caitlin usually didn't shake hands, but she found herself extending hers nonetheless. He hesitated before taking it in his and kissing it. Her cheeks went red and she wondered if anyone had ever kissed her hand before. Her hand felt warm when he let go—which made her blush even more.

"What happened to your shoulder?" he asked her.

"A dog bit me," she said.

"It looks painful," Dylan remarked.

"I heal fast," she said as if it was nothing.

"Do you need me to find you a healer?" he asked in a caring manner.

She could not understand why he would help her if there was nothing in it for him. His eyes didn't leave her wound. *Maybe he feels sorry for me?* she wondered. She thought about Healer Dan and shook her head. There was no way she was going back to a healer. "My family will take good care of me."

"That's what family is for," he said with a smile.

Caitlin's eyes strayed to his left hand and saw no ring on his finger. She wasn't sure why she checked. There was a moment of silence before she stood up.

"I should probably go."

"You don't have to," Dylan smiled. "I was enjoying your company."

"But we were sitting in silence."

"Comfortable silence," he corrected. "Besides, I was studying you."

"And what did you find?"

"You look like a fighter." His eyes lingered on her wounded shoulder.

"Is that good?"

"I guess it depends what you are fighting for."

She looked at all of the weapons strapped to his body. "What are you fighting for?"

"I fight to protect those who can't protect themselves," Dylan told her.

She heard the pride in his voice. "Quite the hero," she winked.

"Something like that."

"Goodbye, Dylan." She had to get back to her family to show them that she was alright. "It was nice meeting you."

"I'll see you around then?"

She nodded and started walking. When she was about ten feet away, she stopped and turned back to face him. "Dylan."

"Yes?" he looked up from the water.

"It's good to want to save people. But it's alright if you only save yourself."

She didn't know where those words came from.

Dylan brought out a deeper and wiser part of her that she didn't even know existed. After saying those words, she turned and walked away.

Dylan didn't respond but his eyes followed her.

# CHAPTER 37

RAFE RECEIVED NEWS from one of the guards that Caitlin was being released. He wondered why she was being released this early. He thought that they would keep her for much longer. It was a miracle.

His heart raced as he made his way to the room where they told him she would be—he couldn't wait to pull her close and breathe in her scent. He was happier than he had been in a long time.

He was hurrying along a corridor when he suddenly stopped at the sight of a beautiful courtyard filled with ferns and flowers and stone paths. He could hear the water falling from the dancer statue in the fountain: it sounded like tiny bells ringing.

But Rafe's eyes didn't linger on the beauty of the place. They were glued to the young man sitting at the fountain. He was, without a doubt, a hunter. The thought made Rafe freeze. The man hadn't seen him. He was staring at the water and was most likely lost in his own mind. *And there's no way he could know that I'm a shifter. So there was no reason to be scared,* Rafe reasoned to himself but kept his guard up anyway. He clenched his firsts. He knew coming to the castle was dangerous. He knew that the people here wanted him and his kind dead.

Then to his surprise, he heard her–Caitlin. She was speaking to the hunter. Rafe, as an experienced shifter, could use his wolf-like hearing without growing wolf ears. So that's what he did; he listened. And he watched. He could see her blush when the blond man kissed her hand. It made Rafe angry and nauseous at the same time. He had to stop himself from storming over to them and pulling her away from that terrible man, a killer of his kind.

He usually wasn't one to eavesdrop, but he couldn't walk away from their conversation. He had never heard Caitlin talk to anyone like that before. She was speaking as if she was old and wise and knew a lot more about the world than she actually did. He didn't know this side of Caitlin existed. He actually liked it and wished that she had chosen to share this side of her with him instead of with that man.

Rafe listened impatiently although he knew it was wrong to eavesdrop. He had enough self-control to stay where he was and wait for their conversation to end. When it finally ended and Caitlin left, he saw that the hunter stared after her with hungry eyes.

Rafe took a minute to collect himself before following Caitlin. He also wanted to stay out of the blond man's sight. It would be much safer for Rafe if the hunter knew nothing of his presence in Sky Castle.

As he hurried to catch up to Caitlin, his heart raced with excitement again. He couldn't wait to wrap his arms around her and pull her to his chest. Then his progress was stopped by a voice—

"Hello, Caitlin." A beautiful voice, like a songbird.

Caitlin jumped, startled. She looked to her right, where Lady Katherine emerged out of a dark hallway. Her midnight-blue dress pooled to the ground around her as she walked. The beads sewn in her dress matched her earrings and glittered like a thousand little stars. Her corset was tight and elegant. Her dark eyes were fixed on the younger girl.

Caitlin squirmed under Lady Katherine's gaze. She felt judged. She felt like she had to behave at her best. She felt the need to display her best manners, to stand up proudly. But even when she tried her best, she felt like it wasn't good enough.

"Milady," Caitlin said and then noticed that Katherine wasn't accompanied by her retinue of guards. *Maybe she feels safe walking around this part of the castle? There aren't many people here anyway.*

Caitlin realized that this was the first time she was completely alone with this king's right hand. She was sure not many people have been in a position like this.

Then she remembered all of the terrible things Rafe had said about the woman. So she tried her best to appear to be respectful because she felt that Lady Katherine would punish her for doing the smallest thing wrong.

But the woman didn't look evil to Caitlin. She looked mysterious and slightly intriguing, even beautiful. Her long lashes touched her cheeks when she blinked at Caitlin.

*"I think she's the only person who hates us more than the king."* Caitlin could still hear Rafe's words in her mind.

*Where is he anyway? Is he looking for me?* The thought of Rafe looking for her made her heart skip a beat. *Of course he won't stop until he finds me. But he'd probably never think of looking for me here in this beautiful court-yard, hidden deep within the castle.*

"I'm surprised to find you here," Katherine murmured in a low voice. "I thought you would be with your family by now."

"I was actually on my way to them," Caitlin said, although she had no idea how to get to their house. But she needed to find them soon so they would know that she was alright.

"How are you feeling?" the king's right hand asked with a raised eyebrow.

Caitlin knew the woman didn't care about her. She only cared about her people and was also suspicious of her. But Caitlin reasoned, *If she thought I was really dangerous, she wouldn't have let me go. She would have had me killed by now.* "I'm fine," she settled on a half-truth. She felt tired and sore but not sick at all. She didn't feel sick like yesterday—she felt like she has been fine all along.

"I didn't think you were going to make it," Lady Katherine said. But there was no sympathy in her voice, only astonishment. "You looked very ill yesterday. I find it strange that you made such a fast recovery."

Caitlin shrugged. *Strange.* She didn't like that word. If Lady Katherine Black thought something was strange, she would surely look into it. Caitlin didn't want to be investigated. She didn't want people watching her. "The healer probably knew what he was doing," she said with a half-smile.

Katherine didn't respond to that. She twirled her hair around her finger and looked Caitlin up and down with those judging eyes. Caitlin shifted her weight from foot to foot uncomfortably.

Then Katherine got to the point. "Someone in the castle wants you dead."

"What?" Caitlin blurted, her eyes widening. Lady Katherine's words were so unexpected and sudden that Caitlin needed a moment to process the fact that she was being warned. That was the last thing she expected to hear from the king's right hand.

"And this someone wants you dead badly," Katherine emphasized. There was nothing threatening in her voice.

Caitlin felt that the warning came from a genuine concern, and this surprised her. "I don't know what to say," she said. Her thoughts went to Nicolas Campbell.

If he had spoken to Lady Katherine, she would surely have had Caitlin killed by now because Campbell would have led her to believe that Caitlin was a witch, and the king's right hand wanted all witches killed, just like he did.

"He is, in fact, so serious about killing you that he has hired a famous assassin to do the job." Katherine sighed. A flicker of irritation lit her eyes before she read the confusion and surprise on Caitlin's face. "Yes, Nicolas Campbell. That man is an idiot to bring Black Blade here. He is a total moron for thinking that I wouldn't know. I know about everything that happens behind the castle walls."

"Apparently... But why are you telling me all this?" Caitlin asked.

"It would be a shame to see you dead after everything you've been through."

Caitlin thought about her town, now in cinders. She thought about all of the dead villagers. She felt the pain in her shoulder from the shifter's bite. But she didn't feel sad or traumatized. She actually felt just fine.

"Thank you for your concern, Milady, and for the warning," she said.

"You don't have many people to protect you here. You'll have to rely on yourself," Katherine said. These words meant that she didn't know about Rafe, and that made Caitlin feel relieved and happy. "My guards won't care much about a peasant like you. They will

347

only intercede if you cause a big enough scene. And then you could be thrown into the dungeons, along with your would-be assassin. I would prefer that my guards don't fight Black Blade. Dead guards are terribly costly to train and replace."

"I'll try to not get killed," Caitlin said, trying not to smile. "And I'll also try not to ask your guards for help."

"Ask your family for help instead," Katherine advised.

Caitlin's jaw dropped. "My family? But they are simple farmers. Not fighters."

"As are you," Katherine tilted her head to the side as if she expected Caitlin to object.

The younger girl realized just how different she viewed herself from her family. She wasn't scared to fight but her family would be. She remembered how scared they were when the wild dogs attacked. Until recently, they'd had little experience with violence. "I don't want to see them get hurt," Caitlin said.

"So if I were you, I'd leave the castle," Lady Katherine said. She didn't say it in a mean way. She didn't say it in an unwelcoming way either. She had merely resumed her role of court advisor.

Caitlin swallowed hard. She didn't want to leave. Where would she go? What would she tell Maggie? Her family would be worried, and she would be alone unless Rafe came with her. But he was keen on finding answers to his own questions here. She knew she wouldn't get him to leave easily. "I can't run out on my family," she told the lady. "It wouldn't be right."

"You're very loyal," Lady Katherine observed. "I hope it doesn't get you killed."

Caitlin had nothing more to say. They took stock of each other for a moment.

"Have a good day." And with that, Lady Katherine took her leave.

Caitlin started walking aimlessly down the corridor. She still didn't know which way was home.

# CHAPTER 38

"RAFE!" CAITLIN EXCLAIMED. She threw her arms around his neck and he pulled her into one of the tightest hugs ever. For a moment they just stood there, body against body. She leaned her head against his shoulder and closed her eyes. She didn't want the moment to ever end.

But it did end.

Rafe straightened his arms and gently pushed her a few inches away from him so that he could look at her with those beautiful gray eyes. Those storm-cloud eyes... "How are you feeling?" His eyes lingered on her shoulder.

"I'm fine. My shoulder will heal fast."

Rafe nodded but he didn't look convinced. He touched her bandages and she couldn't help but twitch. It was still sensitive.

"I am so sorry," he whispered.

"For what?" she asked confused.

His eyes met hers again and he clenched his jaw. Usually he would have taken a step back by now. Today he did not. "You weren't supposed to get bitten. I should have protected you."

"Don't feel guilty," she rolled her eyes. "I chose to save you."

"You shouldn't have," Rafe said. For once he was serious. His eyes burned into her and she felt like a child being scolded.

"What?" She took a step backward, suddenly irritated. He didn't even thank her. "Rafe, if that dog had bitten you instead of me..." She didn't have to explain what would have happened to him. She didn't want to say it out loud anyway. It was as if saying it out loud would have made it more real and worse.

"But you got sick," Rafe pointed out. "A non-Magic got sick from a Magical disease."

"Yes, that was strange, and I can't explain it," she replied.

They stood there thinking about it for a moment. Rafe studied her like there was something about her that he didn't know. She herself didn't know what that something was. She didn't know much about herself. Then she thought of something and decided to ask him. "Rafe, is it possible that I have Magic?"

"I don't know," Rafe said. "Maybe. Some people go their whole lives without knowing."

"Is there a way to tell?" she asked. "I remember how you could tell that Roxy was like you."

He shook his head. "That was different. I picked up her scent and I could tell that it was an animal scent, so that meant she was like me. I can't smell Magic in the general sense."

"Oh," Caitlin mumbled.

"This isn't really the place to talk about it," Rafe told her.

He extended his hand and she took it willingly. For the first time, she laced her fingers with his. Her thin fingers with long nails were the perfect counterpart to his big hands and cracked nails. His hand sent sparks up her arms and her heart beat a little faster. Rafe smiled at her and she wondered if he was listening to her heartbeat. She squeezed his hand. It felt so right.

He sniffed the air.

"What is it?" she asked.

"I thought I smelled something," he said. Then he shook his head like he was shaking away the thought. "Let me take you home."

She nodded. But with Rafe by her side and her hand in his, she felt that she was already home.

Daisy started crying when she saw her older daughter. Tears of happiness rolled down her cheeks and onto Caitlin as she embraced her. Two weeks ago, this would have bothered Caitlin. She might even have found it gross. But now she just let the woman hug her and cry it out. Caitlin wanted Daisy to feel better, and if this was what it took, then Caitlin could stand still for a while.

"It's alright," Caitlin said in a soothing voice. She wasn't very good at comforting people. "I am alright."

Rafe stood behind her, watching them. He heard Daisy call Gerald and Maggie. Both of them came out of the house. They were smiling.

"Sister!" Maggie yelled and ran toward Caitlin. She threw her arms around Caitlin's waist and squeezed. Then Caitlin picked her up, making the six-year-old laugh. Maggie touched the necklace around Caitlin's neck, the one that she had made for her sister's birthday. She knew that Caitlin never took it off.

Gerald embraced them both as Daisy wiped away tears with a handkerchief. She couldn't stop smiling. Having her daughter back was the best feeling in the world.

"What did they say?" Gerald asked. "The healers?"

"Not much," Caitlin confessed as she thought about Healer Dan and how she had fled from that room. "They don't know why I got sick. They only know that I am better now."

"You being healthy is all that matters," Gerald said. He wasn't crying but he was just as happy as Daisy.

Rafe leaned against the wall watching the reunion. He kept his distance and didn't say anything, but he didn't feel out of place. He wasn't one of them but he still shared in their happiness. They wanted him with them.

"You should see the house!" Maggie exclaimed.

"And there's a beautiful pool for swimming nearby," Rafe told her.

"Really?! Can we please go swimming?" Maggie asked, her face swinging from Caitlin to Rafe and back again.

Caitlin laughed as she agreed but first she wanted a tour of the house. Then she needed a bite to eat.

Daisy and Gerald decided not to accompany the kids to the pool for swimming. Daisy was still setting up house and wanted Gerald's help. He said that he was starting his new job tomorrow; he was going to be training as a blacksmith. He was excited because the job paid much more than cutting wood in River Town. He wouldn't need to farm to feed his family anymore.

Living in the castle was much nicer than living in a small town. They had everything they needed, and more. There were more than enough shops to buy food. There were shops for everything, not just for food and necessities—shops for fabrics and clothes, jewelry, toys for kids, furniture, trappings for horseback riding and carriages, and the list went on and on. The castle even had a bookstore. If someone needed something, then someone was sure to be selling it somewhere.

Gerald watched his two girls walk away with Rafe.

Maggie was skipping around and talking nonstop about the marvels of a man-made pool for swimming. Caitlin was looking up at Rafe through her eyelashes. They both looked happy.

Gerald reluctantly turned his attention to what he was doing. He didn't like doing housework, especially decorating. Although he was good at fixing things, the house was in good order and didn't need any fixing, so he was fast getting bored. He was relieved when a young blond man knocked on the door. He could stop working to talk to the guest.

"Hello," the young man said, holding out his hand. "I am Dylan Archer."

Gerald's eyes widened as he immediately knew who the boy was. He'd never met a hunter before, and this one was much younger than he thought a hunter would be. He certainly carried a lot of weapons. "I'm Gerald Wilde," he said and shook hands enthusiastically. The boy had a strong handshake which made Gerald like him immediately. "It's a pleasure to meet you. What brings you here?"

"The king asked my father and me to come to the castle, as he requires our services. I heard about what happened to your town and was wondering if I could ask you some questions."

"Of course," Gerald invited him inside. "Would you like anything to drink?" As he asked this, he realized that they only had water. There hadn't been any time to buy ale or anything else. Luckily the boy declined.

"What is it you would like to know?" Gerald asked as he took a seat in the living room. The couches and chairs were comfortable, stuffed with horsehair and feathers, much nicer than anything they had owned in River Town.

"What happened to your town?" Dylan asked.

"Didn't the king tell you?" Gerald asked.

"He has only spoken to my father" Dylan said. "Besides, I would like to hear the tale directly, from one of the survivors."

"Alright," Gerald said eagerly. He felt proud: he and his entire family had survived. He told Dylan about how the bear lady ripped the town apart and about all the villagers dying. But he didn't mention that the villagers had wanted to burn him and his family.

"I am sorry about your town," Dylan said.

Gerald imagined that this wasn't the first time Dylan had heard a story like this. He had probably handled many similar situations with ease. He had probably killed many monsters in his young life.

"How did the bear die?" Dylan asked.

"My daughter killed it," Gerald said proudly.

"She killed it all by herself?" Dylan asked with raised eyebrows. He thought about the girl he had met at the fountain. *You look like a fighter*, was what he had told her and he had been right. He was usually right when it came to judging people.

"Yes," Gerald said with his head held high.

"How is that possible?" Dylan asked. "She's just a

farm girl."

"Well she's very smart. She killed it by stabbing it with a pitchfork in the stomach." Gerald continued to talk. "I'm not even sure how she did it. But she did what no one else in that town could do."

Dylan wasn't there to talk about the town or the shifters. He was hoping to learn more about Caitlin Wilde so he continued to press along this line of questioning. "That's impressive," Dylan admitted. "Does she have a fighting history?"

"Well no," Gerald said. "Living in River Town is peaceful. Growing up, she never had to learn how to fight—although she does like getting into arguments."

"Don't all women?" Dylan winked.

"She's a little worse than most," Gerald confessed, answering with a grin. He loved his daughter, but she was very stubborn and believed that her way was always right. That was one of the many character-istics that she didn't share with the rest of her family. "I'm sorry that she isn't here to meet you."

"Where is she, if I may ask?" Dylan tried not to sound too curious although he was dying to know what this girl did with her free time.

"She's swimming with her little sister and our travel companion. They went to that pool made just for swimming."

"Travel companion?" Dylan asked. "Is she also from River Town?"

"He," Gerald corrected. "No, he is from Southpaw."

Dylan frowned. He only went to Southpaw once, and he was a kid back then. He didn't have a good recollection of the place. "That's far away."

Gerald nodded. "Yes, he came here seeking work."

Dylan thought about this. Why would someone travel that far for work? There should be more than enough work in Southpaw. "That's a bit odd," he said.

"Rafe is an odd guy," Gerald affirmed. "But he has a good heart."

Dylan asked about their journey and Gerald told him about the attack by the wild dogs on their way into the castle. "My whole life I have only heard about these monsters. And now in two weeks my family and I have been attacked twice!"

"The shifters have been acting crazy," Dylan told Gerald. Dylan was worried but there was no way he would confess his fears to Gerald. It was his job to reassure people and make them feel safe. But keeping people safe was getting harder and harder. If the shifters kept acting crazy, the hunters would have to start thinking of a better plan to get them under control.

Dylan tried to find out more about Caitlin and wondered when Gerald would notice that he was asking more questions about his daughter than about the shifters. But he didn't learn much. Only that she was hot-headed and headstrong and grew up in one town. This was the farthest that she had ever been away from home.

Dylan thought about what that swamp witch had

told him about the girl. He wondered if he had found the right Caitlin Wilde. She didn't seem dangerous at all. Maybe the witch was batty.

Then Dylan remembered that the witch had said that she had actually met Caitlin Wilde. What had the girl been doing at the witch's house? Surely, she knew that she could be killed for going there.... He'd have to get to know her better to find out. Something told him that she was very different from other small-town farm girls.

"Dylan?" Gerald asked.

"I'm sorry. I was just thinking about something.... Would you mind repeating the question?"

"I was asking how many shifters you plan to kill before you retire?"

Dylan knew the answer. "All of them."

# CHAPTER 39

"STOP THAT!" CAITLIN said as Rafe splashed her in the face. The pool for swimming was amazing, its walls and floor were lined with stone mosaics of water lilies and fishes. The water was cool, clean, and clear.

"Fine," he said.

Then he grabbed her and pushed her head under the water. She squirmed and he let go. She tried to dunk him too but he was stronger so she couldn't.

Maggie also didn't know how to swim. Rafe started teaching her but she was a much slower learner than Caitlin. She tired quickly and decided to stick to the shallow end of the pool.

"It's very strange that you two can't swim," Rafe said to Caitlin. "There is so much water in the Riverlands...."

"I can't explain it either."

"Caitlin!" Maggie called. She climbed out of the pool.

"Look at the kitty!"

Caitlin's eyes followed her sister's to where a black cat was sitting on the wall beside the pool. The cat sat with her head held high, like she was royalty, and coolly observed them looking down at them like they were vermin. She was a typical cat—thinking she was above everyone else.

Maggie got out of the pool and reached for the cat.

"Don't pet it!" Caitlin said. "She could be sick! Stray cats have all kinds of diseases."

But Maggie didn't listen. She stroked the cat's head. The cat looked at her with a bored expression. Eventually the girl scratched the right spot on her back. The cat purred and arched her back in pleasure.

"I don't think she is a stray cat," Maggie said. "She is in great condition."

"She's most likely someone's pet then," Rafe said. He stayed in the pool as he didn't want to scare the cat off. He always scared away animals by simply being himself.

"So we can't keep her?" Maggie asked, the hope in her tone contradicting her words.

"No," Caitlin said sternly. "We can't take someone else's pet. They will miss her. How would you feel if someone took Star?"

Maggie's eyes went to the ground sadly. She understood that she couldn't have the cat. It wouldn't be right.

"Maybe she will come visit us," Maggie said with the hope of a child.

361

"Maybe," Caitlin said, although she doubted it.

The castle was big, so they were probably never going to see the cat again. Caitlin wondered if they could get Maggie a pet. The little girl needed something to love and her heart hurt after two of their horses ran away. She wondered if Gerald was going to sell Star and Misty. Now that they lived in the castle there was no need for them anymore.

"What are you thinking?" Rafe asked. For the first time in his life he really wanted to get to know someone. He wanted to know what she thought and why. He wanted to get to know her better than anyone else. Maybe he would even get to know her better than she knew herself.

Caitlin realized that while she was thinking, she was also staring at Rafe. His wet hair clung to his face and he was shirtless. There were no scars on his side where the bear had sunk in its claws. She was glad her parents weren't here to see that. They would have found it odd and disturbing.

Rafe was smiling at her and was standing very close. In times like this, it often felt like they were the only two people on the planet. Like everything else around them just faded away.

"Wow," Rafe said. "I take my shirt off and you are at a loss of words."

"I have decided it's good that you flatter yourself," Caitlin shot back. "Because no one else is going to do it."

"Ouch," Rafe laughed.

She splashed him again and he splashed back. He grabbed her arm and pulled her closer. She knew he was going to dunk her even before he did. There was nothing she could do to stop him. She gasped for air when he let her up and she tried to pull free.

"Maybe you should pick on someone your own size," Rafe teased.

She tried to slap him playfully, but he caught her arm and held it behind her back. Her body pressed against his. Usually she hated looking up at people—it made her feel small and weak. But when she looked up at Rafe, she felt safe and protected.

"Actually, I'm glad you're bigger than most wolves," she breathed.

Rafe gave her a dirty smile.

"I didn't mean it like *that!*" Her cheeks were blood-red as she pulled free. A small space separated them. Rafe was smiling way too arrogantly and so she splashed him again.

Neither of them saw Campbell—Nicolas Campbell, who was staring at them from one of the windows high in the castle.

She was right there in his sight. He stood by a huge window in one of the lower towers that overlooked a good part of the castle grounds, including the pool.

At first he thought his eyes were deceiving him, but they weren't. Caitlin Wilde had finally come to the castle. She was alive and well. Despite the bandage on her shoulder, she looked healthy and happy. She was laughing like a little kid and splashing around foolishly.

Black Blade hadn't killed her yet. Campbell wasn't going to depend on the assassin either. He didn't want her to get away again.

His eyes studied the young man with the dark hair. His skin was very pale. He couldn't be from the region. The two of them were acting like they had known each other forever. It took Nicolas Campbell a moment to realize who the man was. He remembered the wolf that had so annoyingly saved her from burning in River Town. But why would a shifter be dumb enough to come to Sky Castle?

It didn't matter to Campbell. If there was a shifter in the castle, it should be killed. And everyone who knew about it and reported it should be killed too.

Campbell smiled. Getting rid of the girl was going to be easier than he thought. He turned from the window and went to request an audience with the king.

He was important enough for the king to hear him out. Lady Katherine was going to be furious that he didn't consult her first, but he didn't care. He wanted the king to have the girl and the wolf killed before the day was done.

He arrived in the throne room and waited. There were guards on either side of him. They didn't stand too close to him and he was thankful for that. He hated feeling boxed in or treated like a prisoner. The guards didn't want to intimidate him anyway. He wasn't a threat; he was simply there to help. He was there to see that justice would be done.

The king entered and sat down on his throne. He was a big man with hairy arms and a beard. He was very intimidating although he didn't have any weapons. "Campbell," he said in a deep voice that rattled the throne room walls.

"Your Highness," Campbell said with a low bow.

"What brings you here?" the king asked.

"A terrible crime has been committed," Campbell stated. "And I must report it. I just had to tell you, My Lord."

"Well, get on with it, man. What is it?" the king growled. He didn't have time to waste on groveling idiots. He wanted the man to get straight to the point.

Campbell knew the king didn't like having meetings with his people. That's why he had Lady Katherine as his right hand. She did most of the work while he lay back and relaxed.

The door opened again before Campbell could answer, and Lady Katherine walked in. Her lips were pressed together and her eyes burned into Campbell. She walked with a fast pace, bowed to the king and then took her seat beside him. "I wasn't told that you wanted to speak," she said to Campbell, not bothering to hide her annoyance. "Why waste the king's precious time and not just come to me instead?"

"I felt that this was a matter for the king, Milady." Campbell said, casting his eyes down toward her feet instead of her face. He could feel the anger radiating from her.

"I have a feeling you're only here to waste time," she said bluntly. "What is the matter?"

"There is a shifter in the castle," Campbell said, raising his eyes to meet the king's and not Lady Katherine's.

King Leonard leaned forward in his seat. "WHAT?" he roared.

Campbell felt relieved. Now he had the king's attention.

Lady Katherine sat as still as the grave. Although the king was shouting, she was the one that scared Campbell the most. She was unpredictable, explosive —you never knew when she would explode.

"What shifter? Where is it?" the king boomed.

"This is rubbish," Lady Katherine said calmly. Then she fixed her dark eyes on Campbell. "Lying to the king will get you beheaded."

"I am not lying," Campbell insisted. His fists were clenched at his side. He was aware that his hands were shaking.

"No shifter is stupid enough to come to this castle,"

Lady Katherine said. They hadn't had a shifter problem in the castle in years. Shifters only strayed into isolated areas and small towns where few or no threats to them existed.

The king held up his hand to silence her. She obeyed but Campbell could tell she was annoyed from the way she drummed her fingers on her chair's arm. She didn't like following orders—even if those orders came from her king.

"The girl, Caitlin Wilde, has brought a shifter into the castle. She is his friend. She is his ally," Campbell explained.

"Where do I find these two?" the king asked.

Campbell tried to hide his smile. "They are swimming in the nearby pool, Your Majesty."

The king ordered his guards to apprehend them immediately and the guards marched hurriedly out of the throne room. The sooner they got this done the better.

Campbell remained in the throne room and waited patiently. He was going to enjoy watching Caitlin Wilde and her wolf friend die.

# CHAPTER 40

DYLAN HID BEHIND a stone pillar near the pool, watching Caitlin splashing around. Everything about her seemed normal. She laughed a lot and was playful. She was beautiful, and although she seemed a little uncomfortable in the water, she was a strong athlete. Her wet clothes clung to her hourglass figure showing off her physique. She was so pretty and didn't look like a typical farm girl. Dylan tried to focus on studying her behavior instead of her body.

"*By the time you hear of her being a threat it will be too late,*" the witch had said. "*The castle isn't a good place for her. You should take her away.*"

But there was nothing dangerous about her and she looked happy in the castle. She was also with good parents who cared for her. A blind man could see that her little sister looked up to her and her family adored her.

It was the man that was with her that was different. Dylan guessed he was the travel companion that Gerald had mentioned earlier. Gerald didn't need to tell him that Rafe was from Southpaw for him to know. The man's skin was as white as milk.

Dylan watched the way he looked at Caitlin. Rafe didn't come to the castle just for work but also for her. Dylan could tell by the way he was looking at her that he wanted her all for himself. This was obvious from his flirty smile and the way he tried to make her laugh and the way he touched her every chance he got.

Dylan could tell that Caitlin enjoyed the attention. She blushed and giggled like a little girl. She acted nothing like the wise and calm woman that he had met in the courtyard.

Dylan stepped around the stone pillar and walked up to them. "Do you mind if I join?" he asked politely.

"Dylan!" Caitlin exclaimed and splashed him playfully. She was still smiling and didn't greet him formally. But that did not matter because she looked at him in a welcoming way and that made him never want to leave her side. He took a few steps backward and laughed as the water dripped off his body.

"Don't you have work to do?" Rafe asked the hunter. His smile had faded the moment he saw Dylan. His lips were pressed together tightly and his eyes were cold. Most people looked at Dylan with respect and fear. But Rafe looked at Dylan with antagonism and Dylan immediately sensed it.

"I'm taking the day off," Dylan said evenly. He would have shaken Rafe's hand if Rafe hadn't looked at him like he was going to bite his head off. Dylan wondered if he had made a bad first impression. And if so, what had he done?

People didn't like to befriend hunters; they were scared of them. But usually their fear triggered respect. This time it was different.

"I didn't mean to intrude," Dylan continued. "I've only just arrived at the castle and I don't have any friends here."

"I can't imagine why," Rafe said under his breath. His eyes were on the bow that, as always, was strapped to Dylan's back.

Caitlin looked from one to the other. Rafe was tense and that made her tense too. She wasn't used to seeing him behave rudely or meanly toward another person without reason. It put her on edge. "Rafe, this is Dylan; Dylan, Rafe," she said awkwardly, trying to bridge the hostility between the two young men.

Rafe looked at him and climbed out of the pool so that he didn't have to look up at the man. "Why do you carry your weapons everywhere?" Rafe asked. "You're in the castle. It's as safe from Magic as any place."

Dylan tilted his head. It's not often that someone

said the M-word, and if they did, they were a little scared of saying it out loud. They would say the word slowly and cautiously, in a low voice, or stutter, or simply mumble it. This arrogant man stood there, blurting it out like it was an everyday word. In short, Dylan didn't like him. He didn't like his attitude. He didn't like the way Rafe treated him. He didn't like the way he walked around like he owned the place. He didn't like that Rafe was the only man he'd ever met who didn't show a hint of fear toward him, a hunter. "You never know what's waiting where," Dylan answered after a pause.

"Are you sure you're not just scared of your own shadow?" Rafe asked with a snicker.

Their eyes locked. Neither of them looked away.

"What's going on?" Caitlin asked. She felt excluded and didn't understand why both of them were acting this way.

"I'm leaving," Rafe said. "I want to explore the castle a bit. Come with me?" He turned his eyes away from Dylan and looked pleadingly at Caitlin.

"But I'm still enjoying the water," Caitlin said. It wasn't a lie. The day was warm and the water was perfect, cool and refreshing. Besides that, she didn't want to be with Rafe when he was acting this way.

"Please," Rafe begged.

Caitlin shook her head. She had made up her mind and there was no changing it.

Then little Maggie ran to Rafe. "I'll come!" The cat

was still sitting on the wall, staring longingly at Maggie who had just abandoned her.

Rafe tugged on his shirt and hesitantly took the six-year-old's hand. Then the two walked away without a backward glance—the smaller one was skipping happily, while the bigger one was marching stiffly.

"I'm sorry," Caitlin said to Dylan who just stood there. "Usually he is much nicer. I don't know what his problem is today."

"I'm his problem," Dylan laughed.

"Why would you be his problem? He doesn't even know you." Caitlin frowned.

"But he knows what I am," Dylan said.

She looked at him with a confused expression on her face. She swam to the edge of the pool so that she was closer to Dylan and didn't have to raise her voice. "What are you?"

"I am an arch warrior. I'm more commonly known as a hunter. I hunt and kill Magical creatures."

Caitlin tried not to look shocked. No wonder Rafe wanted to get away as fast as possible. Caitlin now regretted not going with him. How had she not realized what Dylan was? She looked at the strong, protective clothes he wore, at all of the weapons he carried.

Dylan caught her gaze and put his weapons down. Then he removed his shoes and socks, put his feet in the cold water, and sighed.

"I didn't realize," Caitlin said honestly.

"It's alright if you want to run away from me now," Dylan said sadly. "That's what most people do."

"I'm not scared of you," she smiled at him.

A part of her told her that she should leave. Her loyalty was with Rafe and he had all the reason in the world to hate hunters. But Caitlin related to Dylan. She understood his loneliness and how it felt to be different. He was looking sadder than he had at the fountain. She didn't like that, so she splashed him again. "Are you scared of the water? Is that why only your feet are in?"

"I thought you might not want me swimming with you," he said honestly. "I'm used to being the outsider."

"If you only kill monsters and not non-Magic folk, why would people be scared of you?"

"Well, some hunters have made mistakes before. They have killed innocent people because they thought they had Magic." Dylan confessed.

"That's bad," Caitlin said although she felt no pity. She didn't care much about most people or what happened to them. She only had a few selective people that she cared about.

He nodded. "And I'm different. People are scared of 'different.'"

"But there are others like you," she said.

"Yes, there are. We are scattered throughout the Silver Kingdom."

Caitlin looked at his weapons. There were so many of them. She wondered how many shifters he had killed.

She wondered if he enjoyed killing. "*I fight to protect those who can't protect themselves,*" Dylan had told her.

"Do all hunters fight to protect normal people?" she asked.

He nodded. "We take great pride in keeping everyone safe."

"And what about the shifters who can't protect themselves?" Caitlin asked in a low voice. All of her playfulness had vanished. She didn't intend to start a fight but at the same time she couldn't keep her mouth shut. "Do you kill them too?"

Dylan's expression changed to an irritated one. "Of course. They are still Magic folk."

"But what if they aren't killers?"

"All shifters are killers," Dylan glared. He didn't want to talk to her about this anymore. She didn't understand. *Why doesn't she understand?* Most people disliked hunters, but they still supported them. They understood how important a hunter's job was. If hunters didn't kill shifters, innocent people would die.

"How do you know that?" she asked.

She pictured Rafe in her mind. He was a shifter. But he wasn't a killer. He wasn't a bad person. He most certainly did not deserve to die.

"Are you sympathizing with the Magic folk?" Dylan asked. He didn't give her time to answer. "It's a risky thing to do."

Caitlin's anger boiled over. "Are you threatening me?" She felt like picking a fight. She felt like punching him in his pretty face. She didn't agree with him and he wasn't even trying to understand her point. She was about to get nastier with him but—

"There!" a voice yelled.

Both of them turned in unison to see ten guards rushing toward them as if they were fugitives.

"Seize them!" one yelled.

"What's going on?" Dylan asked them.

He was answered with a punch in the face that knocked him sideways. He sprang to his bare feet. He could easily take out the five guards that crowded around him. But what was the point in fighting? He knew he didn't do anything wrong. This was all just one big mistake. Two guards grabbed his hands and tied them behind his back. He let them do this without resisting.

Another grabbed a handful of Caitlin's hair and pulled her out of the pool. She screamed and then punched the guard. It was a good, hard hit that sent him to the floor. The other men went for her.

"Don't fight!" Dylan advised. "This must be a misunderstanding."

Caitlin struggled against them but tried not to fight. She didn't want to make the situation worse, but she also didn't want to lose a fight. She was terrible when it came to surrendering. The men handled her roughly, tying her hands behind her back, and that made her want to punch them even more.

The guards dragged them through the corridors and

into the throne room, where many heads turned to stare at them. Caitlin was too angry to be embarrassed and Dylan was used to people gawking at him.

Caitlin had no idea why they were being taken to the throne room. Then the doors swung open and her eyes met the familiar eyes of an old man—Campbell. He smiled at her, clearly pleased with himself.

# CHAPTER 41

RAFE WANTED TO slam his fist into a wall. Why did she have to be so stubborn? Why couldn't she just do the one thing that he'd asked of her? It wasn't like he asked much.

He didn't want to leave her with Dylan. Everything inside of him screamed that he should take her away from that monster. She should not be anywhere near that murderer.

For now, he had to control his anger. Little Maggie was with him and she wouldn't understand why he was so angry. She was an innocent and didn't need to know what Dylan was or what he did for a living. Rafe looked down at Maggie as she held his hand. She followed him wherever he walked and pointed to flowers and people and pretty houses. She was at the age where the world was still a beautiful place. Rafe admired how she found good in everything.

"Can we go shopping?" Maggie asked him.

Rafe hated shopping but he couldn't say no to those cute wide eyes. So they headed to the shops. He ended up buying her a news dress and a string of pearls that were much too expensive for the Wilde family to afford. Rafe didn't have a lot of money either, but Maggie's face lit up when she saw the outfit and he didn't have the heart to tell her that she couldn't have it. So he bought it for her and carried the bag while she skipped around him.

They decided to take a different route home.

"Is that a library?" Maggie gaped as she pointed at a big building.

It was truly impressive. The windows were decorated with glass art and the door had huge ancient handles. Inside were rows and rows of books that they could glimpse through the open doors.

"It sure looks like it," Rafe said.

"Can we go look?" Maggie asked. "I've never seen a library before. I've only heard about them from visitors to our village. Can we go in?" She didn't give Rafe a chance to answer. She dashed right in.

He followed her inside and wondered how well the little girl could read. He knew a lot of people who grew up in small towns and never learned to read or write.

"I love stories," she told him once he'd caught up to her.

Rafe had been inside a few libraries which existed only in large cities. He valued the institution and the idea of safeguarding knowledge for future generations. He guided her to a section furnished with small tables and chairs. Its walls were decorated with happy, colorful pictures. Its shelves were filled with books for children.

Rafe looked around but he didn't see any children besides Maggie who immediately grabbed a book with a gold spine and started paging through it, her mouth ajar, oohing and aahing over the many colorful illustrations inside. She marveled at the exquisite handiwork of the book clerics who lived in silence and seclusion and spent most of their lives quietly scribing, illustrating, and binding one book after another.

"If you want you can choose some books and I will rent them for you," Rafe offered.

"You're the best!" she exclaimed. "Will you read them to me too?"

"I think you should read them to me instead," Rafe replied.

She thought about this for a moment and then she started sorting through the books. She looked at some that contained a lot of pictures. "I'm not a very good reader," she confessed shyly.

"Maybe you just haven't had enough practice. I can teach you." Rafe's eyes scanned over the library's collection. It was the biggest one he had ever seen. There were books on every subject. There was so much he could learn from these pages. "Maggie," he said. "I'm going to go look at some other books while you look at those. Take your time, but stay in this section so that I can find you easily."

She nodded but didn't look up from the books.

Rafe walked toward the librarian. She was a short woman with droopy skin and tangled hair. She looked quite old. She wore spectacles with thick lenses and her nose was stuck in a book.

"Excuse me," Rafe said to her. "Do you know where I can find books about the Silver Kingdom? Books containing detailed maps?"

"Of course I do!" the librarian said and closed the book she was reading. "I've worked in this library all my life, young man."

Together the two of them walked up a flight of stairs and then she pointed down an aisle. "You should find everything there is to know about the kingdom here."

"Thank you," Rafe said.

The old librarian slowly walked back down the flight of stairs. She grunted as she walked and then settled back to studying her own book.

Rafe walked down the aisle and scanned the book topics. The librarian was right—there were books on everything about the kingdom and its castle. He even found a book about the castle's gardens. But he didn't care much about gardens. The real reason he was here was because he had been wondering about River Town for a while now. He didn't know that the town had even existed until he had accidently found himself there. But then he had never seen a map of the entire kingdom and so it wasn't strange that he didn't know it was there.

What was strange was that no one else seemed to know about it either.

"*River Town was small and not many people know about it*," Lady Katherine had said. "*You will not tell anyone where you are from. I don't want the people to be frightened, or to know that the shifters destroyed a whole town. You are welcome to stay in the castle. I will arrange jobs for everyone here and you will be safe. As for the shifters, I will hire the best hunters to kill them.*"

Caitlin had told Rafe what Lady Katherine had said when they were touring through the house earlier. So Lady Katherine knew about the town, but most people didn't. How many people knew about the place?

Rafe thought back to when they were visiting Ears. Ears had guessed that Caitlin was from Sky Castle. But when Caitlin had corrected her and explained that she was from River Town, the witch had said that she'd never heard of it. And Ears was supposed to know A LOT. She was supposed to know about a lot of people and a lot of places. Rafe couldn't help but find it strange that no one, especially Ears, knew about this town.

He went through the books until he found a detailed map of the Silver Kingdom. He studied the map and located the region where River Town should have been. But it was not there. He closed the book and looked for another book with maps. He found many books and many maps but none of them even mentioned a place called River Town in the Silver Kingdom.

It was as if the place never existed. Rafe continued searching but found nothing.

"I'd say you're from the castle."

Had Ears truly guessed wrong?

# CHAPTER 42

CAMPBELL'S SMILE FADED when he saw Dylan. This blond-haired man wasn't the one he had seen swimming with Caitlin earlier. That young man—the one he had thought was a shifter—had dark hair, but maybe he was just a friend she had recently made here at the castle. Did that mean this blond man standing before them now was the shifter? He didn't resemble the wolf as much as the dark-haired one did....

Campbell wanted to speak up. He wanted to tell the king that he wasn't sure if this was the man. He didn't want to look like an idiot. But when he opened his mouth, Lady Katherine silenced him immediately.

"Is this the girl?" the king asked.

"Yes, Milord." Campbell said through his teeth. He wanted to say more but he felt suffocated.

Five guards surrounded her, but she didn't look

scared, only angry when they forced her to her knees in front of the king. One guard's face was purple and Campbell knew she had hit him.

"Then this must be the monster," the king said and looked at Dylan.

"Actually–" Campbell started but the king spoke over him.

"Kill them both," the king said.

Campbell had a moment to feel victorious and then Lady Katherine interrupted with a laugh. "My Lord," she purred. "It appears to me that this man has lied to you."

"What?!" the king asked. He looked toward his right hand. He trusted Lady Katherine and he listened to her. He believed her word above everyone else's.

Campbell felt his knees wobble. This wasn't the way he had wanted things to go. His hands fumbled nervously at his sides and he resisted the urge to speak out.

"I know both this man and this woman," Katherine said. "Neither of them have Magic."

The guards stood their ground and awaited further orders. They still held onto the prisoners' arms, expecting them to fight or run away. But Caitlin knew that if she tried to escape, she would be killed immediately.

Dylan looked irritated. He had been invited to the castle and this was how he was treated–like he was the bad guy. He looked at Caitlin and waited for her to explode. Luckily she didn't. He then looked at Lady Katherine as she spoke. *Is she the only one with brains around here?* he fumed.

"This woman is a victim of Magic. Her town was destroyed by it," Katherine explained. "She came to the castle seeking refuge."

Caitlin tried to meet her eyes. She was trying to figure out what the woman was thinking. Why was she helping them? She owed them nothing and surely she had better things to do than intercede on their behalf? What was it to her if they died?

"This man was invited here by us," the king's advisor continued. "He is here to help get the shifter situation under control."

The king looked more closely at Dylan. "I spoke to Liam Archer yesterday. You resemble him."

Dylan held his ground and met the king's stare. "I am his son, Dylan Archer, Milord."

Most of the anger disappeared from the king's face as he realized that he had the wrong people. Then his eyes found Campbell's and the anger returned.

"I can explain!" Campbell cried out in fear.

At a nod from Lady Katherine, the guards let go of Caitlin and Dylan and untied their hands. It felt good to be free. Caitlin rubbed her wrists where the ropes had constricted the blood flow.

Two guards grabbed Campbell and forced him to his knees in front of the king. He was trembling like a scared child. He started mumbling desperately.

"Be quiet!" Katherine told him.

Campbell ignored her and turned his frantic eyes to the king. "Milord—"

"Gag him," Lady Katherine ordered. "I don't want to hear another lie from his mouth!"

Caitlin watched Campbell try to wiggle free. His eyes were watery and his body was shaking. She felt no sympathy for him.

"My King," Lady Katherine said. She stood from her chair and turned to face him. "This man has lied to you. He has deceived you and he has wasted your precious time." The corners of her mouth twisted into a nasty snarl. "He has also brought an assassin to the castle. He is a threat to us all."

Lady Katherine was a very smart woman. She chose her words wisely. Caitlin watched as the king listened to everything she said. Caitlin wondered briefly who was really ruling the kingdom.

"Behead him," the king commanded.

Campbell's screams were muffled by the gag. He was dragged out of the throne room. He kicked furiously, trying to break free, but was no match for the guards.

"You two should go watch," the king told Dylan and Caitlin. "Watch as he dies the way he wanted you to die." There was a moment of silence. "Why did he want you dead?"

Caitlin didn't know why Campbell wanted her dead, but she was sure that he wanted Rafe instead of Dylan. It was just good luck that Rafe had left the pool before the guards had shown up. She didn't say anything.

"He was a Magic sympathizer," Lady Katherine came to their aid again. "He wanted the famed hunter of the shifters and his friend both killed. So he falsely accused them of being Magic folk so that you would condemn them to death."

The king believed her. Caitlin wondered if the king would believe anyone else as easily—probably not.

King Leonard stood from his throne and left. Caitlin felt more relaxed after his exit. It felt like a mountain was lifted off her shoulders.

"My apologies to both of you," Lady Katherine said kindly. "Would either of you like to watch the execution?"

"No, thank you." Dylan said. "I take no pleasure in death."

These weren't words that Caitlin expected to hear from a hunter. She watched him bow and then leave the room with a confident stride.

"Unlike my friend, I would like to watch him die," Caitlin confessed.

Lady Katherine walked down to Caitlin and together their left for the execution block. Caitlin followed Lady Katherine to a balcony where they had an unobstructed view of Campbell. He was crying as his head was forced down onto the block—a large hunk of wood stained dark with the blood of many men.

A small crowd of people had gathered to watch him die. Caitlin searched their faces, but she didn't know any of them. None of them looked very sad. Caitlin wondered if Campbell had a family that would miss him.

"Does he really deserve to die?" Caitlin asked the lady softly. She actually didn't care about him, but he might have provided her with answers, or at least clues, about her past. *He knows who I am. Why else would he want me dead so badly?*

"I would think you'd be pleased to see him with his head on a block," Lady Katherine said. She turned her big eyes to Caitlin.

Caitlin found it a little intimidating to keep eye contact. "I am," she admitted, forcing her voice to sound normal. "But I still don't know why he wanted me dead so badly."

"Does his motive really matter?" Lady Katherine said. "The way I see it, the situation is simple. He wants you dead and you want to live. All that matters is that you get what you want. The rest is irrelevant."

Caitlin knew she wasn't in a position to argue. She wanted to talk to Campbell badly though. She had so many questions to ask.

"But there has to be a story behind it," Caitlin told Katherine. "He was the leader at River Town. He wanted me dead even before the town was destroyed."

"So what is it you want to ask him?" Lady Katherine asked. "Why he doesn't like you?"

"I want to ask him who I am that he wants me dead so badly," Caitlin said.

"Don't ever ask someone to tell you who you are," Lady Katherine advised. "That is for you and you alone to decide." She turned away and Caitlin knew the discussion was over.

Lady Katherine cleared her throat and then addressed

the people. "May this death serve as an example to us all that lying to the king and sympathizing with Magic are unforgivable crimes."

The executioner lifted his blade as Lady Katherine held up her hand.

Campbell's eyes met Caitlin's and he stared at her with such hatred. She stared right back.

Lady Katherine dropped her hand and the executioner dropped his sword.

Campbell's head fell into a bucket—his unblinking eyes still staring at Caitlin.

Caitlin's chest tightened. But she didn't feel sad for the man who had just died. She felt hopeless: the chance of finding answers to her past died with the executed man.

Black Blade watched the old man die. He didn't really enjoy watching it. Yes, he liked the fact that the old man was dead—especially since he'd already been paid —but he would have liked to have taken that life himself.

Black Blade observed the crowd. Quite a few people had gathered to watch him die. He wondered how many people knew him. No one cried or showed any remorse.

Two men stood out from the rest: they looked worried. One was really big and the other had a scar across his face. They stood near the execution block, staring in disbelief. Black Blade had a feeling that they knew the old man.

Black Blade studied Caitlin Wilde as she stood beside Lady Katherine. He kept his hood up and his head low so that she wouldn't see him. He actually didn't have to bother hiding. Caitlin stared at the dead man's head instead of looking around at the crowd. The girl didn't look happy at all. *Now, why aren't you happy, girlie?*

The assassin was ready to kill her—despite the fact that it was no longer necessary. The man who'd paid to have her killed now lay dead. Black Blade wanted to kill her because she had angered and insulted him. He wanted to kill her to prove to himself that he could do it—he had failed the first time. It was a matter of pride. But he didn't want to attack in front of a crowd like this. He didn't want Lady Katherine sending her guards after him. He had to be patient.

When the people started walking away, he decided to follow Caitlin. He kept his distance so that she didn't notice him. But when he realized in what direction she was going, he decided to cut her off. He decided to get ahead of her by using a shorter alternative route. Then he would kill her and make his escape.

He hurriedly veered off into a side corridor and broke into a trot. He was ahead of her now. He decided to hide behind a wall so that he could ambush her as she passed. He pressed his back against the bricks and waited. No one else was around. Maybe he could kill her and run away without anyone noticing. *Wouldn't that be nice?*

He waited in anticipation. He had a knife in his right hand and he held it close to his chest. This was it. He was finally going to kill her.

Then he heard something breathing behind him. At first he thought he was imagining things. He was standing against a wall and walls don't breathe. He listened intently for a while. He was not imagining it. He could clearly hear inhaling and exhaling. He turned his ear against the wall. There was something moving inside! It was not a rat. This something was big. Its breathing was heavy and its footsteps loud. Black Blade listened to it move. It was coming closer to him.

Black Blade seldom got scared but at that moment he was terrified. He couldn't remember the last time he had felt the need to run. He moved away from the wall and started running toward the stables where his horse was kept. His heart pounded and he forgot all about wanting to kill Caitlin.

When he reached the stables, he was panting and trembling. He gripped the knife with white knuckles and made his way to Jasmine's stall. She whinnied when she saw him and walked to him. He rested his arms on the stable door and she sniffed his hands for food. He stroked her face and tried to calm down. He tried to focus on breathing. He closed his eyes and breathed in the scent of his beloved mare.

He tried not to think about what sort of a creature lived inside the castle walls.

# CHAPTER 43

CAITLIN WANDERED HOME feeling miserable. How was she ever going to learn about her past? How was she ever going to find out who she was?

"*Don't ever ask someone to tell you who you are,*" Lady Katherine had advised. "*That is for you and you alone to decide.*"

But she didn't understand Caitlin's situation. She didn't understand that Caitlin couldn't just decide who she was. Caitlin had a dark past and not knowing exactly what her past was, or who she actually was, haunted her.

Caitlin thought about her dreams. She told herself that tonight she was going to use the dream catcher. She needed to face her fears and start finding some answers.

The walk to home was long and Caitlin decided to

take her time. She needed to think. As she walked alongside the rest of the crowd who had gathered to watch the execution, she was lost in her thoughts, paying no attention to her surroundings. But she was jolted into the present when two men walking in front of her caught her eye: one was large and the other bore a scar. She recognized them immediately. They were the two men she had seen in Waterfall Haven—the two men who had taken Roxy and tried to take Maggie. Caitlin's stomach turned. She remembered how she had fought with Brutus and how they had fallen into the river. Oh, how she wished he had drowned!

The two men didn't spot her. So she hid behind a group of people to avoid being seen. She watched them. They were dressed like peasants and didn't stand out at all. They did look a bit miserable. Their shoulders slumped and their heads hung as they walked away in silence. They didn't have any children with them, which was good. *Why are the child thieves here? Are they bringing the stolen kids to the castle?* she wondered silently.

Caitlin kept her distance and tried not to look suspicious as she followed them. They were walking farther and farther away from the crowd. *Do they live here? If so, why were they in Waterfall Haven?*

The streets grew darker and quieter. The crowd thinned to almost nothing and Caitlin had to hide behind walls, shrubs, and trees. But they didn't look back. Their footsteps were loud on the stone path.

Caitlin tiptoed behind them. She tried to keep her breathing soft and under control so that she could listen....

"I can't believe he is dead," Scarface said.

"I can," Brutus replied. "He had it coming. He was told to stay in the castle instead of going to River Town. But he just couldn't stay away. He just couldn't help himself."

"He'd been on the MOP for so long, and he really worked hard," Scarface defended him. "I understand why he wanted to go to that town so bad to see how it played out."

MOP? Caitlin had no idea what that was, but she didn't like the sound of it.

"I don't think he went there for the MOP," Brutus argued. "He had lost interest in the program long ago. He was more focused on the weapons that they were making for the king."

"But the weapons failed?" Scarface said. "Didn't they all die?"

"Or they escaped," Brutus said. "We can't be sure. They don't tell us anything, do they?"

"We're just the kidnappers," Scarface said miserably. "How many more kids do they need anyway?"

"I'm guessing a lot, after River Town was destroyed. They need to start the whole program from scratch."

"It's a terrible monster that did that."

"There are terrible monsters here as well," Brutus said. "They are hiding in the castle."

"You are just trying to scare me!" Scarface said. "It won't work."

"Then why do you keep looking behind your back all the time?"

Caitlin was hiding behind a wood pile now. She huddled down so that they couldn't see her. But the wood pile also muffled the men's voices so she couldn't understand most of their conversation. She really needed to hear more, so she put her hand on the top of the wood pile in order to push herself up so that she could better hear the two men, or at least try to read their lips.

She didn't realize that the wood pile was unstable. The moment she applied pressure, the two topmost logs tumbled to the ground with a loud CHUNK-THUNK!

She ducked back down, shut her eyes, held her breath, and didn't move for several heartbeats. If the two men attacked her, would she be able to fight both of them off?

"What was that?" Brutus asked.

"Let's get out of here!" Scarface said.

The two men took off. Caitlin waited a moment before following. She had to stay a good distance behind them so as not to be seen.

The two men ducked into a narrow alley. She slowed her pace and hugged the wall of a building. She neared the alley entrance and braced herself.

As she moved into the alley, she stopped. The men

were gone! The alley was a dead end; the only way out was also the way in. There was no way the two men could have slipped past her. So where were they?

She stared at the dark alley. The two men seemed to have disappeared into the walls.

"Look who is back," Rafe said.

Caitlin walked up to their porch. Daisy was baking bread inside the house and the smell filled her nostrils. Caitlin's stomach rumbled. She hadn't realized how hungry she was.

"Did you miss me?" she asked Rafe.

"Not really." He leaned back lazily in his chair.

Maggie was playing in the garden. She wore a beautiful and expensive gown that Caitlin hadn't seen before. She immediately knew that Rafe had bought it for her little sister—he was so nice! "Well I missed you," she said and took a seat beside him.

Rafe looked at her from under his dark messy hair. "But you had a new friend to keep you company," he said. His eyes studied her reaction.

She didn't deny that Dylan was a friend. She wasn't sure if he was joking or angry at her. "Are you jealous?" she asked, neatly sidestepping his comment.

"Me? Jealous? Of course not!"

"Good," she smiled.

"But we can't be friends anymore," he said with a straight face.

"Well... then I'm sorry for your loss," Caitlin said.

Rafe started laughing and she knew he wasn't angry at her anymore. His laugh was truly a beautiful sound. It made her laugh too.

"You're very cheeky," he said when he got his breath back.

"Rafe, we need to talk about something," she said, and he could tell she was serious. Their laughter died down. "But I don't want to talk here."

"We can find a more private place," Rafe said and got up. "Let's take a lunch with us."

They packed a bag with some fresh bread, fruit, and water. Rafe didn't complain that there wasn't any meat, and together they left the house.

"It was nice of you to buy Maggie that dress," Caitlin said.

"How did you know I bought it?" Rafe asked.

"It looks expensive. Daisy wouldn't spend that much money on a growing child," Caitlin explained. "And if she had bought it, she wouldn't let Maggie play in the garden while wearing it. That could ruin the dress."

"I'm sure Daisy would get you a nice dress if you asked," Rafe said.

"I don't think it would suit me," Caitlin confessed. She could admire a pretty dress but couldn't picture herself in one. "And I don't want one anyway."

"What do you want?" Rafe looked at her so intently that her heart skipped a beat. He had a way of looking at her, as if she was made of glass and he could see right through her.

Caitlin's mind went numb for a moment. "To talk," she said.

Rafe looked away and she knew that wasn't the answer he was hoping for. "Well," he said. "I want to hold your hand."

She loved his confidence. He didn't ask for permission as he intertwined their fingers. The electric waves went through Caitlin's hand and arm again. Rafe was smiling and she knew he was listening to her heartbeat.

"You're blushing."

"Shut up," she said.

"People will notice."

"I don't think anyone will mind my red cheeks." She knew he wasn't talking about that. What he meant was that other men would see her holding his hand and assume she was taken. This diminished her chance of finding a husband. She did not mind. She actually felt proud to be seen with Rafe.

Rafe led her away from the crowds and then up some stairs. The stairs were built in a spiral and seemed to never end.

"Where are we going?" she asked Rafe.

"It's a surprise," he responded.

The stairs went up in a tower that seemed to climb

to the heavens. Once on top, Caitlin's calves were burning. She caught her breath not because she was tired but because she was wonderstruck.

They were in one of the castle's highest towers, one with the best view. Down below them she saw tiny houses and tiny people. She saw the mountains and clouds drifting by. The tower had a roof supported by four pillars. There was no surrounding wall for safety, but Caitlin wasn't scared of heights. She walked to the edge and looked down. On one side were houses and on the other side was a huge cliff. It wasn't as intimidating from up here.

The wind rustled through her hair and she pushed it out of her face and tucked it behind her ear. It was pointless to try and control her wild hair in this wind.

Rafe took a seat at the edge of the tower and she wondered if his knees were wobbly. He didn't show fear. He motioned for her to sit beside him as he removed his pack and opened it to take out their lunch. It looked tastier than the bread they had eaten when they traveled. Rafe sniffed it before he handed her a piece.

"This is the most bread and fruit I have ever eaten in my life," he told her and took a bite.

"I was wondering when you were going to start complaining," she said and dug in. She took three huge bites and then realized her mouth was too full to chew. At that moment she realized how unladylike she was being and felt very self-conscious. She chewed with her mouth open and tried to force the food down her throat as fast as possible.

"Do you think you can get any more food in your mouth?" Rafe teased.

"If I tried to, then yes," she mumbled between chews. *He doesn't look grossed out. That's good.* She still felt her cheeks heating up.

"So what did you want to talk about?" Rafe asked.

"I don't even know where to begin," Caitlin told him. She tried to think of a starting point. "I had a bad day."

"Next time you should spend it with me instead of some blond-haired freak."

Caitlin ignored the remark. "Dylan and I were dragged from the swimming pool by the king's guards after you left. I think they had mistaken Dylan for you when they took him."

Rafe raised his eyebrows. "You were brought before the king? Why?"

"Campbell told him that I was a Magic sympathizer and that I had a shifter companion with me."

Rafe choked on his bread. Then he cursed. He took the news hard—like she knew he would.

"How did you get free?" Rafe asked worried. He lost his appetite.

"Lady Katherine helped me."

Rafe gaped at her. Now he really couldn't eat anymore. He put his half-eaten piece of bread down and turned his full attention to Caitlin.

"What?" she asked.

"It's just odd." He frowned. "First, it's odd that Campbell went straight to the king instead of going to Lady Katherine. Second, it's odd that she helped you out."

"Well, she might really think I am innocent. She knew who Dylan was."

"It doesn't matter if she thought you were innocent. If that woman hears the word Magic, she goes crazy. I can't believe she didn't send you to the execution block herself."

"The king sentenced Campbell to die." Caitlin recalled his lifeless eyes staring at her with a hatred she had never seen before. "I watched him die."

Rafe studied her face. It didn't look like Campbell's death had scarred her.

"I don't know what to do, Rafe," she said. "He was the only person who knew about my past. I have no leads now."

"This isn't a lead," Rafe said. "But I did learn something today."

"What did you learn?"

"I was in the library. I went through so many books about the kingdom. I saw many maps, but none of them had River Town on their maps. None of the books even mentioned River Town."

"What does that mean?" she asked.

"That River Town doesn't exist," Rafe said. "Think about it: no one we've talked to knows about it."

"Of course it exists!" she said. "You were there!

You know it's real. Brutus and Scarface know that it's real."

"The child thieves?" Rafe gaped. He wasn't sure how they had come into the conversation.

Caitlin then told him about how they had watched the execution, how she had followed them and eavesdropped on them, and how they had disappeared into thin air.

"MOP?" Rafe said. "I have no idea what that is." Then his expression turned angry. "Why would you go and follow them? What if they saw you?"

"I can take care of myself," she growled back.

They had been sitting there for a long time. The sun was setting. Its rays drew a golden line around Caitlin's hair. Rafe tried not to focus on how beautiful she was. He was reprimanding her. "Can you?"

"I'm not the one we should be worried about!" she said. "You're the one they want dead!"

"I'm not going to die," Rafe rolled his eyes.

"How do you know that?" she asked. "Campbell told King Leonard and Lady Katherine that I have a shifter friend…. If they start looking into it—"

"They won't," Rafe interrupted. "If they thought there was any threat, I would already have been killed."

"And me to for helping you," she added.

"Are you accusing me of placing your life in danger?" Rafe met her eyes. He had saved her so many times and had helped her so many times. How could she possibly think he would do anything to hurt her?

"Indirectly, yes," she said. "I think you should leave the castle." Caitlin cared about him way too much. After seeing how fast the king was to kill Campbell, she wanted Rafe to get away as fast as possible. She didn't want something like that to happen to him. She'd rather lose him than see him dead.

"And when I leave, who is going to protect you from Black Blade?"

"I can protect myself," she glared.

"And I can't?" he asked back.

Her anger was flaring up. Why was he so stubborn? This stubbornness was going to get him killed. "Don't you understand?" she asked loudly and was glad no one could hear her scream at him from up there. "You are in the most dangerous place in the Silver Kingdom! Everyone here wants you dead! Do you realize how selfish you are for staying here? Have you ever thought about me? Have you ever wondered what it would do to me if you got killed?"

"I am not leaving," Rafe said curtly.

"Well I am!" she screamed and jumped to her feet. She had had enough. He didn't even try to see things from her point of view, and she had to get away from him before she completely lost it.

"Caitlin..." Rafe said as she started making her way to the stairs. He was up in a flash and ran toward her. He grabbed her by the arm and pulled her back forcibly.

"What!" she screamed.

He kissed her.

Her heart skipped several beats and she forgot how to breathe. Then her arms twisted around him and she leaned in. His hands moved from cupping her face to her waist and back up to tangle his fingers into her hair. The kiss lasted for several minutes until Rafe pulled away.

Caitlin wanted to lean even closer to him. She looked up at him and wished he would kiss her again.

He didn't. Instead he spoke to her. "Caitlin, you are never going to lose me."

She believed him.

# CHAPTER 44

THEY SAT UP THERE, in the tower, watching the sun set. They kissed and laughed and stared at each other for hours. Caitlin had never felt more alive and she'd never been happier. She let go of all her anger as she melted in Rafe's arms.

It was almost midnight when they decided to go home. Caitlin wondered if her parents were worried that she had stayed out so late. Probably not, she was with Rafe after all.

They climbed down the stairs and walked hand-in-hand back to the house. They opened the door slowly but it still creaked. Then they tiptoed inside.

"Do you have to move out?" she asked Rafe.

"Your dad won't want me moving in," Rafe said and she knew it was true.

"So just stay the night," she asked and looked at him

with big eyes. She knew there was no way he could say no.

They made their way to the couch where Rafe lay down on his back. The couch was padded with goose feathers and horsehair and was bigger and softer than the wooden couches they had in River Town. Caitlin put off going to her room and took the opportunity to snuggle with Rafe, lying with her head on his chest. She could hear his heartbeat. It was a soothing sound.

She wondered if his heart beat as fast as hers when they kissed. She didn't recall much of her past, but somehow she knew that she had never kissed anyone else.

Rafe, on the other hand, was a skilled kisser. He had probably kissed many women. That's why he was so confident. She did not care who he had been with before her. They were his past while she was his present.

She tangled her hands in his shirt, breathed in his scent, and felt his warmth. He was smiling at her again. She could tell without looking. "I'm not sleepy," she murmured.

"You have to sleep," Rafe said. "You have to focus on your dreams, remember?"

She grunted. "I forgot about that."

He pulled the dream catcher out of his pocket and handed it to her. She fumbled with it on his chest. "Do I have to use it?"

"Can you think of anything else?" Rafe asked. "You want answers, don't you?"

"I do..." She did not sound certain and focused on the dream catcher in her hand as she lay on his chest. There was a moment of silence. "Talk to me," she asked him.

"But then you'll talk back and you'll never sleep."

"Sing to me," she asked softly.

"What makes you think I can sing?" Rafe asked.

"I just want to hear the sound of your voice," she said and closed her eyes.

Rafe wrapped his arms around her and sang softly. He didn't have a breathtaking voice, but Caitlin would choose listening to him sing over any professional singer.

Caitlin fell asleep in his arms feeling happy and safe. Once she was asleep, she rolled onto her side and Rafe slid the dream catcher under her pillow.

This time her dream was different. It was like watching a movie instead of starring in it. In all her previous dreams, she was there as a participant, just younger. Younger Caitlin looked about fourteen years old. But in this dream, her face had blood on it and her body looked bruised.

Caitlin stared at her younger self, pacing four steps to the far wall and then four steps back, four steps out and four steps back, back and forth and back and forth in measured, even steps. She was all alone in a tiny room furnished with one small bed, one small chair, and one small table set against a wall. The room was lit by one torch tucked into a sconce above the table. There were no windows and the only door out had no visible knobs or handles. No one could see her—or her imprisoned self—and no one could speak to her. She felt trapped and started to hyperventilate.

Suddenly, Caitlin found herself standing in a different room, one that looked like no other room she'd ever been in. The room was sparkling clean and spacious, with walls made of a polished white stone. There was a cold metal table in the center, its surface polished and gleaming. The table had leathers straps hanging from its sides. The room didn't have any windows but was lit by torches ensconced along the walls and by a large chandelier hanging from the ceiling above the metal table. As a result of all the torches, the room was warm and thus did not need a fireplace for heat.

Counters set with countless bottles surrounded the table. There were jars and containers that kept fluids and long, incredibly thin glass tubes with pointed tips that looked like Daisy's sewing needles, except they were hollow. Somewhere in the back of her mind, she knew they were in fact called needles and were used to inject small amounts of liquids into the body. Caitlin did not know what any of the jars and bottles contained, but she knew they were not meant to save lives. There were razor-sharp knives too. On one counter, Caitlin saw transparent tubes made of what looked like intestines of various lengths and sizes. Some of the transparent skins were shaped more like pouches and contained what looked like blood—the sight of which horrified Caitlin.

The room was filled with people as well. They did not wear the rough, ragged clothes that peasants wore. They also did not wear leather armor and they carried no weapons. Their clothes were white, crisp and clean, made of a fine fabric. These people weren't farmers or fighters; they were healers.

"Hello," Caitlin said but none of the people turned to look at her. "Can someone tell me where I am?"

No one answered her. She reached out to touch a woman, so that she could get her attention, but her hand went straight through the woman's shoulder. Caitlin swallowed and for a moment she wondered if she was dead.

Then she saw a familiar face. His dark hair was a little shorter than it had been when he had introduced himself this morning. "Healer Dan?!"

He was dressed in a white smock with a close-fitting white cap and was looking down at some papers that were secured to a thin, rectangular wood board with a metal clip along the top edge. He held the clipboard out in front of him. When he finished paging through the papers, he put the clipboard down on the counter. "Alright, bring her in."

The doors swung open and Caitlin watched in horror as a younger version of herself was dragged into the room by two patronizers. They forced her onto the table, their metal fingers digging into the skin on her arms. Their bony faces were hidden under red hoods.

Two more patronizers stood behind the two handling younger Caitlin. Although cloaked in the same red hoods, they sported actual knives instead of fingers. They had orders to kill her if she got out of control.

She watched as younger Caitlin was pinned to the table. The straps were fastened around her wrists and ankles. Her kicking and screaming were futile.

"Give her a sedative," Healer Dan said.

"She's already had two full doses earlier," a nurse informed him. "It doesn't work. Her body fights off any medication."

"I hate you!" younger Caitlin cried. "I hate you all."

Caitlin walked to the metal table. She tried to touch the leather straps so that she could undo them, but her fingers went straight through. She realized that she was not dreaming—she was watching a scene from her past and she couldn't change a thing.

"She and Divan are the only survivors," a nurse said. "The rest of the children's bodies couldn't handle the change."

"She was always the most dangerous," another said.

"I'm going to kill all of you," young Caitlin swore. She was ignored, as if they had heard her empty threats many times before. They treated her like an object, not a human being.

"I see her attitude hasn't improved," a familiar male voice said.

Caitlin didn't have to turn to know whose voice that was.

Nicolas Campbell strode into the room and looked down at her younger self, disgusted.

It was strange to see him alive and well after she had just seen his head separate from his body hours earlier. She had the urge to punch him, but she now understood that her fists would have no impact.

"No," Healer Dan agreed with a sigh. "It hasn't."

"You should kill her before she follows through with her threats," Campbell said.

"We cannot kill her," Healer Dan objected. "She's just angry. It's not her fault that she's always angry. We made her this way as a child when we mixed that blood with hers."

*That blood.* *What blood?* Caitlin watched her younger self fight. There was nothing either of them could do in this situation.

"It is because of that blood that she will kill us all," Campbell said. "Can't you see that your test subjects are all dead? Your whole operation is a failure. You'll never be able to turn this creature," he gestured to young Caitlin, "into anything other than what she is."

"Please leave," Healer Dan asked.

"We should throw her into the MOP program," Campbell suggested. He didn't leave as asked and Caitlin didn't think he was going to go away any time soon.

"If we do that, she won't remember ANYTHING," Healer Dan said. "Then all of her training would have been for nothing. She wouldn't be who she is today."

"If she can't remember anything, she will be less dangerous," Campbell said.

"She is a weapon; she is supposed to be dangerous," Healer Dan said.

"You'll have better control over her if she doesn't remember all of these terrible things that you've done to her," Campbell pressed.

"I'm done with this conversation," the healer said. "Let's begin."

Caitlin watched in horror as they started poking at her younger self with the glass needles. They drew her blood into the transparent tubes that emptied into an attached transparent pouch. She was not sure what they were going to do with her blood, but it made her sick. She watched her younger self scream in agony.

"Stop! Stop it!" Caitlin cried. She kicked the table in anger, but her foot went straight through. She felt her younger self's pain and her anger, felt the tears barely kept in check. She heard screams ringing in her ears. Both Caitlins were screaming at the top of their lungs.

413

"Caitlin! Caitlin, wake up!" Rafe was shaking her.

She closed her mouth and sat up. Gerald and Daisy were by the couch and Maggie was standing in the doorway. Rafe had both his hands on her shoulders and was looking at her in horror.

"What happened?" Gerald demanded as he rushed into the room.

"Are you alright?" Daisy asked.

"I had a bad dream," Caitlin said. She looked around at the pale faces around her. Her body was bathed in sweat. She was too freaked out to feel embarrassed over her sudden outburst. "I'm sorry, I didn't mean to scare all of you."

"What on earth were you dreaming about?" Daisy asked.

"I can't remember," she lied.

All of them just stared at her in silence. As she calmed down, she began feeling awkward and was thankful when Daisy offered to make them all something hot to drink. She had a feeling none of them would be able to go back to bed now. On any other night she might have felt guilty for keeping them awake. Tonight was different. Her heart was still beating too fast and that dream—no, that memory—was fresh in her mind.

"I'm fine," she reassured Maggie as her little sister came to hug her.

"It was just a nightmare," Maggie said. "Nightmares can't hurt you."

*But the past can,* Caitlin thought.

# CHAPTER 45

THE NEXT DAY everyone was a little quieter than usual. Before Gerald went to work, he gave Caitlin an extra-long hug. She tried not to show everyone how tired she was. She tried to block out the dream and act normally.

Daisy mentioned something about her finding a job, but Caitlin was only nodding and not listening. They still had enough money left to sustain them for a while.

"What school did you choose for Maggie?" Gerald asked.

"I was looking at some of the more selective schools first," Daisy said. "The one I wanted to send her to is called Evelyn's School."

"That sounds expensive," Gerald said.

"Amazingly, it isn't," Daisy said. "I went there and talked to the people. But they said they weren't taking new students at the moment."

416

"Maybe they are full," Gerald said.

"It didn't look like it," Daisy said. "And it's strange because the mothers of some of the brightest children were complaining that their kids weren't accepted either."

"So where did you end up enrolling her?" Gerald asked.

"I placed her in a local school. It's close to home." Daisy then turned to Maggie and said, "Have you got everything you need? Are you ready to go?"

"Yes, Mom," Maggie said. "Do you think I'll make lots of friends today?"

"It may take a little time, dear, but yes, eventually. They'll see what a special person you are." Daisy said as she adjusted Maggie's new outfit, a pretty pink dress bought especially for the first day of school. "Now let's hurry or you'll be late."

Caitlin watched Daisy scoot Maggie out the door, followed by Gerald who was off to work at the smithy. She then turned her attention to Rafe, who was sitting around looking bored, staring at the ceiling. Caitlin wondered if he was also going to look for work. She also wondered where he was going to find the answers he was looking for.

She studied him closely. She could tell that he didn't sleep well. He had dark smudges under his eyes. He was exhausted and she did not think he would get up from the couch any time soon.

Caitlin made some tea for him and then sat down

next to him. He accepted the tea but did not smile as much as he normally would. He was worried about Caitlin and her mental health. He didn't show it, but his silence gave him away.

"Do you think I'm a freak?" she asked him.

"Yes," he said.

She looked down and suddenly her chest felt tighten. It felt like he had jabbed a knife into her heart. When had she become so sensitive?

"But that's one of the reasons I like you so much," he said and put his hand on hers.

She smiled at him and the pain faded. Then she couldn't help herself—she had to hug him. When she leaned in, he wrapped his arms around her and held her tight.

"I'm sorry. I didn't mean to upset you," she whispered in his ear.

He squeezed a little tighter and then he let go. But she wasn't ready to let go. *Why is he always the one who lets go first?*

"Tell me about your dreams," Rafe said.

"I don't like the dream catcher," she confessed. "It makes the dreams more vivid."

"Did it help you to remember better?"

"It changed the whole experience." It was very hard for her to open up. It was very hard for her to tell Rafe about all of the dreams. It was hard for her to explain to him what a hateful girl she was in her dreams. It was hard for her to tell him about the pain she'd endured.

But she did her best.

Her hand held his as she spoke. She held on tighter and tighter the harder it was to open up. He got pulled into the story and eventually he stopped holding her hand. When she was finished, she looked down at her empty hands before looking at Rafe and said, "I don't feel that I am the girl in my dreams anymore. I feel I've changed."

For a while, Rafe just sat in silence, taking it all in. It freaked her out to see him quiet. She was waiting for him to make a joke to lighten the mood.

"Rafe."

He looked at her.

"Please say something."

"I don't know what to say," he admitted. "There's so much we don't understand." Then he moved closer to her and put a soothing hand on her cheek. "Hey," he whispered. "It will all be alright."

"I hope so," she said. But still she couldn't shake the feeling that something bad was going to happen in the castle. It felt like someone was watching her.

Rafe lay down on the couch for a little while and then he fell asleep on the pillow that Caitlin had slept on last night—the one that had the dream catcher under it.

Caitlin was tired but she knew she couldn't rest. Her mind was too busy and she still felt eyes on her. The feeling of being watched made her uncomfortable and so she stood up and looked around the room.

*Meow.*

She jumped and then turned to the kitchen. On the kitchen table sat the black cat that Maggie had petted the other day. It was the cat that had lain on the wall, in the sun, by the pool.

"My sister will be glad to see you," Caitlin told her.

The cat looked at Caitlin, the way all cats look at humans: as if they were superior. Caitlin walked to her and stroked her head, but the cat didn't look very pleased.

Caitlin gave up trying to please the cat and decided to go for a walk around the castle instead.

Dylan rose early that morning. He went running and came back home dripping with sweat. After taking a bath, he was surprised to find his father packing.

"Dad, why are you packing?" he asked.

"It's time for me to go," his father responded.

"Go?!" Dylan started at him. "But we've only just arrived!"

"As you know, I spoke to the king yesterday," Liam said. "He's paying me well to go kill some shifters in the west."

"I'll start packing then," Dylan said.

"You're not coming," Liam said to his son's surprise.

This was the first time his father said something like this. They always hunted together. They never left each other behind. Every hunter knew that hunting solo was asking for death. You needed a partner to watch your back.

"I don't understand," Dylan said. "Did I do something wrong?"

"Not at all," Liam said. "The king requires your services here. He will speak to you today."

"When will I see you again?" Dylan asked. He wasn't thinking about what an honor it was to be employed by the king.

"I don't know," Liam admitted. "I'll come back to the castle and get you once my work is done."

"Are you going alone?" Dylan asked and tried not to sound worried. His father would hate it if he was worried about him.

"I am," Liam said. "But I am meeting Aunt Lillian there."

"That's good," Dylan said and meant it. Being a hunter was dangerous but hunting alone was even more so. His aunt was a capable hunter and so Dylan felt his worries ease a bit, but only a bit.

"Don't look so worried," Liam told him.

"I'm not worried," Dylan said abruptly.

Liam wasn't convinced. "I know you better than that, son."

Dylan watched as his father put his last few things into his suitcase before closing it. "Don't forget I taught you everything you know. I'll be fine out there in the west," Liam added with a wink at his son.

Dylan nodded. His father had taught him a lot. Liam was a great teacher and a good hunter. He was a survivor too. "Do you know what the king wants me to do?" Dylan asked.

"I don't," Liam said. "He only said that he had a special job for you."

Dylan nodded.

"You should look more excited," Liam said. "It's a great honor to be hired by the king. He must think highly of us."

"I am excited," Dylan said, "and honored."

"At least try to act like you mean what you say," Liam said.

Dylan walked his father to the stables and watched him saddle his horse. His father looked eager to go and kill more shifters. Dylan wondered if he ever got tired of it.

"Father," Dylan said, "where do you see us in five years from now?"

"Excuse me?" Liam looked baffled.

"I mean, what would we be doing after five years have passed?" Dylan asked.

"We'd be hunting, of course," Liam said. "You might also have a pretty huntress by your side by then."

Dylan didn't know many women who hunted but

he was pretty sure he didn't want any of them. He thought about Caitlin. She was very feisty, and she'd be a good hunter....

"What's on your mind, son?"

"I was just thinking that maybe there is more to life than hunting," Dylan confessed.

"What more is there?" Liam asked.

"I don't know," Dylan confessed. "But I'd like to find out."

"What are you trying to tell me?" Liam asked. "You don't want to be a hunter anymore? Hunting is what makes you who you are."

"I know," Dylan said. "I just get tired of it sometimes."

"Dylan, we prevent the deaths of innocent people every day. It's very selfish to grow tired of that."

"I know," Dylan repeated.

"It's time for me to leave," Liam said with a sigh. "Push those thought aside. Your life has so much more meaning than most people's lives."

Dylan hugged him. "I love you, Dad. Please come back soon."

"I never leave family behind," Liam said, cupping the back of his son's neck with both hands and touching his forehead to Dylan's. Then he mounted his horse and rode away.

Dylan watched his father ride out the castle gates. He thought about what his father had said. His father was right: his job was important. If he decided to quit hunting what would he do afterward? Who would he be?

He thought about the three rules an arch warrior lives by:

1. I run toward what I fear.
2. I never leave family behind.
3. I protect those who can't protect themselves.

Yes, his job was important. He should think about others instead of only himself. He should keep doing what he was doing.

Dylan walked to the throne room to meet with the king.

# CHAPTER 46

THE THRONE ROOM doors were open. Dylan nodded to the guards who stood on either side of the door as he walked past. They nodded back and watched him walk into the throne room. He took long confident strides and then bowed low to the king.

"Your majesty requested to see me," Dylan said with respect.

"Yes," the king said and made a motion with his hand to signal that Dylan could stand at ease. Then he turned to the guards. "Leave us," he commanded.

They left the room and closed the doors behind them without a word. The throne room was quiet and empty. It felt strange to be the only man in the king's presence.

King Leonard stood up. He was slightly taller than

Dylan. He walked from his throne to the young man. It was unusual for Dylan to look up at someone—although he didn't look up by much.

"I have heard a lot about you," King Leonard said.

"I hope your majesty has only heard good things," Dylan responded.

"I have heard many good things," the king said with a flicker of a smile. "I've heard you are a fantastic hunter, one of the best actually."

Dylan bowed his head in modesty. He didn't feel intimidated to have the king standing in front of him. Was he supposed to tremble or feel honored?

The king made eye contact. "Tell me, how seriously do you take your job?"

Dylan thought about how often he felt like quitting. How tired he grew of moving around so much and how he longed for a place to call home. He looked into the king's eyes and said, "Very seriously, My King."

"Good," the king said. "I know you think I've asked you here to kill shifters, but that is not the case."

"Then what service do you require of me?" Dylan asked.

"Hunting," the king said. "I want you to hunt something much more dangerous than shifters and I want you to tell no one about it."

"What is it you want me to hunt, My Lord?"

"Follow me," the king said.

Dylan followed him like a dog on a leash. The king didn't say anything as he walked to Lady Katherine's jeweled chair. He grabbed its arms and moved the chair to the side. Under it was trap door that the king opened to reveal stairs that led down into a dark passage under the castle.

"A secret passageway!" Dylan exclaimed. He realized that in that moment he sounded like a little kid that was ready to go exploring.

The king smiled. "One of many," he said.

And then they climbed down the stairs and into the darkness.

As Caitlin left the house, the black cat ran past her. Then she stopped, looked back at Caitlin, and meowed again. When Caitlin walked toward her, she ran farther, and Caitlin followed her again.

*I must be crazy,* Caitlin thought, *to be running after a cat.*

Every time she got close, the cat ran a little farther and then stopped to wait. Caitlin wondered if the cat was leading her somewhere. Then she realized how stupid that was.

She probably just didn't want to Caitlin to get too close. Cats come and go as they please. Maybe she was heading back to her home.

Caitlin was about to turn back when she realized where she was: the alley in which Brutus and Scarface had vanished. The black cat had run into it.

As Caitlin walked toward the entrance, she expected to see the cat at the end of the alley. But she couldn't find the cat. Just like Brutus and Scarface, the cat had disappeared.

*That's really weird*, Caitlin thought as she walked into the alley. It was narrow and flanked on both sides by tall stone walls. She walked until she reached the dead end and found nothing but a stone wall there too. She started pressing on some of the stones but could not find anything odd about them. They were all similar in shape and color. She moved from wall to wall, but she didn't even know what she was looking for.

There was nothing special about this place. She felt like an idiot and turned to face the exit. A feeling of hopelessness washed over her. *Am I going crazy? Am I imagining things?*

She had to get herself together. She needed to think. So she leaned back against the wall and just as she closed her eyes, part of the wall gave way. She fell backward, landing on her buttocks. She groaned and then got to her feet to inspect the camouflaged door. She found a handle on the other side of the door.

She took a deep breath and then walked into the passageway. It was very dark and only partially lit by sunlight streaming in through the open door. The deeper into the tunnel she walked, the darker it got. Caitlin didn't know if the passageway contained any torches that she could use. She looked back into the lit alley. She didn't dare leave the door open. What if someone else saw the secret passage? But she also wasn't keen on closing it and risk wandering around lost in the dark.

After few heartbeats, she made her decision, sighed, and took hold of the door handle and closed the door. Darkness engulfed her. She stood still, waiting with her hand on the door handle for a few minutes—enough time to let her eyes adjust to the dark.

She saw that there were tiny cracks here and there in the stone walls that let light in. So she moved forward, walking through the passage until she came to a fork. The left passageway looked a lot like what was behind her. But the right side led to stairs that went down, under the castle.

Something felt familiar. Have I been here before? Caitlin murmured softly to herself. *Turning left feels safer*, she thought as she nevertheless found herself turning right and climbing down the stairs anyway.

Once under the castle she heard two very familiar voices....

"These passages were built centuries ago," the king explained. "Some were used as escape routes and others lead nowhere. Some lead to rooms filled with secrets."

The king lit two torches and handed one to Dylan who was grateful to hold it. It made him feel like he had more control.

"I've known about these passageways even before I became king. I've been using them for years now," King Leonard told him.

"What for?" Dylan asked. Surely the king didn't need to sneak around in his own castle.

"For experiments," the king said. "I've been conducting experiments on Magic and Non-Magic folk."

"Excuse me?" Dylan said. His knees suddenly felt weak and it was not because of the walking. Even with a torch Dylan felt uncomfortable in the dark. "I don't quite understand."

They reached a heavy, metal door. The king opened it, and they walked into a room that looked like it hadn't been used in a long time. It was a spacious room and the walls were made of a polished, white stone. There was a shiny metal table in the center. Strong leather straps with buckles were attached to the sides of the table. Counters ladened with knives and bottles and what appeared to be glass needles surrounded the table.

Dylan knew this was a torture chamber. He could imagine bringing enemies and shifters here, strapping them to the table, and jabbing the knives and glass needles into their flesh.

"This is where it all started," the king said with a nostalgic look on his face.

"What started?" Dylan asked. He felt uneasy and he wished he could run away. But he couldn't run from the king. *I run toward what I fear,* he reminded himself.

"I was told that Magic folk were returning. I was told that they were forming an army and that they were planning to overthrow me," the king's voice was angry now. Just thinking about a Magic army made his blood boil.

Dylan looked around the room. He didn't like what he was seeing, and he hated what he was hearing.

"Of course, I'm always ready for a fight, but I heard that this Magic rebellion was very strong," the king met Dylan's eyes. "And despite the Magic folk, the Forevermore Kingdom, our neighboring kingdom, has been plotting against me for years."

Dylan listened to every word.

"I was advised to build a weapon. This weapon was supposed to be so strong and scary that it would stop a war before the war could even begin."

"And how would one create such a weapon?" Dylan asked. He wasn't sure if he wanted to know the answer.

"We tried using adult humans at first." There was no remorse in the king's cold eyes. "We mixed their blood with Magic blood or the blood of Magic creatures. The humans all died. Their minds weren't strong enough to handle the transformation." The king paused and his eyes glazed over in recollection.

431

Dylan looked at the king and tried to keep his face expressionless. *The king killed non-Magic folk. He killed his own people!* Dylan tried to see the bigger picture, tried to see the situation from the king's viewpoint: a weapon to protect and save the entire kingdom. He just didn't think that developing that weapon was worth sacrificing lives.

"Then we also started the MOP program," the king resumed, excitedly moving on to describe another one of his initiatives.

"MOP?" Dylan asked. He wondered how much worse this story could get.

"Magic Obliteration Program," the king explained. "We built a device that can take away memories and rebuild someone's mind. Basically, we used a potion called Blankness and made it better. We improved it by pouring it into this device. This device can't take away Magic, but it can make people forget that they have it. Unfortunately, it still has flaws. Sometimes it doesn't work and sometimes people start remembering things."

Dylan had no idea that what he was hearing was even possible. The idea of being brainwashed terrified him. He wanted nothing to do with it. But—*I run toward what I fear*, he thought.

The king continued telling this story and Dylan didn't interrupt him. "At first, we tried it on adults and we found that their memories could indeed be wiped. But they became stupid. We turned them into weapons

432

called patronizers. The blacksmith built them sharp dagger-like fingers, long sword-like arms, and strong metallic legs. The only problem was that he couldn't reconstruct their brains as well. They became mindless creatures, completely void of personalities—zombies, if you like. But despite their flaws, there was one small consolation: they followed orders blindly. So far I've only kept them down here."

Dylan thought that was a wise decision. If the king let creatures like that roam through the castle, his people would be terrified. Many might even turn against him.

"At first, the patronizers were tasked solely with protecting and restraining my newly created Magical weapons, but now they're also used to guard the children," the king explained.

"What children?" Dylan asked. At this point, his mind was so overloaded that he could focus only on the last bit of what came out of the king's mouth, ignoring much of what came before.

"We have been collecting Magical people to test the effectiveness of the Magic Obliteration Device. We've found that the MOP works much better the younger they are. We have used it to make them forget that they have Magic. We have made them love and support me."

Dylan couldn't keep his face placid any longer. *This whole situation is absurd!*

"Don't look so horrified," the king laughed. "We've only been using Magical folk. The kid's minds are easier to wipe and they are easier to control. So far it has worked very well on the children."

"And the adults?"

"We've had recent advancements in the MOP. We've started using the Magic Obliteration Device on adults. None of them have been turned into patronizers, and their brains don't fry like they used to. This is proof that our efforts to improve the device have been very successful."

Dylan felt sick.

"Each test subject has a number tattooed on the backs of their necks so we can keep track of how many there are. The ultimate experiment happened when we created a home for them: River Town. Sending them there was the hardest part: we had to keep them sedated. The test was to see if the Magic Obliteration Program would be effective in the long-term. We wanted to find out if these Magical people believed everything we told them. And it seemed to have worked. They believed that they belonged to the families we assigned to them, each provided with beautifully detailed histories—and that they didn't have Magic. They even feared Magic. And they believed that they loved me as their king. Finally, they could live a normal, humble life, a fully human life."

"But did it work in the long-term?" Dylan asked.

"Unfortunately, shifters with Craybies destroyed the entire town. The development of Craybies is one of our most successful projects, but it did ruin the Magic

Obliteration Project. Now the MOP has to start all over again."

"Craybies was created here?"

"Yes," the king said. "One of the healers accidently created it when they were experimenting with a shifter's mind. Something went wrong and the shifter got sick from all of the tests and escaped."

"And who was held responsible for the things that went wrong?"

"Nicolas Campbell, the Magic sympathiser."

"Are you sure he was a Magic sympathiser? Why would he do all of this then? Why would he experiment on Magic folk to make a weapon for you?"

"So that he could use all of it against me. He was willing to sacrifice some Magic folk, but in the bigger picture, he planned to overthrow me."

Dylan thought about the old man who had mistaken him for a shifter when he was at the pool with Caitlin. He could imagine a disease that drove shifters crazy, a disease that was concocted from the potions down here, one that warped the minds of shifters. "So there is no cure?"

"I don't know, nor do I care," the king said.

Dylan thought about all of those lives lost. But they were mostly Magic lives. They were people who didn't matter. So why did he feel so sick thinking about their deaths? "Were there any survivors?" Dylan asked.

"One family," the king said. "They are being studied closely. So far MOP has been a huge success. What

435

hasn't been a success is my weapon. That was a separate project that started off smoothly. Sixteen years ago, we got a few willing peasants and paid them well...."

Dylan didn't like the sound of this.

"We knew adults struggled to adapt to change. Children also struggled. So we decided to experiment on unborn babies of non-Magic folk."

"How?" Dylan asked with a tight throat.

"We used Magic blood—blood from different creatures —and injected the Magic blood into the wombs of pregnant non-Magic women. These children were born, but we found that the Magic blood was too strong for them. They grew up in these tunnels under the castle where we have fed and trained them to be the perfect weapons. Unfortunately, despite all the care that my patronizers lavished on them, most of these children died before they reached the age of sixteen. Such a shame, really," the king sighed and made tut-tutting noises. "They showed so much promise...."

"Most of them?" Dylan prodded.

"Two survived," the king said. "I thought both of them would push through. One girl and one boy. I never saw either of them."

If the king never saw them, it meant he didn't care much about the project, Dylan thought.

"Anyway, the girl ended up in the Obliteration Device and was sent to River Town."

"And the boy?"

"He escaped. He is angry and unruly and nothing at all like what he was supposed to be. It was a stupid idea to create this monster. I should have listened to my own advice."

"So where is this monster?"

"It is running free in the castle walls. It has killed many people."

"And you want me to hunt it?" Dylan asked, but he already knew the answer.

The king nodded. "I want it dead."

Dylan swallowed. "I can do it."

"Good," the king said and motioned for him to follow. "Don't scream."

"Why would I scream?" Dylan was slightly offended. He had never done anything of the sort before. But as the words left his lips, he saw the patronizers. They were very tall and bony. Their red capes fell to the ground like blood. Their sword arms glinted in the torch light. They were horrible things!

Dylan *almost* screamed. He was glad he didn't. At that moment, he wanted nothing more than a weapon. But of course he hadn't taken a weapon with him to the throne room....

"Don't worry. They won't harm you," the king said with an amused expression. "Behind those doors is the MOP. I'd prefer you stay out of there as you search for the abomination."

Dylan nodded. His eyes were on the patronizers.

"I'll show you where the other entrances to these

passageways are," the king said. "You can't use the one in the throne room."

"Agreed," Dylan managed.

"And Dylan..." It was almost a growl. "If you tell anyone about this, even your father, I will have your head and theirs on a spike."

THE STORY CONTINUES IN BOOK 2:
SECRET OF THE CASTLE

# ACKNOWLEDGMENTS

This book has been such an adventure! I would like to thank everyone who was there for me before, during, and after I wrote it. Shani, Tucker and Margot, I appreciate your endless enthusiasm, support, and motivation. Thank you for always understanding when I'm too busy to hang out because I've locked myself in my room to write for days and days.

Dad, thank you for telling me not to quit and for believing in me, even when I didn't. I have dedicated this book to you because you are my number one supporter and one of the people I love most in the world.

JP, we have had so much fun with our many photo shoots, and I just want to say thank you for my beautiful author photo.

I would like to thank everyone as Aionios Books for the time and hard work that went into editing, designing, and publishing this book. Gerri, thank you for seeing the book's potential and for helping me turn this story into a novel that I'm so proud of. I admire your eye for detail, ability to read between the lines, and work ethic. Thank you for teaching me to

439

be a better writer and for designing such beautiful, eye-catching covers.

A big shout-out and thank you to everyone who reads this book! Your support and interest mean the world to me.

# ABOUT THE AUTHOR

Mermaid. Heroine. Actress. Assassin. Princess. Dragon rider.

Tayla Jean Grossberg was all of these things as a child—she had overactive imagination. She grew up on a game ranch in South Africa, among animals such as leopards, buffalo, zebras, and giraffes.

She expanded her horizons by traveling to America and Europe. Her experiences, the people she meets, the places she visits, and the animals she loves inspire her to write novels. Now Tayla spends her time reading, writing, and continuing her crazy adventures.

The only thing she can't do is reach the top shelf.

You can connect with Tayla on social media:
- Instagram (@tayla.jean.grossberg)
- TikTok (@taylajeangrossberg)

She'd love to hear from you!

AIONIOSBOOKS.COM

Made in the USA
Las Vegas, NV
26 April 2021

22065174R00261